CARLO GÉBLER

THE BULL RAID

A free version of the Irish prose epic
Táin Bó Cuailnge
Or *Cattle Raid of Cooley*

EGMONT

For Cressida and Charles

EGMONT
We bring stories to life

First published 2004
by Egmont Books Limited
239 Kensington High Street, London W8 6SA

Text copyright © 2004 Carlo Gébler
Original background texture © Getty Images

The moral right of the author has been asserted

ISBN 1 4052 1255 1

1 3 5 7 9 10 8 6 4 2

A CIP catalogue record for this title is available from the British Library

Printed and bound in Great Britain by the CPI Group

Fame will outlive life
Irish Proverb

Contents

Contents

Part Two:
The HAPPY DEATH

Acknowledgements

The Bull Raid is a re-telling of the narrative given in the ancient Irish prose epic, *Táin Bó Cuailnge* or *Cattle Raid of Cooley*. The *Táin* was written in Irish and there are several variants in existence. I used a number of English translations of some of these when writing this, as well as several works on Irish pre-Christian culture. These are all listed at the rear. This book could not have been written without these.

I gratefully acknowledge the financial support of the Arts Council/An Chomhairle Ealaíon and the Arts Council of Northern Ireland during the writing of this novel.

I would like to thank Jason Thompson for his close reading of the manuscript, Joe Moran for his advice on the topograpy of counties Louth and Down and Polly Nolan for the guide to the pronunciation of Irish words reproduced at the end.

All mistakes are my own.

Part One:

The SHORT LIFE

Prologue

The Tale's tale

In the year AD598, on the spring day and at the hour chosen, every poet and apprentice filed into the hall. Senchán, the chief poet, had called everyone because he wanted to hear *Cattle Raid of Cooley*.

Bresal, an apprentice poet, was twelve years old and the youngest present. Anxious to avoid two new poets, who delighted in persecuting anyone younger, he skirted up the side of the hall where a sort of passage was made by the hall's exterior wall and the row of pillars that partly supported the roof. These were made of yew and gave off a bitter smell.

Unfortunately for Bresal, he still had to pass his tormentors. The one on the bench closest put out his hand and grabbed Bresal's wrist.

'Will you look at what I've caught?' he said. This young poet was thin and straight, with a long face and bulging eyes. His name was Airmed though behind his back the apprentices called him The Stick.

Beside him sat a poet with a body like a boulder, a head like a rock and two tiny eyes like wet dabs on his stone face. His name was Goibniu but the apprentices knew him as The Rock.

Goibniu stood up and called out across the rows in front of him to the old poet at the front.

'Senchán,' he called.

'Yes,' said the senior poet.

Though his voice was thin and had a wavering quality it had authority too. The hall began to go quiet.

'Isn't our friend here a bit young?' Goibniu pointed at Bresal whom Airmed still had by the wrist.

'A bit young for what, exactly?'

There was now absolute silence.

'A bit too young to listen.'

'Didn't you understand all those tales you heard in here when you were a boy?'

'Of course.'

'So why wouldn't this apprentice?'

'Because he's not very clever.'

'What, and you were?'

There was nothing Goibniu could say to this.

'Do you know what you're going to be famous for?' said Senchán. 'Jealousy, that's what you and your equally lovely friend will be remembered for.'

There were a few titters.

'Stop it,' said Senchán sharply. 'Silence. I want a quiet assembly not a raucous one.'

Shaking his head, as if he was utterly mystified, Goibniu sat heavily. Airmed, equally puzzled, let go of Bresal. The apprentice promptly sat down on the floor well out of his tormentors' reach.

Senchán clapped his old hands. The door keeper closed the great doors.

For a long time Senchán had noticed that *Cattle Raid of Cooley* had not been told as much as it had been. The younger poets preferred newer stories. As one man after another now recited, from memory, the different sections he knew, Senchán found, as he had thought, that parts were missing.

'But it was not always so,' said Senchán, when the recital was over. 'Hundreds of years ago, didn't Riga the Breton give the book that at the time contained all the knowledge then known in the world in exchange for the entire story?'

They all agreed.

'Who will go to Brittany?' he said. 'They can take back their book of knowledge and ask for our story in return. As they're Celts like us, they're bound to cooperate.'

Bresal noticed that Airmed and Goibniu did not volunteer so he put his hand in the air.

A few days later Bresal left with Senchán's son Muirgen, a senior poet called Lir, and two scribes called Finnian and Gamal. They headed off across the middle of Ireland.

On the evening of the third day they came to a grave mound. It was topped by a stone covered with Ogham.* The name spelt in strokes and lines was that of Fergus Mac

---

* This was the writing system that was used in pagan Ireland and that was replaced by the Latin alphabet that came with Christianity.

Roi, who if not the first hero of *Cattle Raid of Cooley*, (for that honour was surely Cuchulainn's), was certainly the second. And though the travellers didn't read Ogham they already knew whose grave this was.

'I'm weary,' said Muirgen. 'Go and find somewhere we can sleep tonight and I'll stay here until you fetch me.'

On a little hill above a small brown stream, the other four found a compound. There was a ditch filled with great brown bunches of old hawthorn, and a rampart behind built of earth that came from the ditch. The face of the rampart was daubed with lime and the hawthorn growing on top of it was heavy with blossom so what they saw was a great white ring on a green hill.

They crossed the ditch by a bridge and inside the rampart they found a level space with several huts. In the middle there was a small mound and on top of this sat the largest hut. A man with sagging cheeks and grey hair emerged from here and scuttled down to them.

'Friend,' said Lir, guessing he was addressing the most important man in the compound.

The man with grey hair nodded. 'I am Erigu,' he said.

'We are travellers.'

There was another nod from Erigu.

'Can we stay here tonight?'

A warm fire, strong beer and meat were promised.

'Go back and fetch Muirgen,' Lir said to Bresal.

Bresal retraced his steps. As he hurried along he passed under dripping trees. In the sky hung great clouds lit from below by the sun. They looked like rocks that were in danger of falling on his head.

When he got near to the grave he found a fantastic fog had sprung up while he was away that covered just the barrow and the ground immediately around it. It was very thick and he couldn't see into it.

'Muirgen?' Bresal shouted.

He took a few steps into the murk but could see nothing. The cold air hurt him as it went into his chest yet the ground under his feet was hot as if a gigantic fire was heating it from below. There was a smell too, a mix of earth, the deep inside of a cave and rotting meat.

'Muirgen?' he shouted again.

Bresal heard the creak of the leather arm fasteners on a shield, the thwack of a sword in its scabbard banging against a leg, the clump of leather sandals with brass fittings. He knew a warrior's ghost was on the move somewhere nearby.

The twelve-year-old ran back to Erigu's compound and burst into the hut where Lir and the two scribes were seated round a fire.

'You'd better come,' he said. 'Muirgen's gone . . . hidden in a fog . . . and there's a ghost with him.'

Lir received the news without any show of either excitement or anxiety. He thought the ghost was most probably Fergus and he thought the best plan was to go and wait as close to Muirgen as possible, in case he should need them for some reason.

Having told Erigu to send food and drink after them, the party returned to the edge of the fog that hid the barrow. In the distance they could hear a muffled voice, dark and heavy, like waves rolling on a shingle beach, while above them monumental clouds floated in a pigeon grey sky.

Bresal and the other three built a fire. The sooty black fog bank showed up the sparks nicely as they hurried upwards. The voice inside the fog changed. Two women came from Erigu with watery beer, a slab of hard cheese, and a bag of goose eggs boiled hard and still warm. The voice in the fog changed again. It changed many more times over the night that followed . . .

In the morning the fog vanished. The grass, the barrow and the gravestone were all scorched brown. Muirgen was lying exhausted on top of the stone.

Bresal, Lir and the two scribes dashed forward and formed a curious circle around Muirgen.

'Well, tell us what happened,' said Lir.

Muirgen eased himself down from the stone.

'I'm so stiff,' he replied.

'Tell us what happened,' replied Lir.

'I was tired,' said Muirgen. 'While you all went away, I sat down and addressed the gravestone. "Fergus, you could save us the trouble of this journey, if you came and told me the story now."

'The grass blades trembled, the ground grew hot, and that fog sprang up. I had to climb up on the stone to stop my feet getting burnt and I heard bellowing coming from deep in the ground.

'Fergus's ghost appeared. He had long brown hair, wore a green hooded cloak over a red tunic and heavy sandals with bronze fittings, and he carried a great sword. The blade was hidden in the scabbard but I could see the end. The handgrip was made of twisted bronze; the pommel at the top was set with a large red stone, and the hand guards, they were also bronze and set with small green stones.

'"So you want *Cattle Raid of Cooley*? That will not be easy. It is a complex story with many heroes."

'"We've lost it,"' I told him.

'"That is different." He agreed to fetch the participants from Hell, where as pagans they had gone when they died, and from where he himself had just come.

'All through the night he brought them before me as he promised and they chanted their parts. It's all in here now.' Muirgen touched his head. 'We can go back to my father. Our search is over.'

They returned to Senchán's compound.

'Why back so soon? Did you decide against the journey?' asked Senchán.

'We found what we went to find in Ireland,' his son answered.

A few days later all the poets and apprentices met again in the hall that smelt of bitter yew wood. After prayers and music, Muirgen closed his eyes and began to declaim what he had heard in the mist. As he chanted he became the people in the story. He began with Crunnchu and ended with the death of Cuchulainn. Everyone listened very carefully. The scribes wrote it all down on large portions of thin vellum stretched over writing boards. Bresal found the story he heard more exciting than anything he had ever heard before in his short life.

Chapter One

Macha's curse

Crunnchu was a small fellow with bandy legs and big gnarled hands. His hair left him early. His bare head, he was once told, shone red like a lobster's back after boiling. He had a wife called Badh, but she died and he was left alone with their sons, Art and Cet. Crunnchu and his sons worked together well and none minded the absence of a wife or mother.

Crunnchu was a farmer and he lived in a lonely place set high in the hills of Ulster. He had two compounds. He lived in one with his sons and a few serving women, while in the other lived his animals, his herdsmen and the rest of his servants.

Each compound had a circular ditch inside which was an earth rampart with hawthorn growing along the top and a single entrance cut through it. To cross the ditch into the compound there was a bridge and at night this was raised.

Immediately outside the entranceway into each compound there was a small wooden chamber set into the rampart. The watchmen stayed here at night, ready to challenge anyone who approached. The watchmen had drums to beat should they need to summon help.

Inside each compound there were several huts made of stakes driven deep in the ground. Screens of interwoven willow shoots were fixed between these in pairs and the narrow gap between the screens was packed with brown bracken and dry moss. The roofs were thatched with straw. This kept them dry. The huts were painted with lime on the outside, so they were a dull white to the eye. This kept them warm. Some of these huts were for men: others were for animals.

Behind Crunnchu's compounds rose a small mountain. In summer he grazed his sheep on its steep sides, while in winter the fern would show brown through the snow that always dusted the slopes.

At the mountain's top there was an old fort. The deep outer moat, the high earth ramparts inside this, and the four entrances that were once stopped with piles of thorn bush and briar, could all clearly be seen from Crunnchu's compounds below.

Hundreds of years earlier this fort, along with the thousands of others just like it that were scattered across the island, was home to the Tuatha De Danaan, the Tribes of the Goddess Danu.

Then the Celts arrived from Spain and beat them in battle. The Tuatha De Danaan decided to abandon the surface of Ireland. They burrowed under their sidhes, as their forts and earthworks were known, to create fabulous hidden palaces, and then they vanished into these. Deep underground everything was opposite to what it was above ground. The Tuatha De Danaan knew neither grief nor sorrow nor death; they stayed young forever and became gods.

Thereafter the two occupiers of Ireland lived largely separate lives. Only now and again did the two get tangled up: usually when one of the Sidhe fell in love with a mortal, as happened now.

She was called Macha and the object of her affections, improbable as it may seem, was the farmer with the bandy legs and the shiny head.

Without his knowledge she began to watch him after the death of his wife. In the beginning she was simply inquisitive. But as the years rolled on she began to see there was more and more to admire in the man. He was so diligent. He was so prudent. He had such a talent for enduring and for prospering. Her initial curiosity gradually turned to interest and that turned into affection and that finally became love.

After watching for twelve years, Macha decided that, as Crunnchu was not going to take an ordinary woman as his second wife, he could have her instead. She would leave her people and go to him.

One morning, when Art and Cet were out in the fields, Crunnchu was alone in the living hut lolling on a couch of wood and feather cushions when he heard the sound of footsteps on the flags outside the door. It was a woman judging by her footfalls and this puzzled him.

'Who's there?' he called out.

The doorway was stopped with a wattle screen. It was lifted aside and a shaft of light slanted into the hut, crowded with spots of trembling brightness. A dark shape stepped over the threshold. It was a woman. She was of middling height, middling age. She put the screen back over the door space and the slanting light vanished. The stranger moved through the gloom to the couch across from his. She sat down on the end, sideways on to him.

Crunnchu squinted across. He saw black hair, gold earrings, a dark dress fastened at the shoulder with a clasp.

'You're welcome,' he said.

Macha stared ahead. He waited. She said nothing. Why was she just sitting? He sighed. Well, he wasn't going to talk to her if she didn't want to talk to him. This was typical; for all his patience and care, he had a habit of making his mind up very quickly, especially when it came to judging others.

Without moving his head he squinted the other way at his bronze sword. It was in its scabbard, standing against the osier wall. It had a gorgeous fat handle that fitted snugly in his big right hand. It was double-edged and he had sharpened both blades the day before. He could slice off her hand with this lovely weapon as easily as split an apple.

Crunnchu decided to pretend to fall asleep. Then he would jump up, seize the sword and give her a few sharp thwacks with the flat – these would hurt but not cut – and then he'd drive her out. Next time she walked in on a householder, she'd not be so quick to carry on like this.

He lowered his lids and was breathing deeply as if drifting towards sleep when he was startled by the sound of a log falling on embers. He opened his eyes.

He hadn't heard her stand but there was the strange woman, standing over the pit, feeding wood to the fire. There were sparks shooting up towards the smoke hole in the roof above.

Macha sensed him looking. She turned, caught his eye and smiled. Her face, which he had not seen properly until now, was wide and calm. Perhaps, after all, he'd let her stay and see what happened. Once again he had changed his mind but then that was Crunnchu: he was changeable.

Macha and the farmer spent the morning by the fire in silence. In the afternoon Crunnchu's sons came in from the fields; she said not a word. Later still, without either being asked or being shown, she found a kneading tray and a sieve with a copper mesh and began to prepare food. In the evening, and still she had not said a word, she went out to the cow and milked her.

When she returned with the pitcher full of frothy warm milk, she went to the cooking hut and now she spoke at last. She gave directions to the women servants. At the meal that followed she sat beside Crunnchu and now she was silent again. After the meal, when everyone went to his sleeping couch she remained and prepared the fire for the night. Then she followed Crunnchu to his couch, undressed and got under the pelts beside him. If this wasn't surprising enough, she then laid her hand on his side.

'My name is Macha,' she said.

This was the start of their life together as man and wife.

By the autumn of the following year, Macha was pregnant and her stomach was huge.

At the end of this season, on the day designated as the first day of winter, the annual fair was held. Crunnchu always went. It was held under the patronage of the Ulster High King, who at that time was called Almu.

Early on the day of the fair, Macha sat Crunnchu down outside the living-hut to get him ready. It was a clear cold day and the light was clean and hard. She had a thick pin to clean his nails, water to wash his face and a knife to cut his hair.

'This is not the day to be boastful or careless in what you say about me,' she warned.

'Why would I?' he asked. 'Aren't I always quiet?'

She eased a round of blue dirt from under one of his cracked yellow nails with the point of the pin. It fell to the ground.

'It would be better to stay here,' she advised.

He shook his head. So she did not trust him? Well, he would show her.

He set off in ill humour, walked from the hills where he lived and reached the fair. It was held on the vast meeting ground in front of King Almu's fort. The grass was entirely hidden by people when Crunnchu arrived. It was a joy to know that, for a while at least, he would be among so many. His bad temper vanished like mist before sunlight. He now felt cheerful but was cautious. For the rest of the day he was as good as his word to Macha. He said nothing about her unusual origins.

At the end of the day, King Almu emerged from his fort in his chariot and was driven to the fair for the final race.

King Almu's was a typical chariot, a sleek structure with wicker sides and two seats: one for the charioteer, the other for the warrior. In front of each seat there were leather foot-bindings fixed to the floor and at the side there were leather ties. In battle or a race like this, men stood with their feet in the bindings and the ties knotted around their waists to help them stay on board. King Almu and his driver were standing and tied.

King Almu's chariot circled the crowd and the king glanced about with a haughty expression on his face. Several lesser kings would be taking part in the race against him and King Almu wished to signal his indifference to his challengers.

In fact King Almu was anxious. This race would have huge consequences for him.

If he won, his authority would be reaffirmed, at least for the time being. If he lost, however, the lower kings would start whispering that the time had come to replace him.

The competitors lined their chariots up behind the starting mark. The steward raised his sword. In each chariot, driver and passenger dug their feet deeper into the foot-bindings and tightened the ties around their waists.

The steward dropped his sword. The drivers cracked their whips. King Almu and the lesser kings bellowed. The animals galloped away. Their hooves threw clods of earth into the air and the chariots juddered behind. One lost a wheel and veered sideways. It hit a second and capsized it. The other chariots raced on. For a while as they chased across the grass they were in a pack, but then King Almu's chariot began to surge ahead and passed the end mark first.

The watching crowd shouted, clapped and whistled. King Almu's driver wheeled the king's chariot round and trotted past the crowd. The king undid the ties and sat down on the warrior's seat. From here he acknowledged the crowd's applause with waves and nods.

In the middle of the crowd the man beside Crunnchu cheered like the rest. As he did he jostled Crunnchu with his shoulder and the farmer, in turn, irritatedly shoved his neighbour back. Crunnchu hoped this would make him more mannerly. It did no good; his neighbour was too intent on securing King Almu's attention to notice.

Now King Almu got really close and, as he did, the neighbour roared, 'There's nothing alive could beat those horses of yours.'

He wanted King Almu to hear this praise and remember him when he came to ask him a favour. There was a girl he wished his son to marry but he had not the bride price to pay her male relatives: only with King Almu's help could he pay.

King Almu appeared to hear him. He turned. Having caught the king's attention, Crunnchu's neighbour raised his hand to wave and as he did he clipped Crunnchu's chin.

That was it for Crunnchu. The words sprang out of his mouth before he could stop them. 'My wife could beat those horses,' he boasted. This was a mistake. Fighting, quarrelling or any action likely to spoil the sport of the fair attracted the harshest penalties.

'Who?' asked Crunnchu's neighbour as the king passed on. His manner was easy.

'I told you,' said Crunnchu aggressively, 'my wife, you fool.'

'This man says his wife could outrun our king's horses,' the neighbour shouted derisively.

'What?' asked another man. 'He says his wife's faster than what?'

'The king's horses,' repeated the neighbour.

'He's a braggart,' said a second.

'That's an insult, plain and simple,' said a third. 'The fool deserves the worst. Don't we have punishments for ones like him who cause trouble at fairs? Will someone tell King Almu what he said?'

Crunnchu decided to slip away. But as he moved sideways, the men he wanted to pass blocked his path.

'You're not leaving,' one said. 'Troublemakers like you must pay for their crimes.'

'Get out of my way,' Crunnchu cried.

They pushed him back and he was seized from behind.

The harder he now struggled to get away, the harder the men gripped him.

King Almu heard the disturbance and turned to see figures jostling and pushing in the crowd. Perhaps they were drunk? Here was an opportunity for him to consolidate his authority, and as he was elected he never ignored any opportunity to assert himself.

'Drive over to where those men are fighting,' King Almu said to his charioteer.

The driver wheeled about and drove there. King Almu got down and walked across to Crunnchu and the roiling knot of men around him.

'What is going on?' he asked.

The entire crowd fell silent.

'This man says he knows someone faster than your horses.'

'Does he?'

'He does,' said the man with the favour to ask. This was forgotten, of course, because what now consumed him most was preserving his own life. He needed to prove Crunnchu was the troublemaker and he was innocent.

'He says his wife is faster than your horses.'

'Oh,' said King Almu warily. So this man had insulted him? There was only one penalty for this. The trouble was, having Crunnchu killed now would do no good. All the crowd would remember was there was a woman and she supposedly could run faster than his royal horses.

'You in the crowd,' King Almu shouted at Crunnchu's captors, 'have you got a good hold of this idiot?'

'We have,' they shouted back.

'Good. Don't let him go because I propose to fetch his wife here and race her. We shall see who's faster then.'

Crunnchu, his arms tightly grasped, stood with his mouth closed and his heart thumping, his gaze fixed on the distant point where the clear deep blue sky shaded into the dark purple hills. It was too late to speak. If he said he was lying the least he could expect was a thick blade dug into his gut. Let King Almu fetch Macha. While they waited the crowd's fury would subside. No fire could rage if it wasn't stoked and by his silence he could help there. Then, when Macha appeared and King Almu saw she was pregnant, he would call the race off, wouldn't he? If Crunnchu was very lucky and the king was merciful, perhaps he might be spared and allowed to leave.

'Where is your farm?' King Almu demanded.

Crunnchu told him. A messenger was dispatched. King Almu addressed the crowd again.

'Aren't you lucky today?' he announced sarcastically. 'A woman is going to run against these horses and win.' King Almu pointed at his beasts. 'And you must never forget that you only got the opportunity to see this remarkable event because of me, your king,' and here King Almu patted his chest, 'who so generously agreed to allow his winning horses to be defeated by a woman.'

While the crowd jeered, Crunnchu silently begged the gods to intercede. Let Macha's labour begin now. Or if not that, then put the thought into her head that she must go to her people in their palace under the mountain.

'If she leaves now,' he whispered, 'she'll be gone by the time the messenger calls . . .'

Neither happened. When King Almu's messenger arrived he found Macha at the fire. He explained his business to her.

'I'm surely not expected to come and run now,' said Macha, showing the messenger her huge swollen belly. 'Look at me.'

'You do as you wish, but if you don't come your husband will be killed.'

'I have no choice then . . .'

When the messenger and Macha reached the fair, the crowd was still as ugly and excited as before. They closed around the chariot. Everyone wanted to see this woman.

Macha slid down from the warrior's seat and landed heavily on the ground. She doubled over. Her waters broke and wet her skirt and the ground around her feet.

'You should not stare at a woman in my condition,' she said to those in the crowd nearest her.

'Why wouldn't we?' said a wag. 'We've never seen a woman who's faster than a horse. Of course we'd want to look.'

Gusts of cruel laughter swept through the crowd. King Almu's chariot approached. When he was close enough to see, King Almu stood up and called over the people's heads, 'Get her over here.'

'I can't run now,' protested Macha. 'The birth has

started. You can see for yourself, surely?'

'Those with swords get ready!' shouted King Almu. 'When I give the word, you can hack her husband to bits.'

'Will you not help me?' said Macha, appealing to those closest to her. 'Let me bear my child the way your mothers bore you.'

'Well, your husband shouldn't have opened his mouth, should he?' someone shouted back nastily. 'Otherwise you'd be at home now, wouldn't you, having your baby on your own birthing couch?'

Hands grabbed Macha and she was hustled over to the king like a log borne down an angry river.

'What is your name?' King Almu asked from the back of his chariot, where he was standing waiting, with an expression that combined anger and impatience.

'Macha,' she said. She grabbed the rim of the chariot's wickerwork wall for support.

'Please,' she said, looking up at him, 'let the birth come first.'

King Almu frowned. 'Your husband gave his word. You would outrun my horses. He said nothing about having to give birth first.'

'If you make me do this, you and all here will be paid back, hurt for hurt.'

King Almu looked down and said, 'Let us race.'

Macha knew she had no choice. King Almu heaved her into the chariot and put her on the warrior's seat and then he sat beside her. King Almu's charioteer then gently trotted the horses to the starting point. When they got there the king pushed Macha down.

'Take your starting mark there,' he ordered. King Almu's charioteer positioned the chariot between the two staves. Two more staves marked the winning place. They were a long way off and to get to them they would both have to pass the crowd. The driver and King Almu put their feet in the foot-bindings and fixed the ties around their waists.

A steward raised his sword and let it fall.

An enormous shout went up from the crowd. It was a mix of contempt for King Almu's competitor and delight at the king's imminent victory.

The king's charioteer whipped his horses. King Almu bellowed. Macha lifted her skirts high. Macha and the horses both bolted forward.

Crunnchu watched from the crowd. He was waiting for the horses to move ahead and for Macha to be left behind. But instead, as the pair thundered along, the chariot did not pull away. Macha kept abreast and then, slowly, she started to pull ahead. She moved so fast her legs, like the horses' legs, were a blur, indistinguishable to Crunnchu's eye.

King Almu's charioteer whipped his horses again and again and the king bellowed. The animals speeded up but as they did so did Macha. This went on as they came closer to the winning place – King Almu's horses straining and failing, Macha striving and extending her lead slowly and steadily.

Suddenly, Crunnchu realised his wife was going to win.

What would everyone in the crowd say to him then? He was filled with hot pleasure. What a wonder to win and be proved right.

The finishing place was just a few strides ahead. In the time it took to close his eyes and then open them, victory would be hers and his. Suddenly Macha faltered and then, with an awful wail, she fell to the ground. King Almu's horses sped past her prone figure, the chariot juddering behind, then thundered between the staves that marked the winning place.

Crunnchu felt his stomach curdle. Macha had lost. He wanted to cry like a child.

He watched King Almu's charioteer rein his horses in and turn the chariot round. He watched the king, still standing, repeatedly bowing his head towards the crowd and waving with his right hand at them. He watched the crowd waving and shouting back. They were like men after their first drink but before their brains become stupid and addled.

'An excellent outcome,' he heard someone shouting. 'She ran well but the king won in the end, which was only right.'

'Yes,' Crunnchu agreed. He tried to sound as if he was both happy, and as if he was chastened and regretted his boast.

He wanted to go to Macha but his captors still held him fast. He saw King Almu was now speaking to his messenger, who then walked up to him.

'King Almu says you are to let this fellow go,' announced the messenger.

Everyone approved of Crunnchu's release. Those who held Crunnchu let him go and then thumped him in a friendly if bumptious way. Their blows were hard enough to hurt but not so hard that he would take offence. Even the man who wanted the bride price was friendly. He said to Crunnchu, 'Your wife, she did well she did, even if she was never going to win.'

Crunnchu considered saying, 'If she wasn't pregnant, she would have won,' but thought better of it. So he just smiled and nodded at his erstwhile tormentors and then when their attention moved back to King Almu, who was now making a victory lap around the crowd in his chariot, Crunnchu slipped away from them. He pushed on carefully through the crowd, taking care to bump into no one, and finally he burst free on to the open grass. Macha was on the ground ahead of him, her skirts up, her bare body showing.

He ran over to her. While the curious stared and the incurious walked around them, first a son and then a daughter slithered out on to the grass.

'Fionn and Fionnuala,' Macha said.

Crunnchu slapped first one and then the other infant and then bit through the umbilical cords. As Fionn and Fionnuala gave their first cries, Macha began screaming. The sound she made was ugly and hard. The crowd fell silent as the terrible noise spread over them.

Then, without warning, King Almu and every fighting man in the crowd doubled up and fell to the ground.

'Oh my stomach,' cried one stricken warrior.

'Oh my guts,' shouted another.

'I'm dying,' moaned a third.

A collective wail went up. It was very horrible and very loud.

A woman darted out of the crowd and loomed over Macha and her husband. Her hair was scraped back from her bony face and fixed with a gold clasp at the back. She had thin legs sticking out from under her skirts.

'What is happening?' she demanded.

Another woman appeared beside the first. She carried a sword that was obviously too heavy for she held it with both hands.

'What have you done?' this second one said. 'You've done something. I know you have.'

Macha groaned but did not answer.

'Let's cut the woman's throat,' said the woman with the sword.

'No, lop off her breasts, cut out her womb and *then* cut her throat,' said the one with the bony face. 'Let's make it hurt.'

'Better still,' said the one with the heavy sword.

A few other women moved up beside the first two. Their hands were behind their backs and Crunnchu guessed they had weapons they did not want him to see.

'Our men are dying,' one of the newcomers said.

'They are not dying,' said Macha viciously. She lay on the ground, blood on her thighs, with Fionn feeding at her right breast and Fionnuala suckling on the left one.

'They're being punished. Those are the pangs of birth

they're suffering, the pangs that every mother knows and that no man until now has known.'

The women murmured anxiously. Witchcraft and spells in a story were one thing. It was quite another when it affected them directly.

'Why are they suffering like this?' asked Bony Face, her tone suddenly reasonable. 'These men have their own pains, the ones of battle. They should not have ours as well.'

'Oh yes, they should. Your men made me run when my birth pangs had begun. Well, now I've paid them back. Now they know what I felt.'

'And for how long will they suffer?'

'For this season. Today is the first day of winter. This is how they will stay until the first day of spring.'

'And then what – they recover?'

'For the time being.'

'What does that mean? These pangs are coming back?'

'Oh yes,' said Macha, joyously.

'When?'

'The worst time imaginable.'

'What does that mean?'

'When your men can least afford to be stricken.'

'When is that?'

'When do you think?'

'This riddle is beyond us.'

'Whenever invaders cross the border and enter Ulster, these pains will come and they will not end until the season in which they began gives way to the one that follows. Your men will have to stay in their beds and without them to defend you, think what will happen to you. You'll all be giving birth in nine months to the children of your invaders, assuming that is they let you live.'

The women were appalled.

'And don't think this curse will end in your lifetime,' Macha continued. 'Your sons and the sons of your sons, forward for nine generations, will suffer the same pains if they are fighting men and Ulster is invaded.'

'We'll be destroyed,' moaned Bony Face and began to cry. 'Are there any exceptions?' she asked, wiping her eyes with the heel of her hand.

'Women, boys and anyone with a parent like me who is a Sidhe.'

When they heard this last word all the women started as if each had been pricked with a poison thorn. Macha was a woman not to argue with, much less to talk of killing. If they angered her further she would punish them as she had punished their men.

The women slunk away. On the ground behind they joined all the other women and children who were searching for their men. When they had found them, they gathered them up and carried them away. The lamentations that had filled the air gave way to silence as the ground emptied. Crunnchu built a fire and lit it. The light leeched away from the winter sky and dusk fell.

'What have you done?' Crunnchu asked Macha.

'Nothing less than what they deserve,' said Macha.

Later, while Macha drowsed, he stared into the flames. He saw justice in her position yet he felt sick in his heart on account of his stupid boast and the trouble it had begun. Every predator in Ireland and elsewhere, once they heard of Macha's curse, would storm his province. All women would be raped, all children enslaved, and all compounds looted and burned.

Happily he was wrong. He forgot that human beings are most inventive when they are most in trouble. Once King Almu recovered from his pangs he immediately created a corps of warriors known as the Boy Spears. They were youths. They had no hair on their faces. Therefore the curse did not affect them.

When the first invasion came after Macha had laid her curse, the Boy Spears went out into the field to meet the enemy. Their style was unusual. They did not engage in mass battles or single combat as grown warriors did. Instead they harried and raided and kept the enemy at bay. With these tactics the Boy Spears stopped the invaders sacking forts, stealing children and hurting women.

The men warriors, meanwhile, lay in their beds, stricken with the birth pangs and unable to fight. When the season ended – and in those times the seasons had definite days on which they started and ended – the pains left them. They got out of their sickbeds and marched out to meet the invaders.

Battle was joined. The Ulster warriors gave the enemy no quarter. They slaughtered every one of them. Then they cut off their heads (these were taken back by Ulster's warriors as spoils of war; preserved and stored in the house of the Ruddy Branch), and they stuck the bodies up on poles along the border to warn those who were thinking of raiding what they could expect. In no short time the men of Ulster acquired a reputation for extreme violence. Incursions across the border, though they never entirely ceased, certainly declined. So Crunnchu's stupidity produced a good result in the end.

Years later, when he was old and close to death, Macha took Crunnchu to visit a druid who was said to be able to see what lay in the future. Crunnchu had one question. Would Macha's curse, he asked, produce any more unexpected consequences like the Boy Spears?

The seer told him that long after he was dead a royal pair, Maeve and Ailill, queen and king of Connacht, would march north with a great army to capture Ulster's great Brown Bull.

Because of Macha's curse all Ulster's warriors would be disabled by the birth pangs and the enemy would be too numerous and formidable for the Boy Spears to resist.

However, there would be one warrior in Ulster who sprang from the same stock as Macha and so he would be immune to the pangs: Cuchulainn. He would keep Maeve and Aillil's great army at bay, at great cost to the enemy and also to himself, until the warriors recovered, and in the process he would become famous.

Crunnchu died knowing that his stupidity would be the making of a great hero. No man could ask for a better outcome to his actions and he died happy. Macha returned then to her people in the palace under the mountain, taking Fionn and Fionnuala with her and leaving Art and Cet behind to work their father's land.

Chapter Two

Conor's birth and his rise to power

King Almu's fort had become known as Emain Macha, meaning the twins of Macha (for this was where Fionn and Fionnuala were born). The middle of the fort was a vast mound covered with all sorts of huts and halls. Around the mound lay a huge rampart and circling the rampart was a deep ditch.

There was one entrance cut into the rampart. It was stopped with huge wooden gates and a drawbridge took one across the ditch. Immediately in front of the gate there was a lawn mostly used by women. On both sides of this and running all the way round the walls were many more living and sleeping, cooking and storage huts, along with several halls. These were big wooden structures, of which the grandest were those of the High King. And in front of the lawn stretched the vast meeting ground where fairs and assemblies were held, and where Macha had raced and fallen, given birth and made her curse. Now it was where the Boy Spears and the warriors trained.

One day, when the curse still had generations to run, Nes, who had come to Emain Macha from her own compound which lay away in the east, sat at the edge of the

33

lawn not far from the gates. She was the daughter of Nestor, one of Ulster's lesser kings and so a queen in her own right. She was a small slim woman with a small neat face, dark eyes and beautiful breasts of which she was inordinately proud. Her manner was solemn and she was known to be sharp. Many believed she didn't have a sense of humour. This was true, she didn't.

Cathbad, the druid, passed Nes by. He was a heavy man with a brisk manner, a wide still face on which his feelings never showed, large hands and surprisingly small feet. He was a seer. He was able to look into the future and to understand the meaning of dreams as well as being very learned. He specialised in the healing arts. He knew how to make sick men well and how to drive away madness.

'What is this hour lucky for?' she asked him.

'For conceiving a king with a queen,' he replied without thinking. 'A child conceived now, at this hour, will be spoken of in Ireland for the rest of time.'

'I'm a queen,' she said. 'Are you sure?'

'Yes,' said Cathbad.

'I'm a queen,' she said again.

Nes led him away to the sleeping hut she was using and within the hour she had conceived. She returned to her compound in the east with the child in her belly. The foetus took three years and three months to grow to full size. Then the waters broke. The child that was born was Conor.

The first great event in the boy's life came when he was seven.

At this time Fergus Mac Roi was High King of Ulster. He was a large square man with a square head and a long freckled face and penetrating eyes. Though he was large and powerful his presence was comforting rather than threatening. He had many gifts of which the principal were intelligence, charm and loyalty.

Fergus at this time had no wife and as the beautiful Nes had no husband, he had determined to ask her to marry him. He and his entourage left Emain Macha and travelled to her compound where he proposed to her himself rather than through the customary intermediary.

'To have someone as fine as I am, you must surely expect to pay,' she said quickly.

Fergus nodded.

'Of course,' he said. 'No bride comes free.'

'I wasn't thinking of the bride price in gold though,' she said.

'Weren't you? What were you thinking?'

'I come encumbered,' she said.

'Encumbered?' He smiled. She was fooling. 'You don't have a husband. At least I don't think you do. Do you have a husband?'

'I was thinking of my son.'

'Ah. Of course, I will help him . . . and look after him and . . .'

'No bride price,' she said quickly. 'Instead, resign your kingship and install my son in your place. Then, when Conor has a son, as one day, though he's only a child now, he surely will, that child will be known as the son of a king.'

'And why would I do that?' Fergus picked at skin at the side of his thumb. 'We might have a son who one day might follow me.'

'We might,' said Nes sweetly. She had noticed the way Fergus was worrying away at his thumb.

'I'm not asking you to give up the kingship forever,' said Nes. 'Oh no. That would be too much. No, in a year's time, Conor will resign in your favour.'

Fergus went to take counsel with his people outside. Yes, he wanted Nes but did he want her enough to accept her terms?

'Oh give her what she wants,' said one of his entourage.

'What harm is in it?' said another. 'You'll really still be king, won't you? Her son'll just be the king in name. He's only a child.'

'And,' said a third, 'in a year's time you'll be king again and you'll have a delightful wife too and at no cost, no bride price. And she is so beautiful. This is a really good proposition.'

Fergus went back in to Nes. 'All right, I agree,' he said.

Nes and Fergus became husband and wife. They returned to Emain Macha taking Conor with them. He was now styled High King. Fergus continued to make decisions of course.

Nes was well liked. She became even better liked when she gave all her gold and silver to the same Ulster warriors who had first elected Fergus and then, when they were in her compound, advised him to marry her.

Her action perplexed and bewildered Fergus. He assumed it was in the hope of what her son might gain from these same warriors one day. He did not like this.

Fergus by nature was not combative. He hadn't lived as long as he'd lived and got as far as he had by the exercise of force. He was clever and cunning and he never picked an argument unless he was certain he would win.

He waited until he and Nes were in bed together one night before he broached the subject in his typically indirect way.

'You're a generous woman,' he said.

'I am.'

'Very generous.'

'If you say so.'

'All your wealth you've given away and what is that if not generous?'

'What other way could I show my thanks to your good warriors?'

Fergus lay still in the darkness.

'I heard everything that was said out in my courtyard. Without their persuasion you wouldn't have taken me, would you?' she said.

'Oh but I would,' said Fergus. He had not expected the conversation to take this turn. 'Of course I would.'

'I wanted you, you know, and so I made a vow that if they made you take me, I'd give them everything I had.

Everything. And having made the vow and then you taking me, well, I had to give them everything, didn't I? I couldn't break a vow.'

This answer took Fergus completely by surprise. He was charmed by it. He was flattered by it. He believed it. And he wanted to believe because that was better than knowing he had been duped.

Exactly one year to the day after the marriage, Fergus invited Conor to resign, as Nes had promised he would before he married her.

But when the same warriors who had advised him to marry heard Fergus making this announcement, they demurred.

'We're not certain about this. We'll have to talk about it.'

Fergus and the warriors gathered together. Their talk was heated. The warriors were angry.

'You've obviously no regard for us who elected you king in the first place,' said one.

'That's not true, of course I have,' Fergus protested.

'No, or you wouldn't have traded your position like a chattel.'

'I did not,' Fergus protested hotly. The warriors rejected this denial. Fergus went on pleading but they would not hear him. They expressed their position with this simple single phrase:

'What you sold, Fergus, should stay sold, and what Conor paid for, he should keep.'

Now Fergus understood that he had been very foolish when he believed Nes's explanation. She had given all her money away to get them on her side. The truth bore down upon him and he could not deny it. He had wanted to believe he had married a kind woman, not a schemer. But she had betrayed him and it was too late to do anything about that now. The warriors had swung against him.

It was at moments of crisis that Fergus's thinking was clearest. He was not a man for complaining or feeling sorry for himself. When things were bad he would look at them coldly and without emotion and determine what was the best thing to do.

He had resigned his kingship for a year. Now he wanted it back but his warriors, on whom he depended for election, did not want to let him have it. They wanted this child to remain.

If he went against them, what would happen?

They would win.

He was outnumbered and out-manoeuvred. He could fight and lose. Or he could concede and survive. Given the choice there was only one possible decision he could make.

'All right,' he agreed. 'Conor is king.'

Fergus went to find Nes. He found her on the lawn outside the fort.

'Why did you do it? Why did you trick me?'

There was no answer she could give that would make him happy, so Nes stared at the sky and said nothing.

'I am not your husband any more,' he said.

Again, there was nothing Nes could say so she stayed silent.

Fergus went back into the fort. Later the same day Conor sought him out.

'Are we still going to be friends?' asked the boy. He spoke gravely and without guile.

'Why do you ask? You think we wouldn't be?'

'Yes.'

'Why would you think we wouldn't be friends?'

'Because my mother tricked you and you're angry.'

'Well, that's true.'

'But are you angry with me?' said Conor.

How did he answer this little boy? Conor's question was so pure and direct and uncomplicated. But how should he answer? What were his feelings?

His thoughts came. They were quick and deft, just like his work with the sword. Had this been the boy's doing? Well, obviously not. His mother, Nes, was the one who plotted and bribed. Conor hadn't had anything to do with it, had he? In which case was it fair to hate him? Well, no, clearly it wasn't. He couldn't hate someone for what his mother had done.

Then there was the complicating factor of affection. He had come to like this solemn, high-minded child over the year he'd known him, hadn't he? Yes, he had. And were those feelings there still?

It didn't take Fergus very long to recognise they remained unchanged.

Could he gather them up and throw them away?

That was hardly likely, he decided. In which case there was only one answer he could give.

'No,' he said finally, 'I'm not angry with you.'

'Well, if you're not angry will you stay?'

'Why?'

'In order that I can talk to you every day?'

'And will you listen?'

'Of course.'

'Whose idea is this?'

'No one's.'

'No one's suggested you ask me?'

'Of course not.'

'You're sure Nes didn't put you up to this?'

'No one put me up to anything.'

He said this so emphatically Fergus felt certain it was true.

Fergus pondered. What if he accepted this? And what if the young king not only asked his advice but acted on it too? Wouldn't that be rather wonderful? As an advisor he would have power and prestige, wouldn't he? Yet he'd never need to worry that he was surrounded by men who wanted to usurp him. Wouldn't that be marvellous, to have authority without the burden of fear? He might even decide in the end that the way things had worked out was for the best.

'So what do you say?' asked Conor.

'I'll do as you ask,' Fergus replied. 'I'll stay.'

He stayed while his mother, Nes, whom Fergus soon divorced, returned to her compound and thereafter almost never saw her son. The years passed. Having started as friends, Fergus and Conor grew closer and closer.

Then Conor became a man. At this point they might have parted. Conor could have jettisoned the influences of his youth. Fergus could have grown jealous. It was one thing to serve a minor. It was another to serve a king who was so adored that when a man married he sent his new wife to Conor for the wedding night.

But Fergus was as clear-sighted as he was wise. He saw that the kingdom was more prosperous and calm and secure than it could ever have been under him.

Time passed. By early middle age Conor was a handsome man with a household as handsome as he was and three magnificent homes as well. Their names were the house of the Ruddy Branch, the house of the Glittering Hoard and the house of the Red Branch. The first two were within the ramparts of Emain Macha, while the third was outside.

The spoils of war were kept in the first, the house of the Ruddy Branch. These were the smoked heads, brown and wrinkled, or the lime-preserved brains, grey and hard, of Conor's enemies.

The weapons and precious objects were kept in the second house, the house of the Glittering Hoard. These were swords and javelins with gold chased into their handles, shield plates and shields with shining silver rims, goblets, cups and drinking-horns with gold and silver parts. There were also rooms where the king could stay in an emergency, such as an invasion.

However, other than at such times, the king was always in his main residence, the house of the Red Branch, which was red, the colour of royalty. It was enormous (which was why it couldn't be inside the rampart, it would have taken up too much ground in there) with a hundred and fifty inner rooms, each of which slept three couples. Conor's room was in the middle and the walls were made of sheets of copper. In this room he kept the rod he used for keeping order. It was silver with three gold apples on the end. He only had to shake this once and everyone would fall into such respectful silence you could hear a needle drop to the floor.

Fergus, as the second most important man in the kingdom after Conor, had his room next door to the king's. He came and went as he wished. He still gave advice and his advice was followed more often than it was ignored. These were very good years and Fergus often remembered the day when the boy Conor had asked him to stay. Now he knew his decision had turned out for the best. Now he knew there was no better man than Conor to be king.

Chapter Three

Sétanta's birth and early life

A vast flock of thrushes landed on the lawn in front of Emain Macha where the women often sat and worked at their embroidery if the sun was shining. The thrushes devoured the green blades and shoots that showed above the ground. Then they pulled out the white earthy roots and ate them too. The thrushes worked in pairs that were attached to one another by silver chains.

The guards on the ramparts summoned Conor and he rushed to the rampart.

'They've the lawn destroyed already,' said Conor, staring down at the great blanket of thrushes below him, chewing everything in their way. 'They'll have the meeting ground finished next and then they'll empty the plains beyond. If something's not done there'll be nothing left growing in the whole country.'

He ordered nine chariots harnessed and collected together a small retinue. Among those in the party were Fergus as well as the king's sister, Dechtire. Conor's usual driver, Ibar, was sick and he had decided Dechtire would drive his chariot today. Dechtire was a nervous woman, who wore her red crinkled hair swept back from her face and was inclined to sweat when she was anxious. Her most prominent features were her great broad forehead, her red eyebrows, and her large blue eyes.

The nine chariots loaded with drivers and warriors went careering out the gate and across the bare earth where the lawn had been, the hooves of the pulling horses pitting the earth, and the metal-rimmed chariot wheels scoring lines in it. And as they hurtled forward, the charioteers in their seats at the front shouted at the tops of their voices, while Conor and the others on their seats at the back pounded their throwing spears on their shields of iron plate on a wooden frame.

The thrushes heard these noises. How could they not? But they were not startled. They did not rise quickly making a great banging noise with their wings. They simply floated effortlessly upward and flew away slowly over the plain that ran on from where the meeting ground ended.

'Stop,' Conor ordered.

The charioteers obliged. The retinue watched the birds moving away.

'They've gone,' said Conor.

'Only into the sky,' Fergus pointed out.

The birds drifted down to the plain beyond the meeting ground and resumed eating again.

'Look at them,' said Conor, 'they're shameless. Come on, after them.'

The nine chariots thundered after them, unimpeded by dykes or walls, trees or ditches. There was nothing between them and the thrushes but flat green turf and clear warm air.

When the chariots had almost caught up, the thrushes flew off again and landed on a more distant part of the plain and the chariots were obliged to chase after them again. The pursuit went on for the rest of the day until a pair of birds detached itself from the flock.

'Follow them,' said Conor.

The chariots raced after them across the flat plain, the eyes of the drivers fixed on the two brown dots moving across the white sky. As afternoon shaded towards dusk, a great gash appeared in the ground ahead – it was the river Boyne. In the distance the huge ancient tomb of Newgrange rose up. Snowflakes began falling, a few to begin with and very soon many more. The thrushes wheeled into the dappled sky and vanished.

'Stop here,' Conor ordered.

Reins were tugged. The chariots stopped.

Fergus slipped down through the opening at the back of his chariot and went off to look for shelter. Close to where the chariots had halted he found a sturdy earth rampart – it looked newly built to him – with fresh new huts inside. The sole occupiers were a solitary young couple. This was odd but he thought nothing of it because he was in such a rush to find somewhere before it got dark. The man was tall with a smooth pleasant face, while his wife was handsome, with a pointed, freckled face, exceedingly white skin and a hugely swollen belly: she was hugely pregnant.

'We need shelter for the night,' said Fergus. He explained how many and who they were.

'You are all welcome,' said the man.

Fergus looked at the woman to see that she agreed as well. Her eyes were black, he noticed, as she nodded.

Fergus returned to the chariots, then led the party back across the snowy ground. It was dusk when they arrived, not quite night but nearly, and the rampart and huts showed up as dark stark shapes against the white drizzle tumbling from the sky.

The visitors crowded into the living hut, warm and smoky. The handsome man was alone.

'Where's your wife?' Fergus asked.

'She's in the storage hut giving birth,' he said. He indicated the direction of the hut with a sweep of his hand. Had there been more light Fergus might have noticed the seven fingers. He might also have noticed the four pupils in one eye and the three in the other. But all he saw in the murk was that the hands seemed unusually big and the eyes unusually wide.

'Is your wife alone?' asked Dechtire.

'She is,' said their host.

'I'll help her.'

Dechtire glided out of the doorway, through the snow and into the storage hut.

The woman lay on pelts on a couch.

'Who is that?' she called.

'A friend,' said Dechtire.

In the middle of the night, with Dechtire's help, the woman with the white skin and freckled face gave birth. It was a boy, quite perfect except each hand had seven fingers and each foot seven toes. In the room, lit only by firelight, this was not noticed. The baby's eyes were closed so the four pupils in one eye and the three in the other were not noticed either.

At the same time a hugely pregnant mare appeared in the compound, whinnying and stamping her hoof. Conor's party, who were very cheerful by this stage for their host had plied them with beer, came out to see the mare in her pangs. As snowflakes fluttered and trembled all around, she dropped two foals, one black and the other grey. The newborn animals immediately struggled on to their long spindly legs – these did not look as if they could support their bodies but they did – and then stumbled after their mother. They found her teats and started to suckle. The men watching applauded and went back inside the hut to have more beer.

Early the next morning Fergus awoke. He sat up and brushed the snow from his face. His cheekbones ached. The others were stirring around him. They were dusted like he was with snow.

Fergus looked around. He was on open ground. The hut where he had fallen asleep with everyone else was gone. The other huts were gone. The new rampart with its neat flanks was gone. And so were the heavy gates.

In the distance he spotted the chariots and the horses

where they had left them the previous evening. He noticed the new foals were tethered to the spars that stuck out from behind Conor's chariots.

'The mare is gone,' he said, to no one in particular, 'and so is everything else, but not the foals.'

'And not the child,' said Dechtire.

Fergus squinted over and saw a lump under Dechtire's cloak. 'He doesn't move though,' he said.

Fergus went across and lifted the cloak aside. There was a newborn lying there. He was still and might have been asleep but when Fergus touched the head he felt the scalp was cold.

'He's dead, isn't he?' said Dechtire. She could tell from Fergus's face which she was staring at.

'He is.'

'Fergus,' said Conor. The king was up and standing close behind him. 'A word.'

They moved away from the others, the new snow crunching underneath their feet and the flakes that had fallen on their cloaks overnight falling away in little powdery puffs. When they were far enough away that they were sure they could not be overheard they stopped.

'Where is our host and his pregnant wife now do you think?' asked Conor.

Fergus nodded at the distant mound that was Newgrange.

'Yes, I think that too,' said Conor, carefully. 'They're Sidhe. They must come from there.'

'The thrushes were a lure,' said Fergus. 'To get Dechtire here.'

'I agree.'

'Once they'd given her the baby they went home, but without their presence everything vanished.'

'Which surely was why the infant died too,' said Conor.

They put the corpse in a small hollow in the cold ground and heaped stones over his body. Dechtire wept horribly and afterwards asked for a drink of water.

Fergus filled a beaker in the river and carried it back. He didn't notice that there was something floating in the water. Nor did Dechtire. She emptied the beaker without looking.

The retinue set off for Emain Macha . . .

That night Dechtire dreamt she was in an empty place full of light. Their handsome host with the large hands appeared.

'Are you a Sidhe?' Dechtire asked.

'Lugh,' he said. He held up his two enormous hands. In the light Dechtire saw their size and the extra fingers. 'Meaning long-handed.'

'The thrushes were a lure?'

He nodded. 'Nothing existed that you saw that night except me.'

'Not even your wife?'

He smiled. 'You were my wife.'

He explained that while she thought she was helping at a birth, she was in fact with him. They had slept together and the child on her breast in the morning was their child. He had a name: Sétanta. Though he had died, Lugh was not giving up his intention of having a child by Dechtire. His seed was in the water Fergus had fetched in the beaker and she had swallowed this and now Sétanta was in her womb again and growing already.

Then Dechtire awoke. She felt her belly in the darkness. She felt nothing yet she was certain it was true. She was pregnant.

Dechtire was right. She began to swell and, as she did, a nasty rumour spread too through Emain Macha. This was that Conor, her brother, had slept with her in the course of the strange night by the Boyne and made her pregnant. After all, wasn't he drunk from all the drink the strange host with the big hands had passed round to everyone?

The king, appalled by this slander – as was his sister too when she heard it – promptly married Dechtire to Sencha, the judge, and one of Fergus's relatives. On the wedding night Dechtire, her belly by now very swollen, was too ashamed to go to bed with her husband, Sencha, in the state she was in. Pleading sickness she slept alone and when she woke in the morning she found her thighs sticky with blood. Lugh's child had splashed away in the darkness.

The foetus gone, Dechtire was no longer mortified and she went to her new husband. Nine months later she bore a son. He was a perfect child in every respect except for the seven fingers on each hand and the seven toes on each foot and the four pupils in one eye and three in the other. She called him Sétanta.

After the birth, as was the custom, Conor nominated

another of his sisters, Finnchoem, to foster the infant. This caused considerable dissension as many in the king's court, certain that Sétanta was going to be special (he had been conceived three times after all), were adamant they should be the ones chosen as his fosterers instead.

In the end, the arguments over who would foster Sétanta caused such bitterness, the matter went to the judge, Morann. He ruled Finnchoem should be foster-mother to the child and nourish him at her breast. Her husband, Sualdam, should be his foster-father, and her son, the champion Conall the Victorious, should be foster-brother to him. But the strictures did not end there.

Since Finnchoem was Conor's sister, the king, as his foster uncle, should be Sétanta's special patron. Sencha, the judge, Dechtire's husband, should train him in oratory. Blai, the royal quartermaster, should see to his material needs, providing clothes and anything else he needed. Fergus, the warrior, should teach him to fight. Amergin, the poet, should pass on his storytelling gifts. Cherished by many, the judge said, the child would become the supreme chariot-fighter, prince and sage of the age. This was Morann's prophecy.

Sétanta was reared by his fosterers in their home made of oak at Dun Breth. As a child he was lively and agile and compact, he had a broad face, a lovely smile and skin that was slightly golden.

At the age of six he heard rumours of the one-hundred-

and-fifty-strong corps of warriors at Emain Macha, the Boy Spears. They were so impressive as they trained or played on the meeting ground in front of the fort, the king spent a third of his royal day watching them.

Sétanta went to Finnchoem and begged to join the corps of Boy Spears.

'You can't just go,' she said. 'We must wait until someone from Emain visits us who can bring you back there.'

'I can't wait that long,' said the child.

'You must be introduced. They're fierce, even vicious. They kill strangers. You must be vouched for.'

'I won't wait.'

His position was immovable. Finnchoem recognised that.

'How do I find Emain Macha?' he insisted.

She had no alternative. She pointed the way.

He set off. He carried a toy javelin, a wooden play shield made of twigs plaited together, a ball and a hurley stick. Hurley, a fast-moving game played with a broad stick and a hard ball, was Sétanta's favourite pastime.

To shorten the journey, he invented a game. He hit the ball with the stick. Then he hurled the stick after the ball. Then he threw his javelin after the stick. Then, with all three still flying, he ran ahead and caught each item in turn before it fell to the ground. This passed the time nicely until he reached the meeting ground before Emain Macha.

The sight he saw there quickened his heart. The Boy Spears, divided into two enormous teams, were engaged in a violent and exhilarating game of hurley, each side contesting the ball and trying to hit it through the opposition's goal.

Sétanta ran towards the players whooping with joy. Some of the Boy Spears, seeing him coming, waved their arms. This was to warn him away.

What he did not know was that the members of the Boy Spears had all made a *geis* or pledge to kill anyone who interrupted their activities without permission. It was only safe to enter the field during play if Folaman, Conor's son by his first wife Ceithlinn and the Boy Spears' troop leader, had promised safe conduct.

Sétanta, knowing nothing of this, interpreted the waving arms and the other gestures as the typical reaction of older boys who were intent on blocking a younger lad who was trying to join them. Didn't older children always reject a younger one? But that would change, he thought, oh yes, that would change once they saw him play. He ran on.

Folaman, who was a little older and taller than the others, detached himself now from them and turned towards Sétanta.

'You!' Folaman shouted at Sétanta. 'Yes, you, the idiot, go back. You can't join our game. You are not invited.'

Sétanta felt a little prickle of annoyance, hot and sharp, needling around his belly. He reminded himself that he must not slide into rage. He must overlook the insult. He was there to play not to fight and once they saw how skilful he was at hurley they would welcome him.

Sétanta reached the edge of the ground where the game

had been taking place. He slipped nimbly in amongst the Boy Spears. He trapped their ball between his calves and escaped, hopping now rather than running. The members of the Boy Spears threw hundreds of blows at his head and body but he was so agile not even one blow was landed on him.

When he was some distance away he turned and cracked the ball past their heads and over the post.

And yet still, to Sétanta's amazement, the Boy Spears did not wave at him, indicating he was to join them. They turned their backs instead and formed a tight circle around the taller boy, the one who had shouted so rudely at him earlier. In his place in the middle Folaman now addressed his fellow troopers.

'He must be the son of a minor chieftain who doesn't know better and hasn't any manners,' said Folaman, 'which is why he's come on to our field without permission and with no promise of safety. But ignorance is no excuse. He's insulted us and there's only one way to pay him back. We all know what our pledge is, don't we?'

The Boy Spears murmured in agreement.

'Punish him, lads, and don't stop until he's dead.'

The Boy Spears drove every hurling-ball they had at Sétanta. Using his chest as if it was a palm, Sétanta caught every one without losing breath or faltering his pace.

Next, the Boy Spears began flinging their javelins at him and this so infuriated Sétanta, that as he stopped the weapons with his flimsy shield of sticks, the rage took hold of him and his small body began to distort.

Each hair on his head stood up so straight and hard it seemed each one was hammered into his head. The tip of each hair burned red hot as if it had just been lifted from a fire. He closed one eye so tight it was as small as the eye of a needle and he opened the other as wide as the mouth of a goblet. He folded back his mouth baring not just his teeth but his gums and even his gullet, all red and wet and fearful. A bright beam, the size and length of a warrior's whetstone, shot out of the top of his head. This was the hero-light. To the unaccustomed eye it appeared it was filled with a red mist. In fact it was packed with boiling gouts of blood that looked like cloud because of the way they swirled about although they were actually heavy and dense. In his distorted state, with his hero-light showing, Sétanta would fight without remorse.

He charged, stabbing with the javelin in one hand, flailing with the stick in the other. With the javelin point he slashed and stabbed, cutting cheeks open to reveal the mouth inside, taking off eyebrows, and snapping the tender webs of skin between fingers. With the stick he smashed and whacked, showering teeth on the ground like pebbles, cracking collarbones and snapping fingers like kindling twigs.

Fifty Boy Spears fell to the ground, gushing blood and spittle everywhere. The rest fled with Sétanta in pursuit. Some fled through the gate and disappeared into Emain Macha, while others bolted into the house of the Red

Branch, which was outside the ramparts. Sétanta decided he would follow them. He pulled back one of the heavy doors and went forward.

Once inside he found himself in a great hall, with columns supporting the roof. In the middle of this hall sat two men, Conor and Fergus. Sétanta did not know them. They were playing fidchell. The boys he had been chasing cowered at the other end of the room, well behind the men.

Sétanta sprinted forward, scattering the rushes that were strewn on the floor as he went. As he passed the fidchell players, Conor stuck his arm out and snapped his heavy fingers about Sétanta's boyish wrist and stopped him in his tracks.

'Why so rough?' the king demanded.

The definite action and then the emphatic question had a miraculous effect which in later years, when Sétanta's rages were much more powerful, they most definitely would not. The hero-light waned. The skin of his mouth and cheeks slipped forward. The wet red gullet and the gums and the teeth vanished. The needle-sized eye swelled back to its normal size and the goblet-wide eye shrank. The red-hot tips at his hair ends vanished. The nail-like hairs lost rigidity and fell across his head and lay as his hair normally lay. The rage was over. Sétanta was himself again.

The boy now sized the speaker up. This was no ordinary man, Sétanta guessed. His face was broad and moonlike. His beard was fair in colour and forked into two points. His hair was partly yellow and partly red and swept back in parallel ridges so the shape of his skull showed through.

He wore a cloak that fixed at the shoulder with a gold fastener. The shield at his side was black iron with a rim of yellow gold, while resting across his lap was an embossed scabbard. The handle of the sword in the scabbard was made of bronze with a silver fist guard and a big blue stone set in the pommel. A well-shaped spear with an iron tip leaned against the wall behind.

Everything about the speaker struck Sétanta, though he was a child of six, as regal. It had to be Conor, he decided, though until now he had never seen the king and so he would have to answer the question that had been put to him with great care.

'It's nothing less than what they deserve,' he said eventually.

'Oh. And what did they do to make you so fierce?'

'They attacked me.'

'Did they?'

'Without warning and for no reason.'

'I see.'

'I just wanted to join their game.'

'Had you their consent?'

'No. Did I have to?'

'With these boys you do.'

'Why?'

'It's their *geis*. If anyone steps on to their field or interrupts their play, they kill them.'

Sétanta looked glum.

'I didn't know that.'

'Who are you?' asked the king.

'Sétanta, your sister Dechtire's son.'

Conor pondered this unexpected piece of information while the young boy watched his face carefully. Sétanta saw nothing. The king did not look embarrassed or appalled. But the king did not speak either. Behind the blank expression, Sétanta guessed, he was disturbed. For Sétanta was not any child. Their kinship gave him an advantage and he decided to use this now.

'As your nephew I'd no idea I could expect this,' Sétanta said pointedly, 'and theirs was no way to treat a guest.'

'They had the right. They grant protection, you can join in. If they haven't, you stay away.'

Sétanta shrugged.

'I knew nothing about their rules, as I said.'

Conor turned to the Boy Spears cowering at the far end of the hall. 'Right,' Conor shouted at them, 'he is now granted protection, do you understand?'

'Yes,' they shouted back, wary but relieved.

'Go back and take this boy with you and tell the others to make him welcome. He's one of you now.'

Sétanta and the Boy Spears left the hall. Conor went back to his game of fidchell. He had made only one move when a guard from the ramparts appeared. He informed Conor that the Boy Spears and a boy he did not recognise were fighting. The struggle was ugly.

Conor hurried to the meeting ground. He found fifty

wailing youths lying about on the grass. The others who were still standing were defending themselves as best they could, which was not very well, against Sétanta. He was in a rage again.

Conor waded through the seething knot of boys. When he reached Sétanta in the middle he snapped his heavy fingers about his nephew's boyish wrist.

'Stop this now,' he shouted.

As in the hall earlier, the king's action had a miraculous effect. Sétanta's cheeks slipped back into place and covered his mouth, his eyes evened up, and his hair went soft and floppy. The rage vanished. He became a boy again.

'Is this supposed to be play?' asked Conor.

He pointed at the moaning boys scattered about the grass.

'You took their protection. That should be the end of fighting.'

'I did,' said Sétanta, 'but then, when I got out here I thought, I'll knock each and every one to the ground unless they come under *my* protection like I came under *theirs*.'

'But of course we will,' moaned one of the figures on the ground. 'Why wouldn't we?'

The king recognised the speaker. It was his own son Folaman.

'So everyone is happy and this business ends now?' said Conor.

'We are,' said Sétanta.

He turned back to the meeting ground and re-joined his heroes. He was a Boy Spear now.

Chapter Four

Deirdre, the child

Conor, the king of Ulster, and his warriors – or some of them at any rate – were drinking one night in the home of Felimid, the king's principal storyteller.

They were in a long hall with recesses along the sides and three big fires in the middle and clean rushes strewn on the floor. Felimid's wife, Eithlinn, who was huge and about to give birth, spent the evening moving through the throng with heavy flat-footed steps, carrying meat on wooden platters and drink in horn beakers to her guests.

When it got late and the guests were nodding off on the couches in the annexes or staggering away to their sleeping huts, Eithlinn left the hall and went into the courtyard.

The flags sunk in the ground glowed faintly in the moonlight. Supporting her heavy belly from below with her two hands, she trod wearily from stone to stone, following the path that led to her sleeping hut. Suddenly a shudder ran from the mouth of her womb right up her body, followed by a horrible piercing cry that came out of the deepest place inside her being.

In the hall the warriors heard the noise. They started to their feet in panic. Had a terrible enemy vaulted the rampart and was this enemy now about to kill them? They had no weapons on them. These were in an adjoining room where by custom they would always be left. This was to prevent the warriors killing each other if they argued when they were drunk.

The cry sounded again. It was like the screech of a fox only louder and harder and bigger.

The warriors stumbled into the arms room, drunkenly drew their swords and buckled on their shields, then rushed out. In the courtyard they found only Eithlinn, her face wild and pained as she stared at the place in her middle from where the sound now came a third time.

'Fetch her inside,' said Conor.

The men filed back and Eithlinn was led in. The hall smelled of wood-smoke, while the warriors reeked of drink and meat and something musk-like, an odour Eithlinn identified with fear. The interior was lit only by firelight.

'That unnatural sound that came out of you,' Felimid said to his wife, his voice trembling with dread, 'what was it?'

Eithlinn was filled with dread too. She peered around until she found Cathbad the druid. He was quiet and calm as the best sages were. He never started a panic and he could often stop one. He must help her, Eithlinn thought.

'I don't know what it was shrieking inside here,' she said, holding her waist, 'the same way I don't know whether I have a boy or girl, or one child or two. No woman knows what she's carrying until after the birth, does she?'

Cathbad nodded.

'But you're a seer so you tell me what it was and why it screamed then.'

Cathbad closed his eyes and started to hum something to himself. Then his body jerked, his fingers trembled and his eyes rolled up and he started to speak in the other voice that he only used when his eyes stared back into his head.

'It is a girl that you have in you. She will be beautiful and when she is grown she will be envied by women and desired by men.'

Cathbad shuffled forward blindly.

'Where are you?'

'Here,' said Eithlinn.

Cathbad found her and put his hands on her middle. Her belly bulged forward against the thin dress that was all she wore, stretching it tight. With his fingers Cathbad felt the skin rippling and then the infant within kicking furiously against the womb.

'Her name is Deirdre and she will cause a war.'

Eithlinn trembled and the warriors remembered their swords dumped in the arms room when they came back in and wondered, if they had them to hand, would they unsheathe them and hack their host's wife to death on the spot? Since Macha's curse no man in Ulster had dared to harm a pregnant woman, not even the wives of their enemies. However, what Cathbad had foretold was so appalling, the warriors would have gone ahead and not cared what happened. One or two of them even glanced towards the arms room. But Conor was in front of the door

to prevent any warrior entering. They could not kill
Eithlinn or the infant in her womb.

In was early dawn the next day. The clouds were grey
except where the rising sun played along their edges and
made them silver. Between the clouds the clear sky behind
showed pale pearl white.

In her hut Eithlinn delivered Deirdre. The midwife
slapped the newborn, whose lusty cries filled the hut, and
cut the cord. Cathbad took the child and carried it to the
hall where Conor and the men were waiting.

'This is Deirdre,' Cathbad said, holding up the infant so
they all were able to see her. She had a small face, a little
red along the edges of the cheeks, and short black down on
her spongy crown. Her enormous slate-grey eyes were
wide and fathomless.

'She is lovely now. She will be lovelier still later. Her
loveliness will lead inevitably to love and from there to
jealousy is no distance. In the lifetime of all here listening,
the sons of Usnach will go into exile. So will Fergus and
Conor's own son, Cormac. There will be war. I have looked
into the future and seen it all.'

The warriors were in no doubt about what they wanted
now. The infant should be taken outside. The head should
be cut off. The body should be burned. The remaining
charred bones should then be flung into a bog hole.

'Kill the infant,' one or two murmured.

'No.' Conor shook his head. 'Answer some questions

before you act and try to think in the process.'

As he gazed around the warriors fell silent.

'Is it true that Ceithlinn, my wife, is dead?'

This question was as true as it was unexpected. There was silence.

'Well,' said Conor grumpily, 'who can answer this perfectly simple question?'

Believing any more prevarication was only going to make the king's mood worse, a warrior called Lothar muttered quickly, 'Well yes, she is.'

It was true. Ceithlinn, the mother of Folaman and Cormac, had died the previous winter after a rabid dog had bitten her.

'And is it therefore true I am free to marry again?'

Lothar considered, uneasy at the answer he guessed the king wanted.

'Well?' said Conor impatiently.

'Well, yes,' answered Lothar.

'Thank you, friend. So, I am free to marry, that is not disputed. Well, I can now announce that I have made my choice. Here she is.' He indicated Deirdre. 'She will not be killed. Tomorrow, I will send her to fosterers. They will rear her in a private place where no one will see her until she is ready for me. There will be no war on her account. This is my decision. I have spoken.'

Conor met the eye of each warrior and each man, in turn, when the king's gaze fell on his face, looked down at the rushes strewn on the floor. It was as if Cathbad had never spoken.

How different everything would have been had he heeded the appalling auguries. This was thought and said later but those who thought and said this did not know Conor. The foetus may have screamed in the womb and Cathbad may have made his prophecy, but Conor being Conor and Conor being king, he thought he could float above destiny, as ordinary men could not. And such was his authority that no one, not even Fergus, could have challenged his decision, let alone made him change his mind.

The next day Conor's most trusted messenger, an old woman and sometime satirist called Levercham, took Deirdre to Abcam and Eve, the fosterers he had selected. This childless couple lived in a lonely compound with high ramparts some distance from Emain Macha. Despite the compound's isolation Conor ordered that Deirdre must be kept behind the rampart at all times and the compound gate must never be left open, so no passer-by would ever have a chance to glimpse her. These strict conditions were to be maintained, he added, until Deirdre was thirteen, and a suitable age to marry him.

When Conor sent Deirdre away it was as if he let fly the stone he was holding in his hand. Once the stone was away, there was no way he could chase after and catch it. It could only travel forward until it arrived at the end where it was destined to go the moment it was thrown.

Everything Cathbad said came true. There was strife in Ulster and good men and women died. Slaughtering the infant would have prevented all this. Yet Conor never felt the slightest shred of shame because he kept Deirdre alive for himself.

'Look at what the trouble produced,' he would claim later. 'The great hero and champion Cuchulainn would never have found the fame he found but for my original deed.'

It was better Cuchulainn had the chance to prosper, Conor believed, than that he did not. On this account, he said, everything was for the best in the end and when he went to his death, long after tragedy had struck, he went a happy man. Such are kings for you. They never regret and they are masters of self-justification. The same is often said of tyrants and evil men.

Chapter Five

The new name

It was an honour for householders to entertain Conor.
They would vie with each other for the privilege.

When Sétanta was seven – he had been with the Boy
Spears for a year now – the glory of providing hospitality was
accorded to a man called Culann. He lived in a compound on
the plains a short distance away from Emain Macha.

On the morning of the day Conor was due to visit,
Culann appeared at the house of the Red Branch in search
of an audience with the king. Culann was a large fellow
with dark black eyes, thick wrists and thumbnails swollen
and black from accidents. He was a blacksmith by trade.

When he was brought before Conor, Culann explained
that all his wealth he had earned with his two strong arms,
his hammer, his anvil and his tongs.

'I can only feast a moderate number of prime warriors,'
he added shyly.

Conor, whilst he was imperious, could also be
sympathetic when necessary.

'I will only bring a small company,' Conor promised.

Culann returned home to make the final preparations.
Conor stayed in his hall and played fidchell. At the end of

the day he dressed in his light travelling clothes. Then he summoned Fergus.

'Come with me,' he said.

Fergus guessed where they were going. It was to the meeting ground. The king wanted to bid the Boy Spears goodbye. This was his custom whenever he went away.

When the two arrived they found Sétanta in the middle of the field and the rest of the troop lined up in front of one of the goals. The troop was so numerous they filled the entire mouth of the goal.

Sétanta tossed a hard ball in the air and smacked it. A moment later the ball appeared on the grass behind the goal. Despite the efforts of the entire troop it had not been possible to keep it out. Sétanta fired several more balls and each shot ended the same way. Every ball went in.

The two parties swapped. Sétanta went into the goal and the troopers lined up on the field.

'On my word,' shouted Folaman. 'Right, go.'

In unison every youth threw his hard ball in the air, swung his stick and struck ferociously. Sétanta, holding two sticks in each hand (both hands were not only exceptionally large but Sétanta had the advantage of seven fingers on each as well), ran forward whirling his arms at an incredible speed. There was a succession of cracks as he stopped the flight of the numerous balls, followed by the thump of the balls hitting the ground. When Sétanta dropped his arms to his sides, a great pool of balls lay on the ground at his feet. Not even one was in the grass behind the goal.

Next Sétanta and the troop wrestled one another. Though every Boy Spears that grappled with the child tried to hurl him down, they all failed and were thrown to the ground. Eventually there were so many prostrate bodies that the competition had to stop. There was no room left where Sétanta's opponents might fall.

Last, they played the Stripping-Game (where each boy had to remove the cloak, tunic, leggings and sandals of his opponents while keeping his own clothes on), and it was not long before all the Boy Spears were naked while not so much as the brooch from Sétanta's cloak was gone.

'This is a lucky land,' said Fergus.

'Why?'

'Having him.'

'He'll only be of solid use,' said Conor, 'if he fulfills his promise.'

This remark surprised Fergus. It was grudging. He wondered if it masked something much less attractive. Was the king jealous? Did he fear this prodigy would grow into a champion and supplant him on the throne?

It was possible – every king had such fears, as Fergus knew from his own time as king. Yet at the same time it was difficult to imagine.

In Fergus's experience, ambitious adults invariably showed their grasping natures from the beginning whereas the Sétanta he knew was made of very different stuff. Yes, he was impatient. He was impetuous. He had a keen sense that his life would be short and he needed to make the most of the time he had. He was anxious to learn. He was competitive. He not only had to win everything but everyone had to know that as well or he was not happy.

At the same time he was agreeable and biddable. He made friends easily. He liked being liked as well. He did not seem especially cunning – or at least he had given Fergus no indication that he had any talent for duplicity or lying, the basic skills required by any that wanted to depose a king. Indeed, Sétanta was blunt and straightforward in a way that was almost naïve as well as delightful.

Fergus knew he might be wrong but, on the evidence he had, this child did not lust for power. What Sétanta wanted was fame. He wanted his reputation secured.

Yet still Conor feared him. Or he seemed to, judging by what he had just said. Jealous or anxious kings caused trouble, Fergus reminded himself, and he determined he would probe and find out if Conor really did fear his nephew.

'Is there any reason he won't?' Fergus asked quietly.

'Won't what?'

'Fulfill his promise?'

'Well, boys don't always grow into the men you hope they'll become.'

'That's true,' agreed Fergus, surprised by Conor's reply. So he didn't fear Sétanta would be a threat. He feared he would be a disappointment.

As he thought about it now, watching the Boy Spears gathering up their clothes and dressing, Fergus conceded there might be some sense in this. Talented youths did not always amount to very much as adults. They were often content to live in the shadow of past glories.

Except though, he thought, these were mortals. And for the young boy in the distance didn't different rules apply?

Sétanta was partly an immortal. His father was the handsome host who had lured them with the thrushes. That must mean that the arc of his life would follow a smooth neat line, rising steadily upwards until it ended (as it must end since he was part mortal). The doubts and confusions that beset ordinary men would not hinder him. He would achieve glory. That was his fate, though his ultimate end, his death, he could not dodge no matter what he did.

Sétanta had started as he meant to continue and the life still to follow, at least where his feats were concerned, would be unsullied by mess and confusion. The outcome of his marriage, if he made one, and his relationship with his children and his wife, that would not necessarily be perfect. In fact, that would very likely be as good or as bad as any man's. But as far as the deeds were concerned the prodigious skill he already showed on the field would be matched later in battle, for his destiny was to be the greatest warrior Ulster would ever know, surely.

'I am in no doubt,' said Fergus emphatically, 'that as he gets older his deeds will get bigger.'

'Is that so?'

'Now he's a boy and he excels on the pitch among boys in boyish things. But when he's a man he'll excel in manly things on the field of battle. I know it.'

'I like that thought,' said Conor.

Fergus watched the king carefully. This was a statement of fact, it seemed to him. Conor was not jealous or troubled or threatened. He wanted Sétanta to succeed. What puzzled Fergus was why this was so. Then a moment later, as if he had read his mind, Conor made everything clear.

'Every successful champion is good for a king. It makes him feared and liked.'

This was typical of Conor, Fergus thought. He judged everything in terms of what it would do for him.

'You know what?' said Conor.

'What?'

'I'm taking the elite, whose ranks Sétanta's destined to join, to Culann's compound, and he should be there tonight too, shouldn't he?' Protocol, as was usual with kings, was never far from Conor's thoughts.

'Yes.'

'Have the child called, so he may come with us and share this banquet.'

Sétanta was brought over and invited.

'But I can't come now,' he protested.

'Why not?'

'I still want to play and so do the Boy Spears.'

'Well, we can't wait until you've all had enough,' said Conor. 'That will take too long.'

'You don't have to. I'll follow you.'

'You don't know the way.'

'I will follow the tracks the chariot wheels make.

I'll see them in the grass easily enough.'

'Good enough. Run along now. We'll see you there.'

Sétanta sprinted off. The chariots were prepared and the small party of guests – Conor had stuck to his word to bring just a small number – got aboard. Fergus and Conor sat side by side in the back of the royal chariot.

The charioteers cracked their reins. The headstalls and bridles on the horses jangled. The wheels rumbled. The chariots jerked and creaked. The king's party circled the meeting ground that was teeming with boys and loud with their cries, then moved off across the darkening plain beneath the sky that was empty except for a few clouds piled along the edge.

Conor and his retinue reached Culann's compound as dusk fell. The host brought them into his small hall. There were fresh rushes laid, and two good fires burning in the middle of the floor. The guests were seated on couches and food and drink were brought to them.

Outside, the last of the daylight drained away. Stars glimmered in the night sky. There was a moon, too, young and white. Her pale light flooded over the plains below, creating the illusion that the ground was lightly dusted with silver.

In the smoky hall, Culann sidled up to his guest of honour. The king was eating a piece of roast mutton and there were patches of mutton grease on his beard. Because of the noise the host leaned close to Conor's ear.

'O king,' he began.

He hoped he struck just the right note of humility and familiarity with his address.

'Has anyone promised they would follow you here tonight?'

'No,' Conor whispered back, forgetting the arrangement he had made with Sétanta. 'You won't have to give food or drink to any more of us.'

'That's not why I asked,' said Culann, who was worried now in case Conor thought he was mean.

'It's my dog,' continued Culann. 'He's that fierce I wouldn't put him out to guard my cattle if anyone else was coming.'

'Go ahead,' said Conor, reaching for his beaker.

Culann slipped outside. It was cold but clear under the starry sky. He released the dog from his pen. He was an enormous creature covered in grey scrawny hair. His pads were vast and two sets of sharp white teeth glistened in his wet mouth. He bounded though the entrance and disappeared on to the plain. Culann closed up the gateway. He did not expect the hound to be back before morning.

Out on the plain, Sétanta followed the lines scored by the chariot wheels in the turf. These were filled with black shadow while the grass that showed on either side of the parallel lines was silvery grey with the light from the moon. He imagined he was walking on the unusually pale skin of a cave-dwelling giant, following the veins that trailed under the surface.

To shorten his journey Sétanta played his usual game.

He hit his hurley-ball with the stick. Then he flung the stick after the ball. Then he threw his toy javelin after the stick. Then he ran ahead and caught each in turn before they hit the ground.

After a while Culann's compound came into view. He saw the steep sides of the rampart glimmering faintly in the moonlight. They were coated in lime and they were the same colour as the moon.

Culann's dog was in the place where he habitually lay on the meeting ground in front of the compound. He sensed the approach of Sétanta in the distance. He lifted his heavy head from his huge paws and stared into the darkness.

The monstrous animal gave a horrible snarl, jumped up on to his vast legs, and sped off across the plain barking ferociously.

Inside the hall, Conor looked up from his beaker of drink and demanded, 'What was that?'

'My dog,' replied Culann. 'He scents a thief.'

'That's no thief,' said Conor, now remembering what he had forgotten before. 'That's a boy of seven.'

'This is bad,' said Culann.

'Call him back.'

'He won't be called back. Nothing will stop the hound now.'

'This is very bad,' said Conor glumly.

Fergus and one or two others had heard the hound and now they noticed Culann and Conor talking. They guessed by the expressions on their faces that something was wrong.

Meantime, out on the plain, Sétanta, having heard the dog's cry, was peering carefully into the darkness. First, he saw nothing though he heard the great feet pounding on the ground and the vicious snarls the animal made as he ran. Then Sétanta saw the outline of the body. It was a dark ugly shape with the lighter black of the sky behind and it was hurtling towards him.

He blinked and the great joy that he felt playing his throwing game vanished, and he was filled by rage. The hairs on his head went rigid. The ends glowed like boiling metal. He dropped the ball, stick and javelin he had just caught.

The great dog, that was now only the length of his body from the child, sprang forward. His lips were pulled right back to show his two sets of huge teeth buried in wet gums, while his tongue trailed from the mouth and down the side of the thick neck like a wet cloth.

Sétanta sidestepped and the beast, instead of flying at him, was now going past him. Sétanta reached up with one hand and grasped the throat-apple, while with the other he reached for the dog's back and grasped as much warm loose flesh along the backbone as he was able to hold.

Culann's hound whimpered, the noise as close as he ever got in his long violent life to the expression of surprise. It would also be his last sound.

An instant after, Sétanta flipped the dog on to his back as if he was of no more consequence than a stave. Then he brought him down on a stone that stood out on the plain. As the vertebrae collided with immovable rock they splintered, making a noise like cracking ice, and his four legs jumped out of the sockets. A moment later they flopped sideways and hung down limply; they were only attached to the rest of the body by the animal's hide.

In the hall Culann's guests had been silenced by the noises from outside.

'This is an unlucky trip,' said Conor bleakly.

'It is,' said Fergus who, remembering the agreement Conor had made with Sétanta, was filled with the horrible thought of the child in the mouth of the creature he had just heard.

'The little boy, Sétanta, my sister's son, he promised to follow us. I fear the worst with the guard dog,' said Conor.

The doors of the hall were thrown open. Everyone flooded outside.

'No time for the gate,' shouted Fergus.

He stormed over the rampart, forced himself through the hawthorn bushes with his hands held over his eyes, and jumped down on the far side on to the plain. More warriors followed but by the time they got over, Fergus, who had spotted him in the darkness, had reached Sétanta.

'Hello, little friend.'

Sétanta nodded.

Fergus hoisted him on his shoulder to carry him back to Conor. He turned on his heel. As he did, Culann passed with a grim face.

'The hound?' he asked.

Sétanta pointed in the direction of the stone.

As Fergus hurried back towards the fort, Culann covered the short distance to the stone. He found his dog, cold and broken-backed, his four legs attached only by skin, like tree branches after a storm attached only by bark.

Culann followed his guests back into his compound and then into the hall. He went straight to the new arrival and addressed him:

'Little boy, you are most unwelcome.'

'Why?' asked Conor. 'What has he done?'

'It was bad luck to have made you this feast, Conor.'

He turned back to the child.

'That animal guarded my herds. Now he's gone, who will?' He shrugged. 'I'll lose them all, my entire wealth.' He paused. 'That was a valuable member of my family you just killed.'

'I'll repay you,' said the child.

'Will you? How?'

'I'll find a whelp, the same breed as your dog. I'll raise him myself. And while he's growing, I will come every night and be the guard.'

'We should call you Cuchulainn then,' said Cathbad, the druid, who was listening, 'for Culann's hound is what you're going to be.'

'But I like my own name,' Sétanta protested.

Cathbad shrugged.

'Yes, it's a good enough name, but believe me – mine's better, for a hero at any rate. Mine's the one that will fill the mouths of men in years to come.'

Over the weeks and months that followed, just as he had promised, the boy guarded Culann's herd each night from wolves, eagles and thieves while each day he devoted to training the pup he had bought to be a guard dog. And because he was acting as Culann's guard dog at this time, the new name Cuchulainn was used by everyone and the boy gradually came both to like and then to accept it. By the time the small pup was a dog, trained and ready, he was no longer Sétanta: he was Cuchulainn. In honour of his new name he undertook a *geis* never to eat dog, or any dog-like animal, such as wolf, fox or otter. With his new name he was ready to start along the road that he believed would lead to his hero's future.

Chapter Six

Cuchulainn takes up arms

Another year had passed. Cuchulainn was now eight. He stood on the edge of the vast meeting ground in front of the fort. He looked across the grass. He saw boys from the Boy Spears running, wrestling and tumbling. The air was filled with their cries and exclamations. But what interested him was what he saw in the distance, beyond them.

Cathbad was with his students who sat on stones arranged in a circle around him. He talked and moved his hands around. Cathbad – usually so calm he verged on the lethargic – was rarely this animated. His listeners looked particularly rapt as well. What might Cathbad be saying, Cuchulainn wondered? He swivelled his head and pointed his right ear at the little knot of would-be druids and their teacher. He closed his eyes. He pushed all the foreground sounds of the boys out of the way and focused on Cathbad until he could hear the magician's voice, exactly as if he was standing beside Cuchulainn and talking to him.

'You want to know what today is favourable for?' Cathbad demanded.

The pupils murmured.

'We do,' said one. Cuchulainn recognised him. He had

watery blue eyes and ears that stuck out.

'I'll tell you what the day is favourable for.' Cathbad paused for effect. 'Anyone from the Boy Spears, who takes up real arms today, will be known forever. I must add that as well as being famous he will die young.'

'And who might this be?' asked the watery-eyed novice.

'You didn't ask who,' replied Cathbad. 'You asked only what was the day auspicious for. You have your answer. Don't be greedy. Be happy with what you've got. Somebody here, one of these young boys, if he chooses today, will be remembered forever. We simply have to wait and by tonight, we'll know who it is – that is, if one of these boys chooses today to make the move.'

Cuchulainn stopped listening to Cathbad. So today was the day one of them, if he took arms, would become famous. None of the other Boy Spears he saw swimming in front of his eyes knew this. But what would they do if they did know? They would race one another to be the first to handle a real weapon. But he alone knew what Cathbad had predicted. This was his chance.

He dropped his little play shield of plaited twigs and his toy javelin on to the grass. He turned and darted into the house of the Red Branch, then went through to the centre to Conor's private room, with its copper walls and immense royal couch. The king was dozing here but hearing footsteps he opened his eyes.

'Why are you here?' he asked sleepily.

'You are a good king,' said Cuchulainn charmingly.

So he wants something, thought Conor.

'Go on. What do you want?'

'What do I want?'

'Yes. You haven't come in here to inquire about my health or to sing me to sleep.'

'No.'

'So what is it you want?'

'To put away childish things. To take up arms.'

'Aged eight?'

'Yes.'

'Aren't you a bit young?'

'No.'

'Why now? Has something prompted this?'

'Cathbad,' said Cuchulainn, and he paused for maximum effect.

'Cathbad?'

'Yes.'

'Cathbad has prompted this?'

'Yes.'

'Well, if Cathbad says, you shall have your wish.'

He gave the child two spears, a sword and a shield. They came from a collection of seventeen such sets he'd had made for when a boy warrior took up arms for the first time. They were smaller and lighter than full-sized weapons yet there was nothing childish about these. They were as highly wrought, and as splendid and strong, as any weapon made for an adult would be.

'Can I test them?' Cuchulainn asked.

Conor nodded. Cuchulainn was to do as he wished.

Cuchulainn took the first spear in both hands and began to bend the shaft. The wood bowed, just a little, and then with a savage crack it snapped and big white splinters of wood fell everywhere, one even catching in his hair.

He took the second shaft and ran his hand up the haft to the head with considerable force. This was to test how well the point was attached to the end – not very well as it turned out. No sooner had the side of his hand struck the socket that secured the point to the shaft than the whole end flew off. It hit one of the copper walls making a dull clanging noise, and fell to the ground.

Cuchulainn threw the useless shaft aside and took hold of the sword. He kicked away the rushes around his feet to reveal the hard earth beneath. He rammed the point into the earth, burying it a hand's breadth down and then, leaning with all his weight on the hilt, he began to bend the blade. The iron went from straight to slightly round to slightly rounder again and then, with a ping, it snapped.

Cuchulainn was left holding the handle with a short stub attached to it. It ended in a jagged line where the blade had broken. The pointed end was still stuck in the ground. He struck it with the stub. It flew through the air and fell with a soft thud into the rushes at the other end of the room.

Next Cuchulainn beat the end of the sword that he still held on the shield. He hit it once, he hit it twice, and the third time he struck the iron, it buckled, then split entirely.

'Oh,' said Conor. This was not what he had expected. All the weapons in his seventeen-strong sets – now down to sixteen – were supposed to be battle ready. The first set must have had some sort of flaw.

So another set was fetched. But they did not survive Cuchulainn's tests. Nor did the next. Nor did any of them. All seventeen sets were tried and found wanting. Every spear snapped or lost its head. Every sword broke. Every shield buckled.

'O my master,' said Cuchulainn archly, when the weapons lay broken around them, 'these were not very good.'

'No,' agreed Conor.

'What will I do?'

'You can take mine.'

The king gave him his own spears, the Venomous and the Cruel, his sword and his shield. The spears had dark yew shafts decorated with silver rings, and iron heads. Cuchulainn bent the hafts and tested the points: both parts of the weapons withstood their trial.

He turned to the sword. It had a broad iron blade, bevelled on both sides. The handle was iron with kid skin wrapped about it so it was easier to grip. The hand guards were brass and the pommel – the round bulbous piece at the top of the hilt – was gold with a small dark blue stone set into the middle. He stabbed the sword into the ground. He reached up – the handle was higher than his head for this was a huge weapon – grasped the handle and began to pull. He didn't stop until he had the blade bent into a circle and the pommel was touching the earth.

'This is a good sword,' he said.

He released the handle and the blade sprang back and the pommel was higher than his head.

He took the shield. It was made of iron plates attached to a wooden frame, with heavy leather thongs at the back that went around the forearms. The shield was round and the rim was chased with silver. He pulled the sword out of the ground and began to beat the blade on the front. The room resounded with the noise of iron clanging on iron but no matter how hard Cuchulainn thumped, the shield remained hard and firm and did not buckle.

'This is a good shield,' he said. 'These arms are good,' he continued. 'They are worthy of me.'

Conor was so surprised he made no reply. Normally he was never without words.

'To the king of the land, who has arms such as these,' continued Cuchulainn, 'good luck will surely come.'

This was even more startling. This was a boy of eight yet he seemed to have acquired the measured tone of the full-grown warrior. Handling the tools of the warrior for the first time in his life, had he remembered things he had heard other warriors say? In which case this heroic posturing would be fleeting, Conor concluded, and he would be a boy again soon enough.

At that moment Cathbad strode in. He saw Cuchulainn and the king. The small boy had the king's shield on his left arm and his spears in his left hand, and the king's sword in his right hand. They looked ridiculously large. Nonetheless, Cuchulainn held them well.

'Oh,' said Cathbad. 'He's taking arms, is he?'

'Yes,' said Conor, puzzled at the druid's surprise. After all, Cuchulainn had told him this was what Cathbad had wanted.

'For myself I have to say he is one I do not care to see take up arms, not today,' said Cathbad.

'What? But you told him to, didn't you? You prompted him.'

'No.'

'Brat,' cried the king. 'Why did you tell me Cathbad told you to take up arms when he didn't? You lied. Don't you know it's wrong to lie? I've obviously neglected your education. You might fight well but you don't know how to behave.'

'I can explain,' said Cuchulainn. 'He did prompt me. I told the truth there. He just didn't do so directly. I heard one of his pupils ask him what today was special for. He told them that whoever took up arms today for the first time would be more famous than any other man in his time or thereafter.'

'Did I not also say his life would be short?' said Cathbad.

'You did also say his life would be short,' Cuchulainn agreed, 'but better fame than a long life. Doesn't fame outlive life?'

Perhaps, thought Conor, the maturity in the boy's speech would not be as short-lived as he had thought.

'Don't you care,' Cathbad asked, 'that your life will be short?'

'No. Nor would I care if I had only another day or another night, so long as the history of my doings endured after I was gone.'

'Well,' said Cathbad, 'finish what you've begun then. Go out and get into a chariot, boy.'

The two men and the boy went out. Conor also had seventeen chariots ready and waiting for this type of occasion. Like the weapons these were slightly smaller and lighter than a warrior's would be but otherwise they were the same.

The first was got ready. Cuchulainn took the driver's seat, put his feet in the foot-bindings and then galloped the horses off towards the meeting ground. Conor and Cathbad followed on foot. When they got to the ground the two men saw Cuchulainn careering around the grounds, waving his whip at the cheering Boy Spears who were standing around.

When Cuchulainn got to the end of the ground, to the point where the plains began, he turned sharply to come back to where he started. As he did there was a nasty wrenching noise and the shaft with the two horses broke away from the chariot. Cuchulainn released the reins, vaulted over the chariot's wicker walls and landed on the grass. The two horses with the spar between wheeled around and began to gallop back towards the fort, their reins trailing on the grass behind. Two Boy Spears ran behind the animals, caught up the leather straps and reined them in.

Cuchulainn went on to the second chariot and the axle snapped as he manoeuvred it about. With the third the linchpins popped out and the wheels flew off. With the fourth the frame split. With all the subsequent chariots, as he tried them out, it was the same – they all fell apart in different ways and the last fell apart so completely, it resembled a pile of firewood heaped up on the grass.

Cuchulainn walked from the seventeenth casualty back to Conor, who had seen everything.

'These chariots of yours, they're no good.'

'I can see that. You'll have to have my chariot.'

Conor sent word to Ibar, his driver, to bring his chariot round. Ibar obeyed and came.

'There you go,' said Conor, 'try it.'

'I'll test it first.'

He wrenched each wheel spoke but every one held. He jumped on the shaft to which the horses were attached. This held too. He tested the chariot's walls and the standing platform. These held as well.

'This is not like the others,' he declared.

He climbed aboard and fixed the weapons he had got to the mountings inside the wicker sides. He took his seat and put his feet in the foot-bindings. Ibar shook the reins and the chariot set off. The Boy Spears cheered wildly in the distance.

Ibar performed a small circuit in front of the gate then brought the chariot back to the point from where he started.

By the time he got there Cathbad and Conor were gone.

'You can get down now you've had your ride,' Ibar said.

'You might think your horses are precious,' said Cuchulainn quietly, 'but so am I, my friend.'

Like the king earlier, Ibar was surprised to hear this boy talking like a fully-grown warrior. And just like the king he assumed it must be the occasion that was producing such talk.

'Make a circuit round Emain Macha now, would you?' Cuchulainn ordered.

Ibar shook the reins and set off. He was, after all, the driver and drivers followed instructions. He trotted along beside the moat with the ramparts rising behind. There were lookouts on the walls. One or two shouted in astonishment, 'Look, there's a boy in the king's chariot.'

The gate at the front came back into view as the chariot reached the end of the circuit. 'This is a good chariot,' said Cuchulainn. 'It is worthy of me.'

'Good,' said Ibar. 'I'm glad you approve. I'm going to unhitch the horses now and turn them out to graze.'

'No, it's too early for that yet, Ibar. Drive through the Boy Spears. Let them see me.'

'They saw you already.'

'Let them see me again.'

Ibar navigated away from the gate and went across the ground teeming with boys. As the chariot passed they cheered and shouted again. They wished him success in spoil-winning and in first-slaying but at the same time they were sorry to lose him, they said. There was jealousy too but everyone knew better than to let that show.

Cuchulainn ordered Ibar to stop. The boys clustered round.

'It's only a take because it's a lucky day that I've taken up arms today, and I'll be back later, I promise.'

'As wc've stopped now,' Ibar wondered, 'will you let me unhitch the horses?'

'No,' said Cuchulainn. 'Go along this road I see here.'

He pointed at a track that stretched across the plain in a straight line. The road was a thin grey line with bright green grass on either side.

Ibar moved off again and reached the road. The wheels rumbled and crunched on the little stones that comprised the surface.

'Where does this road lead?'

'The Look-Out Ford,' said Ibar.

'What is that?'

'Every day a selected warrior waits there, standing sentry,' said Ibar. 'He has two duties. He has to fight any champion who comes to fight in single combat on behalf of his province. His other task is to deal with the poets and ensure they don't spread their poison. If a poet arrives the warrior must arrange his safe conduct to Conor and that way ensure that when he steps in front of the king and starts to speak his poems will be full of praise. In the case of a poet leaving, the warrior must discover what he feels about his treatment in Ulster. If the poet is unhappy the warrior must give him gold and there's no poet who has ever lived who can't be placated in this way.'

'And who is the warrior on guard today?'

'Conall.'

'My foster-brother,' said Cuchulainn. He knew who he was though he did not know him well. 'Drive on to the ford. You won't lose anything by it. Go on, use your goad.'

Perhaps, thought Ibar, Cuchulainn really had acquired adult thinking. Ibar prodded the horses' rumps with the stem of his whip and set them galloping along the road. Reaching the end and finding Conall at the ford's edge, he pulled the reins. The chariot stopped. On the northern side of the ford stakes stuck with the bodies of headless men marked the border.

Conall strolled over. Peering inside the chariot he could not help but notice that the mounts inside the wickerwork walls held different weapons.

'Have you taken up arms today?' he asked.

'Yes.'

'I hope you triumph when you first draw blood but aren't you rather young?'

Cuchulainn ignored the question and said, 'What do you do here?'

'I keep watch.'

'Let me take over, will you?'

'You could manage the poets, I'd say. Talk does them fine. A warrior, on the other hand, might be a little more than you're ready for.'

'But no one might come at all. Nothing might happen,' argued Cuchulainn. 'You never know.'

'You don't know that's right.'

'I shall have to go on so,' said Cuchulainn. 'That's Lough Echtra, isn't it?'

He pointed at the black water shimmering in the distance way beyond the ford.

'I might find a warrior there to try my luck against.'

'I'll have to come too.'

'No, you won't.'

'Think if I don't. Every warrior from Conor down will want to hurt me.'

Cuchulainn shrugged. He ordered Ibar to cross the ford.

'I'll follow,' Conall said. 'I'll call my driver. He's nearby. It won't be long until I catch up.'

'Ignore him, Ibar,' Cuchulainn said.

Ibar spurred the horses. They pulled the chariot into the water and out on to the far bank. Once over, Ibar hurried the horses towards Lough Echtra, drops of water flying from the wheels as the chariot went forward.

After a while Cuchulainn heard the rumble of Conall's chariot coming up behind. The warrior's chariot drew abreast.

'I said I wouldn't let you go alone,' Conall shouted across. He and his driver were standing up, the charioteer at the front and Conall behind, as if they were going into battle.

'I'm afraid you're going to be sorry you followed me,' said Cuchulainn from his seat.

He was sitting and he thought Conall's chasing after him

as if he was going into battle a bit excessive. On the other hand, that Conall insisted on treating this as a battle required that he did too, didn't it? He must rise to the occasion.

There was a small stone stuck in the leather sole of his sandal. Cuchulainn picked it out and loaded the stone into his sling and then fired it sideways at the closer of Conall's horses. The tiny stone hit the creature very hard on the side of the head. The animal, thinking a wasp or a hornet had stung it, veered violently sideways. The force of the horse's movement snapped off the chariot-shaft. The two horses ran on now, leaving the body of the chariot sliding along by itself with the charioteer and Conall still standing in the back, their feet in the foot-bindings, the ties around their waists.

Next the chariot body dipped forward; then the front lip hit the ground and it flipped over, taking the charioteer and Conall with it. It landed upside down and the occupants were hidden, as if under an upturned boat.

'You can stop and turn round so I can see,' Cuchulainn said to Ibar.

The charioteer reined the horses in and turned them. On the ground behind Cuchulainn saw Conall's horses with their reins trailing, the shaft and the yoke between them. Much nearer he saw the upside-down car of the chariot on the road. He saw the charioteer and Conall, having got their feet out of the foot-bindings and the ties off their waists, crawling out. They stood up, rubbing their shoulders and arms and heads. When the chariot flipped they had clearly banged themselves. For a while neither noticed Cuchulainn and then Conall did look up and saw that he was watching.

'What was that for?' Conall shouted furiously.

'I wanted to see if I'd make a marksman,' Cuchulainn called back.

'Well, bad luck to you and don't think if an enemy takes your head I'll move as much as a finger to avenge you.'

'I'll be dead. Why would I care?'

'Do you want to make a bad situation worse?' muttered Ibar.

'No.'

'Well, you are.'

'Listen, Conall,' Cuchulainn shouted, 'it's your custom, is it not, that if a journey proves perilous you don't go on?' Cuchulainn knew the *geis* of every warrior in Emain Macha.

'And I won't,' said Conall churlishly. He wished this *geis*, one of many onerous requirements expected of him as a warrior, had never been laid on him. But it had and a *geis* was a *geis* and a warrior ignored them at his peril.

'All right, Ibar, let's go on,' Cuchulainn said.

Ibar shook the reins and the chariot clipped away, heading south. From the seat at the rear Cuchulainn stared back. For a moment the figure of Conall did not move, then he turned and began to retrace his steps. He was returning to his post, Cuchulainn decided. He went on watching Conall getting smaller and smaller until finally the green ground swallowed him up and he lost sight of the man altogether.

The chariot rattled on to the edge of Lough Echtra. The black shiny surface of the water reflected the great clouds that hung overhead. There was no one else about. Ibar stopped the chariot. He unhitched the horses. The animals drank. Cuchulainn and his driver rested. The afternoon was come on.

'I would be more than happy if we could turn round and go back now,' said Ibar.

'Why wouldn't you?' Cuchulainn agreed.

Ibar decided to meet bumptiousness with honesty.

'They'll soon be carving the food in the hall back at the fort,' he said. 'Now, lucky lad, you have your place between Conor's knees. Late or early, there will always be a piece for you. I, on the other hand, have to scramble with the jesters and messengers and unless we go back now there won't be anything to scramble for.'

'See that?' said Cuchulainn, looking at a mountain he had just seen. 'What's that called?'

It was a small brown mountain with white stones neatly piled on the summit.

'Slieve Mourne.'

'Will you take me to the stones at the top?'

'No.'

'This is my first adventure. Go on, make it an occasion.'

'It's the first, yes, and if I'm lucky enough to get home again, I sincerely hope it will be *my* last.'

'But you'll take me, won't you?'

Ibar saw he would have to. He yoked the horses.

'Come on,' he said, 'get up.'

Cuchulainn jumped on to the seat at the back. The chariot moved off, its wooden frame creaking. Ibar followed the track that criss-crossed up the side of the mountain to the top. When they arrived Cuchulainn saw there was a plain on the other side that had been hidden from view before. It was dotted by forts and sliced by rivers.

'Will you tell me the names of all the features I can see?' he asked.

Ibar named the hills, rivers and forts with the exception of one with high dark stone walls.

'And the one you missed?' said Cuchulainn.

'That is the fort of the sons of Nechtan. Their father was killed by Ulstermen since when they have killed more of us, they boast, than are living in the province today.'

'Really, we'll go there then,' said Cuchulainn quickly.

'You must be mad, so you can, but I am not, so I won't.'

'You will. Alive or dead, you're going.'

'I'll go alive and come back dead so,' said Ibar. He shook the reins. 'A fine day this is turning out to be.'

He drove the chariot down the track that descended the other side of the mountain and then bowled along the track that led to the fort. When they arrived he stopped and Cuchulainn saw the heavy gate set into the rampart was closed. A standing stone stood in front, the bottom end dug into the ground, the top bound in an iron collar covered with writing.

'Ah, a message,' said Cuchulainn. He scrambled down

from the warrior's seat and ran over to see. 'The warrior who reads this,' it went, 'must fight one of the occupants of the fort. This is a *geis*. The obligation cannot be shirked.' At the end were the three marks used by Nechtan's three sons. These were a shield for Foill (because he was supposedly invulnerable to blades and points), a serpent for Tuachell (an allusion to his slipperiness), and a wave for Fannall (famous for his swimming and for fighting in water).

Cuchulainn uprooted the standing stone, carried it as easily as if it were a little log to a small lake that was close by, and dropped it into the water a little way out from the bank. This done he remained where he was, looking down at something.

Ibar wondered what it was that so absorbed the interest of the boy and went over to see.

From the bank he looked down. The water was brown, the colour of a bog. Nonetheless, immediately below his feet he was able to see the lake's floor clearly. It was covered with little chips of stone, old leaves and twigs and dark brown mud.

Further out, however, billowing clouds of stuff swirled around the water and he couldn't see through to the bottom. The stone must have stirred up the bottom, he guessed, when it went in.

He waited. The water cleared and now he saw what Cuchulainn had been standing waiting to see. It was the stone with the collar at the top. It stood on the lake floor exactly like it had outside the fort only it was the length of a man's arm under the water.

'It's only an opinion but I think it looked better where it was,' he said.

'Did I ask what you thought?'

'I don't believe you did,' Ibar agreed, gently.

'You're right though. No one can read it down there.'

They strolled back towards the chariot.

'It won't be long, you know, before you get what you are looking for.'

'Which is?'

'Violent death.'

'Enough. Be quiet. Get out the rugs. I'm going to sleep.'

'Oh why not?' Ibar muttered. 'Take your ease. What's to worry you?'

He fetched the covers from under his seat and laid them out on the grass. He produced cheese and a pitcher of water. Cuchulainn ate and drank and then lay down.

'Don't wake me if just one man comes out. I'm not getting up for just one. But if more show up, I will.'

'I don't think any of this is a good idea,' warned Ibar. 'These people are foes, not friends. We should leave.'

'Not yet.' Cuchulainn pulled a cover over his face and went to sleep.

Ibar sat in the front seat of the chariot, holding the reins, ready to fly off at the first appearance of the sons of Nechtan.

He heard the gate scraping back. A man emerged into the late afternoon light. His yellow hair was long and ragged. His chest stuck out and he had big dark eyes. He was unarmed.

'You wouldn't be thinking of taking the reins off your horses, would you,' the man called, 'and grazing them?'

'Oh no, friend,' said Ibar. He recognised the speaker. This was Foill, oldest of Nechtan's sons.

'See, I'm holding the reins.' He held up the reins to prove this.

'This is not your land,' said Foill.

'I know, friend.'

'Whose are they, by the way?' he asked gently now. Foill was, Ibar remembered, noted for his deceitfulness.

'King Conor's.'

'I thought that. And what have they carried here?'

'A boy.'

'What sort of a boy?'

'A young boy. He's taken arms for the first time today and he thought to show off his form a bit.'

'He did?'

'He's young.'

'So?'

'Well, bearing his age in mind perhaps we could just leave?'

'Go ahead. I don't fight children. I'd only send him back to Conor less his head if he was old enough to fight.'

'Good decision. He's eight. He really isn't old enough to fight.'

Cuchulainn, woken by the voices, sat up as the driver spoke.

'I certainly am ready,' he shouted.

'I think not,' said the man.

The boy's hair went straight as a nail. One eye shrank, the other expanded. The skin slipped back from his mouth. The hero light shot up from his body towards the sky, swarming with heavy red fluxes of blood.

'Of course I'm old enough.'

'And ugly enough,' said Foill.

'I don't fight anyone unarmed.'

Foill dashed inside.

'Be careful, little one,' said Ibar. 'He's invulnerable to all spear points and all sword blades.'

'You didn't mention this before.'

'I didn't?'

'No.'

'I must have had a reason. Perhaps I didn't want the fun to stop before it even started.'

'It doesn't matter, I know what to do anyway,' said Cuchulainn.

'What?'

The boy produced a small iron ball.

'He's got no charm against that.' He put the ball in the pouch of his sling and then began swinging the weapon round and round, faster and faster, over his head.

A horrible shout went up inside the fort. Foill, a shield in one hand and a sword in the other, pelted out through the open gateway.

'He's going to be sorry,' said Cuchulainn.

When Foill was three spear-lengths away Cuchulainn let fly. The ball smashed through Foill's forehead, re-emerging from the rear. Little pieces of brain and bone showered everywhere. They were both grey. Foill gave a soft groan of surprise and toppled back and landed on his back. Cuchulainn trotted across. He raised his sword and sliced down. The blade cut through the throat apple and came out at the back of the neck. Cuchulainn lifted the head by its ragged hair and stood it up on the ground so that it faced the entrance of the fort.

'What do you think of the view?' he asked the head.

The second son of Nechtan shot out of the gate.

'One meagre trophy and already you're full of yourself I suppose?' he said.

'One is nothing to boast of,' said Cuchulainn. 'Two would be a start though.'

'You'll never do it. You'd beginner's luck and that's all.'

The man disappeared back into the fort.

'Tuachell, the second son,' said Ibar, 'known as Cunning. If you don't get him with the first strike then you can chase him all night and you won't get him.'

'I'll put a hole in his heart with this.' Cuchulainn brandished Conor's spear, the Venomous.

Tuachell dashed out. Cuchulainn threw the spear. It flew forward. The warrior's shield went up. The point travelled through the front as easily as if the shield were tree bark. An instant later the spear pierced his chest. It came out the far side and went on travelling until the point had dug into the earth. Tuachell's arm dropped and his head lolled but his body remained upright, supported by the spear. Cuchulainn took off the head and set it neatly beside his brother's.

The third brother came out.

'Fannall,' said Ibar.

'My brothers were fools to fight on the grass. Come into the lake and try your luck.'

He ran towards the water.

'Also known as the Swimmer,' Ibar whispered as he jogged behind Cuchulainn. 'There's none better in water.'

'So he thinks.'

Fannall jumped in and swam away from the bank a short distance. Cuchulainn reached the edge and dropped everything except for a knife that he clamped between his teeth and then jumped in. He swam out towards his enemy. They met and began to wrestle in the water. Then Cuchulainn appeared to stand up in the water. With the advantage of height he was able to push Fannall underwater and keep him there with seemingly no effort being required to hold him under. At first, as Fannall struggled and thrashed, the surface bubbled and boiled. Then this stopped and the surface was smooth and dark again. Then Cuchulainn lifted Fannall's head up by the hair and cut through the neck.

He jumped off the stone on which he had been standing and launched himself at the bank.

'Now I know why they're called standing stones,'

he said as Ibar helped him on to the bank.

'Let's finish off,' said the boy.

They entered the fort. They rounded up all the servants and the dead men's mother, and drove them away. They pillaged weapons, clothes and other goods of value. Then they set all the huts inside the rampart on fire. They piled their booty in the chariot and gathered up the heads of the three brothers. They tied these, with great ingenuity, to the yoke, so the heads appeared to be looking out from behind the horses' necks. Then they mounted the chariot and took their seats. Ibar whipped the horses and spurred them away. Cuchulainn, his face still distorted, stared around him.

Ibar followed the route they had taken, up the mountain and past the little cairn of stones. They descended by the track on the other side of the mountain. They crossed the plain behind and along the way they passed Conall's smashed chariot. They crossed the ford Conall had guarded and they found he was gone.

Ibar pushed the chariot on. The ground was dry and hard. The early evening sky was white with sheets of cloud. In the distance a herd of deer appeared. They were brown with rounded flanks. At the sound of the chariot's approach they all lifted their heads and then, moving in unison, jumped sideways and started to run.

'Catch them,' Cuchulainn urged.

Cuchulainn and Ibar put their feet in the foot-bindings so they could keep their places on their seats, then Ibar whipped the horses. They went very fast but the king's horses were too plump to make the speed necessary to close on the galloping deer.

'This is not good,' said Cuchulainn. He was exasperated. He sprang from the moving chariot on to the ground and then chased after the deer on foot. He brought down two stags and dragged them, snorting and bellowing, back to the chariot. Ibar attached them with strong leather thongs to the terrets on the spars that stuck out at the back that were specifically for attaching animals.

Cuchulainn got back on his seat in the chariot and the journey resumed with two stags behind. Ibar went more slowly than before and without the pounding of the horses' hooves on the turf and the groaning of the wheels as they turned, Cuchulainn could hear what was going on around.

From the distance came a noise like a sheet of leather being bent ferociously. A flock of swans came in view, their bodies large and white, their wings beating powerfully up and down.

'Are they pets or wild?' asked the boy.

That was a strange question Ibar thought.

'They're wild.'

'If I bring some back, what's better: to present them dead or alive?'

Despite his martial prowess there really was so much the boy did not know.

'I know lots of men who've killed them. That's not hard. But I know no one who's captured one.'

'You are about to.'

Cuchulainn loaded a stone into his sling and fired it into the sky. A bird suddenly stopped as if it had collided with an invisible wall. Then it began to tumble. It fluttered its wings uselessly as it fell and shed a few white feathers. Soon a second and third began to plummet downwards. In all, sixteen birds were knocked to the ground where they lay with their long necks stretched out and their heads twisted sideways. Each looked like a small pile of new snow on the green grass.

Ibar steered to the first and stopped. He fixed the reins to the keeper that they were attached to when he was not on board.

'I'll get it,' he said.

He went to swing his leg over the wickerwork side.

'It looks undignified getting out that way,' said Cuchulainn.

'Not as undignified as getting down at the back and getting caught up with those angry stags would look.'

The stags were pulling and tugging on their leashes, throwing their antlers around ferociously and pawing the ground. The pair had never been tied before. Of course they were terrified and so they struggled fiercely.

'I'll stare them quiet and then you can step out.'

Cuchulainn turned in his seat and showed the two stags his face, with the skin still peeled back from the mouth and the two differently sized eyes and the great red pillar filled with swirling gouts of blood that was his hero-light shooting out of his head. For a moment or two the stags thrashed around as if they were more frightened than ever. Then, suddenly, they stopped pulling on the leashes, lowered their heads to the ground and turned sideways so the antlers were pointing away.

'One look at my face and see how quiet they've gone?' said Cuchulainn. 'They won't gore you now.'

Ibar stepped down from the back. As he slipped between the pacified animals he noticed their strong meaty deer smell. He moved forward on to the grassland, found the first bird and lifted it from the ground. Its feathers were oily and it smelt of rushes and wet. He carried it back to the chariot. He found Cuchulainn had prepared a long leash. He slipped one end around the bird's neck, fixed with a stop so it would not throttle the creature, and he tied the other to the back. All the other swans were attached using the same process.

By the time this was done the birds were recovering their senses. They were struggling to get back on to their big webbed feet, tossing their heads in an attempt to shake free of the leash and honking furiously. Cuchulainn stared at each bird in turn and they fell quiet just like the stags.

'Hurry back to Conor and the court and don't stop,' said Cuchulainn, when the tying was finished. 'The night's coming on'.

'I don't want to drag the swans,' said Ibar. 'That would be a bad end to the day.'

'They'll fly,' said Cuchulainn. 'You just go.'

He gathered all the leashes together. Ibar took his reins

from the keeper and called, 'Walk on.' Cuchulainn tugged the leashes and then shook them deftly, throwing the birds upwards into the air.

'Right. Go,' he shouted, 'and they'll fly.'

Ibar cracked his whip. The chariot juddered forward. From above came the leathery creak of sixteen swans beating their wings in unison.

'Nice and steady and not too fast.'

Ibar loosed the reins and the horses pulled forward. When the pace was right and the swans behind were beating along comfortably, he reined them in.

'No stopping until we're back,' said Cuchulainn.

The chariot moved on through the gathering dusk, the charioteer at the front, the small boy in the back with a bright light sticking up like a pole, three heads lashed to the yoke, two stags tied to the spars sticking out behind and sixteen swans flying above.

From the ramparts of the fort the lookouts saw the bright hero-light first and heard the noise of the horses' hooves and the turning wheels. They called Levercham, Conor's special messenger. She was a woman of indeterminate age. Her body was thin and angular, and there was no fat on it. Her hair was grey and she kept it tied in a long thick plait that hung down her back. Her face was flat and her eyes were dark. It was said she never smiled and it was also agreed she never made a mistake.

When she was given a message to bear she reported her king's words with absolute precision and the same was true of any message she brought back to the king. Nor had she ever betrayed a royal secret of which she knew quite a few. Because of her unique position she was the only one from the court, other than Conor himself, who was allowed into the isolated compound, far from Navan Fort, where Deirdre was being raised by Abcam and Eve for the king's bed.

When Levercham came on to the rampart the lookouts pointed out the approaching chariot as it moved across the darkening plain. She saw the swans and the deer tied behind, the column with the swirling blood rising out of Cuchulainn's head and, when the chariot got really close, the heads lashed to the horses' yoke.

She clattered down the stone stairs in her wooden-soled shoes and ran into the hall where Conor was.

'There's a chariot coming,' she said, 'with animals tied behind and a small warrior who is in the grip of a murderous rage.'

'That's my sister's son,' said Conor. 'He went out earlier and met Conall,' and here he pointed at the warrior lying on a couch, 'who did not enjoy the encounter. I'd say he must have killed today.'

'Whatever,' said Levercham, 'but he cannot come into the fort in the state he's in.'

'So what do we do?'

'Shame him.'

The king was confused.

'We find all the young women we can. We strip them and send them out naked on to the ground in front of the gate. That'll disable him. Then we deal with him.'

Sitting in the back of Conor's chariot, the floor juddering and trembling under his feet, Cuchulainn saw the ramparts and the moat of Emain Macha in front of him. He also saw the gate was open. There were people coming out. As far as he could tell they comprised vast heads with red eyes set well apart, tiny noses and mouths shrouded in black beards. They had tiny little legs sticking out from below on which they trotted along.

'What are those?' he asked Ibar.

'Women,' said Ibar.

'Women?'

'And they're naked,' said Ibar.

Cuchulainn realised that on account of the frenzy that gripped him, he had mistaken their breasts for eyes, their belly buttons for noses, and their pubic hair for beards.

'Oh no,' he cried out. 'I mustn't look at them.'

He threw himself down on the chariot floor between his seat and Ibar's and put his head in his hands.

Ibar reached the gates and stopped the chariot completely now. The swans floated to the ground and two naked women leaned into the chariot and plucked out the cowering child.

'Leave me alone,' he cried. 'I will not look at you.'

They ignored this and rushed him inside the gates and plunged him into the animals' water trough that stood there. The cold water quickly began to boil. The women lifted Cuchulainn out and soused him in a second trough.

When that began to grow hot, they immersed him in a third. This time the water did not heat up. Instead the hero-light flickered and wavered, shrank and finally vanished. His hair went flat and the ends stopped shining. The skin slipped over his mouth and the small eye expanded and the big eye contracted. He went a beautiful pinky red. The paroxysm was over. He was himself again.

That evening Cuchulainn took his place in the hall between the king's knees and Conor, throughout the meal, stroked his yellow hair and praised his achievement.

Chapter Seven

Cuchulainn's wooing of Emer

In the hall in the house of the Red Branch guests packed on to all the couches in the alcoves. Most were men but there were many women too, the wives and the daughters, the sisters and the mothers of the men. The women and girls had all insisted on coming to the hall that evening. They said they wanted to see the warriors compete but really they wanted to see just one warrior, Cuchulainn.

There was cord stretched right down the length of the hall from one door to the other. The competition was known as the apple feat. First, a warrior had to balance an apple on the edge of a sword. This was hard.

Then the warrior had to slide under the cord on his back without dropping the apple and then stand up when he got to the other side. This was harder still. Each time a man managed the feat successfully the cord was lowered a further finger's length so the gap through which the warriors had to go got smaller and smaller.

As the evening wore on one warrior after another dropped the apple as he slithered underneath and was disqualified. Finally, when the space between the floor and the cord was no more than a hand's breadth, only

Cuchulainn remained. He was able to move nimbly under the cord and stand, and then drop back down to the ground and go through the tiny space again and never once drop the apple. It was a feat no other warrior could emulate. He was declared the winner.

The hall was filled with shouts of acclaim. The men's shouts were dignified, proper and respectful, if threaded here and there with little streaks of envy, while those of the women were amorous and passionate and filled with yearning for the young warrior. Such was the hubbub that not everyone noticed the difference between the men and the women but a few did. One was a middle-aged man with grey hair, an astute fellow called Findias, whose wife had not taken her eyes off Cuchulainn all evening. As the applause died away he decided to test her.

'You wouldn't see me down there,' said Findias. He pointed at the rope and then clapped his bad leg. 'I wouldn't manage.' Hunting deer once he had cornered a stag and the animal had gored him in the leg above the knee. He had limped ever since.

'No,' said his wife, Morag. She was a nice quiet woman with a heavy square figure.

'Of course a man is more than his skill at the apple feat.' Findias said this in an innocent open way: this was all the encouragement Morag needed. She was bursting to talk and off she went.

'Oh yes,' Morag agreed. 'There is so much more to that young man. He is dexterous, he is nimble, he is wise, and his speech is sweet. He is also handsome and supple, with dark skin and dark eyes. And have you noticed his hands and feet?'

Findias could hardly have failed. The palms were as wide as a man's face, the fingers were as long as a small dog's legs and the nails were as big as good-sized pebbles. But as he was testing his wife he opted for insouciance.

'No, not really,' said Findias.

'Can you imagine what it would be like to be touched by them?'

Morag sighed lightly and her husband looked away.

On an adjacent couch he saw one of his friends. Aidan was tall with grey curly hair. There were three large scars on his left cheek made with a hatchet in a fight some years before. Niamh, Aidan's daughter, was beside him. She had slim shoulders and little hands and her head seemed larger than it should have been for the size of her body. She had very black hair.

'He has so many gifts,' said Niamh, 'that young warrior.'

'Does he?' Aidan was careful not to sound especially interested although in truth he was desperate to discover if, as he suspected, his daughter was infatuated. Niamh was his oldest child and by custom she must be married before her sisters and he had been aware for some while she was impatient to marry.

'He has the gift of prudence,' Niamh began, 'except when the hero-light shows and he distorts and then that goes, of course.'

'Yes,' agreed her father.

'He has the gift of feats. There isn't one he doesn't triumph at. He has the gift of fidchell, the gift of calculating, the gift of sooth-saying, the gift of discerning and the gift of beauty. Have you noticed his eyes?' she continued.

'He has four pupils in the one eye and three in the other.' Niamh nodded.

'That explains all those many gifts.'

'Does it?'

Niamh sighed. Aidan looked away and saw that his friend, Findias, on the adjacent couch, was nodding in his direction and then jerking his head; he wanted to talk outside.

Aidan and Findias slipped out: the one tall, the other slightly stooped on account of his limp. Once out in the dark courtyard they huddled together.

'How old is Cuchulainn now?' asked the worried husband.

'Fourteen,' said the troubled father.

'He has a fair face and a fine figure.'

'The women think so.'

'When he becomes a man he'll be fairer and finer still,' said Findias.

'The women think so too.'

'I see trouble ahead,' said Findias.

'I agree.' Aidan ran his finger down his deepest scar. It was a habit, when he was troubled, to touch this place.

'He'll infatuate our wives.'

'He will.'

'He'll destroy our daughters.'

'He will,' said Aidan. With two fingers he now stretched one of his scars. It was rigid in a way the rest of his skin was not and there was hardly any give in it.

'He must marry.' Findias jiggled his leg. It hurt when he stood on it even for a short while.

'He must.'

'We must put it to Conor,' said Findias emphatically.

'But we can't say we fear for our women.'

'Oh no.' Findias lent back against the wall of the rampart and lifted his bad leg off the ground to rest it.

'What then?' asked Aidan.

'We say, we know his life will be short.' Findias's voice carried a little thrill.

'Which is true,' Aidan agreed.

'We say, "It would be tragic if Cuchulainn were to die and leave no heir."'

'So for this reason a woman must be found for him at once,' said Aidan.

'Excellent.'

'We must put this to the other men, spread the idea around,' said Aidan.

'And then together everyone will bring the idea to Conor,' said Findias.

'It is a good plan,' said Aidan, which it was.

Findias and Aidan spoke to all the men they knew in private and those men later spoke to all the men that they knew. Within a few days it was the agreed opinion of every man in the kingdom that Cuchulainn must marry.

The men went to Conor and put this to him. Conor agreed.

'I will send messengers out into every province to look for a woman,' he said. He outlined what he saw as the characteristics of a suitable wife. He particularly emphasised that strength of character which he thought a woman must have in order to live happily with someone like Cuchulainn.

The messengers were dispatched. After a year, by which time Cuchulainn was fifteen, they returned. They brought bad news. Although they had looked in every fort and town and house, they had found no suitable king's daughter, noble's daughter or land owner's daughter. There was no woman seemingly anywhere on the island fit to be Cuchulainn's bride.

Cuchulainn did not agree. He knew there was one woman whom he wanted to marry. He knew where to find her and he also had the means to fetch her for he now had a chariot and horses of his own. He had a charioteer of his own now too. His name was Laeg. He was older than Cuchulainn, burly, a tiny bit plump and long-limbed. His face was freckled, pleasant, and he always had a trusting expression from which strangers assumed he was slow and naive. This was wrong. His thinking was deft and his observations were invariably clever and often sly. His hands were strong from years with the reins and his voice, when he sang, as he often did, was low and melodious.

'Harness the horses,' Cuchulainn instructed his driver.

'Why?'

'I know where to find a wife.'

'Where's that?'

'When you're ready I'll tell you.'

Laeg caught the horses. One was white and the other was grey. These were the animals, now fully grown, that had been there on the morning Dechtire woke to find herself covered with snow and the infant dead on her breast.

Cuchulainn and his driver boarded the chariot. Laeg took the front seat, Cuchulainn the rear. They set out. The chariot skirted the meeting ground where the Boy Spears exercised and came at the end to the place where the plains began.

'That way.' Cuchulainn pointed.

'And where are we going?' Laeg asked. He cracked the whip to start the horses moving faster.

'Forgall's.'

'The Wily?'

'The same.'

'I never thought he was a suitable wife.'

'You know I don't mean him.'

'Oh.'

'It's Emer, his daughter.'

Though Laeg was aware of her, the father had made a far greater impression on him. This was inevitable given his reputation for lying, trickery and duplicity, for breaking his word and for only attacking when a man had his back turned. Even Cuchulainn, for all his talents, would have to beware.

'Is this wise?'

'What?'

'You know Forgall's reputation?'

'I'm only interested in Emer, not him. Just drive, will you?'

Emer sat on a bench outside her father's compound with several girls, the daughters of local landowners. They each had a piece of cloth on which they were stitching a design with bright thread. Emer, as their teacher, watched them closely.

She was older than the other girls though one or two of them were taller. She was of middling height and her hair, which was black though very fine, was plaited and pinned up over her ears. She had a smooth face, broad at the forehead and tapering to the chin, but not unpleasantly pointed, and very nice white teeth that showed when she smiled as she often did. She preferred gold to silver, and she wore heavy earrings, as well as many bracelets, necklaces and rings. Her hands were small and fine and she had the habit, when her fingers stiffened, of cracking her joints. Her manner was quiet and friendly. She preferred tact to force when she wanted to get her way. If she had a fault it was a tendency to speak well of herself when she got the chance.

The compound where Emer and the others were sitting outside stood on a hill in a landscape of small hills and shallow valleys filled with woods of ash, rowan and elder.

From the distance came the clatter of hooves, mingled

with the cracking of straps, the grating of wheels, and the clanking of weapons.

'Go and see who that is,' said Emer to her sister, who though she was older tended always to do what Emer asked. Fial climbed the little hummock beside them and gazed down into the little defile beyond. There was a road in the bottom and this was the only way to approach the fort.

'Well,' Emer shouted up to her sister, 'what do you see?'

'There are two horses,' she said, 'one black and one grey. They look fierce and powerful. They are yoked to a fine-looking wooden chariot with wicker sides.'

'Yes, and who's in it?'

'I can't see yet. They need to come closer.'

'I should have gone to see myself,' said Emer.

'No, I can see now. There are two men. The driver is slim and freckled and the passenger is a young warrior with lovely coloured skin as far as I can see.'

'Come down so. We wouldn't want them to think we were spying or worse, eager.' Though Fial had not recognised the visitors, Emer had a fair idea who they were.

As Fial sat back in her place with the others, the chariot swept round the hummock and stopped near the bench.

'Friends,' a voice shouted from the chariot. The speaker climbed down at the back and began to walk over.

Emer saw that it was a youth of about fifteen, well-built, good looking, with a strong wide face and very dark eyes. He wore a beautiful crimson tunic over a white shirt with a hood. He carried a large sword in a fine leather scabbard with bronze plates attached that were finely decorated with circles, spirals and wavy lines. He also had a spear with a blood red shaft and a fine shield with animals chased into the silver rim. Anyone who had taken up arms might have such weapons but there was only one individual that she knew of who had the heavy black eyebrows of this visitor. This, without doubt was Cuchulainn, the fifteen-year-old prodigy from Conor's court. In which case, she decided, the slender, freckled one who was following the warrior over was the driver, Laeg. He wore the charioteer's traditional badge of office – the band around the head to hold the hair out of his eyes – and a heavy brown coat of otter skins.

'Today is it as smooth as always is path your hope I,' Emer said, nodding at Cuchulainn. She said this in riddle form, that only he and she understood.

'Harm to come never you hope I,' he replied, again in riddle.

The rest of the conversation was conducted in the same way, so they understood one another but to Laeg and the girls with their sewing the talk was incomprehensible.

'Where are you from?' she asked. Although she had guessed, she thought it was better to pretend she did not know. She could judge what he said against what she knew. If there were discrepancies she would know not to trust him.

'Emain Macha.'

'That is a long way. Which way did you come?'

He told her. His description was long and detailed. When

he finished, she asked, 'Have you come for any reason?'

He nodded at her.

'No man will carry me off.'

'Did I say anything about that?'

'There are many men inside, not to mention my father. He is stronger than any labourer, more learned than any Druid, more acute than any poet. You do not want to challenge him.'

'I don't?'

'No.'

'But I am formidable.'

'Is that so?'

He nodded.

'What are your qualities?'

'At my weakest I take on twenty. At full strength I can fight a hundred men.'

'But you're still young. Yes, you've taken up arms, but you're not quite fully grown, are you?'

This was taking too long. Cuchulainn decided to press his suit. 'I was brought up at Conor's court among chariot-chiefs and champions, jesters and Druids, poets and learned men. I have all their manners and gifts.'

'Who were they?'

He listed the luminaries from whom he had learned all he knew, including Fergus, Cathbad and his foster-brother, Conall, and the qualities each had instilled in him. As soon as he finished he threw the question back at Emer and asked her who had taught her and what she had learned.

She told him and concluded by saying, 'I was brought up to respect the old virtues. I am well behaved and modest, graceful and beautiful and equal in rank to a queen. I am the most praised and admired woman in Ireland.'

'You don't have a high opinion of yourself. That's endearing,' said Cuchulainn quietly.

Emer watched him, but did not react.

'We should join together,' said Cuchulainn. 'We not only understand each other's riddles but we are well matched.'

'Are you married?' she asked.

'No.'

'But I can't marry until after Fial here, who is older. Go and talk to her.'

'I don't love her,' said Cuchulainn. 'Besides, there's a man who wants her. He's coming. I can see this. He'll go to Forgall and he'll pay the bride price your father wants. So you needn't worry. Fial will be married very soon and long before you.'

He glanced down and saw the tops of Emer's breasts. They were freckled.

'I see a place I would rest,' he said.

'No one comes there,' said Emer, 'unless he has fought three groups of nine, slaying each party with one blow but leaving the man in the middle alive.'

'I see a place I would rest,' he repeated.

'No one comes there until he has killed a hundred men at each of the fords between here and Emain Macha.'

'I'll do it all, everything you say, and I will rest in this place.'

'If you do, we'll be joined together as one.'

Cuchulainn gave her his name and said goodbye. He and Laeg clambered back into the chariot and resumed their seats. Then the horses clattered off.

'What was that about?' asked Laeg, as they followed the road from the compound to the little valley below. 'I couldn't understand a word you or the woman said.'

'I hope not. We spoke in riddles.'

'Why?'

'Would you want those other girls to know what you said if you were courting Emer?'

'No, I wouldn't.'

'There you are then.'

'But they'll know you visited and even if they don't know what you said, word will get back to her father. He won't be long in realising you came and he will guess why.'

'A pity I cannot be invisible,' said Cuchulainn.

He was silent for the rest of the journey back but inside his head he was busy thinking about Emer. He thought about her hair, and the complex way it was plaited and pinned up over her ears. He thought of her smooth face, her broad forehead and her small chin and the nice teeth he had seen inside her mouth when she had smiled. He'd seen her tongue too, red and small and wet, and he wondered what it would be like to touch when they kissed. He thought about the jewellery she wore, bracelets and ankle chains, necklaces and ear-rings, and her fine neat hands and the way she'd cracked her joints once while they'd been talking. He'd liked her manner. She was friendly and humorous even if she did describe herself as the most praised and admired woman in Ireland. Of course, as he had to admit, there was probably a certain justice in her remark and if she wasn't the most admired and praised she deserved to be. She was lovely. He was right before he went to think she was the one to be his wife, and now he'd made the journey he knew she was.

Forgall was a small man with very dark eyes, a pointed nose and, like his daughter, Emer, a pointed chin. His face was sharp and watchful. His manner, on the other hand, was smooth and plausible. He went to immense trouble, at least when he was not angry, to appear genial and decent and honest. He was not any of these as many had discovered. His wiliness was well known. Inside his compound and among his people, however, his reputation was different. He had never tricked or betrayed any of his offspring. His relations with his kin were warm and cordial and loving.

Every evening Forgall played fidchell with one or other of his children. A few hours after Cuchulainn's visit, he went to find Fial. His daughter, though he didn't know it yet, was disgruntled. Though she had not understood the riddles, she had not found it hard to guess why Cuchulainn came and what he wanted, and she resented that her sister was being courted before her.

'Shall we have our game then?' said Forgall.

Fial, a tall girl with long legs and long arms and a long

neck, shook her head. She did not want to play, it seemed.

'But why? I played your sister Emer last night. It's your turn.'

'Emer knows no such word,' Fial sighed.

Forgall was puzzled.

'What word?'

'The word turn. She doesn't understand it. She has no concept of what it means.'

'Doesn't she? Would you care to elaborate?'

Fial shook her head. She had said enough to stir her father into action. He would do the rest. He would weasel out the truth about the visitor and his real motives.

'That's a pity,' said Forgall. 'I'd like to know what you mean.'

'Oh well then, let's play if you want,' said Fial, in a sad and heavy voice. Forgall knew he would not get another word out of her.

They played two games; Fial lost both. She left her father. He knew something going on. It involved Emer. He could ask her but maybe it was better to wait and see what came to him. It was the right decision. The following day, Croach, the father of one of the girls who had been on the bench sewing, came and told him everything.

'So that madman was here and talking in riddles,' Forgall said.

'Yes,' said Croach.

'And now I suppose Emer loves him,' said Forgall.

'Well, I wouldn't be sure you could say that . . . exactly.'

Croach took a step back. He did not like where this conversation was going and he wished now he had not informed Forgall.

'Of course she does. It's obvious.'

'Is it? Can you say so for certain?' Croach wondered if Forgall might lash out at him because he happened to be there and took another step back.

'Don't forget, I know her,' Forgall said, 'and I'll thank you to mention nothing about this conversation to anyone, ever. Is that clear?'

'It is.' Croach felt his face go red. 'I'll be on my way then,' he added, and fled.

Until Cuchulainn approached Emer, Forgall had never given Cuchulainn any thought, except as Conor's prodigy. However, once he discovered what Cuchulainn was up to, he became obsessed by him. Forgall was enraged that Cuchulainn had approached his daughter without his permission and without respect for the proper protocol, which specified that Fial was first in line to be wooed. Forgall decided he would never let Emer marry Cuchulainn. He hatched a scheme to ensure this. He disguised himself as a Gaul and then, with a quantity of wine, he presented himself at the gate of Emain Macha.

'Tell Conor I come from Gaul with a gift of wine from the king,' he told one of the guards.

In the evening Forgall, still in disguise and still unrecognised, ate with Conor in the hall. Cuchulainn and other warriors entertained the guest with feats and swordplay.

'These men of mine are spectacular, are they not?' said Conor to his guest afterwards.

It looked like an innocent inquiry but in fact what the king wanted was that his visitor should praise his warriors and, by inference, himself.

'They are the greatest, are they not?' continued the king.

This was the opening Forgall was waiting for.

'Yes and no,' he said carefully.

'Yes and no?' asked Conor, his affront hidden behind polite words.

'In Ireland, they are the greatest,' Forgall said quietly, 'but not elsewhere.'

Conor said nothing. He was irked but there was nothing for it but to listen politely. The man was a guest – a guest who'd brought him gifts from the king in Gaul – and it would be inhospitable to argue with him. The king gave a small false smile that barely concealed his feelings.

'Send your heroes to Scotland, to Donall,' Forgall continued, quietly. 'He can train them. And when he has finished they can go on to Scathach on her island, the Isle of Scathach. She can teach them her secrets. Then, when they return, they really will be the greatest warriors.'

The king gave a lofty nod. Of course, he had no intention of sending his warriors away. The proposition was ludicrous. But despite his initial resistance he found himself thinking about it later. And then the stranger's counsel was no longer irritating. On the contrary, it was sensible and intelligent. What harm, he thought, was there in his champions going abroad to learn more? When the training was finished, as the stranger had said, they really would be the greatest. He ordered Cuchulainn, Conall and Laoghaire, his three leading champions, to travel to Scotland and then to the Isle of Scathach.

Shortly before he left Cuchulainn went to see Emer in secret.

'Emer, I have to go away.' He told her where.

'I'm surprised you haven't more to say.'

'How so?'

'What happened to your gift of sight?'

Cuchulainn was puzzled.

'It was my father's idea,' Emer told him.

Now he was really puzzled.

'That man who came from Gaul – that was him.'

Cuchulainn had not paid any attention to the visitor. He was just a small man from Gaul, he had thought. Now, according to Emer it was Forgall, and as he thought about this it suddenly seemed entirely possible.

'He hopes you'll never come home. You'll die or fall in love.'

'I won't,' Cuchulainn said. 'Now you make me the same promise.'

She did and he left her, vowing he would return. In his mind it was settled. He must and would marry Emer, whatever obstacle was put in his way.

Chapter Eight

The Isle of Scathach

The three warriors went to Donall and he took them in. First he taught them the flagstone feat. The flagstone was laid on burning coals fanned by a bellows. The stone became so hot it groaned and spat and could not be touched without incurring a blister or a burn. Then Donall showed them how to balance on their toe nails, which were hard and thick, and balanced like this they were able then to dance about on the stone without being harmed or hurt.

Next he taught some tricks with the javelin. How to stick the point in the eye socket and pull out the eye like a choice piece of meat from the pot. How to rotate the weapon while pushing in so the point diced and sliced and increased the size of the wound. How to swing the javelin in a circle while turning on the spot, thus allowing one man to keep many at bay, a feat he called the whirlpool.

Once these were learned, Donall spoke to the trio.

'You know everything I have to teach you. Go on to the Isle of Scathach, to the Shadowy One.' This was Scathach's other name.

The three warriors left the fort and walked to the first fork in the road. One road went north, to the Isle of

Scathach, while the other went south and was the start of the way back to Ireland.

'We're taking this road,' said Conall, indicating the road south.

Cuchulainn was perplexed. 'Why? I thought the plan was to go to Scathach and learn her tricks so we could become the greatest warriors anywhere, in Ireland or abroad.'

'That was the plan when we left but we've decided we want to go home now.'

'Why?'

'Can't you guess?'

'No.'

'We're homesick.'

Cuchulainn nodded. He had heard of it, of course. He had come across the concept in songs and poems but he had never felt it. He had never missed his foster-parents after he left his home at Dun Breth and went to Emain Macha. While staying with Donall he had never missed Conor, or Laeg or even Emer. He hadn't thought of any of them once, even the woman he hoped to marry. His only thoughts had been of fighting and weapons and the skills he was learning.

'Come back home.' The speaker was Conall. Since their first encounter at the ford when Cuchulainn was a boy they had become friends. Conall believed he could persuade his foster brother to follow him and Laoghaire.

'Think of the welcome. Think of your friends. Think of everything. We can come another time. Isn't it time to go home, now?'

Cuchulainn shook his head and indicated the road going north.

'No, I go that way,' he insisted. He was vexed with the other two. He thought they had an understanding and now it seemed they didn't. He never reacted well to sudden changes like this. 'If I'm to be famous, it won't be for ignorance.'

'Oh.' Conall was slightly taken aback. Maybe they were not quite such good friends after all?

Cuchulainn noticed Conall's expression and was slightly baffled and annoyed. Then he reminded himself it would be foolish to quarrel. If they did Conall and Loaghaire would return to Navan with a bad taste in their mouths. They might say things to Conor and he wouldn't be there to counter them. They must part as friends.

'You and Laoghaire,' he said, in his most emollient voice, 'you go back home now and return in a few years. You have long lives lying ahead of you, so you've plenty of time. I, on the other hand, have only a short one. I must seize this opportunity now. You see that, don't you?'

They nodded and embraced. Cuchulainn said goodbye and strode off along the road going north. He was cheerful. He had kept their friendship.

The road leading away to the Isle of Scathach was a yellow-white colour with little grey pebbles stuck into it everywhere. The ground on either side was brown and crumbling. It was covered with coarse grass and great clumps of wiry heather. At the journey's start he was calm and cheerful, but as he went on he suddenly began to feel gloomy and lonely. He missed his friends. Such feelings were as unaccustomed as they were unwelcome. He must master them, he decided, or he might turn round and follow his friends home.

He peered into the distance. He hoped to find a tree or a mountain peak that he could focus on to exclude all the other thoughts that were churning around inside. But all he could see was a small dark spot that was moving towards him. He stared at it and after a while the spot turned into a lion. It was brown with a huge ruff of stiff fur around its head and heavy thick footpads. Cuchulainn drew his sword and lifted his shield but the animal, instead of springing, turned its tail to him and lowered its belly on to the road.

It wants to be ridden, he thought. He swung his leg over and sat on the creature's back. There was a smell of cat. The animal rose on to its legs and moved off, slowly gathering speed. Cuchulainn squeezed with his knees and held the mane. He would not pull it or steer it, he realised. He would let the lion go where it wanted.

After several days the pair reached a still black lake with an island. There were two boys in a small boat near the shore.

'It's as well we're in the boat,' said one boy, pointing towards the pair who had come to a stop at the water's edge.

'Are you sure lions can't swim?' said the other.

'No, but I know when he's eaten that man on his back

he'll sink before he gets to us,' said the first.

'Don't count on it,' shouted Cuchulainn. With his prodigious hearing he had heard the boys just like he had heard Cathbad's prophecy years earlier outside Emain Mecha, the one that had prompted him to take up arms.

He dismounted and the lion bounded off.

'The Isle of Scathach?' he asked the astonished pair in the boat.

'That way,' said one.

He pointed at a wooden house.

'The woman of the house will direct you.'

He walked to the house and knocked. A woman opened the door. Her blue eyes were filled with brown specks. She pulled him into the house. He found himself in an empty hall. The woman disappeared and returned with a piece of roast lamb and a pitcher of water. There was nowhere to sit so he ate and drank standing. As soon as he finished she pushed him out the door which she had left standing open.

'The Isle of Scathach?' he asked.

'Ask him,' she said. She pointed at a youth standing on the grass outside with a wheel in one hand and an apple in the other. Then she slammed the door shut behind him.

'The Isle of Scathach?' asked Cuchulainn.

The youth held up the wheel. 'That way,' he said, pointing towards a plain that ended in distant mountains, 'is the Plain of Ill-Luck. For the first half, roll this wheel ahead. Where it goes, you go. Be careful; when you're out there it's all mud. Touch it and you'll get stuck fast. You won't get away. You'll die.

'The second half, kick the apple in front of you. Where it rolls, you go. Be careful; each grass blade is as sharp as a sword. Step on it and you'll be skewered. You won't get away. You'll die.

'When you get to the mountain go through the pass. On the other side you'll find her camp at the end of the glen but not her. Ask for further directions.'

'Since you know so much,' said Cuchulainn, 'can you see my future?'

'Certainly,' said the youth as he gave Cuchulainn the wheel and the apple. 'A great army will come north from Connacht, led by Maeve and her husband Aillil, and you will stand alone against them for the most part. The bloodshed will be immense, but victory will be yours and your fame will be assured.'

'But my life will be short?'

'Your life is short,' said the youth.

Cuchulainn crossed the Plain of Ill-Luck guided first by the wheel and then the apple. He followed the pass through the mountains and, on the far side, in a deep green glen, he found a cluster of huts at the end of a path. They were within sight and sound of the sea.

These huts were where Scathach's pupils lived. Hearing Cuchulainn approach, several emerged to see who the visitor was. One of these was a slim sand-coloured youth with wide shoulders and improbably narrow hips. His movements were deft and quick.

'Friend,' said this youth.

Judging by his accent, Cuchulainn guessed the youth came from Connacht, the province south and west of Ulster. And now, having heard the youth's voice, Cuchulainn remembered hearing talk before he left Ireland of an extraordinary youth from Connacht who had gone to study with Scathach.

'Are you Ferdia?' he asked.

The youth nodded. 'And you are?'

Cuchulainn gave his name.

'Oh yes.' Ferdia nodded and stared at the muscular, dark-eyed visitor. 'I should have recognised you.'

'Surely you wouldn't have known who I was if I hadn't told you?'

'I would if I'd given it some thought.'

Cuchulainn nodded. He was not unhappy with this. He glanced at the others standing behind Ferdia and nodded at them. He turned back to Ferdia and stared closely at him. The youth had a very broad and smooth forehead with small brown freckles scattered across it.

'I'm looking for Scathach,' he said.

Ferdia pointed down the path. It ended at the sea and some way out lay an island connected to the mainland by a long stone bridge.

'So,' said Cuchulainn, 'she's on the island.' He was puzzled. After his long and arduous journey, he had not expected the conclusion to be so easy.

'If you can get over the bridge,' said Ferdia.

That sounded ominous.

'I'll swim then,' said Cuchulainn.

'All visitors must come *over* water. She won't see you otherwise.'

'I'll row in a boat, then.'

Ferdia shook his head. 'The bridge or not at all. That's the rule.'

'The bridge it is then,' agreed Cuchulainn.

'It will not be easy, friend,' warned Ferdia.

Cuchulainn scanned the faces of the small crowd. To ask about the bridge and its possible dangers would only make him appear timid, and he didn't want to be thought that. And no one, judging by their faces, except Ferdia looked as if they wanted to tell him the secret of the bridge. But obviously Ferdia also felt inhibited by the presence of the others. Well, so be it, Cuchulainn thought. He would find out for himself.

He turned from the staring pupils.

'Be warned,' Ferdia shouted after him. 'Take great care.'

Cuchulainn raised a hand in acknowledgement as he moved down the path.

'Thank you, friend,' he called back.

He peered ahead as he moved forward. The long bridge had parapet walls and was hump-backed. On either side there were great rocks, wet and black, piled untidily along the shore's edge. A wave crashed against these and a sheet of spray shot upwards. There were sea birds clamouring somewhere. The path underfoot was sandy and soft and with each step he sank down a little.

He reached the path's end. Now he was closer he saw the bridge was floored with flags. Another wave crashed and a sheet of spray was thrown up. The sea behind rolled back with a sad soughing sound while droplets showered down and wet his face.

'Beware, friend.'

Cuchulainn turned.

The pupils were standing where he left them and they were watching him. Ferdia, who was slightly detached from the others, was clearly the one who had just repeated the warning.

He nodded and looked at the bridge again. It was impossible to guess its secret from the way it looked.

Cuchulainn sniffed. He smelled salt and kelp. That was the clumps of seaweed scattered everywhere. He picked up a piece. It was slippery to touch and heavy with seawater. He lobbed it on to the bridge. It landed in the middle. The structure shivered and the seaweed flew over the side wall and disappeared towards the sea. Was that why Ferdia had warned him to take care? When weight was put on the bridge it wobbled and the greater the weight, he presumed, the fiercer the reaction. It was going to try shaking him into the sea.

The best strategy was to have as little weight bearing down on the structure for as short a time as possible. If he took a good run and hopped, he guessed he could cross to the other side in three or four bounds in which case, surely, the bridge would not get a chance to throw him off.

He tightened the thongs by which his shield was attached to his left arm. He tugged up the cord from which his scabbard hung from his shoulders and moved his sword from its current place by his left leg to the middle of his chest. He gripped his spear firmly by the middle.

He retreated and ran forward. At the edge of the bridge he leapt into the air. Landing on his right foot the bridge trembled but not quite violently enough to heave him off. He sprung up, his left leg out now, his left foot forward. The trick would be, as soon as he touched down, to spring up as soon as possible so the bridge couldn't hurl him sideways.

To his surprise, however, as he looked ahead, he saw the bridge had parted – it was in two halves – and a gap had appeared across the middle. He had a marvellously clear view of the grey churning sea below.

Alarming though that was, it was nothing to what happened next. The half of the bridge immediately under his feet was now flying towards him, like a hurley stick towards a ball. An instant later it caught his foot and, just like a hurley ball, he was thrown upwards. Suddenly, he was on his back, flying through the air. Great piles of cloud went whizzing by overhead, and he passed a bird so close the point of his spear brushed one wing.

Then he was falling and then, inevitably, he hit the path – thwack! His muscles clenched, his bones knocked, the air rushed out of his body. His head banged on the ground.

Small filigree silver specks floated before his eyes. Then the flecks vanished and he saw the sky. He hurt. In the distance he heard the jeers of the watching pupils. The red of shame spread over his face. He wanted to get back on his feet as quickly as possible.

He rolled quickly on to his side and used the shaft of his spear to lever himself up. Back on his feet he stepped forward quickly from the place he had fallen. He looked ahead.

He expected to see the bridge's two halves sticking up into the air like javelins held by men on guard. But no, the two halves of the bridge had knitted back together again. It was as if nothing had happened. He glanced behind. He wanted to see those watching and he wanted them to know he had heard them.

They still stood in a loose group between the huts. With his extraordinary eyesight he was able to see their faces even at such a long distance. They were smiling. Only Ferdia looked serious. He, alone, had not relished his failure.

Cuchulainn turned forward and contemplated the bridge again. There was only one way to get over. That was to be faster than the bridge. If his run up was longer and harder, he would easily clear it in two bounds rather than four.

He moved back and then pelted forward. At the edge, where the path sheered into the bridge, he launched himself into the air. With his right foot forward he saw the middle of the bridge ahead. He would touch down lightly and spring up again. But just as his foot was about to go down, the gap appeared as before. He glimpsed the grey roiling sea for an instant. Then the half of the bridge immediately under him whipped up, caught him under his foot and threw him into the air again. It was a much harder rebuff this time and he landed far further along the path than the last time he was thrown.

As the filigree bits of silver danced in front of his eyes, the hooting and shouting came from behind, more raucous than before. The red flush of shame coloured his face again but this time he lay still on the ground. He did not move. What was the point in springing to his feet? No action could undo what had just happened. He must ignore their jubilation. What he needed was a new strategy that would deprive the bridge of a third chance to toss him back.

The silver flecks vanished. His breathing became normal again. An idea came to him. The salmon leap. It was a feat he had learned long before with the Boy Spears.

He got to his feet. He dusted the sand off his clothes. He took off his shield and re-strapped it on to his back. Then he got his spear and laid it into the crook of his elbows. Then he folded his arms up to his chest. The spear extended on either side of his body.

Cuchulainn went back up the path. He closed his eyes. He opened his eyes. The next stage was to get angry. Not so angry that he distorted. Just angry enough to give him the energy he needed. He looked around. Ferdia was standing still but the rest, with whistles and hand gestures, were urging him to try and fail again. A small hot nugget of rage began to burn in his middle. He would show them, he thought. They wouldn't be so quick to laugh and scoff at him then.

He shook his head at the crowd. They hissed again. He turned. He was ready. If he waited any longer the rage would grow so prodigious he would distort. With his rage in full spate he could probably clear the bridge but then, once he was across, how would he become calm again? There would be no kind women to immerse him in cold water as there were after he took up arms the first time. He might end up killing Scathach. No, this was just right. He was ready.

He sprinted three or four paces and then, his chin tucked against his chest, he hurled himself forward. His shoulders hit the sand path. He brought his knees to his chest and tucked his feet down. He was a small tight ball with the spear in the middle sticking out like an axle and he was going faster and faster.

He hit the edge of the bridge. He felt the hard stone below even through the iron and wood of his shield. The parapet unfurled in a blur. He rolled on, even faster than before. He felt the bridge judder. The structure was separating, ready to throw him back.

The crucial moment was about to come. He hoped he had judged the distance right. If he was wrong he would be flipped back where he came from. On the other hand, if he had it right, he would triumph.

He squinted ahead. There was the edge of the half he was on just ahead. He stuck his feet forward and uncoiled.

As soon as his feet found the stone lip he pushed up and away with all his strength while the bridge pushed at the same time from below. Only this time, the force wasn't throwing him backwards. No, this time, with his legs pressed tightly together, and his back arching backwards, he was shooting forwards and upwards. And then the point was reached when the arm of the bridge was extended as far as it would go, that he left it and continued flying up, his feet snapping now like a salmon's tail fin, until he reached a height far greater than he could ever have achieved with leaping and hopping unaided.

And then, having got this high and really far forward, and having hung for a moment in mid-air exactly like the salmon, he dropped his head forward and formed a ball again. The other arm of the bridge, the far arm, was there ahead of him, sloping away. He found the edge with his shoulder and let himself tumble on. If it batted him away that was fine. There was only one way it could hurl him now and that was in the direction in which he wanted to go, towards the island. He kept himself tight around the spear as he waited for the bridge to hurl him off. But no blow came. He felt the bridge settling instead. Then he felt hard flagstones give way to soft sandy ground. Then he stopped rolling and came to a stop. He had done it. He was over.

He uncoiled and stood up. The long bridge behind was smooth and whole. He put his shield back on his arm and his sword in its usual place by his leg. He glanced back over the sea. The pupils were not mocking now. They were still and silent. Only Ferdia was animated. He was waving and shouting enthusiastically.

Cuchulainn waved back and then turned. He was himself again. There was a path leading across cropped green grass to a small stone fort.

Cuchulainn walked to the solid gates and with his shaft he battered on the wood. No one answered. He stabbed the wood with the point of his spear, driving the point right through. He drilled several holes like this.

Inside the fort, Scathach lurked with her daughter, Uathach. The mother was old, of course, with a slight but spry body and an enormous head made to appear even bigger by her prodigious grey hair. Her daughter was plump with a small face and grey eyes.

'Our visitor is no ordinary man,' said the witch. 'No ordinary man could do that.' She pointed at the holes in the gate. 'Go and see what he wants.'

Uathach approached the gate as Cuchulainn drove his spear through again.

'Friend, we hear you,' she shouted. 'Stop that now.'

She pulled back one of the gates.

'Who are you?' she said.

He gave his name.

'And your business?'

He told her.

'Wait here,' she said.

Uathach went and found her mother. She delivered a

description of the visitor that mixed praise and desire in equal measure.

'He pleases you,' said Scathach. She knew her daughter well. 'It is not hard to see.'

'This is true,' her daughter agreed.

'He can sleep in your bed,' said the old woman, 'if that is what you want.'

'It would not be a disaster if he wanted that too.'

Scathach slipped out of the fort by a back way while Uathach fetched Cuchulainn in. She brought him to her sleeping hut.

'You stay here with me,' she said. There was only one bed. If this was where he stayed then inevitably he would sleep with this woman. For a brief instant he saw Emer with his inner eye, as she had been the last time he saw her, when he went to say goodbye. Had they made a specific undertaking to one another, he wondered? They had promised one another they would neither die nor fall in love and in addition he had promised to return to her after his journey abroad. Was this woman going to kill him? He did not think so. Was she going to make him love her? He glanced at the plump, grey-eyed Uathach. He thought not. Would she keep him? No, he was quite certain, once he had finished his education here on the Isle of Scathach, he would return to Emer. He made his mind up. He would stay here in Uathach's hut and sleep in her bed. He would not break any word by doing so. It would do him no harm and it might even help him. He'd not had sight of Scathach but if he was patient he felt certain Uathach would direct him to her mother in the end.

Uathach gave him food and water. For three days they were together. Cuchulainn said nothing about his quest until the third morning came and he knew Uathach liked him enough to help him.

'I want to see Scathach,' he said. 'I want to learn from her.'

'She is with her sons at the other end of the island. I'll show you the way. Approach the place carefully and make certain she doesn't see you. Don't approach her, watch from a distance, until the middle of the day when she will climb up a yew tree to rest. Perform the feat that got you over the bridge and get up into the yew. Put your sword between her breasts and extract her promise.'

Cuchulainn followed this advice exactly. He surprised Scathach and put his sword to her heart.

'You're dead, unless you grant me my demands.'

Scathach nodded her broad old head.

Cuchulainn lived on the island in the fort and trained with the pupils who gave him no help when he first tried to cross the bridge though they knew its secret for they had all crossed it themselves. He ignored them with the exception of Ferdia, who became his particular friend.

During his training Scathach taught him to juggle nine apples with one hand and with never more than one in his palm. She taught him how to make a noise equal to thunder. She taught him running feats, breath feats, screaming feats. She taught him how to attach sickles to a chariot the better to cut down warriors on foot, and how to crouch in a chariot before battle and how to spring out. She taught him how to leap over a poisoned blade. She taught him how to sever a head with the sharp edge of a shield. She taught him pole throwing. She taught him sword fighting and shield fighting, and rope and javelin feats. She taught him the stunning stroke, the cry-stroke and the precision-stroke. She taught him how to stop a lance in flight by stepping on it with a foot. She taught him how to truss a warrior with a spear and a rope. And she taught him how to cast with his foot the Gae Bolga, or Bellows Spear.

This was a short stemmed javelin with a long thin tip. The shaft behind the pointed end was hollow. As the end punched through the skin, so it dropped back, into the hollowed-out shaft, and released a sliding ring that held a set of barbs in place. These then opened up inside the body like an expanding bellows, shredding any organs they touched. When the spear was pulled out, the fearsome end did even more damage. No man had been known to survive being penetrated by this weapon, for if it didn't kill on entry, it certainly killed on removal. Cuchulainn so excelled at casting the Gae Bolga (it was the seven toes he had on each foot that made him so adept), that Scathach gave it to him to keep.

After Cuchulainn had been with the witch about a year and a half, Scathach and her people went to war. It was rare for warriors to be led by a woman and in this situation, which was rarer still, both sides were. The enemy were led by Aoife, a woman so fierce even Scathach feared her. After various skirmishes that produced no victory, Aoife demanded Scathach present a champion to meet her in single combat and to settle matters that way. Cuchulainn volunteered to go.

Before the encounter he went to Scathach.

'What does she most value?'

'That is not hard. Her chariot, her horses, her charioteer. She will sacrifice anything for them. Why do you ask?'

'If she's better than me it's as well I know her weakness.'

The two met in the early morning by the side of a stream. It was a small uneven piece of ground surrounded by bracken and gorse, with a clear view of the surrounding hills and the tracks that ran down the side of these.

Cuchulainn had been right when he went to Scathach. Aoife was better. She smashed the blade of his sword and left him holding the hilt with a short and useless stub.

He was dead, or he would have been, except that he took several steps back and pointed up at the nearest hill.

'Your chariot's fallen off the track,' he shouted, 'pulling your horses and your charioteer with it.'

Aoife could not stop herself turning to look. Cuchulainn jumped on her back and knocked her to the ground. In the tumble she lost her sword. Cuchulainn picked it up and put the point to the side of her neck.

'You're dead,' he shouted.

She was still on her front with her face in the grass.

'Turn round,' he shouted, 'slowly, on to your back.'

He kept the sword's point so tight on her neck that as she turned the end tore her skin. She did not doubt that he would kill her.

'Don't kill me,' she shouted.

'Why not?' he asked.

'Because I would have spared you,' she said.

Her skin was light yellow, like mild honey, and her pupils were the deep brown of wet bog. Her face was long and her eyes were not round like most of the women he knew but slanted. He had never seen features like this before.

'Would you?' he asked.

'Of course I would, in return for three demands. So make your demands of me. Whatever you can say in a single breath is yours.'

He considered her offer.

'The end of this war with hostages for Scathach to guarantee the peace. Your company tonight. And a son.'

She nodded her strange yellow face.

They slept together that night and in the morning she reported that she would indeed bear his son.

'A pity I won't see him born,' said Cuchulainn.

'A pity,' she agreed. 'A son should know his father.'

Cuchulainn pulled a gold ring off the smallest finger of his left hand. It had been a gift from Conor. It was gold and the letter 'C' was chased into the metal. It was so unusual he knew he would recognise it in years to come. He handed it to Aoife.

'His name will be Connla,' he said. 'When he's seven, send him to Ireland after me and be sure he brings the ring. Tell him when he comes he is to give way to no man, he is to refuse no man combat and he is to give his name to no man until he has found me. These are my conditions and he must not break them.'

Cuchulainn returned to Scathach's fort with the hostages. He was told his teacher wanted him. He went and found the old witch in her hut warming herself by a smoking fire. He had grown to like her while he had lived with her. She was adept and clever and wise.

'You've finished here now,' she said. 'You've nothing more to learn. You can go home.'

'Before I leave will you look and see what is waiting for me ahead?'

Cuchulainn sat while Scathach chanted and danced herself into a trance. When finally she spoke it was not in her usual clear high thin voice but in a growl. As Cathbad had foretold, she confirmed he was to be famous and die young. As the youth with the wheel and the apple he met on the way to the Isle of Scathach had predicted, there would be an epic invasion from the south led by the queen and king of Connacht, Maeve and her husband Aillil, with Cuchulainn almost entirely alone against the enemy, much slaughter and many graves everywhere, the invaders forced to leave and great fame for him in the end. His defence of Ulster would be the foundation of his fame.

Scathach also saw, which previously had never been revealed to him, what would happen next. This was the re-invasion from Connacht by Maeve and Aillil with another army and his death at their hands. However, Scathach emphasised, this death, far from tarnishing, would enhance his already colossal reputation and seal it as something great for ever . . .

Cuchulainn left happy. He was, at seventeen and a half, the best trained warrior in the world. He returned to his own place and people. He did not think any more about the women he had known when he was in Scotland. His thoughts instead were filled with Emer and he wanted to go to her. He called Laeg, his charioteer Laeg who had had nothing to do while Cuchulainn was away except wait for his return.

'Prepare my chariot,' he ordered. 'We are going to Forgall's fort.'

'Not a good idea,' said Laeg. 'Forgall knows you're back and he has many armed men. The only way you'll see Emer is from the end of a pike when your head's cut off and you're stuck in the air.'

Cuchulainn received this information without comment. Forgall's retinue, he had no doubt, were in a high state of readiness. They would be expecting him to come right away. Well, he would not give them the satisfaction.

'All right,' he said. He would remain at Emain Macha . . .

Nine months passed, Connla was born, and Forgall's

contacts in Scotland sent him an account of the birth. He received the news with malicious delight. His oldest daughter, Fial, had married (what Cuchulainn had predicted to Emer had come to pass just as he said), which meant there was now no impediment to Emer marrying. But Forgall, an obstinate man who would never change his mind once he had it made, had no intention of allowing Conor's insufferable and disrespectful prodigy to have his daughter. It would never happen and so this news about Connla, when it came, gladdened his heart. Here, he thought, was exactly the right information to poison Emer and ensure, in her mind at least, that all thoughts of marrying Cuchulainn died. He put on his sad face and told a servant to bring Emer to him.

'Your Cuchulainn has fathered a boy, Connla, by Aoife, a woman he knew in Scotland,' he said in a tone that he hoped sounded neither triumphant nor vehement. He did not want her to think he enjoyed this, especially as it was going to cause pain. He predicted tears and hopefully a savage denunciation of the wayward suitor by his daughter.

However, to his surprise, Emer simply stared at the ground; then, after a long pause, she said, 'She obviously can't have meant anything to him, this Aoife woman. Hasn't he come back to Ireland? Isn't he staying quietly at Emain Macha? I imagine he's biding his time, waiting for you to let your guard slip so he can steal me away.'

'Wrong,' said Forgall, though actually she was right.

Cuchulainn waited another three months. He was half-way through his eighteenth year and twelve months had passed since his return to Ireland. By now Forgall's men must have grown bored and their guard could not be what it was. He was sure of it. He summoned Laeg.

'Harness the chariot.'

'And where are we going?' asked the charioteer. 'I hope not where I think . . .'

'Yes, Forgall's fort.'

'That wasn't a good idea the last time you asked and it's still not a good idea.'

'Wait and see. You won't be disappointed.'

They crossed the plain, arriving in the early evening. They slept out overnight. Early the next morning, when a few pale stars still glimmered in the sky, Cuchulainn scaled the three ramparts and penetrated to the inner enclosure. Here he found three groups of nine men and killed eight men with each stroke, leaving one standing in the middle of each group. The survivors were Emer's three brothers. Forgall, who was watching, decided to flee but as he scaled the first rampart he fell and broke his neck.

Cuchulainn found Emer in her hut and brought her back over the ramparts to his chariot. They climbed into the back and took the warrior's seat together. There were double foot-bindings and each put their feet in these. Then Laeg shook the reins, turned the horses and galloped off.

From the gates of the fort poured a hundred men, rallied by Emer's brothers. They chased the chariot but as they were on foot it was an unequal contest. So these warriors got chariots harnessed and set off after Cuchulainn's. They met him at a ford on a river. Cuchulainn killed every man and their blood turned the river waters a colour halfway between brown and pink.

The next day at the next ford on the route back to Emain Macha, another party of a hundred from Forgall's fort met Cuchulainn and he killed them all. The next day this happened again at a third ford and he killed that hundred too. By the time he reached Emain Macha on the third evening, all the conditions laid down by Emer were fulfilled. He was her husband now and she was his wife.

'I know you were with a woman in Scotland called Aoife,' said Emer to Cuchulainn as the chariot was trundling along the edge of the meeting ground where Cuchulainn had wrestled and jostled with the Boy Spears years earlier. 'You fathered a boy, called Connla.'

Cuchulainn nodded, his throat apple bobbing, his face colouring.

'We will speak no more about it,' said Emer.

That night, Conor and his warriors gathered in the hall in the house of the Red Branch, and Emer was brought in and introduced to them. She was given food and drink. It was the general opinion that she was attractive, graceful and very charming. Every warrior congratulated Cuchulainn, taking care of course to disguise his relief. They were happy he had a bride, for now their wives and daughters and even their mothers would be safe. The only slight demur came from

Poison-Tongue, as the poet Bricriu was known.

'What an interesting night we have lying ahead of us,' he said out loud to no one in particular. 'I don't think it will be to our young hero's liking.'

'Meaning what?' asked Fergus who, sitting closest to the poet, had heard what he said.

'She will have to spend tonight with Conor, won't she?' said the poet nastily. 'It is our custom, isn't it? For the first night the bride is always the king's, isn't she?' He raised a finger and asked a passing servant to re-fill his goblet with beer.

Fergus knew perfectly well that this was the custom and had been hoping, as Conor had not mentioned it, that in this instance the tradition would be quietly overlooked.

'Why don't you forget it, Bricriu?' Fergus was angry but he was careful to speak under his breath.

'I hardly think Conor will forget she must sleep with him, so why should I?'

He said this loudly enough for Cuchulainn, who was on a couch nearby, to hear. Until now the warrior had kept the thought of Emer and the king out of his mind. Like Fergus he had hoped it would just be forgotten. Now Bricriu had spoken, it would have to happen. The thought of Emer in the king's bed filled him with rage. He shook so violently he split the cushion he was sitting on. All the feathers poured out and gusted round the hall. Cuchulainn got to his feet and stumbled out.

'Oh,' said the king, staring into his goblet where a white

feather floated on his beer, 'what is the matter?'

Cathbad was nearby.

'I don't know but I know who will,' he said.

He had noticed Fergus and Bricriu speaking and from past experience he knew the poet was the likely source of trouble.

Cathbad made his way through the smoky hall to Fergus and then whispered in his ear, 'Come and talk to me for a minute.'

They went into a corner. Fergus related what Bricriu had said and what Cuchulainn had overheard.

'The king was hoping, I think,' said Cathbad, 'this would simply be forgotten. Cuchulainn will kill any man who sleeps with Emer. But if Bricriu brings the business up, how can the king refuse? Oh dear, this is bad.'

Cathbad went back to the king. In some circumstances he was known to suppress the truth. In this situation he decided to tell him everything, and he did.

'Call him in to me,' said Conor coolly.

Cuchulainn was summoned.

'I want you to go out and round up every single wild and domestic animal around this fort for as far as the eye can see in every direction.'

'When?'

'Now.'

'Now?'

'Yes.'

'But it's dark.'

'That will hardly trouble a man like you, will it?'

Cuchulainn raced out into the night and Conor called his warriors to attention. Emer and the women were all in the hall. They heard the discussion that followed. The king was not prepared, he said, to forgo the pleasure of Emer in his bed that night but he was delighted to accept Fergus and Cathbad as well. The four would sleep soundly and in the morning Emer would return to her husband no different from how she had left him the night before.

When Cuchulainn returned later, having penned all the animals he had gathered in a single flock on the meeting ground in front of the fort, his anger was gone. Cathbad explained the arrangement.

The next day Conor paid Cuchulainn his honour-price as he would any new husband. He also paid Emer's bride-price. Though her father and brothers were dead, she still had other male relatives who must be paid as always happened when a woman took a husband. Thereafter Cuchulainn slept with Emer every night until he died apart, that is, from when he was away at war.

Chapter Nine

Deirdre, the woman

In the night snow fell on the isolated compound where Deirdre lived. It was a fine white powdery snow and it fell on the ground and the roofs of the huts, the trees and the coping on the well. As dark gave way to dawn, everything was covered with a fine coat of white.

There was a wind blowing too and the snow, so fine and powdery, gusted into the crevices between the stones that made up the ramparts, between the wicker sides of the chariots parked outside, and between the stalks of the thatch of Deirdre's sleeping hut. The flakes that got in during the night were unnoticed by the young woman that Deirdre had now become. As she lay sleeping under heavy pelts, they floated silently down to the floor and melted away.

Then, early the following morning, one flake landed on Deirdre's left cheek, between her eye and mouth. She was in the halfway state, neither awake nor asleep, and she felt the cold touch immediately, like a finger gently touching her skin. She was curious rather than alarmed and she opened her eyes.

By the pale light that leached in she saw a handful of

other white flakes trembling in the air as they floated down. At the same instant she noticed the unusual stillness and quietness that always came after snow fell. It had been snowing all night, she guessed.

She did not brush the flake away. She lay still and waited. The flake melted into water that then trickled down her face. She opened her mouth and it rolled over her lip and on to her tongue. It had no taste, but was cold and clean. Was this an omen, she wondered?

It was a question Deirdre frequently asked at this time. At just thirteen her life was on the verge of momentous change. For as long as she could remember she had lived alone in this compound with her fosterers, Abcam and Eve (joined by Levercham, Conor's special messenger, who had moved in later), out of the sight of everyone else who lived in Ulster. It was her destiny to marry Conor when she was thirteen and until that time came he had decreed that nobody else could see her, in case her beauty caused other men to love her and upset the king's plans for their future.

She had seen her future husband many times at the compound, and she viewed their marriage that must, she imagined, happen any day now, with trepidation. It was not just the difference in age that troubled her, although she was certainly terrified at the thought of spending the rest of her life with someone so much older. She was also troubled by the conviction that it was not life that awaited her: it was death. She would be cheated of everything other girls' lives might offer.

For so young a girl to be burdened by the knowledge of such an unappealing and seemingly inescapable future, Deirdre should have been sad and unhappy. Yet she was not. She was always cheerful – at least that was the impression she gave Abcam and Eve and Levercham, and Conor too when he visited. And she really was happy because she had a secret. Deirdre was sustained by the inner certainty that the life she would live would be different from the one planned.

She had always been careful to keep this intuition to herself. She had realised early that Conor was not only powerful: he could also be dangerous when he was angry. She knew that if he discovered either what she thought of their marriage, or her belief that her life would be different to the one he had planned for her, he would be furious. And in his rage he might do something terrible to her, or worse, to Abcam, or Eve, or Levercham, all of whom he would doubtless blame for her wayward thinking.

Deirdre had always had to strive hard to maintain the mask that hid her feelings and lately even more effort was required. She was old enough now to leave the only home she had ever known, and go to Emain Macha and marry Conor. She also reasoned her other future must make itself known very soon. How would the tension between the two lives be reconciled? And what was to happen to her? She could hardly wait to know.

So when the snow flake landed on her cheek and melted she wondered if it was an omen at last. Was this the day when her other story would begin? She desperately hoped so.

It was later the same day. Abcam brought a calf into the compound and cut the animal's neck with a blade. The beast gave a moan and blood gushed out into a bowl. The animal's legs buckled and then it toppled sideways. When it hit the ground a little cloud of powdery white snow dust puffed up. The calf's head twitched and the tongue fell out, surprisingly large and pink. Blood from the neck sprayed over the snow all round the head and showed everywhere as little bright red spots like holly berries.

Abcam put down the bronze bowl filled with black blood. He attached the carcass by its back legs to a beam. He caught the rest of the blood and then with the sharp point of his knife he cut through the hide with quick swift movements, taking care not to cut too deep. When he had finished these excisions he was ready to skin the creature. With his strong thumbs he began to peel away the pelt to reveal the flesh underneath, a mix of red wet muscle and white drier patches of fat. While he was working a raven dropped silently to the ground behind and began to peck at the blood spatters. It was a large bird and in the black of its plumage there was a faint hint of blue. Abcam was too busy skinning the calf to notice the bird.

At this moment Deirdre came to the door of the cooking hut, which was close by, to see how the butchering was progressing. She saw everything. She saw the snow-covered compound patterned everywhere with footsteps. She saw the upside-down calf hanging by its back legs and Abcam pulling away the skin. She saw the raven too, lapping the blood. She watched for a moment or two and then turned to Levercham, who was crouched inside by the fire.

'I could desire such a man,' she said.

'What man?' asked Levercham, who was feeding wood to the fire.

'Like the three colours I can see here outside.'

Levercham got up and came to the doorway to see.

'Hair as black as that raven, cheeks as red as that blood and skin as white as that snow,' said Deirdre.

Levercham nodded.

'You could; well then, you will.'

'Will I?' said Deirdre. She was careful to control her inflection so no emotion showed. 'How so?'

Levercham was back at the cooking pit, blowing on to the small wavering flame burning in the middle of the pile of sticks.

'I know someone who exactly answers to that description.'

Deirdre left the doorway and crossed to the cooking pit.

'You do?'

'I do.'

'And who might that be?'

Levercham looked at the grey smoke rising slowly towards the hole in the roof. Her face was flat and her eyes were dark. Her body was thin and angular. There was no fat on it and there never had been. Her grey hair hung down her back, as usual, in a long thick plait like a rope.

When she was younger Levercham was noted for her satirical poetry and her extraordinary capacity to produce pain and hurt with words. She had mostly stopped making poetry but the reputation remained when she became the king's special messenger.

When Deirdre was sent away, it was Levercham who carried the infant and Conor's instructions to the fosterers, Abcam and Eve. Over the years that followed Conor frequently sent Levercham to the compound to check on Deirdre's progress. Levercham got to know and like Deirdre, so much so she decided she would join Abcam and Eve. Conor, who was appalled yet fearful of what Levercham might compose about him if he refused, had had to agree and she moved into the compound.

From the day she took Deirdre away when she was a baby from Felimid's compound, Levercham had always known it was Conor's intention to marry her. At first, when Deirdre was very young, Levercham had found it hard to believe this would happen. She was sure Conor must get tired of waiting, find another woman and abandon this plan.

However, as Deirdre grew older, Levercham had come to realise that Conor really did intend to do as he said. It was unjust, she thought, as well as unfair and unnatural that a young girl should be yoked to an older man without having had the chance to gorge herself on the rest that life had to offer.

Naturally, Levercham kept her abhorrence of Conor's scheme private. If anything happened because of what she said, no matter how fearful her reputation as a satirist, and how great her reputation as an honest broker, the king would destroy her if he had the evidence to blame her.

It would be quite a different situation though, she had decided, if Deirdre indicated that she was unhappy with the path that had been laid down. Levercham would not stand in her way. If Deirdre asked questions, Levercham would answer them. In this situation she could never be accused of having sown the idea of rebellion in Deirdre's heart. Conor could not destroy her if Deirdre was against him.

Because Deirdre was so careful to guard her true feelings, Levercham had never had the sense that Deirdre wished to go a different way from the one she had been allotted. Until this moment that is, when Deirdre stood at the door watching the raven drinking the calf's blood that spotted the snow, and spoke of the man she might love. Here, finally, Levercham was in no doubt, was the sign that she intended to strike in a different direction.

Without hesitating Levercham answered Deirdre's question as fully and fairly as it was in her power to do.

'He isn't far away,' she said quietly. 'He's close by.'

'Who?'

'The man you describe.'

'Who is?'

'Naoise, one of Usnach's famous three sons.'

Deirdre turned away and looked through the door.

'I wish you hadn't told me,' she said.

'You asked; I replied. The man who answers exactly to your description is Naoise, Usnach's son, and he is at Emain Macha.'

'I'll be ill until I see him so,' said Deirdre emphatically.

'Oh stop it,' said Levercham and she threw another piece of wood into the fire-pit, 'you will not.'

It was typical of the young, she thought, to exaggerate like this. She had done exactly the same when she was young and she wanted something.

'You must bring him here,' continued Deirdre. 'I must talk to him.'

'Must you?'

'I will be ill, I promise you I will, if I don't see him.'

'I'll believe that when I see it.'

'And what then will you say to Conor, when I am ill and he asks why you haven't looked after me properly?'

'Oh, I'll find something to say.'

'And when I'm dead, what will you tell him then?'

'You'll never know; won't you be dead?'

Deirdre refused the veal served her that evening. She refused all food the day after and the one after that again. Levercham began to worry she really meant what she said. She really would be ill until she spoke to Naoise.

On the evening of the third day without food she found Deirdre in her hut, lying on her bed.

'If I do what you want, Deirdre, what will you do for me?'

'Whatever you ask,' said Deirdre, slyly.

'If I bring Naoise here, will you start to eat again?'

'Certainly,' said Deirdre quietly.

Levercham went to Emain Macha the next morning and found Naoise. She laid her offer before him. She would bring him to Deirdre, who was anxious to meet him. The invitation frightened and flattered Naoise at the same time. He knew who Deirdre was. He knew what Conor intended for her. He knew no man was supposed to associate with her until she was brought to Emain Macha and married to the king. At the same time he saw this as a wonderful opportunity. What a gift this was that had fallen into his hands. What a story to tell in old age. He would be an idiot to reject this offer.

'No one must know about this,' Naoise said.

'Of course not. No one will see us go in or out.'

'What about later? It can never be spoken of.'

'I won't tell, you can be sure of that,' said Levercham. 'Think of the trouble I'd get into. It will be our secret, I promise.'

That evening, Levercham brought Naoise into the compound through a small forgotten entry at the back. No one heard or saw them. Levercham led him to Deirdre's sleeping hut. A screen covered the doorway. Levercham lifted this aside. Naoise slipped in.

The hut was dark inside. A candle burned on the table. Naoise thought he smelled lilies. Deirdre sat on a stool. There was a second empty stool opposite.

'Take it,' she said.

He nodded and sat.

'Here I am.'

'Yes, you are, I can see you.'

His eyes adjusted. He saw a young girl with small ears, a small nose, and long red hair that was intricately plaited and knotted and pinned to her head. She had thin bare forearms with long hands and slender ankles with small feet and all her nails were painted red. She had a smell that reminded him of something that he couldn't identify and a strong, slightly throbbing voice and she spoke very quickly in the way of the young sometimes when they are excited.

'What was your reason?' he asked.

'For what?'

'For sending the old woman to bring me here?'

'Because I felt unlucky never having seen you.'

'Oh.'

'But my ill-luck doesn't end there.'

'What are you talking about?' asked Naoise. He'd come expecting flirtation and banter, not this gloomy talk. He had imagined a pretty girl, some light talk and then a wistful separation. What he found was someone troubled and brooding and possibly reckless.

'Your future is assured,' he said, 'so you can stop with the bad luck. You have the bull of this province all to yourself. When you marry the king you will become queen.'

'Given the choice,' she said quickly, 'I'd pick a game young bull like you.'

Naoise's heart began to race. This was dangerous talk

and not what he expected. He had to stop it and leave.

'What about Cathbad's prophecy?' he said.

'What about it? Are you rejecting me?'

'I am,' he said quickly.

She leaned across and took his ears with her hands.

'You shall be shamed and mocked if you don't take me away.'

'Leave me alone,' he shouted, trying to twist free.

'You will do it. That is a *geis*.'

'Levercham,' she called as Naoise prised Deirdre's hands from his ears.

The old woman had been waiting in the darkness outside and pushed the screen aside and rushed in.

'You are my witness,' said Deirdre. 'I have laid a *geis* on him to take me away with him.'

Naoise rubbed his ears and exclaimed, 'Why did I come?'

'You knew exactly what would happen,' said Deirdre, 'only you wouldn't dare let this knowledge into your thoughts.'

'I must leave,' Naoise said.

Levercham led him out of the compound. He returned to Emain Macha and found his brothers, Ainnle and Ardan. He explained what had happened.

'Two things are certain,' said Ainnle bluntly. 'We will do what she demands. And evil will come of this. But we won't have you shamed because you failed to fulfil the task she imposed.'

Ardan agreed.

The three brothers gathered warriors, women and slaves and three nights later they fled from Ulster, taking Deirdre with them.

They hurried south to a king in north Connacht. He took them in until word came that Conor and a large body of warriors were approaching. Naoise and his party had to go. They went further south and took protection from another king until Conor and his warriors tracked them down again and they had to leave and go elsewhere. For a year or so, Naoise and his party lived a peripatetic life until eventually, exhausted by endless flight, they sailed across to Scotland.

It was spring. They settled in a remote and uninhabited glen. They lived off wild game and fish all through the summer and autumn. With the onset of winter, though, there was nothing to hunt. They began to steal the cattle of the local people, who were quick to complain about the Irish rustlers to their king. He came with warriors to destroy them. Naoise offered the services of himself and his party as hired mercenaries. The local king accepted.

Naoise and his host moved to the king's compound. They built houses outside the ramparts, solid wooden structures with small doors and no windows. They built their houses in a circle with the doors facing inwards and in the middle of the ring they put Naoise's house. They constructed their settlement like this because they remembered Cathbad's prophecy and they were anxious no one should see Deirdre lest it led to killing.

Their caution was admirable but it had the effect of arousing the intense curiosity of the king's steward. What were they hiding in the middle there, he wondered? Early one morning, as he was passing the camp, glancing between two houses that were part of the outer ring he glimpsed Naoise's house in the middle and he saw the door was open. He rushed across the wet ground, for there was dew on the grass, and slipped into the house without making any noise. Inside he found Deirdre asleep on her bed beside Naoise. She was naked. Her face was turned towards the ceiling with her hair pinned behind her head. She lay very still and took her breath in short shallow draughts. Her body was very white except for a few brown freckles on her flanks and her belly, and her breasts were small. He left and hurried to the king, who was also asleep in his bed. He woke him up.

'I never before saw a woman fit for you,' he said, 'until this morning and this woman is fit to be queen of the whole world. Naoise has her hidden in his house. Have him killed now while he's sleeping, and seize her.'

The Scottish king shook his head.

'She'll never take to me if I do that,' he said. 'She has to choose me. When Naoise and his brothers are away, go and tell her that I love her. Tell her that if she comes to me, I will marry her.'

The steward did this. She declined the offer and when Naoise returned later she told him everything.

The steward came to see Deirdre several more times.

She always declined and she always told Naoise about his visits.

After a month, since persuasion did not work, the king decided to try other ways. He sent Naoise to hunt in woods where his men had laid traps but these never caught him. He sent Naoise to fight impossible adversaries who should have overwhelmed him, yet Naoise always triumphed. Finally, the king realised his steward's initial suggestion was the right one but for fear of alienating his prize he told his steward to visit one last time and tell her what would happen if she did not comply.

When the men were away the steward slipped into Naoise's house.

'This is the king's final word,' said the steward. 'Come now, or Naoise and his brothers will be killed and you will be taken by force.'

Deirdre did not think. She loved Naoise in a hot and intense and slightly desperate way. 'No,' she said, 'we'll take our chances.'

The steward left. Naoise returned later and she whispered in his ear, 'We leave now or you will be dead tomorrow.'

The whole party left immediately and took themselves away to an island from where they could see both Scotland and Ireland.

The news was brought to Conor that because a Scottish king coveted Deirdre, the sons of Usnach had left Scotland with their retinue and moved to an island closer to Ireland where they hoped to live unmolested. Conor was delighted by what he heard though he was extremely careful that no one in the court should know this.

He went to bed early that night, to think. The sons of Usnach must be feeling vulnerable and in addition they were halfway home. Now, surely, was the time to lure them back? Then he could kill them for stealing his bride and making him look like a fool. Of course his warriors could not do this. He needed an instrument to execute his will.

As Conor pondered he remembered the king of Fernmag. He was an old adversary although lately he had indicated he was tired of enmity. Fernmag had a son, Eogan, and Conor sent word that the young man must come to Emain Macha. Once he got the visitor alone Conor explained he was prepared to offer peace on condition Eogan kill the sons of Usnach. As Naoise had killed his brother some years previously, Eogan was delighted to accept these terms.

Now he had the instrument in place, Conor needed to inveigle those on whom he was to wreak revenge to come back. He knew the invitation could not be seen to come from him. It must be from the court. He did not see that this would be a problem.

He organised a feast and invited all his warriors. Wine was served in huge quantities. Once everyone was glad and cheerful and merry, Conor spoke.

'I have a question,' he said, in his lordly booming voice.

'You have only to ask, friend, and you will have your answer,' several guests cried back. They expected the question would concern the king's hospitality. It was well known he liked his guests to have plenty of opportunity to praise his generosity.

'And can I be assured of a straight answer?' said the king.

This wasn't a typical question but this didn't stop several guests shouting, 'Of course you can.'

'Even if you think the answer to my question is going to make me angry, can I be assured of a straight answer?'

The conversation was definitely not going in the direction it usually went but the guests couldn't stop now they'd started.

'Of course, friend,' they shouted. No one had any idea what was looming, though they had no doubt it would be nasty. Only Eogan, though he had no idea how the king was going to do this, had guessed it must concern the sons of Usnach.

'My question is this,' said Conor. 'Is there a household, anywhere in the great world, braver than this?'

An audible sigh whistled from the lips of several warriors. This was not a hard question. There could only be one answer.

'No,' one guest shouted.

'Or, if there is, we have never seen it,' shouted another. There was a mild round of applause. This form of words answered the question as the king would have wished yet left the way open for the opposite truth – that there was a braver household – to be argued, if the king wished to argue it.

'Well, that's good to know,' said the wily Conor, 'but nothing is perfect. What, or maybe I should say who, do we lack that would make our assemblies even braver and greater?'

'You tell us,' shouted one of the revellers.

'No, you tell me,' ordered the king, gazing at the man.

The reveller shook his head. 'I have no idea,' he said quietly.

'The three sons of Usnach, obviously,' said Conor.

This was not how the king usually spoke of the trio. The room went quiet.

'They should not be separated from us on account of a woman, would you agree?'

There was an uneasy silence.

'Well, if you don't speak, how will I know your answer? Is it yes you think, or no? Should they be separated from us on account of Deirdre or should they not? Your silence does not tell me. It's not very eloquent.'

Men stared at the floor, or at the walls, anywhere but at Conor.

'You,' he said.

He pointed at Eogan.

'Me?' said Eogan, who was not expecting to be singled out.

'Do you agree they are remarkable men?'

It seemed to Eogan there was only one answer to give.

'I do.'

'Have you always?'

'Yes.'

'So why have you never spoken?' he continued, pointing at a different warrior. The new target decided he might as well continue in the direction Eogan had started.

'Had we dared we would,' he said. 'They are lions.'

'Well,' said Conor, 'let us send assurances, let us have them back. They will bring honour to our court. We will have to send a messenger to them and he can bring them home.'

'Yes, but who?' several shouted back.

'Well,' said Conor, carefully, 'Naoise will only come if Cuchulainn or Conall or Fergus bring him home.'

Everyone nodded.

'I will decide who of these three will have the honour of performing the task,' said Conor. He clapped his hands and the guests resumed drinking and talking.

The king slipped into an anteroom and had Conall called.

'Tell me, what would happen if you had Usnach's sons and on the way here you were attacked and they were killed?'

'And I'd guaranteed their safety?'

'Yes.'

'I would kill every man sitting out there in the hall.'

'I perceive, Conall,' said the king coldly, 'I am not dear to you. You will go home to your compound. I will call you back when I want you.'

Next he had Cuchulainn summoned. He put the same question to him.

'I will not bring them back here to be killed for anything,' said Cuchulainn bluntly.

'I see you have little love for me. Go away home to your own compound and stay there until I call you.'

Finally, Conor had Fergus brought to him.

'Supposing,' said the king, 'Usnach's sons, while on the way home, were killed, what would you do?'

'And I was their escort?'

'Indeed,' said the king.

Fergus's instinct was to say, 'I would punish the attackers.' Even if the aggressors were acting on Conor's instructions, if Fergus had promised to bring the brothers and Deirdre back safely and they were murdered, he must slay those who harmed them. That was the right way: otherwise, how could he call himself a warrior?

Obviously, if he said this he knew he wouldn't be asked to fetch the exiles home. Some other warrior would have the problem then of responding if Conor behaved treacherously. This would save Fergus much trouble and ordinarily he would always avoid conflict if given the choice. Unfortunately, in this case, he couldn't choose the easier path because it was his longstanding belief that the exiles must be brought back to Ulster. Moreover, he was also certain he was the man most likely to get them home alive.

To get them, therefore, was a task he wanted to be asked to perform, but for that to happen, he would have to frame his reply very carefully. He could not lie and say he would do nothing. Conor would see through that: he just wouldn't believe him. Nor could he speak his mind and promise retaliation: the king would not use him if he did. He had to give an answer that would strike the king as just what he, Fergus, would be bound to say; at the same time it must not annoy Conor but, on the contrary, so please and reassure him, he would entrust Fergus with the task. But what form of words could achieve all that? Fergus stilled his mind and suddenly, like the splash heard at the well bottom when the bucket falls in, he had them.

'If that were to happen,' he replied smoothly, 'if they were attacked on the way back, I could promise not to attack you but I would kill the warriors who were responsible.'

'I like your answer,' said Conor. 'You will go. Now, tell me, what route will you take?'

As Conor expected, Fergus mentioned the road that ran east to the coast and passed the compound of a man called Borrach, and who was at that moment a guest in the hall.

'I want to be sure I'll have them back sooner rather than later,' said the wily king, 'so they must on no account stop when they reach Ireland, either to eat or drink. They must press forward until they are here. Do you understand? Those are my instructions.'

They left the anteroom and returned to the main hall. Fergus told everyone that he had undertaken the safe-conduct of Naoise and his brothers back to Emain Macha. He added that, in order to appear less hostile when he got to the exiles' island, he would be bringing only his son, Fiacha, with him. He said goodbye and left.

Once he was gone, Conor returned to the anteroom and sent a servant to fetch Borrach.

'Friend,' he said, after Borrach was led in. Borrach was puzzled and slightly anxious. What surprise might the king spring on him?

'Have you a feast prepared for me?' asked Conor abruptly.

'Oh,' gushed Borrach, greatly relieved, 'I am always ready and delighted to entertain you at any time.'

'That wasn't the question,' said Conor, coldly.

'Wasn't it?'

'Have you a feast prepared for me?'

How could he? He was at Emain Macha, was he not?

'No feast for your king? How very extraordinary and how stupid of me to have imagined you might.'

The king assumed an expression that combined disapproval and regret in equal measure.

Borrach, momentarily confused, recovered now as he grasped the direction in which he was being led.

'Of course,' he said, 'I would be honoured to feast you as soon as you wish.'

The king smiled.

'Soon is good. It is exactly what I had in mind. Now it isn't for myself, sadly, I'm thinking, but Fergus, who will be passing your compound shortly, on my business. It would please me enormously if you would give him what you would have given me. By the way, he may want to refuse your invitation. He can be tricky. But don't pay any heed. Just remind him of his *geis*.'

Years earlier, Fergus had undertaken never to refuse any feast that had been prepared in his honour.

'I think you should leave early,' continued Conor, 'so you can be sure to have everything ready for Fergus when he passes.'

'I could go now,' said Borrach eagerly.

'No, you go tomorrow morning,' said Conor firmly.

The last thing Conor wanted was Borrach overtaking Fergus on the road to the coast and letting slip there would be a feast waiting for him when he returned. Fergus would then be sure to come back by a different route and his plan would be ruined.

In the early morning, as she lay beside Naoise, Deirdre dreamt that three birds came from Emain Macha. Each dropped a sip of honey from its beak into the mouths of Naoise and his brothers, then each bird, with a savage peck, split their lips and sipped the blood that welled out. She woke straight after and lay still listening to Naoise's breathing. Should she speak to him of this? Had she known that even at that moment Fergus was on his way she would not have hesitated. But the dream was not a warning of an immediate threat, she decided: it was more to remind her that she must always be vigilant for Conor's malice was as vigorous as ever.

Carlo Gébler

Later that same day Naoise and Deirdre sat on either side of a fidchell board outside their hut on top of a low hill from where they were able to see Ireland and Scotland. Naoise's brothers' houses stood beside theirs. The rest of the retinue were housed around a harbour below hidden behind trees.

Deirdre stared at the board. Her king was threatened. Did she hide behind the queen or run for the open? As she considered the alternatives a cry came from below.

'I know that voice,' said Naoise.

The cry sounded a second and third time.

'It's Fergus.'

Deirdre moved her king towards the open.

'Play on,' she said.

'Play on? Why? We have a visitor.'

She wished she had related her dream for of course it was too late now. It would sound like she made it up. She would have to content herself, she realised, with gloomy words that reflected the way she felt.

'Nothing good for us can come out of Ireland,' she said.

Naoise waved his hands.

'This is not just anyone,' he said. 'This is Fergus. He would never harm us.'

He pulled Deirdre to her feet.

'We'll go down,' he said. 'We'll see.'

They set off down the path that led to the harbour. Naoise moved more smartly than Deirdre. He stopped and told her to hurry. She lifted her skirts and hurried up to him.

'This is Fergus,' he said. 'We have nothing to fear from him.'

They reached the harbour. Fergus and Fiacha were on the quayside with Naoise's brothers. Many of their followers had come out of their houses to see.

'Naoise,' shouted Fergus, when he saw the young man coming. 'It is time to go home,' he said, 'and I am here to guarantee your safety.'

'I do not want to go,' said Deirdre.

'We will,' said Naoise.

Deirdre shook her head. 'Why can't we stay?'

'There is nowhere,' said Fergus, 'equal to home. You have been in exile. It is time to return. I will be with you and you will come to no harm.'

The brothers and Deirdre boarded the boat with Fergus and his son. The retinue would follow. As the boat skimmed the blue water, Deirdre kept her eyes fixed on the island's coast. She cried quietly and had to wipe her eyes with her hair so often the ends got quite wet.

They landed at a small port and found chariots waiting to take them on to Emain Macha. Fergus had arranged this, he explained, because the king had insisted that as soon as they got to Ireland they were to be taken to him as quickly as possible with no stopping along the way permitted.

They boarded and the charioteers found the road and began to move swiftly along it. It was a winter's day. Snow lay in patches on the ground and where there was none the bare grasses were stiff with frost. The sky was clear and blue with small grey puffs of cloud in the distance. As the wheels rumbled and the land flashed past, Deirdre remembered the day she saw the calf strung up in her compound, and the raven drinking the spots of blood on the snow. She had always believed this vision had been deliberately contrived in order to awaken her passion for Naoise. Now she saw it was a vision of the future, the one towards which she was hurtling. Naoise was the calf and she was the raven drinking his blood.

As the chariots approached Borrach's compound, they saw Borrach's chariot blocking the road with Borrach standing up in the back behind his driver.

'What is he doing out on the road?' muttered Fergus. 'Why isn't he in his fort?'

'There's nothing good can come out of Ireland,' said Deirdre gloomily.

Fergus's charioteers had to pull on the reins. His party stopped just short of Borrach.

'Greetings.' Borrach raised his hand. He was a round man with blonde hair and eyes narrowed as if he was perpetually in the sun. He was not armed.

'I have a feast for you, Fergus,' he said.

Fergus's face reddened. 'I have to take Naoise and his brothers to Emain Macha. Don't stop me now.'

Borrach smiled. He had no idea why Conor wanted Fergus feasted but he would do it and he would enjoy the king's gratitude in the years to come.

'Fergus,' said Borrach, 'it is your personal *geis*. If

hospitality is offered, you must accept. Well, it is, so now you must come in.'

'What can I do?' Fergus addressed the question to Naoise but Deirdre answered.

'If you prefer to abandon us,' she said, 'go ahead, stay and eat.'

'I am not forsaking you,' said Fergus. 'I am sending you on with Fiacha, my own son, to guarantee your safety.'

Fergus's chariot, followed by Borrach, peeled off the road and headed for Borrach's fort, while the rest of the party headed off along the road towards Emain Macha.

At the end of the afternoon the chariots came off the plain and on to the meeting ground in front of Emain Macha. Eogan and his retinue were standing on the lawn in front of the gates, which were shut. The chariots moved up to them and stopped.

'We are expected,' Fiacha called out.

'I know,' Eogan shouted back. He banged with the butt of his spear on the gate three times.

Inside the fort a great party of women and children were waiting for this. Once they heard it they began to scramble up the steps that led to the ramparts above. They made a noise like wind blowing through long grass. Fiacha and the others did not understand what they were hearing at first, but once they saw the women and children beginning to spread themselves along the ramparts, they understood what it was they had heard.

From below, Fiacha scrutinised the expressions on the

faces. Were they hostile, he wondered? No, as far as he could see they were mild and equable. It augured well, he thought, for the coming ceremony of welcome.

'Where is Conor?' said Fiacha. 'He surely wants to welcome the exiles home?'

'He surely does,' Eogan shouted, 'and he'll surely come.'

The gates of Emain Macha creaked back slowly to reveal a circle of soldiers, their shields over their heads or in front of their bodies so they looked to Fiacha and the others like a vast upside-down pot with legs. These were Conor's hired mercenaries whom he kept in case his own warriors ever turned against him.

'Go,' said a voice inside the shields. It was Conor's. With small careful steps the upside-down pot moved through the gate and out on to the middle of the lawn, and came to a halt.

'Eogan,' shouted Conor, from behind the shields.

'Yes,' Eogan shouted back.

'Go and greet our friends.'

Eogan and his retinue moved towards the arrivals.

'Greetings, strangers,' he called.

Fiacha, Deirdre and the brothers each responded.

'Eogan,' shouted Conor, from behind the shields, 'disembark our visitors and send the chariots away.'

'Friends,' said Eogan, 'Conor has spoken. Step down.'

Fiacha and the three brothers and Deirdre got down on to the grass. Eogan clapped his hands and the charioteers walked their horses away.

'Eogan,' shouted Conor, from behind the shields.

'Bring Naoise and his brothers to me.'

'Friends, come,' Eogan shouted.

'We're going to do as Conor says,' Fiacha whispered to Deirdre. 'Stay here, and we will go forward and greet the king.'

'Nothing good can come out of Ireland,' Deirdre whispered back.

Fiacha and the three brothers moved forward slowly. They stopped when they were the length of a spear shaft from Eogan's party.

Eogan nodded. 'Have you hostile intentions?'

'No,' said Fiacha. 'Have you?'

'None whatsoever.'

Eogan made a small bow. 'Go forward, please. As Conor sees you approach, his mercenaries will move aside and he will step forward to embrace you.'

The three brothers moved forward in a line. Naoise was slightly ahead of the other two. Fiacha followed behind.

Just after they had passed him, Eogan suddenly dropped his great spear and in one swift movement stabbed the point into Naoise's back. The point pierced the skin over the shoulder and pushed down into the web of muscle and tendon that covered the shoulder blade.

Fiacha jumped forward and caught Naoise's body under the arms and wrenched him sideways, pulling him off the point of Eogan's spear. Naoise was injured and winded but not dead. Fiacha threw him on to the ground and then threw himself over him.

'Get them!' Eogan shouted to his retinue and with a terrible cry of joy mingled with rage, he drove his spear down at the pair sprawled on the ground at his feet.

The iron point of Eogan's spear sliced off the top of Fiacha's lung, smashed two ribs and punched out of Fiacha's chest above his right nipple. A moment later the spear point punctured Naoise's chest, ripped through the valves on the right of his heart, exited between Naoise's shoulder blades and buried itself in the cold ground. Blood gushed and the men, stuck like pigs, roared with agonised shock.

Naoise's brothers reached for their swords. Eogan's men had their swords already out. They sliced and thrust, and Naoise's brothers tumbled to the grass. Here they cried out like Naoise and Fiacha in shocked agony, then they died.

A dreadful ululation of triumph went up from the ramparts while a cry of anguish and despair poured from Deirdre.

She turned and began to run.

Some of Eogan's men thundered after her. They caught her, threw her to the ground, wrenched her arms behind her back and tied her wrists tightly with cord. Then they lifted her roughly to her feet and marched her back to the gate. The mercenaries parted and Conor emerged from their middle.

'I wish to kiss Naoise,' she said to the king in a voice robbed of feeling.

Conor nodded. Fiacha's corpse was pulled away to

reveal Naoise's below. Deirdre knelt on the cold ground. She kissed his lips then dropped her head and, with quick movements of her small red tongue, began to lap the blood collected in the hollow below Naoise's throat apple.

Though it was customary for a wife to drink her husband's blood if he was killed in battle, Conor disapproved: this spoke more deeply of Deirdre's passion for the dead man than any words or wails. Yet he knew he would look churlish to forbid it too. So he let Deirdre continue for a moment or two, then he spoke:

'That's enough. Bring her here.'

Deirdre was dragged back to the king.

'Listen, Deirdre, this grief is pointless. From the moment you and Naoise ran off you knew it could only end like this. You had your time together. That is over. Now you have your time with me. We are going to the house of the Red Branch . . .'

In his compound far away to the south, Cuchulainn, his head turned sideways, was listening. With his prodigious hearing he had heard everything that had happened – from the chariots arriving to the slaying of the four men. He had reported it all to his wife Emer on the other side of the fire, and now he told her what he had just heard Conor saying: Deirdre had had her time with Naoise, now she would have her time with Conor.

'There's a horrible truth in what he says,' said Emer. 'He was always going to seize her back. Tell me what you hear now.'

The beech log crackled between them.

'They're taking her to the house of the Red Branch,' he said, grimly. 'The women and children are filing down from the ramparts. The women are silent but many of the children are gabbling. I can hear a boy. He's saying, 'Eogan speared the warriors like two sleeping salmon and pinned them to the earth."

There was another pause filled by the sound of the wood burning.

'The lawn is empty now,' Cuchulainn continued. 'Everyone has gone except for a few of Eogan's men and the corpses. They're cutting off the heads now. There goes Naoise's. There go his brother's. They've got Fiacha's body now. I hear a slash, one, two, three . . . it won't come away. One of Eogan's men is complaining. "Fiacha's sinews are like the roots of a willow tree," he's saying. I can hear fiercer chopping. There's a shout now. They must have done it. Yes, the head's off. Someone's gathering them up now. They're all going in a bag. They're going to be carried to the house of the Ruddy Branch to be stored with the other trophies.'

Cuchulainn shook his head.

'What will Fergus say? His own son killed by his own king.'

'He will say whatever he says,' said Emer sharply. 'His quarrel with Conor belongs to him alone. It is no one else's property.'

Cuchulainn sighed. When he was a child and had dreamed incessantly of taking up arms, an event such as this was inconceivable. Even if a seer had predicted the day's events he would not have believed they could happen. He would have said it was impossible for a king to encourage old enemies to return and then slaughter them, having promised he would not. But this was exactly what Conor had done and this, in turn, had created a horrible situation for Cuchulainn.

Cuchulainn only knew Naoise and his brothers by repute but Fiacha was the son of Fergus, one of his foster fathers. This made Fiacha his foster brother. According to his code he should hurry to Emain Macha, search out Eogan and his band, and kill them all. But if he did this he would then be at war with Conor, to whom he had promised absolute loyalty for as long as he lived.

His stomach curdled and his face grimaced. Emer, who was watching her husband closely, knew precisely what the trouble was. He was torn between his warrior's code – a warrior always avenged his kin – and fidelity to his king.

'You know, Cuchulainn,' she began, 'a king cannot call himself a king if his orders are not obeyed and his wishes are not fulfilled. Conor had Deirdre put away for him and then Naoise stole her. Unless he got her back, he could not have gone on being king.'

Cuchulainn was motionless.

'Why do you think you were sent here, banished in effect to your compound?' she continued.

He shrugged.

'It was an act of kindness, wasn't it, on Conor's part,

albeit of a strange and peculiar kind? You were sent here in order that you would not see and thereby become entangled and torn. Be grateful for that and keep it that way. This is none of your business. Deirdre was always supposed to be Conor's. Naoise wrested her away. Now Conor has wrested her back again. Your task is to mind your own life, not theirs. Your task is to think about your future.'

She paused.

'What is it that you care most about?'

Cuchulainn said nothing. They both knew what it was and he hardly saw why he should repeat the obvious. At least that was what he told himself. At the same time, in the other part of his mind, the part that coolly appraised what was happening, he knew exactly what he was feeling. And he resented what he sensed she was about to say even while he knew it was right.

'Your future reputation and glory,' she answered at last, 'is what you have always said you care most about. Hold fast to that, and do not get involved in this business because it does not concern you and if you do get involved you will not achieve what you desire.'

Cuchulainn stared at the ground. Her counsel was wise. This was not his quarrel. When Fergus discovered the truth he could do what he wanted and Cuchulainn would not be there at his side. He should think only of himself and his ambition that everything he did while he lived would be remembered and revered long after he was gone.

*

Cuchulainn stayed quietly in his compound but he was careful to keep listening to events as they unfolded at Emain Macha. In this way he heard everything.

He heard Fergus arrive outside Emain Macha and learn from Conor's son, Cormac, that his son, Fiacha, was dead and how he died. He heard Fergus rail against Borrach, who had waylaid him on the road with the offer of a feast which he was unable to refuse. Consequently, Fergus had had to leave Fiacha to escort the exiles to Emain Macha alone.

Then Cuchulainn heard Fergus declare he would take his warriors, with Naoise's, who were still on the road, and he would lead them to Connacht, to the court of Maeve and Aillil, Conor's great enemies. He heard Cormac declare he would come to Connacht, too, and bring his warriors as well for he was as disgusted with his father's duplicitious behaviour as Fergus was.

Later Cuchulainn heard Fergus and Cormac and all the warriors they had gathered together moving away along the road towards Connacht . . .

Cuchulainn also listened to Deirdre. He heard her crying and sighing. This lasted several days. He heard Conor finally come up to her.

'You've got to stop this now,' said the king. 'It can't go on any more.'

'This has to stop?' protested Deirdre. 'What are you thinking?'

'You must turn away from the past and embrace the life you have.'

'But I don't want this,' she shouted. 'I want Naoise and his brothers and the life we had. But I can't have it, can I? You took him away, the one I loved, and his brothers and with them went the life we lived. So don't talk about the future. I have none. That is why I don't redden my fingernails any more. I have no one to welcome with my hands. Nor can I sleep or smile either. There's too much noise in my head and hurt in my heart for either. My life is comfortless, joyless, pointless, I am as good as dead, and you, Conor, are the cause of that.'

'I'll leave you then,' said Conor. 'Maybe you need a few days more.'

He left her alone again and she went on crying. After a few days he went back.

'Come on Deirdre,' he said, 'You must have run out of tears by now.'

'I haven't,' she shouted. 'I have enough to last your lifetime, I promise.'

Then she repeated what she'd said previously. He left, threatening to return, and when he did the conversation repeated itself again . . .

A year passed in this way. Then, one afternoon, Cuchulainn heard Conor say to Deirdre, now sixteen years old, in his angry voice, 'Is there anyone you hate more than me?' Cuchulainn judged the king had finally run out of patience.

'Yes,' replied Deirdre at once, 'I hate Eogan more. He killed Naoise.'

'Well, my dear,' said Conor, 'he can have you for the next year then.'

Later, Cuchulainn picked out the sound of a chariot clipping along. It was the king's chariot and Deirdre, Conor and Eogan were squeezed on to the warrior's seat at the back.

'So, Deirdre,' he heard Conor say, 'how does it feel to be caught here in the back of this chariot between Eogan and myself?'

Deirdre said nothing.

'You know what you remind me of, Deirdre,' Cuchulainn heard Conor mutter, 'when you stare down at the chariot floor like you are doing now? A ewe, my dear, caught between two fine rams.'

Deirdre's moan swelled to a wail. It was a deep and awful cry of anguish. A few moments after, Cuchulainn heard the most awful thump. It was frail human bone in collision with something hard and unforgiving. This was followed by horses whinnying, the creak of a chariot being manoeuvred, and incoherent male talk, bright and furious, from Conor, from Eogan, and from Conor's charioteer, Ibar. Cuchulainn knew something terrible had happened with Deirdre, but he had to wait until a traveller stopped at his compound for water a couple of days later to get the full story.

'Deirdre,' explained the traveller, 'was in the king's chariot, between Conor and Eogan, travelling to Eogan's compound. The road wound along between rocks. Some overhung the road. Deirdre saw one low piece of stone looming ahead. Without any warning and certainly before she could be stopped, didn't she stand up suddenly as they were passing under the rock. She hit the stone with the right side of her head. I was told her skull caved in and her brain gushed out and splattered everywhere. She toppled off the back of the chariot. When Ibar got their chariot back to her, she was dead of course. She was buried among the rocks where she fell.'

'She was,' said Cuchulainn.

'Well, the king was hardly going to put her into the ground beside Naoise, was he?'

'I suppose not,' Cuchulainn agreed.

After the traveller left Cuchulainn brooded. When he left his home aged six and started on his journey to Emain Macha with his hurley stick, his ball, his javelin, and his wooden shield made of twigs plaited together, he had no concept that anything like this could lie ahead. Seeing the world as a child – and as he was a child how else could he see the world? – he could only imagine a life of adventure crowned – if he struggled sufficiently hard – by success that would guarantee fame. Over the years that followed he continued to think like this. It was only now that he saw what he should have seen but had not. Besides triumph, life also brought disappointment and dismay. It was only now he was just twenty-two that he grasped the bitter truth: a man may enjoy rewards but he must also suffer pain because of the actions of others over which he has no control.

All his life he had honoured Conor both as his king and as his foster father and he had never had any reason to withdraw that respect – until the sequence of events that started a little over a year earlier. First, Naoise and his brothers, under Fergus's protection, were inveigled to return. Then Fergus was waylaid by Borrach (Cuchulainn by now knew this was part of the king's plan), and when the exiles arrived with Fiacha at Emain Macha they were slaughtered by Eogan and his men. Finally, Deirdre, mad with grief, had killed herself.

The whole story made him feel unwell. It was like a bad piece of meat lying in the belly, poisoning the whole body, with the difference that a bad piece of meat he could vomit up, whereas this he could never get rid of. It was there in his thoughts all the time and there was no way to escape its baleful influence.

For a long time after Deirdre's death, he felt heavy and sullen and melancholy. Nothing pleased him or gave him joy. He found it hard to get out of bed in the morning. He took no pleasure in food or drink. He found all talk with Emer stale and uninteresting. He spent his time thinking when he was awake and his thoughts were bitter. How could he have gone through life for so long and not even have had the slightest sense that these sorts of difficulties were lying in wait for him? He had been a fool and an idiot not to foresee them. He hated himself for his stupidity, for his failure to anticipate.

He also hated the events because they were not part of

the dream to which he had clung when younger. Finally, he hated them because not only could he not erase them from his thoughts, he could not act either on the feelings these events provoked. He could not take revenge. That would have precipitated a war.

Now he could only sit and wait and hope that with the passing of time the power of these dark events would wither. And until that happened he realised that for the first time in his short life, he would simply have to accept he was unhappy.

Chapter Ten

Connla's death

As he lay sleeping in his big bed in the house of the Red Branch, Conor dreamt. In his dream he was on the Strand of the Tracks, a long flat beach on the coast. He saw a small bronze boat floating on the cold green sea. There was a small sturdy lad in the back pulling on gold oars. He was heading for the shore.

Conor woke. This was obviously an important dream. There was a concubine beside him. He prodded her bare shoulder.

'Wake up,' he ordered.

The concubine opened one eye.

'Go and fetch Cathbad now,' he ordered.

The concubine got out of the bed and went towards her clothes.

'No time for dressing,' said Conor curtly. 'Just wrap a pelt around you. I want you to bring Cathbad immediately.'

When she returned, Cathbad was with her. Conor immediately related his dream.

'What does it mean?' he asked when he finished.

'It's a prophecy,' said Cathbad. 'A visitor, important though not necessarily friendly, is approaching our shores.

He is coming now. We must go to the strand and await him. If the boy seems dangerous or unfriendly, we drive him away.'

Conor gathered together Sencha the judge, Amergin the poet, Conall the warrior, Cuchulainn and his wife, Emer, who were staying at Emain Macha, Blai the quartermaster, and Condere. The last was a subtle man whom Conor sometimes used instead of Levercham as an intermediary when he negotiated with enemies. Condere excelled at shuttling between adversaries and effecting amity. The party went to the Strand of the Tracks to await the arrival of the mysterious visitor.

At the edge of the beach there were dunes covered with silvery green grass that rippled like water and whispered mysteriously as the wind blew over it. The beach below was flat and white and studded everywhere with small shells of different colours. Where the sea met the land the sand was dark yellow not white because it was wet and thick pieces of seaweed lay everywhere. The edge of the sea was foamy and white. The waters beyond were grey and further away they were deep blue and green. In the distance a band of bright silver lay on the sea where it met the sky and from this silver band there emerged a small yellow spot. As it drew closer and grew bigger, the spot turned into a boat made of bronze. There was a small boy in the back. He pulled on gold oars exactly as he had in Conor's dream. As the boy heaved on the oars, the boat skidded over the sea towards the shore as smoothly and quickly as a stone skimming on ice.

'Our visitor may be a child,' muttered Conor, 'but he handles his boat like a man.'

'Only a prodigy can spring from a prodigy,' said Emer slyly.

'Meaning?' asked Conor.

'He must be the offspring of someone who was himself as gifted when a child.'

Did she mean he was Cuchulainn's son, the king wondered? He had heard rumours of a child in Scotland called Connla, fathered by Cuchulainn with a woman called Aoife some years earlier. And the boy was rowing from the direction of Scotland. On the other hand, if it were Cuchulainn's son, Cathbad would surely have mentioned it. Conor concluded it was better to concentrate on what he saw and not to waste time with ridiculous speculations.

The cloud that had been covering the sun overhead moved away. The light flooded down. Everyone felt the heat on the backs of their heads. At the same moment they all saw the boy pull in his oars and then stand up in his boat. The boy looked up. A flock of seagulls swirled and clamoured above the boat. The lad produced his sling and circled it lazily over his head. He released one end and a moment afterwards a gull tumbled down into the lad's outstretched hand.

'That was some feat,' muttered Conor.

The boy breathed on to the stunned bird and revived it. Then he threw the bird into the air and it flew away back to its flock.

'As was that,' continued Conor.

The boy repeated the trick a couple more times, while the current carried him closer and closer to the shore. Then he put away his sling, cupped his hands over his mouth, and directed a loud sharp cry at one of the birds over his boat. The bird fell from the sky, as surely as if it had been hit with a shot from the sling. The lad caught the bird, revived it, and sent it back into the sky again, just as he had the others.

'Well now,' said Conor ominously, 'I pity wherever he is headed for. And I fear wherever he has come from. If he, just a mere boy, can do what he can do, then the men from his home place – they will surely destroy us. They will grind us into dust and throw us to the wind, just as he threw the gulls back into the air. One of you must go and meet him. On no account is he to land. Get his name. Find out what he wants. Come back and tell me. We will decide then what course to take.'

'Who do you suggest?' asked Cuchulainn.

Since his wife's remark that the visitor was the offspring of someone remarkable, he had been wondering. Nearly eight years ago, hadn't he fathered a child with Aoife while he was in Scotland? And had he not said that when Connla was seven the boy was to come and find him in Ireland? Well, this strange gifted child looked as if he was about seven years older, so the figures tallied.

On the other hand, as he considered the boat and the boy inside, it seemed to him impossible that he should be waiting on the very beach that his own child was rowing towards.

Nonetheless, in a tiny part of himself he did not want to go down to the shore and intercept the visitor. He did not want to get involved in what might turn to violence. He was therefore relieved when Conor said, 'Condere, you go and find out who he is and what he wants.'

'Why Condere?' asked Conall abruptly. To his mind Condere was just a messenger: he did not have the capacity to frighten the visitor away and that, Conall believed, was what the situation demanded. He felt either himself or Cuchulainn should go.

'Because I have asked him,' said Conor in the tone he used when he wanted to end all discussion.

'Right, I'll go and meet him.' Condere was careful to hide his delight at being asked.

He trotted down the side of the dune to the bottom, and began to lollop across the white sand. Little popping sounds accompanied his journey: these were the empty shells on which he trod as they exploded under his feet. He reached the edge of the surf. The bronze boat bobbed in the shallows, its prow just about to touch the land.

'You can stop right where you are and stay in your boat, young lad,' he said. Condere was renowned for his big bright cheerful voice, an obvious asset for a messenger, and he expected the boy would respond as warmly as he had spoken, as people always did to him. To his surprise, however, the boy smirked in a way Condere did not care for (implicit in the scowl was the sense that Condere was a fool), and then shook his head.

'Take yourself away,' said the boy. 'I give my name to no one and I give way to no one. I'm landing.'

'You can't,' said Condere, 'not unless you give your name.'

'I am going where I want and you no more than anyone else will stop me.'

The prow of the boat touched the sand. The boy jumped out. With a rope he began to pull the boat further up the shore.

'Listen to me,' said Condere. 'Over there,' he pointed at the party on the dunes, 'are the great men of this kingdom and they are gathered around the most important, the king, Conor. They saw what you did with your sling and then your voice. They would have been impressed by any man of any age doing what you did. But as you are a child, their awe was even greater. Answer the question. Give me your name. Let me bring it back to them. You will be welcome once they know who you are. But refuse to give your name, and they will be angry. You will enjoy the opposite of welcome and it will bring you no pleasure.'

'I go where I want,' insisted the boy. 'No one stands in my way. Even if you had the strength of a hundred men, you would not turn me back, any more than your friends up on the dunes could.

'Now, bring this message back to them. I will fight each of them singly, or, if they do not wish to take me on alone, they can fight me together. I do not see anyone who either impresses or frightens me, and I do not believe any of them are my equal in cunning or skill.'

'Very well,' Condere agreed.

He returned to the dune and repeated what the lad had said.

'He thinks he can make fun of us,' said Conall darkly. 'He needs to be taught a lesson.'

'Go ahead,' ordered Conor.

Conall, with his spear, his sword and his shield, clambered down from the dune and began to cross the strand towards the bronze boat that now lay beached. With every step he took shells flattened under his sandals with their thick leather soles and heavy bronze buckles that jingled as he moved.

When he got close enough to be heard, Conall shouted, 'Those were pretty words you had carried back to the king.'

'I am so glad you thought so,' replied the boy.

He circled his sling slowly over his head. Conall raised his shield to protect himself from the shot he expected to come flying towards him. Once it bounced off, he would run forward and hurl his spear at the boy before he got a chance to re-load.

'You leave me no option but to teach you a lesson,' Conall called nastily from behind the iron shield with which he covered his face and body.

'Actually,' the boy shouted back, 'I think you are the one who'll learn something.' He released his shot not at Conall but at the cloud in the sky directly overhead. The shot travelled up and disappeared into the cloud. A moment after, a roar of thunder came back from the sky. It knocked Conall face down on to the sand and winded him badly. Before he could recover, the boy dashed over, undid his shield straps, and tied Conall's arms behind his back.

When Conall recovered his senses, his lips were smeared with sand and his arms were fettered. He heard laughter. He heard the boy whisper, 'You see, I was right. I am more cunning and more skilled than you will ever be.'

A great red smear of shame spread up Conall's neck and across his face. A child had knocked him to the ground and trussed him like an animal. He lifted his head and shouted to the others watching on the dune.

'Send someone else,' he shouted.

'Cuchulainn,' said Conor tersely. 'You know what to do.'

Cuchulainn went down the side of the dune and across the sand. Emer ran after her husband, her skirts flying behind. When she caught up with him, she threw her arms around him from behind.

'Stop,' she begged.

'Get off me,' said Cuchulainn gently. He tried to peel her arms away but she held on tightly.

'You must not go down there.'

'I have been told by Conor to go and I am going.'

'The boy must be a twig from your tree,' Emer told him.

'Why do you say that?' asked Cuchulainn coolly.

'Only a son bred out of you could do what we have seen him do. When that boy gives his name, I know what it will be. He is Aoife's son. His name is Connla.'

The last time she spoke this name they were in a chariot. They were in the warrior's seat, skirting the meeting ground, heading for Emain Macha. It was not long after Cuchulainn had stolen Emer from her father's compound. 'We will speak no more about it,' Emer said at the time and the name had not been mentioned until now.

'I do not care who he is,' said Cuchulainn coldly. 'He rebuffed Condere, he humiliated Conall. I will put manners on him now.'

'And you would kill him even if he is your own son?' Emer asked.

'Yes.'

'For what reason?'

'He has shamed us all. I must kill him for the honour of Ulster.'

'But he is a twig from your tree,' she shouted, 'you surely see that, so why do you want to snap it off? Don't. Restrain yourself. Let him live. If you must go down, go like a father. Fall on the boy and hold him in your arms but don't go down and kill him.'

'I don't want to hear any more of this.'

He prised her fingers away from his shoulders and then he pushed her away.

'Neither my wife nor anyone else will hold me back from the future. I am destined for greatness and if I have to find it on the beach below with that child, so be it. You and no one else will stop me.'

'If you are wise, you will listen to my counsel. If you kill your own son, no amount of fame or glory will make up for it.'

'You're wasting your breath. Nothing you can say will deter me. Nothing . . . '

Emer turned aside as there was no more she could say and Cuchulainn went down to the edge of the shore. He found the child standing by his boat and Conall wriggling on the sand with his arms still tied.

'You've been having fun, haven't you?' Cuchulainn said.

'Two of you have been down here and I haven't given my name to either. Is that fun? I suppose it is,' said the boy.

'Perhaps I should have come first. Perhaps I was the one you were supposed to meet.'

'How would I know?'

'Name yourself, or I'll kill you.'

'I don't think so.' The boy drew his sword. The two fought, the blades crashing into each other and making a din. Suddenly, the boy sliced at Cuchulainn's head and before the hero could duck he had cut off the hair from the top of his head with a stroke of great precision.

'Enough sword fighting,' said Cuchulainn. 'Let's wrestle.'

There were two standing stones close to the edge of the sea. The boy climbed up so his head was level with Cuchulainn's. Then he took hold of the older man's shoulder, yanked him forward and down, and jammed him between the stones. After he had done this three times, they went down to the sea to drown each other. The boy swept away Cuchulainn's feet from under him, pushed him under the waves and held him down for a long time. Cuchulainn struggled free and the boy repeated the manoeuvre.

As Cuchulainn struggled to get out from under the water the second time, the rage flooded through him and his body began to distort. With the strength that came with the rage, he was able to slip from the boy's grasp and stand up. His body went on distorting. This process, once it started, could not be stopped at will and it continued until the hero-light sprung up from his crown and rose high into the air above. In this state he would fight without remorse. With his foot he launched the Gae Bolga at the boy. The short stemmed javelin darted forward just under the surface, and tore into the boy's belly just above his right hip.

'That's a trick Scathach never taught me,' shouted the child. He tore at the stem but the weapon would not come away. The fearsome point had opened out on itself inside his bowel and was held fast.

'You have killed me,' he shouted out, falling back into the water reddened now with his blood.

Cuchulainn took the boy in his arms and lifted him up. He saw the boy's hand then and the ring he wore. It was the ring he had taken off the smallest finger of his left hand and given Aoife.

'I gave that ring to Aoife for you,' Cuchulainn murmured.

'So you are my father.'

With the javelin still sticking out of his body, Cuchulainn carried the boy back to the dune where the king and his retinue were waiting.

'This is my son,' he said bleakly and laid him down on the whispering grass.

'That isn't true, is it?' said Conor.

'It is,' said the child. His voice was weak. The adults had to kneel to hear. 'I am Connla. If only I could have had even five years with you. By my efforts your kingdom would have reached to the far end of the world, Conor. But it is not to be. This is the end.'

He died a few moments later. Cuchulainn cut a hole around the Gae Bolga's neck, then tugged. As the end came out the barbs of the Bellows Spear ripped through the young child's flesh. The procedure left a large hole. Connla's tubes tumbled out and spilled across the sandy ground. Cuchulainn scooped them up tenderly, felt they were still warm, dusted off as much sand as he was able, and packed them back into the body.

Connla's body was buried in the dunes and a stone set on the mound to mark the spot. Then the party returned to Emain Macha, and Conor issued an order. For the next three days of mourning no calf was to be allowed near a cow to feed. The edict was then promulgated throughout Ulster and accepted without demur.

When the three days were over, Cuchulainn returned to his compound with Emer. After Deirdre's suicide he had felt horribly cast down but the despair that overwhelmed him now was far worse. He alone had been the agent of his own son's death. Unhappiness and despair at what he had lost were mixed up with remorse and self-reproach.

For the next few months, Cuchulainn was like Deirdre after Naoise's murder. He slept badly. He barely ate or drank. If Emer spoke to him, he would tell her to leave him alone. Her conversation, all conversation, wearied and bored him. All he wanted was to sit by the fire, stare at the flickering flames and brood. He often found himself bitterly wishing he had listened to Emer's warning and once or twice, when his mood was at its blackest, wondering whether he wanted to be a warrior any more and follow the code that caused him to kill his own son.

Cuchulainn's despair lasted two seasons, half a year. Then, one day, the most unexpected thought came into his head. If his early life, he thought, had been all about learning skills, then his later life had been all about learning to withstand the darkest and most powerful emotions known.

After Deirdre's death, the pain had been terrible but he had recovered, hadn't he, and, he had also found when that happened that he was stronger than he had been at the start of the ordeal. In which case, he reasoned now, would not the same be even more true where Connla was concerned?

The emotions that followed the willful killing of one's own child where surely the worst that a man might know. There was no pain comparable to what he was suffering.

but he would survive them wouldn't he, just as he had survived his previous trial? He felt sure he would. And when the moment came, and he knew he was through the worst, he also knew he would see that Connla's death, just like Deirdre's, was not meaningless but had a purpose, this being to temper his mettle, to make him stronger and harder.

Once he recovered, and suddenly he was in no doubt this would happen from the very fact he was thinking like he was, he would find he was ready, or as ready as he would ever be, for the great ordeal that would test him completely, and in the course of which he would do what would make him everlastingly great in eyes of everybody who was to come after him.

Cuchulainn held on to this thought and this was the start of the process by which he came out of the darkness and emerged back into the light.

Part Two:

The Happy Death

Chapter Eleven

Grunt and Boar's-Bristle, the pig-men

Grunt was the pig-man of Bodb, king of the Sidhe in Munster. Although he was only a man his master, King Bodb, had taught Grunt the pagan arts.

Boar's-Bristle was the pig-man of Ochall, the king of the Sidhe in Connacht. Although he was only a man his master, King Ochall, had also taught Boar's-Bristle the pagan arts.

As like attracts like, so Grunt and Boar's-Bristle were the closest of friends. They would often drive their pigs into one another's territories and let the animals graze together while they talked about or showed off their magic. The men of Munster and Connacht didn't like this. The pig-men should be antagonists, not friends. Hoping to provoke a rift, the envious spread the rumour that the pig-man from the province that wasn't theirs had the greater magical powers.

A great oak fell in Munster, scattering acorns. Boar's-Bristle went south with his herd and his friend, Grunt, made him welcome. While the animals gorged themselves the two pig-men sat on a branch of the fallen tree and talked.

'Our people are trying to cause a rift between us,' said Grunt. 'In Connacht your people say my power is greater, while the my people here say yours is.'

'It is certainly no less,' insisted Boar's-Bristle.

'That's something we can test,' replied Grunt. 'I'll cast a spell over your pigs. Whatever they eat down here in Munster they won't grow fat, while mine will.'

And that was what happened. Boar's-Bristle's pigs lost weight. He had to leave for home. When he reached Connacht the envious saw an opportunity and exploited it.

'It was a bad day you took your herd south,' they exclaimed nastily.

'Grunt put a spell on your herd. We can see it with our own eyes; they're wasting away. But don't expect any pity. Didn't we always warn you? His powers are superior to yours. If you'd listened to us, your animals wouldn't be dying today.'

'I'll invite Grunt up,' replied Boar's-Bristle grumpily, 'and I'll play the same trick on him. You wait and see.'

Grunt brought his pigs north to Connacht the next year, and Boar's-Bristle cast a spell on his animals. Though they gorged on hazelnuts Grunt's animals withered away while Boar's-Bristle's pigs grew fat and heavy. Grunt had to take his herd south and his thin animals attracted the same comments as Boar's-Bristle's had the year before.

They also attracted the attention of King Bodb. He was

appalled at the state of his pigs. He dismissed Grunt. Then he sent a messenger to King Ochall in Connacht. His message went: 'Your pig-man has cursed my pigs and they are dying on their feet.' King Ochall, anxious to prevent a feud between himself and King Bodb, took action. He dismissed Boar's-Bristle and told the messenger to carry this news back to his master in the south.

So both pig-men had lost their position and each regarded the other as the cause of his misfortune. They came together as men and quarrelled. They turned into falcons and fought in the air. They turned into sharks and fought in the sea. They turned into stags and fought in the glens. They turned into fire-breathing dragons and fought in the mountains. But their powers were so finely balanced that neither could defeat the other.

After years of fighting they were both exhausted. They agreed on a truce. They would each become maggots and live in a wet place for a while, grow into flies and gather their strength.

Grunt fell into a river in Cooley in the south of Ulster, far from his home in Munster, and was swallowed by a cow belonging to a local king called Daire. From the stomach Grunt burrowed into the cow's womb, and there he grew into a bull calf.

Boar's-Bristle fell into a spring in Connacht and was swallowed by a cow belonging to Queen Maeve. From the beast's stomach he burrowed through to its womb where he too grew into a bull calf.

After the cows had gone their term, they gave birth, on the same day.

The bull born in Cooley was dark brown, the colour of wet bog, from which derived his name, the Brown Bull. In time he grew into such an immense beast, thirty boys could romp on his back as he grazed and never fall off.

The bull born in Connacht had a red body, as if dyed with blood, and white feet and horns, from which derived his name, the White-Horned Bull. In time he grew into such an immense beast that thirty men could shelter under his belly in a storm and always stay dry.

The Brown Bull was Daire's bull and ran with his herd, while the White-Horned Bull was Maeve's and ran with hers near the royal compound at Rathcroghan. In the beginning, when he knew nothing of his owner, the White-Horned Bull was content and so he might have remained except that one day, seeing Maeve and her steward counting the animals, the White-Horned Bull realised his master was in fact a woman. Not liking this, he waited until Maeve had finished counting and had gone, then he quietly lumbered away from Maeve's to her husband, Aillil's pasturage. Thereafter, the White-Horned bull ran with the king's cows and classed himself as the king's and not the queen's beast.

Chapter Twelve

Maeve and Aillil's pillow talk

Maeve was one of six daughters of a high king who outdid her sisters in every respect. She was the most graceful, and the most war-like. When she was a young woman, her father gave her the province of Connacht and the compound at Rathcroghan to rule from and fifteen hundred soldiers to rule with.

With Maeve then young and single, many men came to Rathcroghan and asked to marry her. She rejected them one after the other. When she was asked to explain her reasons this was what she always said:

'They're either mean or jealous or timid and I will only take a man who is notable because those qualities are absent from his character.'

When pressed to explain what she meant, this was what she always said:

'I can't marry a mean man because I am quick to give and if my husband is not, there will be trouble. I need a man who is my equal when it comes to giving.

'I can't marry a jealous man because I know that whenever I am with anyone, whoever they are, there will always be another waiting in the shadows to replace him.

I need a man who will not mind that.

'Finally, I can't marry a timid man because I thrive, myself, on trouble. I need a man who will be as spirited and lively as I am.

'In the husband I take I only ask – though no woman in Ireland has asked for this before – that he is not mean, never jealous, and never fearful.'

In the end, she found the kind of man she wanted in Aillil, from Leinster, whose brothers were both kings, and whom she claimed wasn't greedy or possessive or sluggish.

When he was asked later why he took Maeve, Aillil always gave one of two replies:

'This was the only province in Ireland run by a woman and for that reason I felt I had to come and take the kingship.'

Or:

'Who better to be my queen than the daughter of a high king?'

One night after many years of not unhappy married life, in their room in Rathcroghan, Maeve and Aillil lay side by side on the royal bed, their heads resting on pillows. They were silent for a while and then Maeve asked, 'What are you thinking?'

'I was thinking . . . it is true what they say.'

'Which is what?'

'It is well for the wife of a wealthy man.'

'What put that thought into your head?' she asked.

'I was thinking how much better off you are now than when you met me.'

'I was perfectly wealthy before I knew you,' said Maeve quietly.

'Well, if you were, I didn't hear or know it.'

'Then you weren't very observant.'

'All I knew of your wealth then was what your enemies were stealing.'

'I am surprised by your claim that you don't remember it,' said Maeve a little sharply. 'When you were promised in marriage, I gave you the width of your face in red gold and the weight of your left arm in light gold, a chariot and twelve fine sets of clothes. How else do you think I could afford such gifts except I had great personal wealth?'

'Whatever you say, you're still better off now,' said Aillil quietly.

'I agree, but my fortune is still greater than yours.'

'I don't agree. Mine is far greater.'

They argued the point in the darkness but could not agree. The following day they decided to compare what they had.

The stewards fetched their ordinary household possessions, their buckets and iron pots, their jugs and tubs, their wash-pails and their vessels with handles. Maeve and Aillil were found to possess an equal number.

The stewards collected up their jewellery next: their finger-rings and thumb-rings, their earrings and brooches, their bracelets and neckpieces. These were compared and weighed and found to be of equal value.

The stewards fetched all their clothes and the other pieces of fabric they owned next. They collected their purple and blue clothes, their black and green clothes, their yellow and grey clothes, and their checked and striped clothes. These were compared and counted and it was agreed they owned clothes of equal value.

Then the stewards went out into the country and rounded up the horses. As far as the mares and colts and fillies went, they were equal. Even Maeve's fine stallion had its match among Aillil's stock.

The stewards gathered the pigs next, from the woods and gullies. The sows and piglets were similar in every respect. Even Maeve's most marvellous boar had an equal among Aillil's herd.

The stewards went out on to the grasslands then and gathered all the cattle. The beasts were counted and it was found they were identical except in one respect. In Aillil's herd there was the great White-Horned Bull but in Maeve's herd there was no equivalent animal. When this was discovered, Maeve grew gloomy.

'I might as well have nothing, if I haven't got a bull as great as that White-Horned one,' she said.

Maeve retired to her chamber and summoned Mac Roth, her principal messenger. He was a gentle if cunning fellow and an expert diplomat.

'Is there a match of that White-Horned Bull anywhere in Ireland?' she asked.

'There is. In Cooley, up in Ulster. He's known as the Brown Bull. He's the property of Daire, a local king.'

'Go to him,' she commanded. 'Ask if he will lend me this Brown Bull for a year. At the end of the year he can have fifty heifers and of course he can have his bull back too. If he seems reluctant to agree, then increase the offer. Tell him he should come here bringing his animal. I will give him a portion of land equivalent to his own, and a chariot, and I will throw in my own generous thighs as well.'

Mac Roth took eight messengers and went to Daire's compound. The king was puzzled that they had come to him but nonetheless he welcomed them into his hall.

'What business do great Queen Maeve's messengers have with a little minnow like myself?' King Daire sat on a chair on a big plump cushion and his visitors sat on couches arranged in a circle around him.

Mac Roth described the spat between Maeve and Aillil.

'The Queen asks,' he continued, 'for the loan of your magnificent Brown Bull, so she can match the White-Horned one.'

Explaining to Daire that he was under no obligation – he could accept or reject the offer as he wished – he outlined Maeve's terms.

When Mac Roth finished Daire wriggled with joy. The cushion burst under him, and feathers flew around the hall.

'The men of Ulster won't like it, but I'll do as I please.'

He would take the Brown Bull to Connacht and enjoy Maeve's largesse.

The visitors from Connacht were taken to a large hut where the floor was covered with fresh rushes and straw. They were given food and drink and, as the night wore on, they grew drunk and noisy.

In one corner, two of the messengers got talking.

'There's no doubt,' said one, 'the man of this house is a good man.'

'No doubt,' said the second.

'Is there a better man in Ulster?' asked the first.

'The king, Conor,' said the second. 'He is so great that if everyone in the province gave him everything they owned, there would be no shame in it.'

Then, because he was drunk and not thinking clearly, the second messenger followed a new line of thought. 'The man of this house was good to lend his Brown Bull. If we'd wanted to carry it away from Ulster, we'd have had to get the rest of Ireland to help.'

A third messenger butted in.

'What are you gabbing about?'

The other two repeated themselves. Conor was better than Daire. The chieftain nonetheless was very good to agree to lend his treasured Brown Bull. Had force been necessary, it would have taken all of the rest of Ireland to seize the creature from the pugnacious Daire.

Daire's steward meanwhile, had entered the hut with plates of food and drink, and was just in time to hear the third messenger, who was very drunk, shouting at his companions:

'What do you mean, it would have taken all of Ireland to seize the Brown Bull? I'd as soon see the mouth that said that spout blood. If this Daire'd said no, we'd just have taken it just like that.' He snapped his fingers to emphasise the point.

The steward was appalled. He set down the food and drink and hurried back to Daire.

'Are you giving away the Brown Bull?' he asked him.

'No, I'm lending him.'

'Why?'

'They made a very generous offer.'

'That was fortunate for you then,' said the steward sharply.

'What do you mean?' The steward's dark expression and terse speech troubled Daire.

'I'm only after hearing one of Maeve's messengers saying that if you hadn't given your famous Brown Bull freely, they'd have just snatched him.'

'By the gods I worship,' announced Daire, who was suddenly as angry as he had been excited, 'nothing leaves here unless I choose to let it go.'

The next morning Mac Roth was brought before Daire in his hall. The burst cushion had been replaced and the feathers cleared away.

'Last night your men were heard chattering,' said Daire coldly. 'And only for the fact that it isn't our custom to murder guests, I should have come and cut your heads off. Apparently, if I hadn't agreed, you'd have just taken the Brown Bull anyhow. So much for the choice I was offered.'

'When men are full of drink,' said Mac Roth politely, 'they might say anything. It isn't worth bothering about.'

'You won't win me round whatever you say. I've changed my mind. I won't lend the Brown Bull and I won't go with you.'

Mac Roth and his party returned to Rathcroghan. Mac Roth went before Maeve. His report omitted the boasting talk.

'Well,' said Maeve darkly when he finished, 'it's his own lookout. He knows that if he doesn't give freely his famous Bull will just be taken. And so it will be.'

Maeve and Aillil sent messengers fanning across Ireland with requests for help. In return men flooded back to Rathcroghan. Maeve also gathered in her own troops as well as summoning Fergus and Cormac and the troops they had brought to Connacht from Ulster years earlier when they went into exile.

After several weeks a great army was assembled. They lived in tents, pitched on the lawn outside the royal compound. Maeve decided that Fergus should be appointed chief scout and commander. Following his appointment he was summoned to discuss the campaign with the royal couple.

'Once we cross the border we trip Macha's curse,' said Fergus, 'and all Ulster's warriors will suffer the awful pangs women suffer in childbirth. However, they only last until the end of the season in which they started. This is autumn:

if we go in now, on the first day of winter, which is only a few days away, the warriors of Ulster will recover. The better course is to cross the border the day winter starts. That will mean we then get ninety days when most of the enemy will be in bed. There'll still be the Boy Spears of course, but they'll be no match, not for a great army this size. That will leave just Cuchulainn, but he's one and we are so many. He won't stop us. We will seize the Brown Bull and get away.'

The royal couple saw the wisdom of this counsel. They would wait until winter had just started before ordering their attack.

Chapter Thirteen

Cuchulainn and the great army

The cloud above the great army's camp outside Rathcroghan was grey but in the far distance, because light from the low sun was playing on it, the cloud was white. It was the morning of the first day of winter and Maeve was in her chariot in the warrior's seat, and her charioteer was in the driver's seat in front. All around her, soldiers and warriors were striking their camp.

'This great army is here for me,' said Maeve. These words were addressed to her charioteer. He was a grey-haired older man, with round shoulders and a small mouth that hung permanently open. 'Today they are cheerful but it will not last. Their mood will change and then they will turn against me.'

Maeve's charioteer didn't care for this sort of talk. He thought it was bad for morale. In his opinion the queen should be oblivious to the opinions of subordinates. She should think only of winning.

'I'm going to turn the chariot rightwards,' he said. 'I will draw down the power from the rising sun and guarantee our safe return.'

The charioteer began to drive the chariot in a series of graceful neat circles. Maeve stared ahead and as the chariot wheeled around she caught sight of many different scenes but all featuring men from the great army. Some were felling tents, others were folding them away, and still others were stowing them in the carts that would carry them. Then, though Maeve did not see how she got there, a young girl was suddenly sitting sideways on the rump of one of the horses and this girl was looking right back at her. The girl wore a cloak with a hood. The hood was thrown back and her hair was elaborately plaited.

'Who are you?' asked Maeve.

'A poet.'

'From where?'

'Connacht.'

'Have you ever seen this girl before?' she asked her charioteer.

'No.' He was as surprised as the queen was by the appearance of the visitor.

'Can you see the future?' Maeve asked.

'I can,' said the girl.

'Then tell me what will become of my great army.'

The girl closed her eyes and began to hum. 'I see it red, I see it crimson.'

'That can't be right,' said Maeve. 'Once we cross the border, the warriors of Ulster will all be forced to bed by the birth pangs. They won't be able to fight.'

'I see it crimson, I see it red,' repeated the girl.

'You're wrong. I have this great army, while my enemies will have nothing.'

'I see it crimson, I see it red,' said the girl again.

'You're wrong,' replied Maeve, even more emphatically than previously.

The girl vanished. The great army moved north. The border came in view. It was marked by a line of poles with rotting bodies skewered on them. The corpses were displayed in all sorts of positions. Some appeared to be sitting on their stakes. Some were speared through the belly, thus allowing the hands and feet to dangle down. Some were pierced through the back and were arched like a bow. The oldest corpses that had lost all their flesh had slipped down the stakes that once supported them and formed little bone piles on the ground at bases of the poles.

Maeve, who was at the front of the great army, gave the order to halt.

'It's all been easy up until now,' said Maeve to her driver. 'Go to that pole.'

She indicated the one she meant. The body on the pole had been speared upside down, with the prong going in through the neck and the legs sticking into the air.

'Cut it down,' she ordered him.

The driver took the axe from under his seat and got down. He cut the base of the pole and it crashed with the body to the ground.

A murmur rippled through the ranks of the great army. They were all watching and wondering what this meant.

'When that pole crashed,' said Maeve, 'every Ulster warrior was felled by the awful contractions of birth. We have a whole winter ahead and apart from a small corps of Boy Spears and a solitary warrior, Cuchulainn, there will be no opposition.'

Maeve was first across the border and the great army followed . . .

In the hall in Emain Macha, Conor was on the rush-strewn floor, stricken with great hot contractions that ran from the bottom of his pelvis to the middle of his chest.

At this moment two men were carrying wood for the fire into the hall. They dropped the wood, picked the king off the floor and carried him to his couch.

'Get Cathbad,' said the king to his helpers.

The druid was fetched.

'Are these the birth pangs Macha cursed us with?'

'The same. Every warrior in Emain Macha has gone down with them. Now tell me what you want me to do.'

'Under no circumstances are the Boy Spears to go into the field,' said the king.

There were great beads of sweat rolling from his hairline. These went down his great domed forehead and caught in his eyebrows, or trickled down to the tip of his nose and then, from there, dripped down to his chin.

'Lose them, and we've no one to defend us here. Post the Boy Spears on the ramparts. Close the gates. Cuchulainn may have heard something and he may already know, but send a messenger anyhow to him, just in case.'

Cathbad dispatched a messenger and mustered the Boy

Spears. As he was in the process of posting them along the ramparts a chariot raced up. There was a driver in the front seat but no warrior in the back. Before the driver could steer through the gate, which was still open, he found his way blocked by a boy warrior with a spear.

'Cathbad,' the boy warrior shouted and the druid appeared.

'I've flown from the south,' said the charioteer. 'Maeve and a great army have crossed the border.'

'How large?' asked Cathbad.

'I don't know. Large is all I can say.'

'Headed where?'

'East, for Cooley,' said the charioteer.

'Let him in,' said Cathbad.

The driver trundled through.

'Now close the gates.'

In his compound, far to the south, Cuchulainn sat alone at his fire. He heard this conversation and the closing of the gates as clearly as if he had been standing in Emain Macha itself. He got up and left the hut. Outside he met Emer. He told her what he'd heard and to expect a messenger from Cathbad with the news.

'When Cathbad's man comes, thank him for his message and send him on his way.'

'Of course,' said Emer.

'I'm going to the armoury. I'd better make certain my weapons are sharp and ready.'

Later that day a chariot roared up to Cuchulainn's

compound and stopped in front of the closed gates. The passenger got down from the warrior's seat and rapped on the wood with the shaft of his spear. Emer went to answer. There was a little hole in the wood. She looked through the hole and saw a man with a large nose and two eyes set close together. She could not make out their colour.

'Have you come from Conor?'

'No, I've come from Fergus,' said the man with the close-set eyes.

From Fergus? thought Emer. But how could that be? Fergus had crossed to the enemy years before. He'd be with them now, wouldn't he?

'Maeve comes with a great army,' said the messenger, 'and Fergus and his troops are among them.'

So she was right: Fergus was with the invaders.

'They have come for the great Brown Bull. Once they have him, they'll go.'

Emer thought quickly. This was a strange message to come from the other side, even if he had once been her husband's friend and fosterer.

'Does Maeve know you're here?'

The messenger smirked.

'No one from the great army knows I'm here. They think I'm scouting for the Brown Bull which, now I've done what Fergus asked, I'm about to do.'

The man with close-set eyes climbed into the warrior's seat. The charioteer shook the reins and Fergus's messenger careered away.

Emer went and found Cuchulainn in the armoury. She told him everything.

'That was good of Fergus,' he said.

'It was.'

'But it won't change anything. I can't skulk in my compound while they go about their business. I'll be called a coward if I do. My reputation would be ruined, forever. I'll have to go out and meet them.'

'You, one man, against a great army – it won't work.'

'You needn't worry, I shan't take them on directly. I'll harry them from a distance and melt away whenever they get close. I'll be deft and nimble. I'll make little cuts in their force each day. Each wound won't amount to much on its own but, taken all together, they'll hurt.'

Conor's messenger turned up. He delivered his message and then Cuchulainn replied.

'Tell Cathbad I will harass the enemy until winter ends and the curse lifts. Then Conor and the others can get up from their beds and come after them.'

The messenger left. Cuchulainn summoned Laeg. His body was still a little plump, his expression was still pleasant and trusting, but his hair was grey at the sides now. He had aged.

'Harness the chariot,' Cuchulainn said.

Laeg harnessed Cuchulainn's two horses, the two that were born on the night of his first birth, the Grey of Macha and the Black Sainglain. Cuchulainn climbed up and sat on the warrior's seat and Laeg drove off.

Cuchulainn instructed his driver to go south and west, the direction from where the enemy was coming. They travelled all the rest of that day and through the night. By the next morning Cuchulainn could hear the great army in the distance. He pointed at a large hill with a prominent standing stone on the summit that lay in the path of the great army.

'Let's go up there,' he said.

At the top, using a piece of rowan from a solitary tree that grew close by, he made a hoop that fitted snugly on the head of the stone: it fitted as tight as Conor's crown fitted his head. Then, he found a flat piece of wood and carved a message in Ogham on its broad front and left this leaning against the stone. Finally, he ordered Laeg to withdraw.

In the afternoon two chariots appeared. There were charioteers on the driver's seats and two warriors on the back seats. Both were minor kings and both had left a young wife and a new first son at their compounds in the south. One man's son was called Erc, the other's Lugaid and both fathers were anxious to succeed on this campaign, to secure their own position and that of their sons later. To this end both fathers had prevailed on Fergus to let them scour ahead for the Brown Bull. The sooner they engaged with the enemy, they believed, the sooner their reputations would be made.

The scouts' chariots reached the hill's summit and the eager kings noticed where Cuchulainn's horses had torn at the grass and where the ground was flattened by the tramp of feet. They saw the hoop jammed on top of the stone. They saw the tablet with the message. They read the message. They were the first in the great army to make contact with the enemy. They felt gratified. This was the start, they had no doubt, of what would be a great story with them in the middle. They made a fire and sat down to wait. The smoke rose up into the sky like a black finger. Fergus, travelling at the front of the great army, saw the smoke and hurried to join them. He was shown the hoop and the tablet. He read the message and then he too sat down to wait. Later, Maeve appeared.

'Why are you waiting here?' she asked.

'Because of this hoop,' said Fergus. He pointed it out to her. It was a plain circle of white wood without a break. 'It came with this message,' Fergus said. He waved the tablet.

'I'll read it: "This is a *geis*. Come no further unless you have a man who can make a hoop like this with one hand from a single piece of wood. I exclude my friend Fergus." Cuchulainn must have made this.'

Maeve summoned her principle druid and asked his advice.

'If you ignore this challenge,' he said, 'and pass this point, he will kill one of us before morning.'

'But the campaign has hardly started,' said Aillil. 'We don't want anyone killed yet. Why don't we re-trace our steps and go round this place through the forest. That way we can't be accused of breaking the *geis* yet we'll still be making progress.'

All agreed Aillil's counsel was wise.

The great army re-traced its steps and entered the forest. Night came and it began to snow. The flakes were thick and heavy and they fell so hard and fast, flake on flake, that soon the snow was as high as the axles of the chariots. A halt was called but it was impossible to pitch tents or light fires. The warriors wrapped their cloaks around themselves, lay down on the ground and slept as best they were able.

The next day Cuchulainn woke early under his chariot. He was wrapped in pelts. He looked out. The sky was clear and blue: the land was blanketed in white. He washed in the brown water of a cold stream and then had Laeg drive him to the standing stone where he had left the hoop. The hoop was where he'd left it on top of the standing stone but the enemy was nowhere to be seen. He could hear them in the forest, cutting around the side. He hurried there and found their tracks in the dense snow under the bare trees.

'How big is this great army?' Cuchulainn asked Laeg.

Though the snow had been disturbed over a wide area, it was mixed with old leaves and broken twigs. There were no lines of footsteps from which the charioteer might work out the size of the forces precisely.

'I can't tell,' he said, finally. 'There are a lot of them, thousands and thousands I'd say.'

'Take us around Maeve's great army,' Cuchulainn said, 'to the ford on the far side.'

Laeg struck out through the forest. He circled the great army and reached the ford. This was the only place to cross the river that bounded the forest's far edge.

Cuchulainn selected an oak. With a single circular sweep of his sword that lopped both top and bottom, he reduced the tree to a pole with four forks. Then he hurled this with one hand into the ford. The stump went deep into the river's bed, leaving the prongs sticking up above the water, looking as if they had always been there. The ford was now blocked. No chariot could pass though a man on foot might squeeze by.

Cuchulainn put Laeg and his chariot behind a screen of young alders, and sat down to wait on the snowy ground. After a while two chariots appeared with the same two scouts sitting in the warrior seats as had found the hoop the previous day.

'Look,' said Erc's father, pointing at the oak in the ford.

'This is our second important find,' said Lugaid's father.

Both felt certain they had stumbled on another addition to the great story in which now they surely were central. But they would not be remembered as warriors who won fame by their deeds. Their importance would be as the fathers of Erc and Lugaid, and it was only long after they died that it became clear why the sons were so important.

'A tree blocks the way,' said Erc's father.

'So it does,' said Lugaid's.

These were the last words their drivers ever heard. Cuchulainn came from behind. He sliced their heads and the heads of their drivers from their bodies and then stuck these on the four prongs of the tree. The heads were warm and dripping and the blood ran down the prongs. Then he turned the horses and sent the blood-drenched chariots, with their cargo of headless bodies, cantering back through the forest in the direction from which they had just come . . .

The frantic horses burst on Fergus at the front of the army. The horses were caught and the bodies discovered tumbled on the floors of the chariots. As he looked at them, Fergus wondered if perhaps the corps of Boy Spears had been sent to waylay them.

He sent a large troop ahead to see. When these men got to the ford they found the oak with the four heads stuck on it, a tablet with Ogham writing on the bank and the track of a single chariot leading away through the snow that covered the ground. As their path was blocked, the scouts decided to wait. After a while Fergus and the royal couple appeared, with the great army behind, great plumes of cold breath coming out of the mouths of the warriors.

'Are they our men?' Maeve asked. She pointed at the four heads on the red-dyed prongs.

'They are,' said Aillil. His tone was grim. 'I am troubled.'

'Of course we are,' said Maeve loudly, 'we've lost four good men.' She was anxious this should be heard and reported throughout the great army. It was important they knew she was a leader who cared about the loss of men.

'I wasn't thinking about our loss,' said Aillil. 'All armies have losses. What surprises me is that our men were beheaded with so little effort. You saw the bodies back there in the chariots. They didn't even get their swords out of their scabbards before this was done to them.'

'No,' said Fergus, 'the real surprise is in the middle of the ford. There was no hole dug for the tree. It was simply thrown so that the end speared the ground and the part we see was left standing as if it had grown there.'

The tablet was brought to Fergus and he read it in silence.

'Well?' asked Maeve.

'It's another *geis*. It says a single man with one movement lopped the branches leaving four prongs and then felled the tree, then cast it with the same one hand into the ford, into the position where we see it standing now. Unless we have a man who can perform this same feat, we can't pass. Once again, I am excluded.'

Maeve took the tablet with the Ogham writing and threw it into the river. The current carried it off.

'*Geis*. What *geis*? Now get that tree moved.'

It took fourteen chariots to pull the oak free. When the warriors got it on to the bank finally, Fergus pointed to the dripping, muddy base that had been buried in the riverbed.

'See! It was felled with a single cut.'

'Who did this?' Aillil asked. 'Was it Conor?'

'How could he? He has pangs like all the others warriors. No, this was Cuchulainn.'

'He may only be one but he won't be so easy.'

'He won't,' agreed Fergus, 'but I never said he'd be easy.'

'True, but you never said he'd be so hard, either,'

said Maeve.

The great army crossed the ford and pitched camp on the snowy ground on the other side. Then Fergus went to the tent of the royal couple. He told them everything he knew about their adversary. He started with the night of Cuchulainn's first conception. He ended with his own last night in Ulster when he defected to Connacht in disgust at Conor's treatment of the sons of Usnach. He had not seen Cuchulainn since then. It took Fergus most of the night to tell the royal pair everything he knew about their adversary's history. When he finished Maeve was first to speak.

'We're too many for him to risk an attack in the open.'

Fergus and Aillil agreed.

'He'll come at us sideways, won't he? He'll pick off our scouts and our outriders and our stragglers, won't he?'

'And if it's only a few, so what?' said Aillil. 'Men die in the field all the time. They get ill, they have accidents. If Cuchulainn picks off a man here or there, no one will complain, will they? We must keep our aim in sight and push on. We're here for the Brown Bull. Once we have him, we're done.'

'Let's not forget that,' agreed Fergus. 'We're here for the Brown Bull, not Cuchulainn, and once we have him we go.'

Fergus was relieved his counsel was accepted. He had come to war to hurt Conor by taking the prize bull: he had not come to war to hurt Cuchulainn. If the great army secured the Brown Bull quickly and left without hurting Cuchulainn, he would be happy.

*

The following morning the sky was empty and blue once again. There was still snow on the ground. Maeve summoned her messenger Mac Roth.

'Let us be off. Spread the word through the ranks.'

The great army packed up and moved off along a road that wound east towards Cooley. The ground here was boggy and the road twisted as it went forward between one dry place and the next. After several hours the great army found the way blocked by another oak. This one had been felled and laid across the middle of the road. There was a message carved into the trunk of the tree. This is what it said:

'This is a *geis*. No one may pass until a warrior has leapt this tree in his chariot.'

At the ford Maeve had solved the problem of the *geis* by simply throwing the tablet away. She could not do that here. The *geis* would have to be fulfilled. The great army pitched camp and several warriors with their drivers tried to leap the tree in their chariots. All failed and in the process smashed their chariots.

The following morning, with the snow starting to melt, water was to be heard trickling everywhere. Maeve summoned Fraech, a warrior of great subtlety and cunning. Like Cuchulainn, he was supposed to be part Sidhe and part human.

'Go and find this Cuchulainn and kill him,' ordered Maeve. 'Having the same mixed ancestry as him, I have no doubt you'll succeed.'

With nine warriors, Fraech hurried off. He found Cuchulainn in a little stream of cold brown water, splashing his face.

Fraech jumped into the water and waded forward. Cuchulainn heard him coming.

'Don't come any nearer,' he shouted. 'I'll have to kill you if you do and that would be a pity.'

Fraech ignored this remark and waded on, the freezing water lapping his thighs, the stones of the riverbed pressing into his feet though the soles of his sandals.

'Choose your style of combat,' Fraech shouted.

'Grappling.'

The two men wrestled for ages. Finally, Cuchulainn threw Fraech into the brown water. He held him down until he stopped thrashing around, then pulled Fraech up again.

'Now, will you let me spare you?' Cuchulainn asked.

'I won't let it be said you took pity on me. I'd look a fool.'

Cuchulainn pushed him down again and this time he held Fraech in the cold gushing water until he stopped struggling. Then he threw the limp body on to the bank and went away. Fraech's followers retrieved the sodden corpse and set off for the camp. Their return coincided with Fergus managing to leap his chariot across the oak tree that had blocked the great army's path.

'Ah, good and bad, success and failure,' murmured Aillil. 'How is it, they always come together?'

Fraech was buried and it was decided to stay until the next day. The men whose chariots were damaged trying to jump the oak went away to the nearby woods to search for timber for repairs. One was Orlam. He was Maeve and Aillil's son and he went with his charioteer. The pair searched until they found a stand of holly trees.

'Those will make good chariot-shafts,' said Orlam. 'Cut them all down and I'll go and find the willow we need for the chariot sides.'

While Orlam went off to forage by a little stream, his charioteer went to the first tree. As he hacked with his axe he did not hear Cuchulainn's tread until the warrior was right beside him.

'What are you doing?' the stranger asked.

'Cutting this tree down.'

'Why?'

The charioteer assumed the other man must be from the great army. It was filled with enormous men like him.

'For a chariot-shaft,' said the charioteer. 'I've to cut all the others too.'

'Do you want me to help?' the stranger asked.

'I never say no to help,' said the charioteer.

'Well, you chop and I'll trim then,' said Cuchulainn.

The first holly tree crashed to the forest floor. Cuchulainn picked it up and, in one deft movement, dragged it through the space between his big toe and the next. The prickly foliage and the bark were stripped away by the action and a shaft produced that was so smooth a fly could not have kept its footing.

The charioteer had never seen anything like this before.

'This isn't your usual work,' he said.

'No,' Cuchulainn agreed.

'And you are?'

'Cuchulainn.'

'So I'm dead then?' said the man.

'I don't kill drivers or messengers or anyone without a weapon – unless of course they don't answer my questions. Who are you?'

'Orlam's charioteer.'

'And he is?'

'Aillil and Maeve's son.'

'And where is he?'

'Cutting willow over there somewhere.'

'I'll race you for him.'

Cuchulainn reached the willow stand first. Orlam was so busy cutting sally rods he did not hear him approach. He did not even hear Cuchulainn draw his sword. However, he did feel the edge of the blade as it struck the side of his neck and for an instant he knew he was about to die. Then the blade cut the tendons and the windpipe and the muscle, his head flew off and he was dead.

'So now I am next,' said the charioteer when he caught up.

'No, I told you,' said Cuchulainn, 'I have no quarrel with drivers, providing they do as I say.'

He fixed Orlam's head to the charioteer's shoulder with a sally rod so the unfortunate man looked as if he had acquired a second head.

'Take this right into the camp. I'll follow. If you don't do as I've told you, you'll get a shot from my sling.'

Orlam's charioteer retraced his steps to the camp. Reaching the edge where the sentries were posted, he decided it must be safe to take the head off his shoulder. He did this and then he carried Orlam's head to Maeve and Aillil and told them the story of their son's death.

'This isn't like catching birds,' said Maeve. She hoped that by talking so matter-of-factly she could stop the tears that wanted to flow out at the sight of her dead son.

'And Cuchulainn told me,' continued the charioteer, 'that if I didn't carry the head on my shoulder right to the middle of the camp, he'd fire a shot from his sling at me.'

'He did?' said Maeve.

At that moment a stone came out of the sky and smashed into the back of the charioteer's head. It broke his skull and scattered pieces of grey brain all over the queen.

'I must clean myself,' she said and retired to her private quarters. She stayed there for the rest of the day crying.

Over the days that followed several warriors chased out into the empty country to challenge Cuchulainn. He killed them all and cut off their heads. This was the work of the broad bright day. At dusk, through the night and at dawn, Cuchulainn used his sling, to send still more living things to their graves. To forestall these depredations, Fergus ordered that no man could move out of his tent without his shield. Yet still the shots kept on coming and men kept dying.

Fergus ordered thorn bushes to be cut and piled about the camp at night so that the great army's men might not be seen. He also ordered that all fires were to be extinguished after darkness fell. Yet still the shots kept coming and men kept dying. Fergus ordered that screens be made from woven osiers. When these went up the entire great army heaved a sigh of relief. If he could not see them, Cuchulainn would not kill them with shots from his sling. But Cuchulainn could see between the tiny gaps between the screens and he made his most audacious strike so far. He killed a woman whom he mistook for the queen: then, even more audaciously, for he did this in daylight when he did not normally use his sling shot, he killed Maeve's pet raven as it sat on her shoulder.

Immediately after this last outrage, Aillil said to another of his sons, 'Cuchulainn can't be far off.' Maine was plump and lazy and Aillil had hoped that this campaign might be his making. 'Can't you go off and kill him?'

Maine went out in his chariot with his driver to the place from where the shot had come. He found Cuchulainn's firing position. The grass was flat. But there was no sign of Cuchulainn.

He went back to his father.

'He's a very hard man to find,' said Maine.

'A hard man to find is he?' mocked Aillil's jester, who was standing, as usual, just behind his master. He was a small man with a sharp, sour face.

'Yes, he's a very hard man to find,' repeated Maine.

A stone fell from the sky. It hit the jester over his right ear. He fell to the ground with a soft thumping noise, like the sound of snow, having slid from a tree, as it hits the ground.

'I swear by my gods,' said Aillil, as soldiers hurried to make a wall with their shields around him, 'if he carries on like this, Cuchulainn is going to kill us all.'

Chapter Fourteen

The Brown Bull's escape

In Cooley, his home place, the Brown Bull stood on his monstrous legs chewing grass, his heavy tongue and his huge teeth all stained green, his heifers scattered around him. On his back, the boys who followed him around were roistering about.

Out of the air a raven dropped down. The bird settled on the Brown Bull's heavy neck close to his left ear. Its weight was so insignificant to the Brown Bull (it was the equivalent to what a grain of sand would be to a man), the Brown Bull did not notice it. But then the raven began to speak into his ear, and he did notice.

'Dark one,' the bird said, 'a raiding party has come. You are their quarry and they are heading this way.'

The raven lifted into the air, flew away and landed on a tree. Here it changed shape into a small naked woman. Her body was smooth and brown like a young girl's but her face, with its dark brown eyes and pointed chin, was old. Morrigu, the Goddess of War, might assume the shape of any animal she wished and might even keep her body young, but her face was beyond her power.

The Brown Bull was infuriated by what he heard. He

was a blameless creature who lived his whole life quietly with his heifers, harming no one, and now he was to be taken against his will. Rage shuddered along the length of his enormous body and the boys playing on his broad back were tumbled violently off. They shrieked as they fell and then hit the ground with horrible thuds. They were all killed. The Brown Bull threw back his vast head and bellowed furiously, then pawed at the ground with his monstrous hooves, mashing the corpses of a couple of the newly dead boys as he did, so the churned earth went red with their blood. Finally, as there was no other way to relieve the terrible feelings that had seized him, he began plunging his huge horns into the grassland, gouging out great clods and tossing them back over his haunches.

Sitting watching his charge, from a place close by, the Brown Bull's herdsman saw everything. Fergal was a lanky man, abnormally tall by the standards of the day, with long tapering hands and feet. As Fergal knew from past experience, in such circumstances it was pointless to do nothing and hope the rage would run its course. Once the Brown Bull was roused, he would, if he was allowed, rage until he fell down dead with exhaustion. Decisive action was the only way to save the Brown Bull from harming himself. Fergal determined they would move. They would go north, cross the long line of distant brown hills and carry on until they got to the northern sea. In that barren place, far from where they then were, the Brown Bull, distracted by his new and unusual surroundings, would forget his troubles and return to his usual easy-going, ruminative ways.

From her perch where she sat on her heels, the Morrigu saw the herdsman stand and whistle. His dogs ran to him. He gathered his weapons and began to walk towards the Brown Bull, his dogs following. Fergal waved and shouted. The dogs ran behind the heifers and drove them forward. The Brown Bull, still tearing up great lumps of turf with his terrible horns, heard his heifer's hoof-falls as they approached. He lifted his head, bellowed twice, then seeing in what direction they were running, set off the same way himself.

The great army reached the district of Cooley, with its moist pastures. The soldiers pitched their tents and threw up their osier screens around the edge of the camp. That night, despite these efforts, Cuchulainn killed dozens of men with his sling. The next morning half the force were sent off with instructions to take everything they found. At the end of the day the raiders returned. They had many prisoners and numerous cattle but no Brown Bull.

'Where is he?' Maeve demanded.

'We don't know,' replied one of the warriors who had gone on the raid. He was a swarthy man with broad shoulders and a high forehead and noted for the fat warts that thrived along his hairline. 'We certainly saw no trace of him.'

'Then we'll talk to the prisoners,' said Maeve. 'One of them is bound to know.'

Before long a small boy with a square head and stiff shoulders stood in the royal tent.

'I saw the herdsman, Fergal, driving the Brown Bull away,' he said. 'The Bull was roaring and shaking with rage.'

'What direction were they going?' said Maeve.

'North,' said the boy.

'Then that is where we go to find him,' said Maeve.

A council of war was summoned. It was decided to split the great army in two. One half would be quick moving and mobile. They would shoot ahead each day, scouring for the Brown Bull and Cuchulainn. The other half would hold the prisoners and the cattle that had been taken and they would move more slowly. They would join the vanguard at the end of the day. Fergus would command the advance force, with Maeve alongside him, while Aillil would command the rear.

This new arrangement perturbed the king. Why did Maeve want to be with Fergus? He suspected the commander and his wife were intimate. He called his charioteer to his private tent.

'Listen,' said Aillil to his charioteer, 'tomorrow, I want you to go with the advance force, watch Maeve and Fergus and bring me back a sign, if you can, of what you find.'

That night, the prisoners were arranged around the camp's perimeter, to form a shield and so deter Cuchulainn from using his slingshot. It was an ingenious plan but it didn't work. That night, as every night before, warriors were killed with stones to the head: not one prisoner was hurt, however.

All through the next day, Aillil's charioteer in a

borrowed chariot followed the queen and Fergus as the couple searched for the Brown Bull with their troops. Towards evening he found them lying on a bank, hidden behind a screen of gorse. Fergus's sword was hanging from a small rowan tree. The charioteer slipped the sword from the scabbard and melted away.

The charioteer found Aillil in the rear with half of the great army along with the prisoners and the plundered cattle. Aillil was driving his chariot himself. The charioteer jumped aboard and sat in the warrior's seat.

'This is unusual,' he said. 'Me back here and you in the front where I normally am. I can't say it's unpleasant, though.'

'I'm sure it isn't,' said Aillil. 'Now have you anything for me?'

'I suppose I have.'

'There's a remark that doesn't put a man at his ease.'

'No,' the charioteer agreed.

'Well, let's get this over sooner rather than later. Show me what you have.'

'You'll have to stop and turn to face me.'

Aillil hauled on the reins and stopped the chariot. He turned to face his driver.

'Here I am. Show me.'

The charioteer lifted his cloak and revealed the sword he had hidden underneath.

'Where were Maeve and Fergus when you took this?' Aillil asked.

The charioteer had already decided to answer any question the king asked but it still wasn't any easier blurting the words out.

'They were lying on the ground together,' he said, quietly.

The charioteer expected an outburst but instead, to his surprise, the king grinned.

'Well, I suppose it's only to be expected,' said Aillil. 'She wants to keep Fergus happy, doesn't she? Without his help we fail. Now keep this sword in good order. Wrap it up in a piece of linen and store it here under your driver's seat. Now hop in the front; you can take over driving. I'm having my usual place back . . .'

Meanwhile, on the bank, Fergus, having discovered his sword was gone from his scabbard, was muttering aloud.

'Oh, this is terrible.'

'What is?' asked Maeve. She was still naked and stretched out on the ground.

'The wrong I've done Aillil,' said Fergus.

'What wrong?' Maeve didn't like this talk. Fergus was no good to her like this. She needed him to be eager and amorous, not preoccupied and troubled.

'I'll have to go into that wood,' said Fergus. 'Wait here for me and don't be surprised if I'm away for a while.'

In the wood, Fergus used his dagger to fashion a copy of his missing sword from a piece of ash. When it was finished and snug in his scabbard, he retraced his steps to Maeve.

'Let's go back,' said Fergus.

Without either saying another word, they set off for the place where they'd left their chariots . . .

Night found Aillil and Maeve sitting together in the royal tent.

'I fancy a game of fidchell with Fergus,' said the king.

'Play me,' said Maeve.

'I don't want to,' said the king.

'Why not?'

'Because I want to play Fergus.'

'But I'm the more interesting player,' said Maeve.

'You probably are.'

'So why don't you play me?'

'Because.'

'Because what?'

'Because I don't want to.'

Maeve pondered. Had they been alone in the tent she could have diverted her husband. But there were servants present so she couldn't do what she wanted.

'Go and fetch, Fergus,' said Aillil now to one of these. 'Tell him I want to play fidchell.'

Maeve felt her palms go hot, though her face remained cool.

When Fergus came into the tent, Aillil murmured, 'Fine sword.'

'It is,' said Fergus, a little too curtly, for this was the wooden replica and he didn't want anyone looking too closely at it.

'I've always thought I'd like to swap one of mine for yours.

I'm sure I could offer you a weapon as impressive as yours.'

'I wouldn't part with it.'

'You wouldn't?'

'He said he wouldn't, didn't you hear?' said Maeve.

'Oh dear,' said Ailill, 'everyone seems very grumpy tonight. It shan't spoil the play, I hope.'

'No one's grumpy,' protested Maeve.

'Oh. Right,' said Ailill mildly. 'Well, Fergus, shall we play?'

Fergus sat on one side of the board and Ailill on the other. They started to play. Fergus lost three games in a row. Ailill cleared his throat as the pieces were cleared away after the last game.

'I want Fergus to stay in the rear and I will go ahead with you, Maeve.'

'Why?' asked Maeve.

'I must lead from the front. If I don't it won't be long before everyone in this great army will think I'm a coward.'

'Won't they think the same of Fergus, then?' said Maeve slyly.

'Not at all. They'll know we have put him there. Isn't that right, Fergus?'

'I suppose,' said Fergus.

'And what if we suddenly need him?'

'We'll send back word.'

Fergus said good night and left. Ailill and Maeve went to bed and fell asleep with their backs turned to one another.

That night Cuchulainn fired more stones with his sling and killed more of the great army.

In the morning the royal pair and Fergus met again. Maine, the sluggish son, was there as well.

'Let me go out and find him,' Maine begged his parents.

Fergus counselled against this. The king and queen over-ruled him. Maine left with thirty men. The great army divided in two. Maeve and Aillil went ahead with troops to scour the country. Fergus remained with the rump. The mobile forces found Maine and his followers scattered around the bank of a small river. Their heads were cut off. The advance force pitched camp here and the rear army joined them. The bodies were buried. Darkness came on. The moon hung in the sky, lighting up the dark clouds that hung about. Fergus slipped out of the camp and drove off across the plain in his chariot. He found Cuchulainn by a fire. The wood in the fire crackled as it burned.

'Greetings, friend,' Fergus called.

'You have a fine army,' Cuchulainn called back.

'It won't be so fine if this goes on,' said the older man. 'You are one, we are many, yet we are taking casualties every night and day and you haven't had so much as a scratch.'

'Is the great army frightened of me?' asked Cuchulainn.

'Oh yes. When a man wants to make water at night, he'll only go to the latrine pit if he has twenty or thirty with him who'll hold their shields up to keep him safe from you.'

'You can tell them not to worry. I never strike at a man doing that.'

'I will,' said Fergus, 'but they won't believe it. By picking men off one by one, you've made the whole army uncertain. Everyone fears the next shot from your sling will be for him.'

'What do you want?' said Cuchulainn. He guessed his old friend would not have come out to see him otherwise.

'Spare my men,' said Fergus.

'Certainly,' Cuchulainn agreed. 'How will I recognise them though?'

'I'll have every man tie a piece of cloth to his spear.'

'Tell Lothar to tell his men to do the same.' Lothar had been there in Felimid's compound when Deirdre was born and the king announced he would keep her. Lothar was the warrior the king had asked whether, since his first wife was dead, he was not therefore free to marry: Lothar reluctantly had to admit that yes, the king was free to marry. It ws an answer Lothar had always regretted having given for he knew, and he had said this to Cuchulainn many times subsequently, that to flout the prophecy regarding Deirdre would lead to bloodshed. And it had: the sons of Naoise and Deirdre were killed. Blaming himself for the deaths as much as Conor – for hadn't his reply helped set the whole sorry train of events in motion? – Lothar went into exile then with Fergus and Cormac, which was why, years later again, he was now in the great army that had come north. Despite his being one of the invaders Cuchulainn, who had always admired Lothar for his honesty, now found it impossible to hate him and the idea of hurting him was intolerable.

'And the healers too,' Cuchulainn continued. 'I can't be hurting them either. What happens when I'm wounded if there's no healer for me?'

Fergus returned to the camp. He went to the royal tent and called Lothar out.

'Listen,' he whispered, 'get each of your men to tie a strip of cloth to his spear. That way Cuchulainn will know not to fire at them. I saw him just now and he promised.'

Inside the tent Aillil heard the two warriors whispering though he wasn't close enough to make out the sense of what they said. Later, in bed, he said to Maeve, 'Fergus was off somewhere tonight and when he got back he had a long private conversation with Lothar.'

'It might have been innocent,' said Maeve.

'It might,' he agreed, 'but still, I don't like it.'

'I have more ploys than all the men in this army put together,' boasted Maeve.

The royal couple lapsed into silence and both lay awake in the darkness, thinking . . .

Meanwhile, Fergus and Lothar were talking to their men. 'Every man tie a bit of cloth on his spear now,' they each said, 'and every man is to carry his spear at all times from now on.' The healers received the same instructions.

In the night Cuchulainn killed again. In the morning the bodies were tallied. Among the dead there was not one man from Fergus or Lothar's troop, nor a single healer.

After the new dead were buried, Fergus went to the royal tent.

'This is getting bad,' he said. 'He's killing men every night, and in the day as well. Meanwhile, we haven't landed a single blow and we can't find the Brown Bull, either. If this goes on like it is, apart from loss of life for no gain, the winter will end, and the pangs will leave the enemy. Then we'll have to face not only Cuchulainn but also all the Ulster men. They'll grind us to grit and gravel.'

'For all his qualities, Cuchulainn is only one man,' said Maeve, blithely. 'He will tire, he will make a mistake and then we will kill him. I do not doubt it.'

Later that day Cuchulainn came on Aillil's charioteer. He was standing in a river washing the wheels of the king's chariot. Although he was a driver and despite what Cuchulainn had previously said about not harming drivers, he decided to make an exception here. The king and his queen would be disturbed by the death of this charioteer in a way that the other deaths didn't disturb them. He killed the man with a shot from his sling. Then he searched the chariot for booty and was not disappointed when he found Fergus's sword swaddled in linen and stored under the driver's seat. He recognised it, of course, and he took it away with him.

That night more men were killed by stones from the sling and the next day several warriors, who had strayed too far from the main body in their quest to find the Brown Bull, were caught by Cuchulainn and beheaded. This was the pattern for days and then weeks without let-up. Individuals were beheaded in the day and scores of warriors were killed with the shots from the sling at night. Meanwhile, Cuchulainn gave no indication he was tired and Maeve's assertion that he would surely make a mistake because of exhaustion began to look less and less likely.

The invaders reached a country of low rolling hills. The ground was open grassland mostly, interspersed with alder and oak copses and great clumps of sharp gorse and numerous little streams and rivers. That night, as usual, shots from Cuchulainn's sling flew in and men with split heads dropped to the ground. Later, it began to snow and the fierce flakes blinded even Cuchulainn. He retired with Laeg to a ford and the two men spent the night under the chariot wrapped in pelts.

In the morning, Fergus and the royal pair met as usual. The night's deaths were reckoned up.

'But for the snow he'd have gone on until dawn,' said Fergus grimly, 'and this morning we'd be burying twice the number we are. And tonight, if it doesn't snow, he'll be killing at his old rate again.'

'We'll have to negotiate,' said Aillil.

'We will,' Maeve agreed.

Mac Roth the messenger was summoned.

'Go and find Cuchulainn,' ordered Aillil.

'How?'

'Just go north,' said Fergus. 'His chariot will have left tracks in the snow. You follow them.'

'He might have gone south.'

'He knows its north we're headed so of course that's where he is – he's blocking our path.'

'And when you find him,' said Aillil, 'you are to make him this offer. Land in Connacht equivalent to his here, the best chariot in Ireland, twenty-one bondswomen and compensation for any of his property we've destroyed. All I ask in return is an oath of loyalty to me . . .'

'You mean to us,' interrupted Maeve.

'Yes, to us,' said Aillil.

'Who are far worthier,' continued Maeve, 'than Conor, who even now is lying in his bed, moaning like a woman.'

Cuchulainn sat on the ground in the camp he had made above the ford. Through he appeared normal and his mood was calm, the blood in his veins was boiling. The heat his body generated melted the snow closest to him into water which in turn became steam that rose up in dense billows into the air. Laeg had camped a little way off. He had a fire and he sat warming himself: he wore a pelt thrown over his shoulders. The chariot was parked nearby and the two horses were tethered to a small bent ash tree with grey bent branches that were like an outstretched hand.

Mac Roth followed the tracks of Cuchulainn's chariot through the snow. Then he saw the clouds of steam in the distance. He assumed these were clouds of smoke from a fire and hurried on.

Laeg saw the visitor first as he approached and called out, 'A man is coming holding a hazel wand.'

'He must be the herald,' Cuchulainn said.

Mac Roth reached the edge of the ford. He was about to cross.

'You can stop where you are. Say your piece,' Cuchulainn shouted over at him.

Mac Roth delivered the message.

'I couldn't accept those terms,' said Cuchulainn.

This rejection, as speedy as it was absolute, surprised Mac Roth. This enemy was altogether different from anyone Maeve had ever sent him to see before.

'Are there any terms you would accept?' He might as well ask, he thought, rather than return with nothing to report except rejection.

'There are.'

'Well, tell me them then,' said Mac Roth. That would be something at least to bring back to Aillil and Maeve, he thought.

'I won't say them,' said Cuchulainn.

'Why not? How can we negotiate if you don't say what you want?'

'Are we negotiating?'

'Yes,' said Mac Roth.

A bird trilled somewhere and the water burbled. Mac Roth was exasperated by this conversation but he took care not to show this. It was folly to ever say more than was strictly necessarily. Look how this whole mess started. His messengers got drunk and were overheard talking nonsense. Had they kept their mouths shut, the Brown

Bull would be in Connacht now and he wouldn't be standing in the snow talking to a demon who was wasting his queen's great army. Reticence was always the better course. Sadly, as he often reflected, most people forgot this if they ever knew it. Or, as was more likely, they had never known it in the first place.

'I thought we were negotiating,' Mac Roth continued carefully.

'Well, you might be, but I'm not,' said Cuchulainn. 'If you want to know what I want – work it out for yourself.'

'You won't tell me?'

'I said I won't.'

Mac Roth knew better than to argue. He made his way back through the snow to the camp. He found the royal pair and Fergus and explained what had happened.

'Well, Fergus, you knew him, can you guess what he wants?' Maeve asked.

'I'd say it's something like this. We send a man to fight him every day at this ford where he's camped and in return he won't prey on us at night.'

'So what does that give him?' asked Maeve.

'He thinks he'll always win.'

'Every day, against every man we put up against him?'

'He does. He thinks he can win every day and that way he can keep us here in Ulster until the first day of spring. Then the pangs go, and Conor and his warriors recover and destroy us in battle. That's his plan, I'm sure of it.'

'There's still a way to go before winter ends,' said Aillil.

'There is,' agreed Maeve.

'I say we accept,' said Aillil. 'It must be better to lose just a man each day than dozens every night. Meantime, we can send scouts north to look for the Bull. There's nothing in these terms to prevent us doing that, is there?'

'No,' said Fergus slowly.

'So, Fergus,' said Aillil, 'go and talk to him. Tell him we know what he wants and he can have it. We'll send a champion out every morning. Don't you agree, Maeve?'

'I do.'

While Fergus waited for his charioteer to harness his horses, Etarcomol, a foster son of Aillil and Maeve, came up to him.

'I want to come with you,' said Etarcomol. He was a dark, attractive young man, with a fierce stare and a reputation for arrogance.

'I'd rather you didn't,' said Fergus.

'But I'd like to see this famous hero with my own eyes. Perhaps he's not be as great as they say.'

'You're insolent and he's ferocious. I can promise no good will come from that combination.'

'But if I go under your protection, I'll be safe and there won't be any trouble.'

'If you come,' insisted Fergus, 'it's on condition you do what I say and you keep your mouth shut.'

Cuchulainn sat in the middle of a perfectly round piece of dry ground rimmed by snow. His blood was still boiling and the snow closest to his hot body melted, then bubbled and then rose as vapour into the cold winter air. Laeg sat by his chariot at a fire he had made some distance away. A rabbit sizzled on a spit over the flames. The sky was pale and blue with feathery, bedraggled clouds lying here and there across it.

Laeg heard Fergus and Etarcomol's chariots rumbling in the distance. He saw the dark shapes moving across the white landscape.

'Visitors,' he called.

From his place in the snow with the steam still whirling around, Cuchulainn raised a hand to show he had heard.

The chariots reached the ford's edge, slowly splashed across to the other side and finally stopped. In front of Fergus was Cuchulainn, seated on the ground, great steam clouds billowing around him, while to his right Laeg sat at his fire.

'Friend Fergus,' Cuchulainn called.

Fergus waved in reply.

'Had I a nice fat salmon cooking, I'd give it all to you.'

Fergus nodded carefully.

'Except today I haven't such a gift to offer. No, today . . .' He turned. 'What's on your fire, Laeg?'

'Rabbit.'

'Stringy?'

'I'd say.'

Cuchulainn turned back to Fergus.

'A piece of stringy rabbit is all I could offer. And you'd have to accept, because your *geis* is never to turn down hospitality.'

Uncertain where this was leading, Fergus remained perfectly still, his face a blank with nothing showing.

'Which is why,' Cuchulainn continued, 'we're here today, isn't it? Had not Borrach waylaid you on the way home with the exiles and pressed the feast on you, the story might have turned out very differently for Naoise and his brothers and Deirdre.'

'It might,' Fergus agreed. 'But then again it mightn't. Anyway, no hospitality today; talk only: that suits me.'

'And it would be unfriendly to make you eat that rabbit,' said Cuchulainn. 'You'd have to chew it for ages. So, talk away, friend.'

Fergus felt the heat from Cuchulainn pressing on his eyeballs.

'I think I know what you want,' said Fergus. He repeated what he'd said to Aillil and Maeve.

Cuchulainn nodded. 'Very good, Fergus, but then you always had that talent, hadn't you?'

'For what?'

'For peering into the heads of others.'

Fergus smiled. 'Only when I have to,' he said.

'I have something to give you. Old friends deserve generosity, don't they?'

Fergus was unsure what was meant but he nodded anyway.

'Laeg, bring our friend the bundle we've been keeping.'

Laeg rooted under the seat in his chariot and pulled out

a white linen bundle. He carried this across the snow to Fergus's chariot.

'This is yours,' said Laeg.

'What is it?'

Laeg glanced at Fergus's scabbard with the wooden replica that Fergus, since he his sword was taken, had been carrying around. With the exception of the sly Aillil no one had looked at it doubtfully before. With this thought Fergus had a sudden intuition as to what was in the bundle.

'Is that what I think?' he said quietly.

Laeg nodded.

'Pass it carefully,' said Fergus. 'We don't want him seeing.' With a slight jerk of his head Fergus indicated Etarcomol, sitting on the warrior's seat in his chariot not far behind Fergus's.

'We certainly don't,' Laeg agreed. 'Think of the gossip.'

'I'd rather not.'

As he took the parcel, Fergus felt the weight of his sword wrapped up in the cloth.

'I'd be destroyed for ever if anyone found out I lost this.'

'We shan't breathe a word, you can be sure of that,' said Laeg.

Fergus put the sword down on the ground.

'I'll get it out when I am back in my tent.'

'You do that,' said Laeg.

'One question though.' Fergus said this in a low voice as he straightened up. 'How did you find it?'

'That's enough, Laeg,' said Cuchulainn, who was

listening. 'Go back to your fire. Your rabbit needs turning.'

Laeg rolled his eyes, signalling to Fergus he'd have told him only he'd been stopped. Then Laeg turned and began to crunch back through the snow towards his fire.

'I accept your gift,' said Fergus, 'and I'll be off now. I don't want to linger too long, in case any of mine think I'm plotting with you to betray them.'

'You definitely don't want them thinking that,' said Cuchulainn.

'I'll tell the royal couple you agree to the terms.'

'You do that.'

'Back to the camp,' ordered Fergus.

Fergus's charioteer shook the reins and the two horses pulled away. The driver turned the chariot round, splashed back across the ford and up the ramp on the far side. Then he shook the reins and the animals broke into a slow canter.

Etarcomol, however, made no attempt to follow: he stayed as he was, sitting in the warrior's seat in the back of his chariot, his dark fierce eyes locked on Cuchulainn.

'What are you staring at?' Cuchulainn shouted from the steam clouds.

'You.'

'See anything?'

'Nothing much – a young warrior with a talent for tricks.'

'Don't annoy me,' said Cuchulainn.

'I might say the same to you,' Etarcomol shouted back.

Cuchulainn stamped across the snow, headed for the

river, little puffs of steam rising from each footstep as he sank into the snow.

'Follow me down to the water,' said Cuchulainn as he passed Etarcomol. He continued walking towards the ford. He dragged his sword and the tip made a line in the snow as he moved.

Etarcomol got down and followed Cuchulainn on foot to the water's edge.

'It's you who wants this,' said Cuchulainn. 'I don't.'

'I agree, you don't have a choice.'

Etarcomol felt the great heat coming from Cuchulainn's body as he lunged with his stabbing spear. Cuchulainn stepped sideways, and slashed away the snow and the sod from under Etarcomol's feet. The young warrior fell on his face.

'Just go away now,' said Cuchulainn.

'I won't leave like this,' said Etarcomol, getting to his feet. There was snow in his hair and his eyebrows and little bits of frozen fern and twig stuck to his chest and arms. 'I'll have your head or leave you mine.'

'It'll be the second for sure.'

Cuchulainn swung his sword over Etarcomol's head, shaving off all his hair to the scalp but drawing no blood. The hair landed on the snow. For a moment it looked as if a bird had fallen from the sky and was lying there.

'Now clear off.'

'No.' Etarcomol stabbed with his spear, nicking Cuchulainn's cheek. The wound was tiny but the effect was a great surge of rage. Cuchulainn's face distended and the hero-light filled with huge blood clots sprang up from his head. He brought the blade of his sword down on the crown of Etarcomol's head and drove the blade on until he had split the youth right down to his navel. The two halves fell sideways like a half-lopped apple and then the body, still joined at the waist, fell slowly backwards. It hit the snow heavily, sending little puffs of white jumping into the air.

Cuchulainn pitched into the river and lay face down. Only immersion in freezing water would cool his body sufficiently so he could return to his normal state. Etarcomol's driver galloped his chariot across the ford, passing Cuchulainn whose boiling body was making the water around him bubble and sending up great clouds of steam. The driver urged his horses up the ramp on the far side of the ford and then sped off across the snow-covered plain following the direction Fergus had gone in.

Cuchulainn's body cooled. The water stopped bubbling and boiling. The steam stopped too. His mouth slipped back over his teeth, his eyes returned to their normal size, his hero light waned and vanished . . .

Out on the plain Etarcomol's chariot overtook Fergus's. When Fergus saw Etarcomol was missing he shouted across to the driver, 'What happened?'

The driver ignored the question and urged his horses to go faster.

Fergus tapped his own charioteer on the shoulder.

'Something's happened. Go back.'

As Etarcomol's chariot ran on, Fergus's turned about and headed back towards the ford. When they arrived, Fergus saw Cuchulainn sitting in the water, Etarcomol on the far bank, his body split and the snow red around him. Laeg on the bank was chewing a piece of cooked meat.

'What have you done, Cuchulainn? I brought this boy here under my protection and you've killed him.'

Cuchulainn stood up, dripping. He splashed forward, going carefully because the stones of the riverbed made him unsteady, and stepped up on to the bank on Fergus's side.

'I had to,' he said.

'You didn't have to kill him. There was no need.'

'I had to. Etarcomol wasn't leaving until he either had my head or he had left his own. Ask Laeg.'

'It's true,' the charioteer shouted across.

'Now, given he wouldn't leave until he had my head or he left his own, what else could I do? I was hardly going to give him my head, was I?'

'I can see that,' said Fergus slowly.

'I wouldn't have done anything had he not insisted.'

'He was arrogant, I suppose,' said Fergus.

Fergus tied Etarcomol's body to the back of his chariot and drove back to the camp.

'Is that how you'd treat a dog?' said Maeve when she saw her foster son's pulpy, bloody, half-frozen, snow-covered carcass trailing behind.

'A whelp like this I would,' said Fergus grimly.

'Why?'

'For being so stupid as to pick a fight with Cuchulainn. But don't take my word. Talk to Etarcomol's charioteer.'

Maeve spoke to the man.

'He wasn't leaving until he had Cuchulainn's head or left his own,' said the driver.

Etarcomol was buried; his memorial stone was planted on his mound and his name written in Ogham on the stone.

That night Cuchulainn murdered no one with shots from his sling for the new terms applied now.

Chapter Fifteen

Cuchulainn in single combat

Various warriors were in counsel with the royal couple in their tent.

'Who,' asked Maeve, 'can we put up against Cuchulainn?'

A warrior chief was mentioned. He was at home in Connacht though several of his people were in the great army and one of these was in the tent.

'He won't fight,' said this man of his chief. 'He thinks he's done enough by sending his men here.'

'Nadcranntail, then,' said Maeve.

This was thought to be a good idea. He was a cunning and formidable warrior. He also was at home in Connacht, which meant he wouldn't be put off fighting Cuchulainn, like everyone else, by the experience of the previous weeks. But to bring Nadcranntail would take days, and in the meantime what was to be done? Cuchulainn expected a champion the next morning.

'I know what we'll do,' said Maeve, 'let's ask Cuchulainn for a truce until he arrives. Fergus, you go out and propose it.'

So Fergus went off and came back.

'He agrees.'

Maeve decided to take advantage of the lull. She selected a body of troops, a third of the entire force in number. The plan was to go to the northern coast far beyond Emain Macha, to take prisoners, girls for preference (Maeve intended these as concubines for her warriors), and to locate the Brown Bull which was known to be up there somewhere.

'That's not entirely fair,' said Fergus, when he saw the soldiers mustering and learnt what they had been tasked to do.

'Cuchulainn never said we couldn't search for the Brown Bull during the truce,' said Maeve quickly.

'No,' Fergus agreed, 'although . . .'

'I'm not interested in your scruples,' Maeve went on. 'I want the Brown Bull and then I want to leave and I'm not interested in what you think about my methods.'

'Fair enough,' was all Fergus said.

From his place at the ford, Cuchulainn heard chariot wheels turning and feet tramping as Maeve and her force left the camp and began the march north.

They're after the Brown Bull, he thought. Did he chase after them? Or did he stay? It only took him a few moments to decide. Let them get the Brown Bull, he thought. What mattered was that he kept the enemy pinned down, here. Once spring came, the birth pangs would lift. Conor's men would get out of their beds. After ninety days on their backs their muscles would be slack and their reactions would be slow. But with exercise and effort they would soon recover their old form. Then they would hurry south. They would be fresh. The enemy, on the other hand, after an entire winter in the field, would be exhausted. In the battle between the two adversaries, there could only be one outcome. The invaders would be smashed to pieces. The unlucky would fall and lose their heads, while the lucky would scramble over the border and run all the way back to Connacht. As for the Brown Bull, he could then be reclaimed with ease.

While scouring the far north, Maeve and her force found Fergal the herdsman and the Brown Bull at the open end of a lonely glen.

As the soldiers approached, Fergal took off. He ran past the Brown Bull and escaped into the glen. He hoped to escape capture by hiding deep inside it.

'After him,' Maeve shouted.

Her warriors took off. Their movement disturbed the Brown Bull. He turned and ran after Fergal. Before long he was level with Fergal. Now the Brown Bull wanted to pass as he was faster than the herdsman was. But the glen was very narrow and with there being no space at the side the Bull took the only route left open. He went forward: he went over the herdsman.

When Maeve's warriors found Fergal, they found his body mashed into the ground, face down. He was dead. They could see the Bull in the distance at the end of the glen. Because the glen had no way out at the end, the

Brown Bull had turned, to face the men. He was pawing the ground and bellowing.

'Stop,' Maeve ordered. 'Stay where you are.'

The troops obeyed.

'You will wait until he's quiet, even if it takes until the first day of spring. Then you will lead him back to our camp.'

She told her charioteer to turn round.

'Now I know we have him, I can return to our camp. Do not fail me,' she shouted at her forces who would be staying behind.

Her charioteer started Maeve's horses and drove on without stopping until they were back at the camp.

'We have the Bull,' she told Aillil when she found her husband in the royal tent, 'but he was angry when I left him and he may still be angry now. We will have to wait a while until he's brought to us.'

'I hope that'll be before the start of spring,' said Aillil.

'So do I,' said Maeve, 'but if not, so what? We'll only lose a man a day between now and then – what's that – forty, fifty at most? When Conor's army come, they'll be slack after a season in bed, whilst we'll be battle ready after a season in the field. We'll pulverise them.'

'I hope you're right,' said Aillil.

Nadcranntail finally arrived. He chose to come by cart not chariot. The chariot was ostentatious and Nadcranntail, being innately modest, did not like to draw attention to himself. He was a large burly man of great strength with a straggling beard and a manner that was so quiet it was easy to mistake him as timid. The day after his arrival he went out with nine spears made of holly, the points charred and sharpened in a fire.

As he got close to the ford where he was told he would find his quarry, Nadcranntail saw Cuchulainn had left his camp and gone out on to the plain to stalk a cock pheasant and his hen. Nadcranntail came up behind and threw his holly spears. Cuchulainn heard the spears and, without taking his eyes off the birds, he plucked them out of the air before they could touch him. Then he dropped the spears and continued pursuing the birds.

Nadcranntail returned to the camp of the great army.

'That boy's a coward,' he said. 'I loosed nine spears and he fled into the country.'

'That can't be right,' said Fergus.

That evening he went out to see Cuchulainn.

'Look here, having fled from Nadcranntail today, I think you'd better hide yourself.'

'Fled, you're saying?' Cuchulainn's tone was dangerous.

'That's what we're hearing.'

'The fellow wasn't armed, he only had a few light holly sticks. I wasn't going to fight him: you know I don't fight unarmed men. If he wants to fight tell him to come armed to the ford tomorrow morning and he'll find me waiting.'

That night the temperature rose and the snow melted. The next morning the clouds in the sky were dull, the colour of old lead, and the ground was spongy and wet under Nadcranntail's feet when he appeared at the ford. He saw Cuchulainn standing on the far side wrapped in a cloak.

'Let's agree upon our rules,' he shouted. That was Nadcranntail all over. He was a man who detested surprises.

'You're my guest,' Cuchulainn shouted back, 'you say.'

'We'll throw spears then and no dodging.'

'No dodging,' Cuchulainn agreed, 'except upwards.'

Except upwards? Nadcranntail thought. What does he mean? He threw his spear. Cuchulainn leapt up and the spear passed under his feet and landed on the wet ground a long way off.

'Cheat,' Nadcranntail cried. 'You did dodge.'

'Feel free to dodge mine by jumping as high as you can.'

Then he threw his spear high into the air so that it dropped down and hit Nadcranntail's helmet from above. It split the iron, then sliced through the back of his head and knocked him to the ground.

'Misery, oh misery,' Nadcranntail cried. He was flat on the ground but he was not dead yet. He still had his shield and a quiver of heavy darts with barbed ends and heavy bodies. A dart in the eye or face would kill a man and in the body it would cause much damage.

As Cuchulainn splashed through the water towards him, Nadcranntail pulled his shield over his body. When Cuchulainn stepped on to the bank, he flung the first dart. The point pierced Cuchulainn's ear and lodged in the side of his skull just behind his ear.

Nadcranntail grasped a second dart. He intended to hit Cuchulainn in the foot with this one. As he took aim he saw his opponent distend. Cuchulainn's mouth slipped back and revealed massive teeth set in red gums. One eye shrank, the other expanded. The hero-light filled with his blood sprang up from his head. Nadcranntail flung his dart. It caught Cuchulainn's ankle, tore the skin badly but did not lodge. Cuchulainn jumped on to Nadcranntail's shield and lifted his sword.

'You are the best,' Nadcranntail cried.

Cuchulainn brought his sword down. The sword point gouged a line through the wet earth before the blade separated Nadcranntail's head from his body. For a few moments thereafter, as he stood on the shield, Cuchulainn felt the body twitching below. Then Nadcranntail's body was still and the blood stopped gushing out of his neck and pooling on the wet brown ground.

Cuchulainn got down from the shield. It began to rain. The drops that came down from the sky were so cold they stung. Cuchulainn pulled the dart out of his ear and tossed it on to the shield. It made a dull clang. He felt blood trickling down his ear. Laeg would have to clean and dress it. His ankle also. He looked at Nadcranntail's blood and the ripples on the surface of the blood pool made by the raindrops. His mouth slipped back over his teeth. His eyes returned to their normal size. The hero-light collapsed and the blood vanished back into his skull. He heard Laeg, who'd been watching from the far distance, driving his chariot towards him.

'If Maeve's party of rustlers passed right now,' he said to his charioteer when he drew up, 'I'd slay every one of them.'

'Of course you would.'

'We'll take Nadcranntail.' He pointed at the head. 'I'll make a nice pole for it to go on later.'

'Of course you will.'

Laeg wrapped the head in a square of linen and stowed it under the driver's seat.

'Let's go before they come out for the body,' he advised.

He led Cuchulainn to the chariot, got him up on to the warrior's seat and drove him away. Nadcranntail's sons came from the camp then. They wore heavy cloaks that were made heavier by the rain that soaked into them. They took their father's body and carried it back to the camp and buried it. Their father's head, meanwhile, Cuchulainn stuck on a pole at the top of a small mountain.

Cúr was the next champion selected to go to the ford and fight Cuchulainn. When Cúr drew blood, even if it was only a nick that Cúr had made, his opponent must die within seven days for his weapons were poisoned.

'If he kills Cuchulainn, we've won, and that'll be marvellous,' said Maeve to Aillil when they were together in bed. 'But if Cúr's killed that'll be one burden less for our soldiers. No one takes any pleasure when Cúr is around, knowing what the smallest cut from his sword will do.'

Cúr went out the next morning. As he splashed through the shallows, he saw his adversary on the other side, sitting on the ground by Laeg's fire and eating a nut.

'I thought this was a warrior's camp,' Cúr shouted, 'but I'm wrong, it's for boys.'

Cuchulainn flung the half of the nut he had left. It went though Cúr's cheek and shot out the back of his head. Cúr toppled back and landed in the water with a crash.

Fergus was watching events from a distance.

'Let's collect the body,' he said, 'then we can take it back and break the news.'

In the afternoon the sun hung low in the winter sky and the light it gave, which was weak and yellow, seemed to lie across the land rather than falling down on to it.

Fergus was in the royal tent with Aillil and Maeve and the sun shone in through the open door and Fergus had to shade his eyes with his hand.

'Who's going tomorrow?' he asked.

'It won't be so easy to find someone after what happened today,' said Aillil. 'Cúr was thought to be unbeatable.'

'This calls for cunning,' said Maeve. She snapped her fingers at a servant. 'Close that flap.'

A moment later the flap was dropped and the tent's interior went dark.

'Whoever we think might do should be brought here,' said Aillil. 'They should be plied with wine. Get our daughter Finnabair to do the serving and have her sit on the man's right hand, and promise her to him if he brings us Cuchulainn's head.'

'No harm in that,' said Maeve. 'If the warrior is killed,

well, Finnabair won't have lost anything. And if he wins, well, she'll find herself betrothed to the greatest warrior in Ireland, the one who killed Cuchulainn.'

Thereafter a great warrior was called in each night and persuaded to go out the next morning with the promise of Finnabair, and each in turn was killed.

This was the pattern over the following days. At first, Cuchulainn's success made it difficult to find champions willing to go into the field to fight him. But then, those who went out from the camp to watch their champions fight Cuchulainn began to notice a change in their adversary. Though he might win each combat, with each day that succeeded it was harder for him and it took him longer to kill his opponent.

One reason was that Cuchulainn was extremely tired. He had not slept properly for weeks. Another reason was that several of those who had gone against him had hurt him before he killed them. Each wound on its own was slight but added altogether they were not. They amounted to a serious catalogue of injuries. And all these cuts and nicks, gouges and slices did not get a chance to heal. How could they? Yes, at night, to be sure, the wounds would dry and the blood would form a scab. But then come the morning Cuchulainn would be fighting and they would open and start to bleed again. These wounds increasingly hobbled the hero. He wasn't defeated yet but it seemed more and more likely that Maeve's calculation that he would tire in the end and then he would make a mistake would turn out to be true. The sense grew Cuchulainn could be beaten. Suddenly Maeve and Aillil found it easier to find men willing to go and fight him, though no champion being willing to fight without some incentive, no man set out without the promise that Finnabair would be his if he brought Cuchulainn's head back. The hero remained unbeaten but among the men of the great army the certainty was growing with each day that passed that it would not be so very long before he was toppled and then his head would be separated from his body.

Chapter Sixteen

Cuchulainn avenges the Boy Spears

It was afternoon. Cuchulainn sat by his fire. He shin had been cut in the combat that morning and the wound was long and raw. He had pinched the two sides together and was waiting now for his blood to dry and close the wound over.

'There's a man coming,' said Laeg.

'From where?'

'From the north.'

'Not from the camp?'

'No.'

'Who is it?'

'I've never seen him before.'

'Describe him.'

'He carries a spear with five points in one hand and a javelin in the other.'

'That's no man,' said Cuchulainn. 'It's one of the Sidhe and I hope he's come because he's taken pity on me.'

The visitor approached. He was tall, broad, and his hair

was blonde, and cut very short. He had abnormally large hands and feet.

'Who are you?' Cuchulainn asked.

'I'm your father,' said the visitor.

Lugh noticed the blood running out of the wound on his son's shin and spattering on to the ground.

'Nasty,' he said.

'Unless my wounds heal,' said Cuchulainn, 'I'll be done for.'

'You'll come with me then,' said Lugh, 'to the grave mound at Lerga. I'll rub ointments on your wounds to make them better. You'll go to sleep and I'll guard you. Laeg can take us now.'

'What about tomorrow?'

'Tomorrow's combat – there won't be one. I'll carve a message and leave it at the ford. I'll say you've gone away.'

The next morning there was no champion at the ford. When this news was brought back to the camp of the great army there was widespread puzzlement. Where had Cuchulainn gone? Could this be a trick? Was he about to attack?

Then, completely coincidentally, the corps of Boy Spears appeared outside the camp perimeter. Tired of permanent guard duty and knowing intuitively that it was impossible for Cuchulainn to sustain the fight entirely alone, they had slipped away from Emain Macha without consulting Conor or anyone and had come to help him, all one hundred and fifty of them. They didn't find him of course. But they found the camp of the great army and as they approached they beat their shields with the shafts of their spears.

'A lucky few may keep their heads,' they shouted, 'when they get home but the rest will leave their heads behind.'

Aillil and Maeve went to the camp's edge and gazed at the troop.

'Cuchulainn has summoned them and together they're going to attack us,' said Maeve. 'I'd say he's out there with them.'

'A thousand men now,' Aillil ordered. 'Go out and kill them.'

Two lines of men sallied from the camp, flanked by chariots, with drivers and warriors standing as was customary in battle. The Boy Spears formed a ring with every youth standing shoulder to shoulder. The chariots swooped round and cut off their line of retreat. The foot soldiers raced forward like two javelins thrown at an enemy, then swung suddenly with considerable elegance and formed a larger circle around the Boy Spears' circle. The chariots left the rear and came forward and formed another, even wider circle around their own troops. Anyone looking down from above would now have seen three circles, one inside the other.

Then trumpets sounded in the field; the sound of the instruments was loud and bright and decisive. The circle of men from the great army dashed forward, like a noose closing around a neck, and the killing started. A few boys fought their way through the great army's ranks but emerging on the far side they found the chariots waiting. As they ran, seeking a gap in the outer circle, the chariots bore down on them and the warriors speared them to death. In a short while the slaughter was over. The entire corps of Boy Spears was dead. A search was now made about the field but, to the invaders' perplexity, Cuchulainn's body was nowhere to be seen.

This news was brought back to the camp perimeter where Fergus and the royal couple stood waiting.

'No Cuchulainn,' mused Maeve. 'What does this mean? Is he dead, do you think? Has he run away? Or has he some scheme underway to surprise us?'

Out on the battlefield the soldiers of the great army were now stripping the dead of their armour and weapons and piling the corpses ready for burial.

'I don't know,' said Fergus. 'The tablet at the ford simply said that he had gone away. I did not recognise the hand that carved the Ogham script. I'd say someone has joined him and taken him away. That's all I can tell.'

Out on the battlefield a trumpet sounded.

'What's that for?' said Maeve. 'Cuchulainn's body is found?'

'I would doubt that,' said Aillil.

A man was running pell-mell across the turf. He arrived breathless.

'The party from the north and the Brown Bull,' he said. 'They've been spotted in the far distance.'

They arrived a little later, driving the great Brown Bull.

'Let's go forward,' commanded Maeve, 'and make our men and the Brown Bull welcome.'

In the afternoon, Fergus went to the royal tent to take counsel with Maeve and Aillil.

'We don't know where Cuchulainn has gone,' said Fergus, 'but we can be sure he will be back. We were wrong to think he was about to attack us with the Boy Spears – their appearance at the moment he disappeared was simply an accident.

'However, their arrival reminds us there is another enemy besides Cuchulainn – Conor's formidable army. They will get up soon, they will muster and they will come after us and with Cuchulainn in support, they will be formidable, perhaps invincible. We have our Brown Bull at last. The moment has come to strike camp and leave.'

'Agreed,' Maeve said.

Aillil nodded.

The orders were issued. The camp was to be struck. The great army was to start the journey home.

Cuchulainn woke on the slope of the grave mound at Lerga. He sat up and glanced down at his shin. The slit he last saw before he went to sleep was gone. The skin was smooth. There was no scar. He checked his ankle where one dart hole had been and his ear where there had been another. These were the wounds Nadcranntail had made and they were gone too. He ran his hands over the rest of his body. Every nick and cut, every slice and gouge that he remembered from before he went to sleep was gone and in their place the skin was clean, healthy and smooth. He wiped his hand over his face. His whole body, from head to toe, turned crimson. He felt a great inward whirling. It was excitement and certainty; it was joy and energy. He had recovered. He was ready for anything and everything.

'How long have I slept?'

Cuchulainn addressed the question to his father who was sitting nearby on a large stone.

'Three days, three nights.'

'That's a shame.'

'Why?'

'That's three days and nights the enemy were free from harassment.'

'Ah, but they weren't. The Boy Spears came down and fought them.'

'I'd say they didn't win though, judging by your tone – am I right?'

'Yes, they lost.'

'A shame I wasn't with them.'

'It was.'

'What happened exactly?'

Lugh told Cuchulainn.

'Where are Maeve and Aillil's army now?'

'They've the Brown Bull now, so they've started the journey home.'

'Let's harry them. Stay with us and we'll avenge the Boy Spears together.'

'I can't,' said Lugh. 'This is when you earn your fame and no one else can share that with you. You must go against the enemy yourself. They have no power over your life at this time.'

Lugh left. Cuchulainn turned to Laeg.

'Arm our chariot and get ready yourself.'

Laeg broke out the scythes and barbs, the blades and the point that attached to the chariot.

The scythes went on the axle ends.

The blades extended from all the corners and edges and the arm that stuck out at the back.

The barbs slotted on to the posts that supported the chariot's wicker sides.

The huge savage point went on the end of the chariot's shaft, turning the chariot, in effect, into a massive flying javelin.

Laeg threw the protective covers on the horses next. These were made of heavy leather with iron plates stitched on and nails and spits sticking out everywhere.

Every part of the chariot and its horses bristled with weaponry. Every angle and corner, front and back, was a ripping place.

Cuchulainn arranged his weapons in the chariot and fixed them to the various mounts around the sides that were for holding weapons. He chose eight short swords and a long sword, eight small spears and a five-pronged spear, a quiver of darts, eight ordinary shields and his special shield with its razor-sharp edge that could split a hair along its length.

Laeg dressed himself for battle then. He put on a surplice of deerskin. The skin was spotted and striped and slit under the arms so as not to interfere with his movement. Then he put on a coat made of feathers. Then he put on the sign of a driver, a circlet of gold that went around his head. Finally, he added his four-pointed war helmet made of light yellow brass.

Cuchulainn pulled on a light tunic made of waxed deerskin. Then he pulled on his leather body armour. This went around his chest. This was to repel spears and spikes, javelins, lances and arrows. Then he pulled on his aprons, the first silk, and the second black cowhide. Finally, he pulled on a cloak.

Now he began to quiver like a bulrush, in mid-current. His heels, hamstrings and calves swelled up. Next his chest and arms expanded like a bladder when air is blown into it. Finally his neck and head blew up and the sinews under his skin stuck out in great lumps as big as his fists. One eye shrank and receded so far back into his skull no wild heron could have reached it with his beak and dragged it out. The other eye expanded hugely, popped out of the socket and spread over the cheek. His mouth twisted and stretched around his jaw until it met his ears. His heart thumped, making a sound that was a cross between the howl of a dog and the roar of a lion. Every single hair on his head bristled hard and made a ferocious point. Were an apple tree shaken over him, no apple would have got to the ground because the points would have caught every one. His jaw dropped and rose clashing his teeth and producing, in the process, enormous sparks. These cascaded out of his mouth and started little fires all around him. The smoke from the fires rose, black and dense, and swirled around the hero-light that rose, higher than the mast of a great ship, perpendicular from his head. Inside, it was filled with his dusky blood.

Driver and warrior leapt aboard the chariot. Laeg went in the front and Cuchulainn in the back. They put their feet in the foot-bindings and fixed the ties around their waists. Laeg shook the reins. The horses, quickly moving from trot, to canter, to gallop, sped off, heading west, the sparks that poured out of Cuchulainn's mouth tumbling to the ground where they formed a red trail that spread out behind. In due course, the invaders' army, a great long line of men and chariots, with the great Brown Bull like a tower in the middle, surrounded by warriors, came into view.

Cuchulainn let out a terrible cry. The cry rolled across the grass and hit the edge of the great army. Those it hit first staggered as if from a blow. Then blood roared out of their ears, and their eyes popped out of their sockets and hung in the air, bouncing on the nerves that reached back into their brains. Then they fell dead to the ground.

'Circle around them,' Cuchulainn ordered.

As Laeg drove the horses forward, the great army stopped moving and began to form a circle around the Brown Bull who, with his great bulk, rose high into the sky above everyone. But the circle was not finished before

Cuchulainn's chariot reached the enemy's perimeter. Laeg galloped skilfully through the rabble of men scrambling to get into position. As he did, men were speared on the point on the end of the chariot-shaft and the scythe that flashed past mowed down men as well. From his position in the rear, Cuchulainn was able to reach over the wicker sides, stabbing with his spear and slashing with his sword, and felling many more men.

Laeg made a second and a third circuit but by the time that was done there were no stragglers left and the entire army was now in a tight block with the Brown Bull in the middle.

'Over there,' Cuchulainn ordered. He pointed at a river he could see in the distance, unfastened his ties and sat down.

Laeg turned the chariot away, untied himself and sat down too. Through the great army word spread: 'The demon is going. The demon is leaving.'

'We camp here tonight and bury our dead tomorrow,' shouted Fergus. His words were passed through the ranks.

As the chariot moved away across the plain, slowly now, as there was no need to speed, the dusky blood drained away and the hero-light, the rigid mast-like perpendicular towering over Cuchulainn, shrank away to nothing. The teeth stopped grinding and the sparks dried up. The bristling hair went floppy. The heart stopped thumping and with it the cross between the howl of a dog and the roar of a lion vanished. The fat eye shrank and melted back into its socket and tiny eye expanded and rose to the surface and resumed its place. The sinews of the head and neck receded. The chest and arms deflated like a bladder when the air inside rushes out. The heels, ham-strings and calves shrank back to their normal size. The body ceased quivering. Cuchulainn was still. He was himself again. He felt vindicated. He had paid the enemy back for what they had done to the corps of Boy Spears yet he had not sustained so much as a cut.

Laeg reached the river and followed the bank. After a while he came to a place where the bank was sheered away. It was possible to drive down into the river and drive up the ramp on the other side.

'We'll cross to the other side and camp there,' said Cuchulainn. 'And I don't doubt someone will be along from the great army soon enough.'

Laeg turned the horses and drove down the slope into the river. The chariot wheels splashed in the water and the chariot rose dripping on the other side and pulled up on to the bank. Laeg turned the chariot so that he faced in the direction that he'd just come from, then, finally, he pulled on the reins and stopped the horses. In the distance the invaders' fires were flickering in the twilight.

'We'll make our camp near those trees,' said Cuchulainn. He gestured at a small clump that grew close to the bank.

'We'll need a fire tonight.'

Laeg turned the chariot and headed for the place Cuchulainn had indicated. In the distance he noticed another much bigger wood set back some way from the river.

Chapter Seventeen

Fergus faces Cuchulainn

That evening Maeve sent Mac Roth to talk to Cuchulainn.

'A truce tomorrow?' Mac Roth shouted across the river.

'No truce. Send someone here to fight me in the morning.'

'And if we do, what happens to the rest of the great army?'

'I won't be able to harass it, will I? I'll be here, won't I?'

This was the answer Mac Roth expected.

'And can they move?'

'For as long as your champion is away from the great army, yes. But once your champion is back, whether he's breathing still or whether he's sprawled dead in the back of his chariot, then the great army stops until the next combat.'

Mac Roth looked at the white water winding past. He could hear something moving that he couldn't identify. An otter perhaps?

'Those are generous terms, wouldn't you say?' continued Cuchulainn.

'Are they?' said Mac Roth. 'I wonder that after today anyone will want to meet you. But I suppose someone will have to, for otherwise there'll be more carnage.'

'The choice is yours.'

Mac Roth returned to the great army's camp. The Brown Bull was moaning and bellowing at his tethering spot in the middle of the camp. Mac Roth went to the royal tent where Fergus and the principal warriors and the royal couple were waiting. He delivered the news.

'We send a warrior, Cuchulainn won't harass us and for as long as the combat lasts, the great army can move. But if there's no champion at the ford tomorrow morning we can expect another day like today.'

The murmurs started instantly.

'Well, I'm not going,' said one man.

'I won't,' said another.

'Someone else can go,' said a third. 'I have no intention of finishing my race tomorrow.'

'Be quiet,' said Maeve. The tent fell quiet.

'Someone has to go. It's going to be much worse for all of us if they don't. Will anyone go?' she asked.

No one spoke up.

'There's not one of you here prepared to test his skill and, if successful, become the greatest warrior in Ireland and, in the process, win the hand of my daughter, Finnabair?'

There was silence.

'It'll have to be you then, Fergus,' said the queen suddenly.

Fergus knew he couldn't go and he also knew Maeve and the others wouldn't rest until they had persuaded him to go. This thought was promptly followed by an inspiration: he saw how to handle the combat if he went. Now all that remained was to create an impression of initial resistance worn away by the pressure of opinion.

'I can't,' said Fergus.

'Why not?'

'You can't ask me to fight my own foster-son.'

Maeve, as he expected, called for wine. Everyone was served liberally and everyone got drunk. Fergus got drunk too. He had his plan already. He knew he was going. But everyone else had to believe that he got drunk and then was persuaded to go.

'You'll have to face Cuchulainn tomorrow,' began Maeve.

'I can't,' said Fergus, his speech slightly slurred now, his face burning red from the drink.

'Oh, but you must,' said a warrior.

'Yes, you must,' said a second.

'Only you have the skill,' said a third, 'and think of the consequences if you don't.'

'Another day like today – or worse,' said Aillil, decisively. 'He'll wipe the lot of us out at this rate.'

'All right,' Fergus agreed.

There was a cheer. The assembled warriors were delighted. There was shouting and clapping and hurrahing. Fergus stood in the middle of the warriors, smiling. His smile was read as the smile of a man who was content with the decision he had made, who knew what was right and had chosen to do what was right. Actually, the reason for the smile was that he had tricked everyone into thinking they'd persuaded him, when all along he'd known that he'd be going. How fortunate, Fergus thought, slowly, for the wine had addled his mind, that none of those in the tent could read his thoughts. They wouldn't be cheering so loudly if they could.

Very early the next day, a little heavy with drink, Fergus got dressed. He took his sword from his scabbard and replaced it with the wooden copy he had cut. Then he left his tent, carefully holding a hand on the wooden hilt of his sword so no one would see it.

Outside there was bustling everywhere. The ground was hard with frost. In every direction he looked men were striking tents and packing away their gear. For as long as he was gone, the great army could move and it was important to take advantage of the opportunity while it lasted.

'Good luck,' several called.

Fergus acknowledged the voices.

'Be sure and don't forget to come back to us,' said one wag.

'I can't promise you that even if I wanted to,' replied Fergus. His chariot was waiting, his charioteer in the driver's seat holding the reins. Fergus climbed up carefully and sat on the warrior's seat.

'Drive,' he commanded.

The driver shook the reins. The chariot wheels turned. Fergus looked up. There was a small moon in the sky, very white, and a few pale stars glimmered nearby.

'Is this the last time I will look at the moon?' Fergus

asked. 'I would be sorry never to see it again.'

'Don't talk like that,' said the charioteer and Fergus felt certain it would not be long – because his charioteer would faithfully report his remark – before everyone in the army knew what he had said.

The chariot crossed the plain and approached the ford.

'Stop here,' said Fergus, although they were still quite a distance from the bank.

'But then you'll have to walk all that way,' said the driver, who didn't understand that Fergus didn't want him to see what he was up to.

'So I will,' said Fergus. 'I'll enjoy it. This may be the last time I ever get to walk the ground.'

'Don't say that,' said the charioteer, as he hauled on the reins and the chariot stopped.

Fergus jumped down from the chariot at the back.

'If I fall, should I fall, bring me back and have me buried.'

'You mustn't talk like that.'

Fergus crossed the cold ground to the river's edge.

'Cuchulainn,' he called over the fast-moving water, white in places, clear elsewhere, with the black and brown stones of the riverbed showing through and glimmering in the first faint light of day.

'Friend,' Cuchulainn called back. 'Come over.'

Fergus splashed across and climbed the ramp up the other side. Cuchulainn left the fire and came to meet him.

'Have you come for the reason I think?'

Fergus pulled his wooden sword out of his scabbard.

'What do you think?'

'I'm thinking you must have some special power if you're coming against me with that today.'

'None,' said Fergus. 'But if I had an iron weapon it would be as useless as this is now – and for the same simple reason. I wouldn't use it against you.'

'Oh,' said Cuchulainn.

'Yield to me now.'

Cuchulainn considered. It was impossible to fight Fergus if he only had a wooden sword. He decided to counter one request with another.

'All right,' said Cuchulainn, 'we'll fight a bit, and I'll yield providing, when I ask, as I will one day in the future, you yield to me.'

'Agreed,' said Fergus.

The two warriors went into the water and sparred tamely. Then Cuchulainn turned and dashed up the ramp, streaked past his fire where Laeg sat watching, and went on running across the grassland behind, before disappearing finally into the large wood Laeg had already noticed. Fergus followed slowly, waving his wooden sword. When he got as far as Laeg he stopped.

'Not a word of this,' said Fergus, dropping the wooden sword back into the scabbard. 'They'll send Mac Roth out to verify my account as I know they won't believe it from me. You tell them we fought and then he ran.'

'I will,' said Laeg.

Fergus went back to his chariot. Though he was at a

distance, the driver had seen enough to know the outcome of the struggle.

'He didn't seem to put up much of a fight and then he ran,' said the driver. 'Was he wounded? Was he tired?'

'Outclassed,' said Fergus emphatically, 'outclassed.' He climbed aboard and took his seat.

'So why didn't you finish him?' The driver shook the reins.

'He ran off.'

'Why didn't you catch him?'

'Well, I tried, you saw. But he was too lively. I couldn't catch up with him.'

'So he outclassed you there?'

'Yes, I suppose you could say that.'

They re-joined the great army and immediately the order to pitch camp rang out for those were the rules. Fergus went to the royal couple and gave an account of what happened as they waited for their tent to be pitched.

'And you didn't catch him and kill him?' said Maeve incredulously, when he finished.

'He was too fresh for me.'

Mac Roth was sent to Cuchulainn's camp to verify the account.

'I ran,' said Cuchulainn, who was helping Laeg to load the chariot with his things. He had his back to Mac Roth so the messenger wouldn't see he was smirking as he spoke.

'He did,' agreed Laeg, who wasn't smirking and was happy to let the visitor see his face.

'We're going to find a ford nearer to where the great army is now camped,' said Cuchulainn, 'and we'll expect another champion tomorrow.'

Mac Roth returned to the camp and confirmed Fergus's account.

It was afternoon. The royal tent was crowded.

'Someone needs to go to meet Cuchulainn tomorrow,' said Maeve.

Every man there knew this. The warriors fell silent.

'Is any man here prepared to go?'

No one was. Various names were canvassed. All declined. No one wanted to go to meet the rejuvenated, irrepressible and unbeatable Cuchulainn.

'What shall we do, then?' asked Maeve. 'We will have to draw lots, won't we?'

'What about Calitin?'

'Calitin?'

'Yes.'

Calitin, like Cúr, used poisoned weapons. If the tip of his spear or a stone from his sling made even a tiny cut, the victim would die.

'But not just Calitin,' the speaker continued. 'We send him and his sons.'

Calitin had twenty sons who were as brutal as their father and as devious. Their weapons were poisoned as well.

'I see,' said Maeve, warming to this idea, 'but how do we justify sending the whole brood?'

'They're a single unit. They eat together, they sleep together, they fight together and they know one another so well they hardly need to talk when they have something to say. One of them just thinks what he wants to say and all the others just know it. They're all part of a single whole, really. Like the arms and legs, the hands and feet of a single body.'

Calitin and his sons weren't in the tent. This wouldn't have been suggested if they had been, for Calitin and his sons were famously truculent and argumentative. Maeve now sent for the father. He arrived and she made her request.

'I decline,' said Calitin.

'Think of the odds,' said Maeve. 'All of you acting as one against him.'

'I still say no.'

'I'll give you and your sons . . .' Maeve continued, and she listed the land and chariots, the armour and bondswomen they would all receive if they prevailed.

The enticements were so prodigious that in the end Calitin heard himself agreeing. 'All right,' he said.

Fergus, who had been noticeably silent throughout these proceedings, returned to his tent where he found his charioteer.

'Go out and find Cuchulainn. Warn him that Calitin and his sons come tomorrow.'

The next morning, the great army struck camp – while the combat was in progress they would move further west – and Calitin and his sons, accompanied by Fergus, went to the new ford where Cuchulainn was camped. Calitin and his sons lined up on the bank of the river.

'Throw,' Calitin ordered.

Twenty-one arms moved as one and released the javelins they each held at the same instant. The weapons flashed over the water, their shafts reflecting on the surface. Cuchulainn lifted his shield and paddled it about. There was a metallic crash as every javelin point collided with the shield. In the normal run of things the sequence should have been the tumbling of the javelins to the ground. But before this could happen Cuchulainn got his sword out and sliced the blade through the shaft of each javelin during the instant that it hung in the air after it had been stopped. Twenty-one javelins became forty-two pieces and these now clattered to the stony ground on his side of the river.

'Rush him,' Calitin shouted.

He and the sons drew their swords, and jumped into the water. The ford was shallow. There was gravel and sand under their feet.

Cuchulainn jumped sideways, so that he was away from the line running towards him. Calitin and his sons got to the far bank. Cuchulainn, holding his sword upright with two hands, sprinted along the edge of the bank and pruned off the sword hands of Calitin and his sons and the swords they held. Twenty-one hands and the swords they held clattered to the ground.

There was confusion and chaos among the belligerents.

Some staggered, some screamed, some tried to reach with their remaining hands for their swords which were still grasped by their severed hands lying on the bank at their feet. But they did not act in unison. They were no longer a single unit. Cuchulainn stepped among them and began the dispatch. Some resisted gamely but ineffectively – they were fighting with the wrong hand after all – and Cuchulainn killed them easily. Some turned and ran and he chased them and killed them in the river or on the ground on the far side. In a few moments it was all over. Calitin and all his sons were dead.

Fergus saw everything from his seat in his chariot.

'Let's go back,' he said to his charioteer.

Fergus was driven back to the great army. He found them moving west, the great looming form of the Brown Bull in the middle. The great army pitched camp as soon as Fergus caught up. Those were the rules. Fergus went before the royal couple.

'Calitin and his sons are dead.'

'All of them?'

'All of them.'

'Mac Roth,' Maeve called.

Her messenger appeared.

'Go to the ford. Collect Calitin and his sons.'

Mac Roth went and returned with the bodies piled on a cart. The heads were separate. Cuchulainn had cut them off.

A group of soldiers were selected and told to make a

mound into which the corpses were to go. The soldiers set about the job with picks and shovels. Among the party were two brothers. They were servants in the royal palace before they came to war, their duties primarily being to fetch water and fuel, and to change the rushes on the floor.

'Well,' said the younger one. He was a short wiry fellow with a left eye that wandered around. 'Is there any end to Cuchulainn's triumphs?'

'Who knows?' said the other. He was older and much bigger and broader though not as clever or dexterous as his younger brother with his bad eye. For this reason he tended to rely on his younger brother and to defer to his decisions.

'It'll have to be Ferdia now, for there's no one else,' said the younger brother. 'We don't have any one left but him.'

'Oh well, he'll have to go,' said the older.

'But will he?'

'Why wouldn't he?'

'They're friends.'

'They were friends in Scotland,' said the older, 'when they both lived in Scathach's training camp. But that was a long time ago.'

'Must doesn't mean he will.'

'Come again?' said the older, puzzled by this construction.

'Ferdia doesn't want to go, does he? He's in his tent all the time when we're not moving. He knows he's going to be asked, and so he keeps himself out of sight all the time so he won't be.'

'He does,' the older brother agreed, for this was true.

'I can see why,' said the younger. 'When those two go to fight, only one's going to be left alive at the end. What a choice – that means it's either you or your friend will die.'

'That's not a choice I'd care to make,' agreed the older. 'But even so, won't he have to go anyway?'

'He won't be so easy to entice with promises of this and that, even when the royal couple throw Finnabair in.'

'As they will,' said the older.

'As they will.'

'So nothing's certain, you'd say?'

'Nothing,' said the younger. 'The royal pair can shout and cajole or make extravagant promises, but he might still say no.'

The brothers fell silent as they dug now. They were so absorbed in their work they did not notice the man behind. This was a pity for this was Calitin's servant, a man with a big head, bright blue eyes and a rolling gait and he was hurrying away from the camp of the great army. This was strange: why was he going before the burial? If the brothers had seen him they could have stopped him and asked him. He would have replied that he was going to Calitin's wife, Tethba, to break the news that her husband and her sons were dead. The brothers wouldn't have thought this particularly remarkable then but later, much later, they would have seen that the moment this servant set out on this journey, it was inevitable that Cuchulainn would be killed.

Chapter Eighteen

Maeve challenges Ferdia

In the royal tent Maeve sat in counsel with Fergus and Aillil.

'There's only Ferdia,' she said.

'He won't do it,' said Fergus.

'Yes, he will.'

She summoned Mac Roth.

'Fetch Ferdia.'

Mac Roth went away and a short while later the tent flaps parted and Ferdia stepped in.

'Before you say you won't go to fight Cuchulainn tomorrow,' said Maeve quickly, 'listen to why you must.'

Ferdia shrugged. 'I won't fight my friend, whatever you say to me.'

'Finnabair,' said Maeve as if Ferdia hadn't spoken, 'see to our guest.'

Finnabair led Ferdia to a seat and pressed a goblet filled with wine into his hand.

'There's the reason you must go,' said Maeve quietly. 'Look at her – isn't she fair, isn't she wonderful? After you defeat Cuchulainn she'll be waiting here to marry you. Think of that.'

Ferdia smelt the wine. It had a slightly bitter smell and

when he drank a mouthful, it had a bitter taste too, and a little shudder ran through him. He was nervous. He might already have said no but Maeve had ignored that and, he could be certain, she was now going to subject him to enormous pressure. The only course left open in this situation was to remember that any trouble he faced here had to be better than going to the ford the next morning to fight his friend. He had to go on refusing: there was nothing else for it.

'No harm to your daughter,' he said, 'but you've promised her to every man you've had in here before he went to fight Cuchulainn but no man has ever returned from his encounter with Cuchulainn to enjoy her.'

'She wasn't promised to Calitin,' said Maeve quickly.

'All right, not Calitin but to everyone else.'

'Do you know what I'll do if you don't go?' said Maeve.

'No,' said Ferdia. He took another drink of wine and steeled himself for something nasty.

'I'll go to the poets.'

'You will?'

'I will and I'll pay them to write poems about your cowardliness.'

Ferdia considered. 'Well,' he said, coolly, 'no one will believe a few bad poems, not after everything I've done. People will hear the poems and they'll say, "Those are just the bitter words of one man. They're not to be believed."'

'Oh, if it were just one or two poems from one or two poets, I agree,' said Maeve. 'They wouldn't be believed. But

I won't go to one or two, or five or six, or ten or twenty even. I'll pay every satirist in Ireland. There'll be hundreds of poems about your cowardice. The place will be flooded with them.'

She paused to let Ferdia absorb this.

'Just think, every poet in Ireland will have a poem with the same message – that you, Ferdia, are a coward.'

'I still say they won't be believed,' he said, though even he could hear he didn't sound particularly convinced by his own argument. 'I have been a warrior for years. My deeds are well known. Poems can't wipe away the memory of all I've done. The truth won't be forgotten. I know that.'

'Oh come on,' she goaded, 'you know how it is with lies. If enough are told with enough vigour, in the end, everyone believes them. And that's how it'll be. With every poet, and I mean every poet, saying you're a coward, it will be believed, I promise you. And no one will know, because the poems will have blocked it out, that you knew Cuchulainn once in Scotland when you were young and that, rather than cowardliness, was why you wouldn't go against him.'

'Well, so be it,' said Ferdia, defiantly. 'If that happens I'll simply have to fight every man I meet if he won't accept the truth from me when I tell him why I wouldn't fight Cuchulainn because he prefers to believe the poets instead.'

'You'll take on every man on this island? Don't be ridiculous.'

'All right,' said Ferdia, 'I can't. But I'm still saying no. You go to the poets, let them do their worst, that's just how it'll have to be, and that's better than the alternative.' Then he added, 'I can always go to Scotland if I want. You can't buy the poets there.'

'Have you heard yourself? Do you know what you're saying? Ferdia, think what it would be like if everyone believed you were a coward. After the life you've lived and the struggles you've undergone it would be intolerable, and yet you're telling me you'd prefer that to what I'm offering.'

'I am,' insisted Ferdia. 'I would.'

'But why?'

'I'd rather it was said I was a coward than that I went against my friend.'

'Would you really?'

'I would.'

'You'd choose ignominy and shame rather than have your reputation assured for the rest of your life, for the rest of time? You'd choose to be remembered as a coward rather than as the man who vanquished Cuchulainn and won Finnabair here, would you really?'

'I would.'

'And yet she is exquisite, don't you think?'

Ferdia glanced at the queen's daughter. Her hair was yellow, the colour of straw, and she wore it in plaits pinned to the top of her head. Her lips were wide and thick and she had nice even teeth showing behind. Her eyes were brown, her figure was full and her manner was warm and friendly. He took another drink. He emptied the goblet.

'More wine for our guest, Finnabair,' said Maeve.

Finnabair bent low over Ferdia. He saw her breasts as she poured the wine. There were worse ways to spend one's life than in Finnabair's company, he thought, but then he reminded himself that nothing could ever be an adequate recompense for going to the ford the next morning to fight Cuchulainn. He had come to say no. He would go on saying no. He would leave later having said no. That was all there was for it.

'She is marvellous,' he said, anxious not to seem impolite, 'but I still say no.'

'Of course,' said Maeve. She had seen how he had looked at her daughter and she felt certain now she could get him to go by listing the riches that he would also acquire. 'You know it wouldn't just be Finnabair waiting for you after your victory?'

Maeve itemised the land, the gold, the weaponry, the chariots, the bondswomen, and everything else that would be Ferdia's after his triumph.

'I still say no,' insisted Ferdia.

'You're a stubborn man, because I know inside you want to say yes even though you're saying no.' She was still thinking about the covetous way he had looked at Finnabair.

'I don't want to say yes.'

'Oh but you do.'

'I don't.'

The conversation repeated itself. Ferdia drank goblet after goblet of wine while Finnabair stroked his hair and his hands. Ferdia should, with each passing moment, have felt less and less cheerful, whereas in fact he felt more and more cheerful.

It was the wine of course. It was Finnabair's attention too. But most of all he was boosted by his own resolution. The more he said no, the better he felt, and therefore the easier it was to go on saying no, and so on.

Ferdia finished his eighth goblet. Maeve now decided she would introduce another argument that she had been saving for when Ferdia thought his position was unassailable and he was full of wine.

'You can match Cuchulainn feat for feat, I believe,' said Maeve, innocently.

Ferdia was puzzled. Why was Maeve now suddenly introducing this new argument? He would need to proceed with care, he thought, and then he corrected himself. Not care, no; where martial prowess was concerned absolute accuracy was the only course.

'I can't quite match him. He has the Gae Bolga. I haven't.'

'But you have a special suit of horn, haven't you?' said Maeve quietly. 'No point can pierce it and no edge can cut it. Wearing that you're invincible.'

'Yes,' agreed Ferdia.

'Yet still you decline to go?'

'I do.'

'So imagine what the satirists will say. Even though he was invincible, still Ferdia wouldn't go. They'll say you brought cowardliness to a whole new level.'

'We've been backwards and forwards over this so many times,' said Ferdia gently, 'but however you put it, however you phrase it, I won't agree. I won't fight my friend. I think people will know why but if you pay every satirist in Ireland to tell a different story and everyone believes I'm a coward rather than a loyal friend, well, I'll accept it. I'd rather that than the alternative. I won't go.'

Maeve stood and began to walk around the tent. She made some sort of gesture to Mac Roth, who was standing by the door, but as her back was towards him Ferdia couldn't see what this was exactly. Then she sighed loudly.

Yes, thought Ferdia, the gesture he couldn't make out was a gesture of frustration. She was losing patience. The queen always got her way. She was the queen, after all. But he was defying her. Of course she was enraged.

Suddenly, the sense of what he was doing bore in on him. He saw how contrary to the normal state of things this was and this, in turn, led him, suddenly, to feel ill at ease and embarrassed. He didn't like going against the traditional order and refusing her while at the same time he knew he had no alternative. All the confidence he had felt before began draining away.

Now he very much wanted to rescue the situation. He wanted amity. He wanted sweetness. He glanced at Fergus and Aillil. He hoped with this look to solicit their intervention. But both men were staring at the ground. They would not make eye contact with him. They were embarrassed by this public row that others, beyond the tent, were no doubt also overhearing. When he left warriors would point at him and say, 'There's Ferdia who refused the queen and made her furious.' That was the cost of the position he was taking. And when the poets denounced him, well, there'd be much more of that, wouldn't there?

'So,' said Macve, interrupting his train of thought, 'it turns out then it's true what Cuchulainn said.'

'What was that?' Ferdia said. He was confused.

'Oh, nothing very important. It was just something he said about you.'

'Who did he say this to?'

'To Mac Roth.'

'To Mac Roth? When?'

'When he went to collect the bodies of Calitin and his sons.'

'And what was it he said?'

'Cuchulainn asked who tomorrow's champion would be,' said Maeve. 'And Mac Roth said he didn't know. And Cuchulainn said there must be someone. Then he said it was hardly a secret that you would have to be next. As he'd defeated everyone it couldn't be anyone else. It had to be you.'

She paused.

'Yes, what's so odd about that?' asked Ferdia.

'Nothing. It's what he said next.'

She paused again.

'Are you going to tell me then?'

'I don't know if you'll like it.'

'I won't know until I've heard.'

'He said your defeat would hardly count, in the light of all the other great fights he's had, as a triumph.'

'He said that?'

'He did.'

'He said that? I don't believe you.'

'Oh he did say it,' she said emphatically.

'Well, maybe he meant something else. When he said this, what else did he say?'

'Oh, that's easy,' said Maeve blithely. 'He said defeating you in combat would hardly rank, that was the exact word he used – not when judged against all the other combats he's had. That's because you've turned out to be a coward who's spent the whole winter skulking in his tent, and are too frightened to meet him. That's what he said.'

Then she turned to Mac Roth. 'Aren't I right? Isn't that what he said?'

Cuchulainn had said nothing like this to Mac Roth but the messenger wasn't going to say that now. Instead he simply nodded his head.

'So, there you have it. Mac Roth's confirmed it. Your so-called friend doesn't seem to hold you in the same esteem in which you hold him. It's hurtful, but there it is.'

Ferdia shook his head. His face was heating up, and his head was spinning. He wanted to rush out into the cold winter night and cool himself but he didn't know if he could excuse himself quickly and adroitly enough and he was afraid he would stumble as he went to the flap. He shouldn't have drunk the wine because now he was at a disadvantage.

'He shouldn't have said what he said,' Ferdia blurted out.

Cuchulainn had insulted him. He must express the rage that was rising inside. He must let the words out even if he didn't know where they were leading.

'He never knew me slow or sluggish in a fight.'

When he got to the end of the sentence he felt still angrier than when he started. But the next sentence would make him feel better, wouldn't it?

'I swear by the gods,' he roared, 'I'll be there at the ford tomorrow morning and I'll fight him.'

He felt much better. Maeve, who up until this point had been scowling, was suddenly smiling at him. She was happy. She had got the champion of her choice. Here was amity. Except who was that champion? He was the champion. He had just agreed to go, hadn't he? What had he done? The good feelings of an instant earlier vanished.

Now he felt bad. At the same time he was aware that Maeve was talking. He turned his attention away from the inner world to the real world around him.

'Listen,' she was exclaiming. 'Up to this moment everyone in this army thought you were loyal to the stranger who was fighting us. That explained why you were sluggish and slow to fight. But now, when you ride out to meet Cuchulainn tomorrow, everyone will see that you have remembered you are the son of a Connacht king who is prepared to fight for Connacht to win. Your reputation will soar. All that remains now for you to do is first to win, then to return here and claim Finnabair and everything else that will be rightfully yours.'

This was supposed to make Ferdia better. But it made him feel worse. He stood. He said good night. Fergus, who'd been there the whole evening stood up and said good night as well.

They left the tent together. There was a moon in the sky. It shone from behind a great mound of cloud and the men's pale shadows moved ahead of them along the ground as they walked away. In the centre of the camp the Brown Bull drowsed. A chain that ran from his enormous nose ring to an oak tree tethered him and the chain clinked faintly when he moved now.

'Do you think Cuchulainn said those things Maeve said?' he asked. If Fergus thought he didn't, it would make him feel a lot better

But Fergus didn't answer the question. He said instead, 'I think I should send my charioteer to warn him it's you, don't you think?'

So, thought Ferdia, Fergus ignored my question. Well, obviously Cuchulainn didn't say it. Or Fergus didn't think he did. Maeve had tricked him then, hadn't she? He'd have to do it now. He'd have to go, and there wasn't anything he could do to get out of it. It was better he went out the next day thinking that what Maeve said was true, even if it was a lie. He'd never survive otherwise.

'So you agree, I send my charioteer to warn him?' said Fergus.

Clink, clink, sounded the Brown Bull's chain again, followed by a snort. What was Fergus saying? The charioteer would warn Cuchulainn, was it? Well, yes, that was good. If Cuchulainn had been warned it would be much less embarrassing than if he surprised his old friend.

'Yes, please, send your driver to tell him.'

'I'll say good night then.'

'Good night.'

Ferdia went into his tent and lay down on his couch. He expected sleep to come quickly after drinking so much wine. He yearned for sleep too, but of course as soon as his head was on the pillow he was suddenly wide awake and his thoughts were racing . . .

Why had he said what he said? It was the wine. Then when he was drunk Maeve told him what Cuchulainn said. Of course Cuchulainn hadn't said it. But Ferdia, provoked, had said he'd go, and now he'd have to. That was the way . . .

There was nothing worse than thoughts following the same course and repeating over and over and over again. He felt worse than at any point in his entire life leading up to this moment. He was an idiot, a fool, and he hated himself . . .

Later he fell asleep, but he woke in the dark and long before dawn with the anxiety of what was to come pressing down on him. In any combat in which he and Cuchulainn met, one of them would not return alive. The knowledge of this was crushing and depressing.

If he lost he would also lose Finnabair and everything else he had been promised and the awful truth, he now realised, was he didn't want to lose them. As far as he was concerned, as far as Maeve and Ailill were concerned, as far as Fergus and everyone in the camp of the great army were concerned, he was going to defend his honour against an old friend's slur because that was the warrior's code. But the horrible truth, he now acknowledged, was that this was a pretext which Maeve had given him and he'd been only too happy to accept. The awful truth was that he wanted everything Maeve promised, particularly Finnabair. With this realisation his inner turmoil grew worse. There was no possibility he would go back to sleep now. None whatsoever.

He got up and woke Miliucc, his charioteer. He was a small wiry man with a strong bony nose, very dark eyes, a very wide mouth and improbably large teeth. His manner was brusque and he had a habit of asking direct and even awkward questions. Strangers when they met him would often find him rude but Ferdia, who had known Miliucc many years, was not bothered by his manners. Indeed, he found the charioteer's straightforwardness and willingness to speak his mind refreshing.

'Get the horses and yoke the chariot,' said Ferdia. 'Load up my weapons, my armour and everything I need for combat.'

'Why?' asked Miliucc.

'We're going to the ford.'

'Is this wise?'

'No.'

'Then don't go.'

'I promised. I can't get out of it'

'You promised to fight Cuchulainn?'

'Yes.'

'Maeve persuaded you?'

'Yes.'

'But Cuchulainn's your special friend.'

'Just get the chariot ready.'

'It would be better I didn't. You know only one of you will come out alive.'

'I don't want to hear. You're wasting your breath. I have to go. That's it. Don't question what I say. Just get the chariot ready.'

Miliucc got up and harnessed the chariot. He returned to the tent. 'It's ready though I still say this is foolish. I still say we stay.'

'You know what happens to a warrior who breaks his word? He's thrown to the poets and they tear him to pieces. I have to go. I said I would. Now I must.'

The two men went outside and climbed into the chariot, the driver into the front, Ferdia into the back. Over the tent tops Ferdia saw the Brown Bull's massive head, nodding on the end of his massive neck, a dark profile against the clouds that hung behind.

Miliucc shook the reins and the wheels began to turn, grinding on the axle as they did.

'I'd better say goodbye,' said Ferdia abruptly.

'To who?'

'The royal couple.'

'Because you won't be back, is it?'

Ferdia decided to ignore this remark.

'Go past their tent,' he said.

'They'll be asleep.'

'I can still say goodbye, even if they don't hear.'

Miliucc brought the chariot to the royal tent and stopped. The flaps were closed and the tent was dark. Nothing stirred inside though there did seem to be noise coming from behind the tent.

'Goodbye,' Ferdia called. He tapped Miliucc on the shoulder. 'Go on . . .'

In the darkness at the back of the tent Maeve squatted, making water. She had heard Ferdia's chariot approach, stop, and go on. She ducked into the tent and went to Aillil. She shook his shoulder. He woke.

'Did you hear?'

'What?' said Aillil groggily.

'Your new son-in-law just passed on his way to combat. He said farewell.'

'Oh did he?' said Aillil.

'And a man who says goodbye like that isn't coming back on his own two feet, I think.'

'Well, if both die it's all the same to us,' said Aillil. 'Still, it would be better if Ferdia lived. He'll be famous and he'll make Finnabair a good husband.'

'Can we talk about tomorrow?' She slipped in beside him and pressed her bare body against his.

'Can't that wait?' answered Aillil. He wanted to go back to sleep.

'But you're awake.'

'Go on then.'

'This contest won't end quickly.'

'No,' Aillil agreed.

'It'll be days.'

'I hope so.'

'So I propose, when we leave tomorrow, we keep going and going and we don't stop except for a few hours when its dark, and the next day we go on, and the day after.'

'Strictly speaking, shouldn't we make camp when the combat is over? Isn't that the condition . . .?'

'Only when it's over, but it's only over when one of the combatants is dead. Until that happens, which won't be for several days, it could be said the fight is ongoing, even if Ferdia and Cuchulainn are resting.'

'I suppose you're right,' said Aillil, chuckling.

'And think, if we hardly stop, in three or four days we'll get our prize to the border. We'll get him over the border.'

'We probably will.'

'And then I don't think Conor and his forces would be so keen to chase after us.'

'I suppose not.'

'Whereas if we stay Conor will come for us with his army and that day isn't far away, you know. It's nearly spring.'

'Oh I know that,' said Aillil.

'I say we leave Mac Roth and some healers and a few messengers here. They can send runners after us if there's any news. In three or four days, by which time we'll be in Connacht, Mac Roth can bring Ferdia, or failing that, an account of what happened. It's the best plan.'

'Yes, I can see that,' said Aillil. He yawned. 'Well, I'd better get some sleep then, if we're going to try and get back while Ferdia and Cuchulainn fight it out.'

He closed his eyes . . .

Meanwhile, Ferdia and Miliucc had left the camp of the great army and were moving across the dark empty ground towards the river and the ford. In the sky overhead great grey and black clouds were piled, one on top of the other, the edges silver with light from the moon.

The two men reached the south side of the ford where Calitin and his sons had died. Miliucc stopped the chariot. It was night still. The water in the river rustled and gurgled as it ran past. One of the horses stamped a foot. On the other side of the river the flames from Cuchulainn's fire flickered in the darkness.

Miliucc spread cushions and skins under the chariot. Ferdia went under the chariot and went back to sleep. At dawn Miliucc banged on the chariot floor. Ferdia woke up and crawled out. The cloud in the sky was the colour of clay and it was very cold. The moon was gone. There was a fire flickering in the far distance.

'Any sign of Cuchulainn?' he asked.

'None,' said Miliucc.

'Are you sure?' said Ferdia.

'Cuchulainn isn't such a little speck I wouldn't see him, you know.'

'True,' said Ferdia, 'but you know I bet that as soon as he heard I was coming he fled back to Emain Macha.'

'You do?'

'I do. That's why he isn't here.'

'That's slander, and I'm sure you don't believe it either.' Then he reminded Ferdia of the time, in Scotland, Cuchulainn had slaughtered a hundred men in order to get Ferdia's lost sword back.

'You did wrong,' said Ferdia grimly, 'not to have reminded me of that before. I wouldn't have come if you had.'

'I doubt that. You wouldn't listen to my advice, so why would you have listened to a story?'

Ferdia went to the edge of the ford where the stony ground sheered into the shallow bubbling river. There was nothing to do but wait for his adversary to arrive.

Chapter Nineteen

The fight of friends

At that moment Cuchulainn was asleep under his chariot. Dawn came and still he slept. It grew brighter and still he slept. This sleeping was deliberate. He didn't want anyone saying later that he had risen early because of fear or dread of the battle. Finally he opened his eyes and looked out. Now he was awake he remembered instantly what was looming. He'd got Fergus's message the night before.

'Laeg,' he called. He wriggled out from under the chariot. 'Fetch the horses, prepare the chariot. Ferdia will be wondering why we're late . . .'

In his place on the south of the ford, Ferdia could see there was activity now at Cuchulainn's far-off camp. Then he saw the chariot moving and heard its creaking as Laeg drove it towards him. He saw Cuchulainn's famous horses – the Black Sainglain and the Grey of Macha. He saw Laeg with the reins in the front and he saw Cuchulainn, a shield on his left arm, a javelin in his right hand, sitting on the warrior's seat in the back.

'How does Cuchulainn look to you?' he called back to Miliucc.

'He looks to me like a warrior to whom no man means anything.'

'Stop that. You praise him too much. Now bring some weapons quickly. I don't want to turn my back in case he drives the chariot shaft into me.'

Miliucc brought the warrior a sword, shield and javelin. On the north bank opposite, Laeg pulled the reins and stopped Cuchulainn's chariot. Ferdia went forward and stood on the edge of the water.

'Welcome, Cuchulainn,' shouted Ferdia.

'Once I relished your greeting but I don't trust it now,' answered Cuchulainn. 'And by the way, I should be the one saying welcome. This is my land. You're the intruder. You've stolen our women and children, our cows and sheep, and our great Brown Bull. We want them back. Return them and go.'

'Well, you've grown since Scotland. I'd hardly recognise the lad who fixed my spears and made my bed.'

'I did all that once but I've come on since then. There isn't a warrior anywhere I couldn't take on and beat.'

'Ah, talk, talk. You're a fire without fuel. When I've finished you'll need plenty of help when you get home, assuming you ever do.'

'Ferdia,' Cuchulainn shouted back, 'Aillil and Maeve promised Finnabair to every man who's faced me, and you know what? I killed every one of them. They promised you Finnabair as well, I'm sure, and that's why you're here. And you know what? I'll kill you too.'

'We've talked enough. What shall we fight with?'

'You were at the ford first, you choose.'

'Do you remember the last feats we learned in Scotland?'

'The throwing feats I do, yes.'

'Let's see how well you remember.'

Each took eight long-handled spears, eight little quill spears, and eight ivory-handled spears. Then they took up position on opposite banks and began throwing and parrying. The spears flew backwards and forwards between them like bees on the wing on a sunny day. Every spear found its target but so good were they both at parrying that neither man was able to make so much as a tiny nick in the other's skin.

At midday Ferdia called out. 'Let's stop this shall we? This isn't going to decide anything.'

'Agreed,' said Cuchulainn.

They both threw their weapons into their charioteers' arms.

'What next then?' asked Ferdia.

'It's your choice until nightfall. You were at the ford first.'

'Let's try the smooth-polished slender spears, bound tightly with flax.'

'Agreed.'

Each took a tough shield and a spear. They hurled these spears at each other for the rest of the day. Their shield work was fine, but their casting was finer. As the afternoon wore on they began to hit one another. These weren't big hits. Neither managed to get the point to lodge in the other's flesh. But they hurt each other, slicing the edge of a shoulder here, the back of a calf there. Finally, it began to grow dark and each man had cuts and gashes all over his body. Each wound on its own was of no consequence but so many together were quite a different matter.

'Shall we stop?' Ferdia asked.

'We will,' said Cuchulainn.

They both threw their weapons into their charioteers' arms. Then they both walked into the river. The rage they had felt before they started had gone. Now they just felt exhausted and hurt. They threw their arms around one another and stood, chest to chest, heart to heart, with the cold white water running around their ankles. They broke away then and waded back to their respective sides. Their charioteers led them away to little shelters with rushes strewn on the floor that they had built during the day. The warriors lay down.

Mac Roth appeared with a healer. The man applied herbs and plants of curing to Ferdia's cuts and gashes. When the healer was done, Ferdia told him to cross over to treat Cuchulainn. He didn't want it said later that he only won because he got more care than his adversary did. Cuchulainn, meanwhile, received some food from a compound on his side. He split the portion and sent half across to Ferdia. He didn't want it said he won because Ferdia was weak with hunger.

Mac Roth took a report on the day from Ferdia and returned to the little rump camp left behind after the great army set off that morning. He selected a messenger who reached the great army in the middle of the night, when the men were resting for an hour in the open around enormous bonfires. The messenger went to Fergus and the royal couple.

'Mac Roth says the fighting was inconclusive. There was no clear winner. It'll take three or four days to settle it.'

'Good,' said Maeve. 'That's what we want to hear. At the first glimmer of light on the edge of the sky we move on and with luck we'll be home in two or three days before one of them is dead.' She turned to one of her servants. 'Pass round this order: at first light we go.'

The message went round the camp from one man to the next. The short wiry brother, the one who had helped to bury Calitin and his sons, was woken and told. He then woke and told his older, bigger brother.

'Listen, we march at first light. We expect to be home in a couple of days, three at most.'

'What?' asked the older. 'March, you said?'

'Yes.'

'I'm tired.'

'You'd rather sleep?'

'Oh yes, please, I could sleep for days.'

'Well, you can't. We've got to get out of Ulster and away from Cuchulainn and back to Connacht with our prize. Two or three days' hard marching and we've done it.'

The great Brown Bull moaned above their heads.

'I don't know if I've the strength,' said the older brother.

'You're going to have to find it,' said the younger. 'In five days winter ends, spring starts. The birth pangs go, and Conor and his men get up from their beds. If we're still on their land, they'll come after us, full of rage and hate, and they'll kill us all. But if we're gone, it'll be a different matter. Yes, they'll be annoyed. We'll have their prize bull, after all. But it's quite a different thing invading a province than it is defending your own. Conor and his forces won't be so keen to come after us. They'll negotiate, or they'll ask for a fine. They won't go to war straight off, you can be sure of that.'

'You're sure?' said the older.

'Absolutely,' said the younger with total confidence. 'And I'll tell you something else. The thought of home so close will fill you with joy. Your feet will go faster and faster in the rush to get back, so much so you won't even notice you're marching.'

'I won't?'

'You'll have your eye fixed on home, just like a dog or a horse at the end of a journey when he rushes to get back.'

'I suppose you're right,' said the older. This did make sense to him. 'So I won't be tired on the last part of the journey. I'll just rush and I won't stop again 'til I'm home.'

'Yes, you and the whole army,' said his younger brother.

Later, as light began to glimmer along the edge of the sky, the entire army set off with the Brown Bull in the middle. The troops, though far from fresh, were bright-eyed and full of energy. No man could wait to be back home and safe in Connacht before Conor and his men got out of their beds and came to get them.

Cuchulainn and Ferdia woke and came to the ford to discuss the day.

'What weapons will we use?' asked Cuchulainn.

'I chose yesterday, so you choose today,' said Ferdia.

'Let's try the stabbing-spears then,' said Cuchulainn. 'Working with them today we may bring the end nearer than we did yesterday with our throwing. Let our chariots be brought and our horses yoked. Today we'll fight from them.'

'Agreed,' said Ferdia.

Each man armed himself with a big shield and a heavy stabbing spear. The charioteers harnessed the horses to the chariots and drove them through the ford, the warriors standing in the back, their feet in the bindings, the ties around their middles. The bed of the ford here was a mix of sand and gravel, so the going was easy. As the chariots passed, the warriors drilled and stabbed at one another over the wicker sides. Once they had passed the drivers turned and re-passed and Ferdia and Cuchulainn stabbed at one another again. The drivers turned their chariots round and as they passed they stabbed again . . .

On and on it went like this without stopping. By the end of the day, when the sun sank behind the edge of the land and the light leeched out of the sky, there was sticky blood all over the chariots' wicker walls and such holes in both men's bodies as small birds could easily fly through.

'Let's stop this,' said Cuchulainn. 'Our horses and drivers are finished and so why shouldn't we be too?'

'Yes,' Ferdia shouted.

Both thrust their weapons into their charioteers' hands and then embraced each other over the chariot sides. They returned to their camps and collapsed on their beds of clean rushes. That night the healer came to Ferdia and food was brought to Cuchulainn and both men showed one another the same courtesy they had the previous night. Mac Roth took a report on the day from Ferdia, returned to the rump camp and sent a messenger to the royal couple and Fergus.

'The second day standing up in their chariots they fought with stabbing-spears and again,' he reported to the royal couple and Fergus, 'there was no clear outcome and it is still not clear who'll win. The warriors will shortly be going into their third day of combat.'

'Excellent,' cried Maeve, and she clapped her hands with glee.

Back at the ford on the third day Ferdia arrived on the south bank as Cuchulainn arrived on the north bank.

'Ferdia,' Cuchulainn shouted across the water, 'do you know you look terrible this morning? Your hair looks darker than yesterday and your eyes look duller and you're stooping too.'

'I'm not frightened, if that's what you think.'

'I didn't say that.'

'There's no one I couldn't beat, including you, my friend.'

'What shall it be today?' shouted Cuchulainn. 'I chose yesterday so it's your turn.'

'Let's use our broadswords. We may bring the end nearer today by hacking than we did yesterday with our stabbing.'

They returned to their charioteers and called for these heavy swords and their heaviest shields. They armed themselves and returned to the ford then jumped into the water and splashed out as far as the mid-way point. Then they started fighting, trading blow for blow, and as they fought they hacked and hewed great pieces of flesh out of each other's shoulders and backs and flanks. By the time dusk came on, each man was scored and gashed all over his body.

'Cuchulainn, let us stop,' Ferdia shouted.

'Agreed,' shouted the other man.

They turned and threw their weapons to their charioteers but today they did not then turn to embrace each other. The day had been so hard, and the fighting so vicious, they had not only hurt one another badly but they had both realised that when they met the next day it would be the last day living for one man or the other.

Each man splashed wearily towards the bank where his charioteer was waiting. Then each man made his way, with help, to his bed of rushes and lay down. The healer came and food came and once again they shared with each other what they had. Mac Roth came too and Ferdia gave him a report. He then sent a third messenger racing to the royal couple and Fergus.

'The next will be the last day of combat,' the messenger said, 'and the fight will be settled once and for all. It is still unclear who will win.'

'By tonight or first thing tomorrow at the latest we'll be over the border,' said Maeve. 'Once we're back in Connacht, it won't matter.'

Ferdia woke on his bed of rushes. They smelt vaguely of brackish water and fine dust. He heard the fire crackling. He opened his eyes. He saw sparks and dark grey smoke trailing into a dark dawn sky. There were patches of blue on the edge of the sky while overhead it was all grey. He'd gone to sleep knowing the coming day the fight would be decided and now he was awake he knew nothing had changed and this was the day.

'My horn suit,' he said to his charioteer, for if there was any day to wear this special garment, this was it. The suit was brought. It came in several small pieces that strapped on in such a cunning way his whole body was covered, bar his feet, his hands and his head, and yet he was able to move as freely and lightly as if he wore no armour.

'My helmet.'

The helmet was brought.

'My sword with the gold hilt, my gold-rimmed shield and my javelin with the gold ring,' he said.

His charioteer brought the weapons. Ferdia took the weapons and set out. There had been a frost in the night and white ice dust covered the ground and the trees.

The frost went right to the edge of the ford and stopped. Beyond the bank the river moved swiftly and noisily along.

He looked across but on the other side there was no sign of Cuchulainn or his chariot although he could see his camp in the distance. There was a fire there and a column of smoke trailed into the air.

Ferdia was relieved his opponent was not there waiting. This gave him time to practise various feats. These were not old feats he had learned in Scotland but new ones inspired by the thought of Cuchulainn and what lay ahead. He hurled his javelin into the air and caught it on the tip of his sword as it hurtled down towards the ground.

Next he balanced the front of his shield on the point of his javelin and by rotating the shaft he spun the shield. Then he flung the shield high into the air. Here the shield turned and started to fall towards him, rim first. Ferdia caught the rim on the point of his javelin and then, with a series of deft wrist movements, he began to turn the shield so it was like a chariot wheel racing along. Ferdia followed this with dozens more similarly marvellous feats . . .

At his camp Cuchulainn woke on his bed of rushes, damp from the night. He heard the fire burning and crackling and smelled the wood-smoke. He threw aside the pelts and sat up.

'This is the day,' he said to Laeg, who sat at the fire. 'This is the day.'

'It is,' Laeg agreed.

Laeg helped Cuchulainn dress and arm himself. Then they climbed aboard the chariot and moved towards the ford. The bare branches of the trees they passed were silver with frost and so was every blade of grass in every direction. The sky was smeared with ragged, grey clouds and through the holes there were occasional patches of blue. In the distance, over the frosty ground beyond the river, Cuchulainn saw Ferdia: with the sky behind him he was just a black shape but what an extraordinary one.

Ferdia had stuck his javelin point into the ground and he was balanced upside down on the other end, supporting himself with just his hand.

Laeg stopped the horses when they got to the edge of the ford. Ferdia was now supporting himself on just the tip of his thumb. This was an extraordinary sight, Ferdia, upside down, his legs in the air, his whole weight on his thumb which rested on the end of the wooden javelin shaft.

'Now there's something,' said Cuchulainn, 'he didn't learn in Scotland. Friend Laeg, you must do something for me today. If Ferdia looks like he's going to win, I want you to insult me. Say your worst. Use words to hurt and shame me. And do not stint or stop until you have made me angry. Goad me with vehemence to finish the job. Do you understand?

'And that's not all. If it seems victory is almost mine, if it seems all I need to do is reach out and seize it, then urge me on with words of praise and shouts of encouragement.

Goad me with sweetness to finish the job. I must not baulk at the end. Do you understand?'

'I do,' said Laeg.

'Ferdia,' Cuchulainn shouted over the water.

The warrior had lowered his belly on to the end of the shaft and was starting to spin. Round and round he went, faster and faster, until he was whirling so fast Cuchulainn could no longer make him out any more but only saw a blur.

'Ferdia,' Cuchulainn shouted again. His voice was much more loud this time and it secured his opponent's attention. In one fluid movement Ferdia wriggled off the end of the shaft and landed neatly, sending little spurts of frost rising like dust.

'I didn't hear you,' he said. 'You haven't been waiting long, have you?'

'What weapons shall we use today?'

'Your choice,' Ferdia shouted back. He sliced his arm through the air so viciously he made a booming noise.

'Swords,' said Cuchulainn, 'but we fight in the ford.'

'Well, why not?' said Ferdia. His tone was light but not his feelings. Cuchulainn never failed when he fought in water. His only strategy must be to seem indifferent, pleased even with the suggestion.

Ferdia took his shield from the ground and began to buckle it on.

'An excellent choice,' he said.

He had the shield on and he pulled the javelin out of the

cold ground and threw it to Miliucc. In return he was thrown his sword.

Ferdia stepped down into the cold ford and strode towards the middle. Here the water reached as far as his knees.

Cuchulainn jumped down from his chariot, got into the water and went over to Ferdia. He put up his shield. Ferdia did likewise. He threw his arm out, hoping to slice into the joint where the horn suit articulated. Ferdia's shield came up and pushed the sword sideways. Now Ferdia drove his sword end at Cuchulainn's belly. Cuchulainn dropped his shield and Ferdia's sword hit the front and glanced away. Cuchulainn lunged at Ferdia's thigh, got deflected, then had to defend himself as Ferdia struck back . . .

At first, because they were fresh, they fought at arm's length from one another. Their feet moved nimbly as they thrust and parried and they let out hard exhalations of breath as they threw their blows.

As time passed though, their strength began to drain away as light leaves a sky at the approach of dusk. They moved their feet a little less deftly. The exhalations of breath sounded more desperate and their blows were less forceful and less accurate. Exhaustion also drove them inexorably closer until their two shields met and began to grind one against the other.

At midday the white round of the sun showed through the cloud above. The watching charioteers saw their champions' fighting had lost its polish and elegance.

Cuchulainn and Ferdia were now two weary men, smashing brutally away at one another, desperate to finish the other off and indifferent as to how it was done. All that mattered to each man now was that he win.

Suddenly, from the driver's seat of the chariot where he sat watching, Laeg noticed Cuchulainn retreating up the ramp that fed into the water. Laeg was surprised, as Cuchulainn preferred to fight in a ford above any other place. It must be part of a plan, he decided, watching Cuchulainn as he followed the bank as it ran downstream.

Ferdia, still on the riverbed, chased Cuchulainn, swinging viciously at his ankles. Cuchulainn had to jump up again and again in order to avoid having his feet sliced off.

Suddenly, Cuchulainn somersaulted forward and landed on Ferdia's shield, his sword raised. So that was his plan, Laeg thought.

Ferdia brought his left elbow up and thwacked the shield from behind. Cuchulainn flew through the air and landed on his back on the bank. He jumped to his feet, rolled forward and landed on the shield again. Ferdia hit the shield with his left knee and Cuchulainn was thrown back on to the bank again. One rebuff was tolerable, thought Laeg, but two in a row were a sign of weakness. It was time to goad Cuchulainn.

'Cuchulainn,' shouted Laeg. 'Ferdia scattered you as easily as the white down of a dandelion is blown away with a puff of breath.'

Ferdia grabbed the lip of the bank. But as he went to pull himself out the clod he had grasped came away in his hand. He stumbled back and sat down heavily. The cold water coursed around his waist and legs, cooling the boiling skin under the horn suit.

'You know, Cuchulainn,' continued Laeg, 'faced with a real enemy, as you are now, your fighting talent is shown to be pitiful.'

Cuchulainn sat up. Out in the middle of the river, Ferdia rose dripping and angry.

'You call yourself a warrior, Cuchulainn, but you delude yourself,' shouted Laeg. 'From this day on, you'll know yourself as a fool and a poltroon. Others will be less polite but closer to the mark. They'll call you a coward.'

Cuchulainn got up and jumped with a fierce shout from the bank. His image reflected in the water below as he flew over the span from land to Ferdia. He landed on the upturned shield. Ferdia moved two steps back, yet did not fall. Cuchulainn grasped the shield rim with one hand and swung his sword furiously at the tiny vulnerable wedge of skin between the edge of the armour and the bottom of Ferdia's helmet with the other. The sword blade never connected because Ferdia shrugged Cuchulainn away, not towards the bank this time but into the middle of the ford. Here he landed heavily, spraying a great gush of water into the sky, a gush so thick that for a moment the sky was lost from view to Ferdia.

And as the water drops fell Cuchulainn swelled up like

a bladder and the hero-light full of black blood shot up and pushed as high as a great ship's mast towards the sky.

Cuchulainn stood with another fierce shout and ran forward. Ferdia raised his shield. Cuchulainn's shield collided with his. There was an awful grating of metal on metal: the securing rivets popped and the iron sheets on the shield fronts flew off.

The warriors parted and flung the shield carcasses aside and went at each other with their heavy swords which they held in two hands now. There was a deafening banging of metal on metal, accompanied by much splashing of water and incoherent shouts. Neither landed a blow but both managed to shear each other's sword off at the hilt.

The warriors turned to their charioteers.

'Javelins,' they both shouted.

The weapons were thrown. They caught them and began to stab at one another. The fighting was so hard and the footwork so intense all the water around them was driven out of the riverbed.

For Ferdia, this was as good as fighting on dry land. The balance of advantage that had, up until now, lain with Cuchulainn, now swung to him. He thrust with his javelin. It was a low, hard thrust. The javelin's point went into Cuchulainn's belly immediately below the bottom rib on the left-hand side. Cuchulainn backed away, wrenching himself off the point. A great spume of red blood shot out of the wound and sprayed the stones on the river bed. Ferdia registered the metallic taste of blood on his lips. He'd landed a blow. One more, perhaps two, and that would be that. He would have won. His enemy would be dead.

He thrust again but Cuchulainn jumped up and back, performing a complete circle, and landed on the ramp that led to dry land on his side of the ford.

'Short spear and Gae Bolga,' he shouted to Laeg. Without Cuchulainn's footwork water from upstream gushed forward in a great torrent and filled the ford again.

'Long shield,' Ferdia shouted to his charioteer.

The shield was thrown to him. As he caught it he felt the water lapping around his knees. He dropped the shield down so the bottom rested on the riverbed – this was to cover his lower body from the Gae Bolga – and as he did he had a dismal thought.

The return of the water meant a shift of advantage back to his opponent. To wrest back that advantage he needed to empty the ford of water and make the riverbed dry again.

With his feet he began to drive away the water. But he had only one pair of feet. He couldn't get all the water away as quickly as when he and Cuchulainn were fighting.

Cuchulainn meanwhile, on the ramp, saw what Ferdia was doing. If Ferdia emptied the ford dry he would lose his advantage. He needed water to succeed.

He bolted down the ramp and splashed through the shallows. Ferdia's shield was low. Cuchulainn saw his chance. He reached over the top rim and got the point of his short stabbing spear between two pieces of horn and into Ferdia's shoulder. Ferdia called out in surprise and hurt. Cuchulainn pulled the point out and lifted his arm back as if he intended to stab Ferdia again. Ferdia brought his shield up to protect himself from another puncture. Cuchulainn, registering the level of the ford was dropping and knowing if it got any shallower it wouldn't be deep enough, dropped the Gae Bolga and caught it with his left foot between his big toe and the next toe down. He threw his leg forward and released the weapon. It skimmed through the water, bumping over the grit and the sand on the bottom, until the point connected with Ferdia's foot. The spear slipped under the edge of the horn that covered his foot and then turned and started to travel up his leg.

'That's it,' Ferdia shouted. 'I'll die of that.'

The Gae Bolga slipped by Ferdia's knee, passed around his hip and pushed up through his belly until it reached his heart, at which point the end opened outwards and barbs pushed in every direction.

Ferdia dropped his sword and shield.

'My heart is all blood,' he shouted. 'I'm leaving this life.'

He pitched forward. Cuchulainn dropped his stabbing spear and caught him under his arms. He dragged the body across the ford and on to the ramp on the north side.

He laid Ferdia on the cold ground where little particles of frost still glistened. Ferdia's breath was going in and out in short shallow gusts. His eyes were cloudy. Then, finally, the gusting breath stopped.

'You've done it,' said Laeg.

'I have.'

Cuchulainn sat down suddenly on the ground. The hero-light that had towered mast-like over his head collapsed to nothing. His inflated body shrank too and suddenly, from having been so big, he was small and even ordinary. He touched the wound under his belly.

'I'm hurting,' Cuchulainn said.

'You are.'

Cuchulainn stared at Ferdia's face. It had all the attributes Ferdia's face usually had. It was wide at the forehead, it tapered to a pointed chin and it was covered with freckles. It was his face yet it was not. Something that had been inside and informed the face had gone away. Now it was really his copy.

'He's dead,' Cuchulainn said bluntly.

It took him a moment or two to know the enormity of what it was he had said. His friend, his great friend, was gone. He really was dead and he would never come back. He would never laugh or sing, walk or eat. Cuchulainn would never hear reports from others about his doings or meet him again. He would never smile and Cuchulainn would never see his smile either. A great surge of anguish ran though the middle of his being and he let out a long low cry.

'He's dead,' he said again.

'He is,' said Laeg, 'and this is what happens when two fight. One dies.'

'When we were in Scotland I thought we'd be friends for ever,' said Cuchulainn bleakly. 'It turns out that wasn't true. Maeve offered him Finnabair and so he came. We clashed and I did what I did. But it's shameful, isn't it, what I did? I have killed him; I have killed my best friend.'

Laeg looked at Cuchulainn's face. He had looked at this face many times at moments like this in the past but he had never seen what he saw now.

Of course it was not the case, as Laeg well knew, that Cuchulainn had never been miserable before. The slaughter of Naoise and his brothers and the tragedy of Deirdre had made him very unhappy for a while. The source of his pain then, apart from the deaths, was his discovery that Conor wasn't the noble king he thought he was. This knowledge had poisoned Cuchulainn for a while. The fact he couldn't move against Eogan – to have done so would have provoked a civil war – this had made everything worse. For that meant Cuchulainn was unable to punish the wrong-doer and purge his emotions.

But what he suffered then was nothing to what he went through after he killed Connla. What he had to face then, besides the pain and the bitter regret, was the awful sense of responsibility that he alone had done it. He might be half-God but, as this episode showed him, he was half-man too, and all too imperfect.

But Cuchulainn recovered from these blows and was stronger because of them. In the battles he subsequently fought against the great army and against the champions Maeve sent against him, he knew a happiness deeper than any he had known before, even in childhood, because never had he fought so well. He had finally become what he was always intended to be, the supreme warrior of his day. And this sense of fulfillment was there on Cuchulainn's face after every combat and Laeg saw it as clearly as he might a cloud in the sky or a tree on a hill.

At least that was how it had been. Now, when he looked down at the face of the man on the ground, Laeg saw what he had never imagined he would ever see. This wasn't the face Cuchulainn showed even during the earlier bad times. This wasn't the face of a man in the grip of despair and a deep unassailable grief. This was the face of a man who wished he was dead. In this circumstance, he must try to rally him.

'What are you doing? Get up,' Laeg said.

'Why?'

'You've won. This isn't something to regret. It's to be celebrated.'

'How can I be happy after what I've done?'

'You won. He lost. This will make you famous for ever.'

'And Ferdia dead is the price worth paying for my fame?'

'For a warrior to be great he has to kill. You've always known that. So why are you complaining about it now? If you didn't want this you shouldn't have become a warrior in the first place.'

Cuchulainn shrugged.

'You don't know what you think any more,' said Laeg, 'because you're completely exhausted. You need to go to your compound and rest and then you'll see what you've achieved.'

Shaking his head, Cuchulainn struggled to his feet.

'Take off his armour,' said Cuchulainn, 'and cut the Gae Bolga out of him. I must have my weapon. Then call Miliucc over to take him away.'

Laeg undid the thongs that attached the armour. The cunningly contrived pieces of brown horn fell away and the body was laid bare. The only sign the Gae Bolga was inside the rib cage was a little bump, sticking up, just above Ferdia's heart.

He fetched a hatchet and split Ferdia's torso open to reveal the end of the Gae Bolga. Then he got a pair of tongs, grasped the barbed head and, with a great effort, heaved the weapon out, all covered in blood.

He carried it to the ford and dropped it in. The water flowed around the weapon, taking away all the blood. When Laeg lifted the weapon out, it was wet and clean. He folded away the barbs.

'Come over,' he shouted across to Miliucc.

'I will.'

Miliucc shook his reins and started to trundle his chariot down the ramp. Laeg turned away with the dripping spear and moved towards his chariot to store it away.

'You might wash his blood from my spear,' said Cuchulainn, 'but you can't do the same with my memory, can you?'

'I can't,' Laeg agreed. 'Memories you must bear but the

great fame that this will bring you, you'll learn how to bear that too in time, I promise.'

'I've had enough of this,' said Cuchulainn. 'Take me home.'

Laeg helped Miliucc to lift Ferdia's body into the chariot. Miliucc thanked Laeg, drove back across the ford and headed away in the direction of the rump camp.

Chapter Twenty

The Clash of the Bulls

Miliucc reached the rump camp and stopped at Mac Roth's tent.

'Mac Roth,' he called.

Mac Roth came out and peered over the wicker sides of the chariot at the body lying on the floor between the two seats. Through the gash running down Ferdia's chest, he saw cartilage and muscle, veins and heart muscles, bone and fat.

'Wash the body,' he said. 'We'll put him in the mound with Calitin and the others.'

Miliucc nodded and rode away.

Mac Roth summoned a messenger.

'Take your chariot, follow the great army. Tell Maeve it is finished. Ferdia is dead.'

The messenger set off and drove his horses as fast as they would go, west after Maeve and the great army.

Ferdia was buried and the gravestone with his name in Ogham set over his body.

Mac Roth and the other mourners returned to the rump camp.

'Pack everything away,' Mac Roth ordered. 'We're leaving.'

The order was met with murmurs of delight. There were two more days of winter left. It was just possible that Conor would send a mobile force to harry them. They were anxious to leave the territory of Ulster before this could happen.

It was early the next morning when Mac Roth's messenger caught up with the great army. They were just crossing the border that was marked by a line of poles with the headless bodies of Ulster's enemies stuck on to them. He was brought before the royal couple and Fergus.

'Ferdia is dead. Mac Roth follows,' he said.

'But we're away,' said Maeve jubilantly. 'If Conor wants his Brown Bull, he'll have to invade us.'

'Don't underestimate him,' said Fergus.

'Meaning?'

'He'll come.'

'How can you be so sure?'

'Well of course he'll come,' said Fergus. 'Think about it.'

'I am thinking about it,' said Maeve. 'Why would he mount a campaign now, when it's too late, and the Brown Bull has gone?'

'I'll tell you why,' said Fergus. 'Because he'll be thinking about the future. If he doesn't come after us, after you and Aillil, then the Munster people or the Leinster ones will say, "Maeve and Aillil invaded. They got away with the Brown Bull, not to mention all the other spoils they seized, and Conor never went after them when he and his men got over the birth pangs. And now the Boy Spears are gone there's nothing to stop us. Let's invade Ulster . . ." He has to come after you. You see that surely?'

'You never said this before,' said Maeve. 'Why not?'

'You'd surely worked it out for yourself, I'd have thought.'

'We'll send the Brown Bull and sixty men home to Rathcroghan by a circuitous southerly route,' said Maeve. 'He mustn't be near us when the enemy fall on us. Meanwhile, we stay here, on our territory, and we advise our great army to prepare to fight.'

The order was issued.

In Emain Macha, in the middle of the night, as winter ended and spring began, Conor rose from his bed. He was not strong enough to go to war immediately and he knew the same was true of his warriors.

Later that day Conor sent scouts south and west. They brought him three pieces of news. Cuchulainn was with Emer, recuperating. Mac Roth and his little force were close to the border. Maeve's great army were camped just across the border in Connacht and were making no attempt to move away. But of the Brown Bull there was no report. He was gone.

Conor summoned Cuchulainn and told his warriors to prepare themselves for battle. It was several days before arrangements were made and the men were ready. Every day his scouts brought the news that the enemy were still camped in the same place on the other side of the border.

Conor moved his forces south and west. When he was

close to the border he split his force in three. His plan was to encircle the great army with two of these three parts and attack them from the rear. These forces would press Maeve's great army back across the border into Ulster. Here, the great army would find the last third of Conor's forces waiting. Conor himself would be in command here. His orders to his men were that they were to take no prisoners. They were to slaughter every man in the great army. When they were dead, their heads were to be cut off, to be taken away to Emain Macha, and the bodies were to be stuck up on poles along the border. There would be thousands upon thousands of them. Seeing this would deter any future prospective invader.

Conor dispatched the two prongs, Cuchulainn leading the troops that went around the west way, and Conall leading the troops that went around the east way. In the coming battle, which would be closely fought and intense, chariots would be no good so all warriors were on foot. Once they were round the great army Cuchulainn and Conall's forces attacked from behind.

Maeve's forces fought back fiercely and refused to be rolled back. Conor, realising he needed to engage the final third if he was to tip the battle in his favour, ordered them to attack. The troops surged forward on foot, Conor moving with them, and fell on the enemy. Maeve's great army was now completely encircled and there was fighting right around the perimeter. The fighting was fiercest where the fresh troops were engaged.

A messenger found Fergus and gave him the news that forces under Conor's command were attacking. Fergus hurried north. In the roiling mass of heaving men he saw the king's gold shield with its distinctive four horns. This was the Ear of Beauty as the shield was believed, by some, to resemble an ear.

Fergus rushed up and struck with his sword three times on Conor's shield. Another warrior holding an ordinary shield would have collapsed with the force of Fergus's blows. Conor did not collapse, nor was his shield damaged by the force of the blows.

'Who holds this shield?' Fergus shouted, though he knew the answer.

'A better man than you,' Conor shouted back. 'One who drove you into Connacht to live in exile with the dogs and foxes. One who'll destroy this army here and kill every man in it.'

Fergus raised his great two-handed sword. This time, he would bear down on the king with full force. He would split the shield. He would kill Conor.

However, as the tip was touching the ground behind and he was about to let it fly forward, Cormac grasped his wrist with one hand, and his shoulder with the other.

'Turn your hand aside,' said Cormac. 'Let Conor live and he will let us live. You will, won't you, Father?'

The last time Conor had heard Cormac speak Deirdre and the sons of Usnach were alive. Then Conor had inveigled the exiles into returning and, when they reached

Emain Macha, Eogan and the others had slaughtered the sons of Usnach along with Fergus's son. Fergus left Ulster then in disgust and so did Conor's son, Cormac. Fergus and Cormac went into exile in Connacht and, when Maeve and Aillil brought the great army into Ulster, Fergus and Cormac came north with them. It had therefore been many years since Conor had heard his son speak; nonetheless he knew the voice instantly. One does not forget the voice of one's own. Nor does one grow indifferent or inured to it, even if one is a great king. On the contrary, the voice of one's child can bend a great king. Conor no sooner heard Cormac speak than he knew he could not fight on. He could not let this go on. His son might be killed and anything was better than that. He must agree.

'If I must,' he said.

'So stop this now,' said Cormac.

'And you'll go?' For all that he was moved by his son's request, Conor was still thinking like a king and still determined that an agreement would be reached that left him looking like the winner

'We'll leave,' Cormac agreed. 'Won't we, Fergus?'

'We will,' Fergus said.

'Done.'

Conor turned and shouted to his trumpeter, 'All fighting stops now. Blow your trumpet so everyone knows.'

The notes floated across the battlefield. As one man after another heard the notes and recognised what the message signalled, the fighting stopped. It stopped first closest to

Conor and last at the other end of the field. Cuchulainn was in charge here and he was puzzled by this unexpected order which came from his own king.

'Why has Conor ordered us to stop?' he asked. No one could answer. No one knew. He found Laeg and his chariot in the rear. 'Take me back to Conor,' he said.

Laeg began to circle the great army, heading for Conor. As the chariot moved forward, Cuchulainn saw the great army was changing disposition from fighting to marching mode. He saw Fergus was in the thick of it, driving round in his chariot and organising the troops. Meanwhile, all around the edge of the great army, men swarmed over the ground where the fighting had taken place. They were gathering up the dead and the wounded of the great army and loading them on to carts that would carry them away.

'It looks like the great army is going to slip away,' he said to Laeg, from his seat in the back. 'Forget Conor, take me to Fergus.'

Laeg drove through the milling ranks of the great army and stopped near Fergus.

'Friend Fergus,' Cuchulainn called, 'I've come to finish you.'

'Have you?'

'I'm going to dispose of you as easily as if you were a small boy and I was your loving mother. One cuff and you'll wail, two and you'll fall, three and you'll beg, four and you'll be dead.'

Fergus brought his chariot right up to Cuchulainn's. The

two chariots were so close their axles were touching.

'You'll do no such thing,' Fergus said in a low voice so no one could hear him.

'Oh, why won't I?' said Cuchulainn. His body trembled and he felt the first stirrings of the blood inside his head that would pour out into the hero-light when it burst out of his skull.

Fergus saw what was happening. He must act quickly and decisively to stop Cuchulainn getting angry.

'Once you ran from me,' he said in his most reasonable voice, 'but now it is my turn to flee, as I promised you I would, and I'll take this great army with me when I go.'

Cuchulainn, who had forgotten this arrangement they had made at the ford, now remembered it.

'Good enough,' he said. The trembling in his body stopped and the blood inside his head became still.

'I'd say you must have been a fox once,' said Cuchulainn. 'You can outrun us all.'

'Well, if I am a fox, I have to thank the greatest hunter for letting me live.'

Cuchulainn acknowledged the compliment with a nod.

The order was given to the great army to march. Conor's troops, who surrounded the great army like a net, watched as they slipped past and headed south and west in the direction of Rathcroghan, like a slippery fish swimming to freedom.

Maeve, who had been in the centre of the great army, now found herself at the very rear of the line. Fergus joined her and together they moved away, their chariots moving in parallel.

'Wasn't it as well I sent the Brown Bull ahead?' said Maeve.

'It was,' Fergus agreed.

Conor now issued orders to his forces to pitch camp. Most men obeyed, but a few hundred, dismayed by the outcome of the day, formed a raiding party and slipped away in pursuit of Maeve. They caught up with the queen and the rear of the line at Athlone, as they were crossing the river there. The raiders surged forward with lusty cries, hacking at the men closest to them. Maeve, who was almost across, called out from her chariot to Fergus in his.

'Look at my legs,' she said.

He looked over the side of her chariot and she showed him her thighs and he saw the bright line of very red blood spreading slowly down each one.

'I can't command my troops like this,' she said. At this time in her cycle that was forbidden. That was her *geis*.

'You picked a bad time for this,' said Fergus.

'I can't help it,' she said.

'I suppose.'

'Will you help me or are you going to leave me to the enemy?'

'I wouldn't do that,' said Fergus. He turned to Maeve's charioteer. 'Get the queen's chariot on to dry land,' he said. Then he rallied the men, had some form a shelter of shields around the queen, and with the remainder he turned to face the raiders. The fighting that followed was short and intense. The raiders, finding the resistance was more stout that they had expected from an army in retreat, fell back themselves. Maeve's troops resumed their journey. Fergus and Maeve found they were side by side again.

'That was a shambles today,' said Maeve. 'It was also an occasion of great personal shame.'

No, thought Fergus, it was worse. They had followed the rump of a misguided woman and she had led them, eventually, to what could have been disaster. But then, his thoughts continued, when the herd was led by the mare, it always ended in tragedy, and the herd either strayed or was destroyed.

Of course Fergus gave no indication that this was what he was thinking. Instead, all he said, very carefully, was, 'Yes, I suppose it was,' followed a moment after by an equally inscrutable remark.

'I wonder if we can say this is over now?' he asked.

'I doubt it,' said Maeve.

The great army arrived at Rathcroghan. Though she had not won a great victory and Cuchulainn had defeated every warrior she sent out to fight him, and moreover she had been shamed at the ford near Athlone, Maeve was not totally downhearted. She had her prize. She had got what she wanted and there he was, tethered to a tree outside the royal compound – the great Brown Bull.

'Send him out to pasture,' Maeve ordered.

A warrior was sent up to the top of the tree and with great difficulty he detached the chain from the ring in the Brown Bull's nose. It made a great crash when it hit the ground. Fergus was behind the Brown Bull with a switch. He swiped it gently against one of the animal's back legs.

'Go on,' Fergus shouted, 'go on.'

The animal lifted his head and looked into the sky. Here were great foamy spumes of cloud lit from above by the sun but dark underneath. In the distance between the clouds there were patches of washed blue.

'Go and meet the White-Horned Bull,' Fergus shouted.

The Brown Bull meandered slowly away across the grassland that stretched behind Rathcroghan, the heifers stolen with him following, their low cries mingling with the Brown Bull's hearty bellows.

At first, as he went, the Brown Bull saw grass. His head was down so what else would he see but the ground immediately in front of his hooves? He liked the look of this pasture that he saw. It seemed green and rich to him. Then he heard an animal bellow and he knew by the sound it was an animal like himself. He did not care for this as much as what he had been seeing. If there was another like himself then that would mean that all this rich pasture would either have to be shared or conquered.

The Brown Bull lifted his head. In the distance he saw the White-Horned Bull. He saw he was an animal not only of his own type but also his own size. He had never seen a bull of his own size before.

The Brown Bull roared. The deep powerful noise rolled away over the ground. A moment after the reply rolled back. This was an equally deep and powerful noise.

The Brown Bull moved slowly on, one hoof going in front of the other, the ground shaking with his great weight, his gaze fixed on the truly amazing sight of the White-Horned Bull. To Fergus who was following and watching there was no sign of any hostility between the two. The Brown Bull had seen the White-Horned Bull and now he was going forward to greet it. Fergus felt the reverberations of the beast's tread as a trembling in his legs.

The Brown Bull reached the White-Horned Bull's side. He moved his great wet nose up and down the White-Horned Bull's flank and, as he did, he snorted. The air that roared out of his nose rippled over the White-Horned Bull's pelt like wind over long grass before a storm.

Fergus, watching at a distance, wondered if this smelling was like talk between men. Were the Bulls greeting one another? He was surprised by the lack of hostility. Fergus looked into the sky. The Brown Bull had no idea, he thought, how many had died to bring him to this place. In a short time he would move off. He would put his mouth to the turf. His vast teeth would tear a hunk of grass. He would chew. He would live the same life he had lived in Cooley, one unconcerned by the affairs of men. It was an admirable existence, Fergus thought, almost enviable.

But then, suddenly, as he was having this thought, the Brown Bull butted his head into the White-Horned Bull's side. The White-Horned Bull, surprised by the push, pitched sideways and hit the ground with a heavy thud, sending up a cloud of dust and grass and sending tremors along the ground that Fergus felt in his chest.

The White-Horned Bull rolled on to his back in preparation to rolling on to his legs and then heaving himself on to his feet. Fergus had seen animals perform this movement many times but he had never seen what happened next. Before the White-Horned Bull could roll back and get on to his feet, the Brown Bull put his heavy hoof on the White-Horned Bull's horn closest to the ground and pinned it down. The White-Horned Bull now tried to roll sideways, waggling his legs, wriggling his torso, bellowing frantically, but he wasn't able to move his head from the ground. He was caught fast, pinned by the hoof on his horn to the ground.

'Is that the best you can do?' Fergus shouted to the Brown Bull. 'Because if it is, it isn't heroic enough. Thousands of fine men have died because of you.'

The Brown Bull pushed his hoof down. With a terrible shearing noise the White-Horned Bull's horn snapped off. Free, suddenly, the White-Horned Bull rolled on to his legs and sprang to his feet. He let out a great moan and with his single remaining horn slashed at the Brown Bull's flank, tearing the pelt and exposing the white ribs.

The battle of the Bulls lasted through the rest of the day and through the night. In the morning the Brown Bull appeared outside Rathcroghan with the White-

Horned Bull's liver stuck on one of his horns and blood all over his body. The White-Horned Bull was presumed dead, an opinion later confirmed when the carcass was found. Some of Maeve's men were for killing the Brown Bull now but Fergus intervened.

'Kill him,' he said, 'and I kill you.'

The Brown Bull was allowed to wander off. Bellowing wearily he found his way back to Cooley, his home place. This was where he lived before he was taken north by his herdsman, Fergal, where he was then captured and brought away to Connacht. He knew this terrain: this was *his* terrain and he soon found the small glen that, in those easy-going days before his troubles, he had always imagined as the place where he would one day die.

He turned and backed into this place, so he could see out the end, then sank on to the ground. The glen was so small he filled it to the brim, from back to mouth. Now he had settled he let out a final great bellow and then his heart burst. Then a great amount of dark red gore vomited out of his mouth, his heavy head sank to the grass and he was dead.

Chapter Twenty-one

The death of Cuchulainn

Calitin's wife, Tethba, had been brought the news of her husband's and her sons' deaths when she was about to give birth. As she lay on her birthing couch a little later, the contractions in her belly pulling fiercely at her, she was filled with rage.

'Cuchulainn, I hate you,' she shouted. 'I hope the children I am about to bear will kill you.'

She gave birth to six children, three males and three females. Their bodies were heavy and bulky, their faces were squashed and misshapen, and each had a full set of yellow teeth inside their huge mouths.

After she had recovered from the birth, Tethba took her six newborns to Maeve.

'These are no ordinary babies,' she said to the queen. 'Look at their teeth.' She opened the mouth of one. 'Feel the weight of that arm.'

Maeve took the arm Tethba proffered. It was heavy.

'If anyone can hurt Cuchulainn,' said Maeve, 'it's these ones, once they've grown.'

Since the Brown Bull's death, the queen had brooded incessantly on the campaign. The reason it was such a failure had become obvious to her; it was Cuchulainn. He had held her army up by himself, without aid, for the whole of the winter, not just killing all her champions but leaving Finnabair without a worthy husband.

Then ignominy was heaped on failure when, instead of commanding her troops at the end, she was forced to cower behind a wall of shields.

True, the Brown Bull was there at Rathcroghan when she got home but then he had been killed in his great struggle with the White-Horned Bull, and so she had lost her trophy.

Since then there had been talk. She had been mocked. She had been teased. The poets had produced poem after nasty poem cataloguing her disasters and praising Cuchulainn's achievements. If she didn't hate Cuchulainn when she got back from the raid, well, she certainly did by the time the poets had finished spreading their poisoned words around the place.

Now all she wanted was to pay back her old adversary for all he had done to her great army. She desperately wanted to kill him and suddenly here were the means – these six infants of Tethba.

'I'll leave them,' said Tethba, 'if you promise you'll rear them to destroy Cuchulainn.'

'Oh I will,' said the queen. 'You can be sure I will.'

Tethba departed, leaving her brood behind. Maeve sent Mac Roth to round up the strongest wizards and druids to be found and to bring them back to Rathcroghan. He did. She put the men and the children together with instructions that the wizards and druids were to teach them all the charms and spells they knew. Once the children had matured – and in three years they matured as much as an ordinary child did in eighteen years – Maeve sent them away to learn more. First they went to magician friends of their father, Calitin. Then they went abroad . . .

Tethba's brood had been away a year when, one afternoon, Maeve heard a fierce wind start up and blow about the compound. It was summer, not winter, and this sudden wind puzzled her. She stepped outside. The sky above was clear and blue and the sun was shining yet the wind was still howling. For a moment she was puzzled and then she saw, standing on the ramparts, her six foster children.

'You are welcome home,' she called up to them. 'You've finished your learning?'

'We have,' one said.

Maeve felt a great surge of joy. She had bided her time. Now she would strike.

She summoned Mac Roth to her chamber.

'Go to every king in Ireland. Ask them to send troops for a new invasion of Ulster.'

'And what is the purpose of this venture?'

'To kill Cuchulainn and then to plunder the province.'

'Does Aillil know this?'

'He will when I tell him.'

'And Fergus?'

'Only when I tell him.'

'Will Fergus join this time?'

'I wouldn't think so.'

'A wise decision,' said the messenger.

Mac Roth went from kingdom to kingdom repeating Maeve's request. In those kingdoms where the descendants of men Cuchulainn had killed now ruled, he emphasised the opportunity for revenge. Many said yes and two of the most eager takers were Erc and Lugaid, whose fathers had been the two scouts Cuchulainn slaughtered at the start, along with their drivers, and whose heads he stuck on the four-pronged oak that blocked the river. In those kingdoms whose rulers had not participated in the previous raid, Mac Roth emphasised the opportunities for pillaging and personal enrichment that the campaign offered. Many more said yes.

A new army mustered at Rathcroghan. They marched north and crossed the border and immediately, all over Ulster, warriors were driven to their beds by the searing pains of childbirth in their bellies. With gusto the invaders began burning forts and compounds, taking prisoners and seizing cattle and goods and women.

In his bed in Emain Macha, Conor lay under pelts groaning and moaning, great beads of perspiration pouring from his face, hot thoughts rattling around his head.

It must be Maeve, he thought. Who else could it be? And it was in order to kill Cuchulainn, he guessed, his thoughts running on, that she had now come. If she killed the warrior then the poets would have to produce poems celebrating her victory and her reputation, as a result, would soar. He needed to act. If he left Cuchulainn in Dundalk, the invaders would catch him and kill him. Conor decided he would have him brought to Emain Macha. Cuchulainn could protect the fort and, in turn, the fort could protect him from the enemy.

Conor summoned Levercham, who had brought Naoise to Deirdre. He still trusted and used her because he did not know this.

'I have a task for you,' he said when she appeared.

Levercham nodded. She was now a very old woman. Her flat face was a mass of lines and her once grey hair was now quite white and tied in a plait that dropped behind her back.

'Come close so I can whisper.'

Conor knew Cuchulainn, who was in his compound in Dundalk, could not hear him when he whispered. Conor did not want Cuchulainn to hear about the invasion in case he armed himself and rode out to meet the enemy and his death. He wanted Cuchulainn brought back and the best way to get that was to keep him in ignorance.

'This invasion must be led by Maeve,' whispered Conor.

Levercham nodded.

'They want Cuchulainn. Go to Dundalk and bring him back here. Emer too.'

Levercham set off. She found Emer in Cuchulainn's compound and sent her back to Emain Macha with Laeg. Then she found Cuchulainn on the Strand of the Tracks close to the mound where Connla was buried. He had been stalking a flock of seafowl all morning but uncharacteristically, though he had fired many shots from his sling, he had not hit one bird. It was a sign, he thought. Something was wrong. Then he heard Levercham calling, 'Cuchulainn!'

'Levercham, what brings you?'

'There's an invasion.'

'I was right. I knew something must be wrong.'

Cuchulainn wanted to arm himself and ride out straight away. Hadn't it worked before?

'Conor wants you with him now,' said Levercham.

'Well, can I go to my compound for Emer first?'

'I saw her already. She's gone.'

Cuchulainn and Levercham went back to Emain Macha. Meanwhile, the new army, under Tethba's brood reached Cuchulainn's compound. The hero might have slipped away but they did their worst anyway. The troops slaughtered everyone they found, burned everything they could and then set the compound on fire.

When the destruction was complete Tethba's brood were brought to Maeve in the royal tent.

'Well,' said Maeve, 'he slipped off again. He must be at Emain Macha. I rather fear that will be hard to take even if it's only Cuchulainn himself manning the walls.'

The oldest of Tethba's brood raised a hand. 'March north, camp near Emain Macha. We will lure him out and then the entire army can kill him.'

'Agreed,' said Maeve.

The brood went outside. They summoned a wind that carried them all north and set them down on the lawn in front of the great gates of Emain Macha. They squatted down and began to pull the grass growing there out by the roots. They tossed the blades into the air where they swirled around. They added twigs and dust and little stones to the cloud. They ran to the ramparts where dandelions and thistles grew along the bottom edge. They tore these out and threw the stalks and fuzz balls into the air. Then they whispered and danced and whirled their arms around and the swirling incoherent mass of material became an army of heavily armed warriors. These then formed themselves into fighting groups, and began stamping their feet, banging their swords on their shields and shouting in the manner of soldiers before battle.

Cuchulainn, sitting in Cathbad's hut with the druid, heard the awful din coming over the ramparts.

'That's an army about to attack,' he said.

He bolted out, Cathbad in pursuit. The compound was filled with children and women, drawn from their quarters by the terrible noise. From the ramparts one of the new Boy Spears from the troop formed after the last one had been wiped out, shouted down, 'Enemy at the gates!'

Cuchulainn scrambled up the ramparts, Cathbad following.

'Don't look,' Cathbad shouted. 'Come back down.'

Cuchulainn reached the top and looked over the

parapet. He could not see the lawn for the thousands and thousands of men standing below, beating their shields and shouting their hoarse war cries. There was indeed an army at the gates and they were readying themselves to swarm over the ramparts and seize Emain Macha.

'I must arm myself,' he said.

He turned to go and found Cathbad blocking his way.

'You're not going outside,' said the druid. 'You're staying here.'

Cathbad turned and addressed the women and children milling below.

'That's no real army out there; only phantoms made out of grass and thistle stalks. They can do nothing but stamp their feet and shout and bang their swords. They cannot attack. Go about your business. You have nothing to fear.'

'What are you talking about?' shouted Cuchulainn. 'That's an army down there and you know what they're going to do? They're going to scale the ramparts, kill all the men, take the women and children, and burn this place to the ground.'

'They can't. They don't exist.'

Cuchulainn was incredulous. 'Those beating swords, those stamping feet, that shouting, that isn't real?'

'Listen,' said the druid. He addressed both Cuchulainn and the crowd below. 'This army was made by Tethba's brood from bits and pieces they found outside the fort. I know. With the power I have I recognise the power of others. This is an illusion.'

'It can't be,' said Cuchulainn.

'They are a lure, created to draw you out and lead you away across the plains to the real army who are waiting to destroy you.'

To Cuchulainn, these were real. He would ignore the druid and act.

'Let me pass,' he said.

'I can't.'

A vast black crow appeared over Cuchulainn's head. This was one of Tethba's brood.

'It's a strange thing, a big brave man like you holding back,' said the bird, 'and with everyone from your compound killed and your place burned down. I'd have thought you'd be eager to avenge what has been done.'

'I am eager,' shouted Cuchulainn.

'He is,' shouted someone in the crowd.

'So come out and fight,' said the bird. 'The army's waiting.'

'He will,' shouted the crowd.

'He won't,' said Cathbad.

Cuchulainn tried to push forward but Cathbad still blocked his way.

'They've burned my compound . . . let me pass.'

'And everyone in it,' said the bird. 'We lopped off their heads – women, girls, men, boys, infants – not one of your retainers is left living.'

'I have to go out,' said Cuchulainn.

'The power to conjure up these apparitions doesn't last,' said the druid. 'In three days, the lawn below will be piled with grass blades and thistle stalks and the army will be gone, you'll see.'

'Three whole days?' said the bird. 'Why, that's long enough for word to get round all of Ireland that the great Cuchulainn wouldn't fight.'

'I shan't let that happen,' said Cuchulainn. 'I'm coming out.'

'You aren't,' said the druid.

'I am . . . out of my way.'

'You'll have to throw me off if you want to pass,' said Cathbad.

'And you would if you were serious,' said the bird.

'Don't do that,' someone shouted from below. 'Persuade Cathbad to step aside.'

'Of course I won't,' said Cuchulainn. 'What do you think I am?'

'A coward,' said the bird. The voice was cool and clear. 'Who won't fight.'

'I am not.'

'That's why you believe what this druid says. But don't imagine any of us are fooled. We all see. It's because the great Cuchulainn doesn't want to fight he's let himself be persuaded this is an illusion.'

'I don't believe him and I'm coming.'

'Ah, good man,' said the bird, 'so you are a true warrior after all.'

'Out of my way, Cathbad.' Again Cuchulainn tried to pass but still Cathbad wouldn't move.

'Why don't you throw me off like the crow says?' said Cathbad.

'Yes, why don't you?' said the bird.

'You see the men with scaling ladders?' said the druid, pointing down. 'Why aren't they coming forward? Why aren't the soldiers locking shields over their heads and bodies as soldiers always do before they storm ramparts? I'll tell you why . . . they're fakes, built out of bits of earth and fuzz balls, and all they can do is stamp and shout and bang swords.'

Cuchulainn couldn't stop himself glancing down. He saw the men with the scaling ladders were making no attempt to run forward, nor were the rest of the soldiers locking shields. This, on top of the conviction with which Cathbad had spoken, made him think perhaps it was true and no sooner had he had this thought than he knew Cathbad was right.

'Perhaps,' he said, 'they are as you say.'

Cathbad turned to the crowd below.

'Tell the warriors in their beds there's no army about to break through the gates and slaughter everyone in the fort. This is a sham army they can hear and they'll be gone in three days. Now go about your business and ignore everything you hear.'

The crowd began to disperse. The druid and Cuchulainn went back to the hut. They spent the rest of the day ignoring the pandemonium made by the army of spectres on the other side of the ramparts. In the evening Tethba's brood withdrew and their army reverted to its constituent parts.

Night came and Cuchulainn fell asleep. Cathbad and Emer took counsel. They assumed Tethba's brood would return the next day and try to lure Cuchulainn away again. They decided to take him to the Glen of the Deaf. This was a glen where a great waterfall poured over a cliff making a thunderous din, and where it seemed hardly possible that even one whose hearing was as acute as Cuchulainn's was could hear anything coming from outside amidst the water's roar. They had chariots harnessed, including Cuchulainn's. Then they woke Cuchulainn before dawn and together they slipped out of Emain Macha.

The next day dawned. Tethba's brood returned to Emain Macha and recreated their army from the mounds of stuff lying about the lawn. Then the racket started up, the same as the day before, but this time there was no response from inside Emain Macha.

'Why doesn't Cuchulainn come?' asked one of Tethba's brood.

'I'll see why,' said another.

She transformed herself into a crow as she had the previous day and flew over the ramparts. From above she saw women washing clothes and lighting fires and grinding meal. She saw children playing games. She saw Conor in his bed, in the room in the house of the Glittering Hoard which he used when he had to come inside the ramparts, clutching his belly and rolling about in pain.

Then she spotted the roof of Cathbad's hut. There was

no grey woodsmoke trembling through the smoke hole and coiling into the sky as there was from all the other huts in the compound. She landed on Cathbad's roof and peered over the sooty rim. On the floor below she saw sleeping couches heaped with pelts. These had clearly been slept on recently but they were empty now.

She flew back to her brothers and sisters.

'Cuchulainn's gone,' she said.

The children of Tethba dissolved their army and created a fierce wind. They roared over the whole of Ulster and searched every cave and glen, every forest and valley, every riverside and mountaintop. Eventually they reached a flat piece of wooded ground near the pass to the Glen of the Deaf. There were chariots here and horses too, including Cuchulainn's, the Grey of Macha and the Black Sainglain.

Tethba's brood floated down from the sky. From pinecones and fern leaves, nettles and rock mould, bullrushes and gorse needles, they produced another army at the entrance to the pass. These apparitions, in turn, produced a vile dirge that combined the thunder of war drums and the moans of dying men, the clash of swords on shields and the menacing tramp of feet. And mixed in with this were the whinnies of the real horses tethered at the entrance to the pass, terrified by all they heard, as they struggled to break free.

The noise was incredible. It was louder than the day before but Tethba's brood knew they had to make a phenomenal racket to compete with the roar of the waterfall. And they succeeded. Cuchulainn heard it, albeit only faintly, from where he stood inside the glen.

'What's that?' he said.

The cacophony of battle swelled, causing the small trees and the rocks on the ground to tremble.

'What?' said Emer. She had heard it too but she had no intention of letting on she had.

'That's the sound of battle,' said Cuchulainn, 'and men dying. Don't you hear it?'

'I can hear the sound of water pounding the rocks,' shouted Emer, 'if that's what you mean.'

'And my horses, they're in the middle of it.'

'That part's true,' said Cathbad, 'but that's all. Look, they're trying to lure you out again. There are no armies fighting out there.'

Cuchulainn and Cathbad argued as they had on the ramparts and once again the old druid prevailed.

Meanwhile, outside the glen, Tethba's brood debated.

'He won't be lured out,' said one. 'That much is obvious.'

'What do we do then?' asked a second.

'We'll try another ploy,' said the daughter who'd previously assumed the shape of the crow.

Her body shrank, her face rippled, her hair changed colour. When the motions ended she was Emer. She entered the glen and conjured a thick, nearly liquid fog that filled it right up to the brim like a beaker filled with water.

Cuchulainn's party – Emer, Cathbad, Laeg and Cuchulainn himself – were engulfed by the fog and everyone immediately lost sight of everyone else and became confused. Cuchulainn started to search for Emer. As he did, he heard what he thought was his wife shouting over the roaring water and clamour of battle, 'Cuchulainn, where are you?'

Mistaking the fake for the real Emer, he called back, 'Here I am.'

'Cuchulainn,' shouted the imposter, 'lead me to you.'

He called out again and she found him.

'Cuchulainn,' the fraud said, 'Cathbad's been lying.'

'He's been lying?'

'I found one of the Boy Spears in the pass that leads into this glen,' the deceiver whispered, 'with his side split, and his guts on the ground.'

'What . . .'

'These sounds . . . they *are* the corps of Boy Spears and Maeve's new army battling it out just beyond the pass. The dying boy told me he'd been sent to fetch you. They need you. If you don't go, they're finished.'

'But Cathbad said . . .'

'I know what he said. It was a lie.'

'Why did Cathbad lie?' Cuchulainn was confused. 'I don't understand.' Then he turned and shouted, 'Cathbad, those are real soldiers fighting a real battle we're hearing this time. It's our Boy Spears and the new army and we're losing.' His angry voice filled the whole glen.

'That's no battle we're hearing,' Cathbad's voice came back from the fog, only just audible over the roar of the waterfall and the raging battle.

'Cathbad, I've Emer here, she's been out of the glen and she knows the truth.'

'That's impossible,' the real Emer shouted from deep in the fog. 'I'm here and I'm lost in the fog. I've been nowhere. I have seen and heard nothing.'

'That's not Emer,' the pretender at Cuchulainn's side whispered. 'I am Emer. That's a fake conjured up by Cathbad to make you stay.'

'How do I know you're my wife?' said Cuchulainn.

She pressed herself against Cuchulainn. She put her mouth on his and touched his tongue with hers.

'Don't you recognise me?' she said.

'I suppose . . .'

'Isn't it only your wife who kisses the way I do?'

Cuchulainn thought, well, yes, it was.

'We must go now quickly,' she said, 'come on, follow me.'

The dissembler turned and disappeared into the fog.

Cuchulainn went to follow and, as he did, he stepped on the hem of his cloak. The material tugged and the brooch that secured it at his shoulder sprang out. The brooch tumbled to the ground pin first and the sharp end stuck into his foot.

'That's bad,' said Cuchulainn. He pulled out the brooch and re-attached it at the shoulder.

The fog lifted as abruptly as it had fallen. He saw Emer and Cathbad in the distance, while Laeg was closer.

'You're liars,' he shouted to his wife and the druid. 'There is a battle out there. Come on Laeg,' he said to his charioteer, 'let's go.'

He started along the path towards the pass.

'Come back, Cuchulainn,' Emer and Cathbad called from their different parts of the glen.

He ignored them.

'Laeg, don't take him,' they shouted.

'Don't listen to them, Laeg,' said Cuchulainn. 'Just do as I say.'

He hurried on, his charioteer following him, Emer and Cathbad already faint and growing fainter, the further Cuchulainn and Laeg moved away.

'Come on, Laeg, hurry up,' he said.

He broke into a run and his charioteer started to run too. They ran through the rest of the glen and through the pass and emerged on to the small piece of flat ground where the horses and chariot were. They had expected they would be able to see the fighting from here but at the very moment they had emerged from the pass the sound of battle moved away.

'One army's fleeing and the other's pursuing them,' said Cuchulainn. 'Let's hope it's not the Boy Spears who are running. Harness the horses quickly and let's go before Emer and Cathbad catch up and try to stop us.'

Laeg got the horses yoked to the chariot while Cuchulainn pulled on his armour, buckled on his shield and picked up his arms. When each man had finished the two took their places, Laeg at the front, Cuchulainn in the rear, both standing in their foot-bindings, and both tied with thongs to the chariot sides that would hold them in and stop an enemy pulling them out.

'Go,' said Cuchulainn.

Laeg shook the reins, the horses picked up their feet and the chariot hurtled off.

'Follow the sounds of battle,' Cuchulainn ordered.

Laeg steered the chariot out of the hills and down to the plains. Cuchulainn and his driver expected to see soldiers in battle here but instead they only heard the noise of fighting in the distance and as they advanced the noise receded.

'Drive the horses harder,' said Cuchulainn. 'We must catch up.'

Laeg struck the horses with his goad. The Grey and the Black sped forward across the plains but the faster they went the faster the battle noises went away.

And it went on like this for a long time, with the chariot chasing the sounds of battle as they kept withdrawing further and further to the south . . .

It was afternoon. The horses were slick with sweat and great puffs of frothy saliva had bubbled up around their mouths.

'I must rest these animals,' said Laeg.

He pulled on the reins and slowed them to a walk. In the distance Cuchulainn heard bugle calls and the clatter of careering chariots, the cries of dying men and the din of iron thudding on iron yet he could still see nothing. The battling armies remained tantalisingly, frustratingly, just out of sight. Then he heard a burning log crackle and hiss and he noticed – because he had been scanning the horizon so intently it had escaped his attention until now – a cooking fire was just ahead. Three old women squatted on the ground around it. There was brown meat on a spit made from a rowan branch roasting over the middle of red and yellow flames. It was a lamb or a goat, he thought, but as his chariot drew closer he realised by the sour smell of the meat it was dog.

'Go around them,' he said to Laeg, 'before they see us.'

Laeg pulled with his right hand, intending to drive the animals rightwards. As he did one of the women sprang up and ran in front of the horses. Laeg had to stop. The woman had one eye that was wet and blue and one that was dead and white.

'Will you come over to the fire, Cuchulainn, and take something to eat?'

'I won't,' he said.

On the day he took his new name he swore a *geis* never to eat dog.

'Why not? Because we're poor women and this is only a poor bit of meat we have?'

Her companions had stood and were urging Cuchulainn to come over to the fire.

'If we were queens you'd stop.'

'I won't let her get away with that,' said Cuchulainn. 'Stop,' he ordered Laeg.

The charioteer pulled on the reins. Cuchulainn unhitched the ties, clambered down through the gap at the rear and walked over to the fire.

One of the other old women hacked off a piece of flesh and offered it on the point of her knife. Cuchulainn took the piece of meat with his left hand. It scorched his fingertips. He blew on it to cool it down. He put it in his mouth, chewed, then swallowed. As the meat travelled down his throat a pain spread up his left arm, down the left of his body and along his left leg to his left foot. In the distance the clamour of arms and men and horses flared up. He thanked the women and limped back to the chariot, and heaved himself aboard with some difficulty.

'What's wrong with your leg?' said Laeg.

'That was dog they gave me,' said Cuchulainn, re-fixing the ties.

'Then turn back,' said Laeg.

'No, go on,' said Cuchulainn.

Laeg shook the reins and moved the horses over the grassland, following the sound of fighting. A river appeared. Laeg steered for the ford. When they drew close they found their way blocked by a figure with a girl's body and an old woman's face. She had a great cloak sopping with blood. She dropped it in the river and trod down on it and the water round her ankles went red.

'It's the Morrigu, isn't it?' said Laeg, meaning the goddess of War. In the form of a raven she had whispered into the Brown Bull's ear with news of the invasion. Today she was the Washer at the Ford, the one who washes the blood from the clothes of the man who is about to die.

'That's the same cloak as you're wearing,' said Laeg, as she lifted up the cloak. The water sheeting down was brown with blood.

'It is,' said Cuchulainn.

'And the same clothes you're wearing are there on the bank.'

Laeg pointed at the pile. They were soaked with blood too.

'This is not good,' said Laeg. 'Let's go back.'

'I haven't come all this way to run away now,' said Cuchulainn.

'Who said you'd be running? Isn't this a sign, telling you not to go on?'

'We'll catch these fleeing armies if it's the last thing I do.'

'In which case it *will* be the last thing you do,' warned Laeg.

He drove the horses into the ford and up the other side. He drove forward over the plains, circling around hills and splashing through more fords until finally an army came in view. This was not the illusory army that Cuchulainn had been chasing. It was Maeve's new army and they were arranged in a block. As Cuchulainn's chariot came into view, the new army's warriors roared and stamped their feet, then locked their shields above their heads and in front of their bodies, presenting Cuchulainn with a gigantic band of metal. They were like an ingot lying across the landscape.

Cuchulainn warped into fighting mode and with that the pains on his left side vanished. His head and body swelled like a bladder filled with water. One eye shrank and the other expanded. His mouth slipped away, baring his teeth, his gums, and his gullet. The hero-light filled with churning dark black blood shot up over his head.

'Forward,' he said.

Laeg drove right through the middle of the enemy, the horses scattering men with their great hooves, and the wheels knocking them sideways and sometimes cutting them in two. Cuchulainn stood in the back of the chariot, slashing and hewing with his great sword and his long spear at every warrior within reach. Men were split like ripe fruit and their insides were thrown about like apple pips and plum stones.

The chariot emerged at the back and turned about. Cuchulainn noted with satisfaction that the great solid band of metal was now in two pieces with a hole in the middle where dying and injured men were strewn about. Now, according to convention, he must wait while the new army got ready to face him again.

Erc was in the middle of one of the warrior blocks. He gave orders for the two halves to join into one unit. The two blocks moved and became one. At either end he put out a pair of champions and a druid. The champions were ordered to pretend to fight and the druid to act as if he were judging the outcome.

'Circle around them this time,' said Cuchulainn. 'We'll see what these champions have been put out for.'

Laeg drove the chariot forward and leftwards. One of

the druids shouted when Cuchulainn was close, 'Separate these champions, will you?'

'Certainly,' said Cuchulainn.

From his vantage on the chariot platform he gored both fighters with his spear and they fell to the ground. Laeg stopped the chariot.

'You separated those two all right,' the druid said. 'Their fighting days are done. Now give me that spear, Cuchulainn.'

'I can't.'

'And to think I believed those who said you were always generous,' said the druid, 'and you always gave whatever was asked.'

'You know I need it.'

'Don't think I won't tell everyone you refused me,' said the druid. 'And imagine what everyone will say about you when they hear that. The poets will tear your reputation to shreds.'

'All right,' said Cuchulainn. 'No one will be able to say I didn't give what was asked.'

He reversed the spear and threw it from the place where he stood with his feet in the foot-bindings. The shaft went in through the druid's chest and came out at the back, pulling his lungs with it. The spear and the lungs landed on the grass beside Lugaid. The lungs were pink and trembling. Lugaid picked the spear up.

'Whose name is on this?' he asked.

'A king's,' said Tethba's children together from the ranks behind.

Lugaid hurled the spear at Cuchulainn but caught Laeg instead, the head burying itself in the driver's bowel.

'Now I've learned my lesson,' said the charioteer. 'I should have turned round.'

Cuchulainn undid the ties around Laeg's waist and laid the charioteer down on the floor between the seats. Then he pulled the spear from Laeg's belly. As it came out the contents of his bowel came too.

'Turning back wouldn't have done any good,' said Cuchulainn. 'My spear would have found you somehow. You can't change what's meant to be.'

Laeg shuddered. He opened his mouth and a huge bubble, half-blood, half-saliva, slowly formed, then popped. His eyelids closed. Cuchulainn felt a little tug deep inside. This was the first glimmering of grief and if he didn't act at once he would be flooded with feeling. If he let that happen he would have even less chance of surviving.

Cuchulainn unhitched the tie that fixed him and heaved Laeg's body on to the ground. Then he put his feet in the charioteer's foot-bindings, fixed the charioteer's ties around his middle and grasped the reins. He began to turn but found his way blocked. The two warriors and the druid who'd been having the sham combat on the other wing were there.

'Will you separate these champions?' shouted the druid who was judging the pair.

Cuchulainn gored the pair as he passed with the spear

that had killed Laeg and was smeared with his charioteer's blood and mess.

'Now give me your spear,' the druid shouted after him.

Cuchulainn turned the chariot to face the speaker.

'I can't.'

'Why not?'

'I need it.'

'But I asked and you're the warrior who never says no, or am I wrong?'

'You know I need it.'

'So your good name is based on a lie,' the druid said. 'I can't say I'm surprised.'

'I defended my good name once today already,' said Cuchulainn. 'Now you make me do it again.'

He reversed the spear and threw it. The spear's butt went in though the druid's left eye and came out at the back of his head and landed on the grass. All along its length the spear was now smeared with grey matter from the druid's brain.

Erc bounded from the ranks and picked up the spear, slippery and slimy with so much human waste.

'Children of Tethba,' he asked, 'whom will this kill?'

'A king.'

'You said that before Lugaid threw and it killed the charioteer.'

'And we were right. Laeg was king of the charioteers.'

Erc cast the spear at Cuchulainn but hit the Grey of Macha in the side instead. The horsed whinnied and its blood spurted out and sheeted its flanks red. Cuchulainn pulled the spear out. The horse snapped his harness, fell to the ground, and began to thrash his legs around. Then his legs stopped moving and his head flopped sideways. The grass nearby was now as red as his body with blood. Cuchulainn knew he was dead.

Pulled by just the Black Sainglain now, Cuchulainn drove through the middle of the new army, knocking men sideways and stabbing with his spear at anyone close enough to reach with a thrust. He came out on the far side. He turned and saw the new army was in two halves again and the gap between the ground was strewn with men. While the army reformed Erc sent another pair forward with instructions to stage another sham fight on the ground between Cuchulainn and the new army. A druid went with them and when the warriors began sparring he called to Cuchulainn to separate the pair. Cuchulainn drove up and killed both with a stab from his filthy spear, after which the druid asked for it.

'This is the third time I've been asked and for the third time I say no.'

'No?' said the druid. 'Really? And you supposed to be the one who says yes to every request.'

'You know I need this spear. You shouldn't ask.'

'But I am asking. A man may ask for whatever he wants. And if the one to whom the request is made refuses, he must accept the consequences.'

'Which are?'

'That I will tell everyone you are mean.'

Cuchulainn reversed the spear and threw it. It went in through the druid's belly button, broke the spine as it passed through his body, and came out the far side.

Lugaid ran forward and picked up the spear from the ground.

'Children of Tethba,' he said.

'Yes?' they replied from the ranks behind.

'You told Erc a king would fall when he threw this.'

'And one did. The Grey of Macha was the king of the chariot horses.'

'And will it kill another king?'

'It will.'

'The king of warriors?'

'It will.'

Lugaid flung the spear. The point struck Cuchulainn at the side of his chest on his left side, passing neatly through the tiny space where his chest and back armour were jointed. The point went through the skin behind and smashed two ribs. The point punched on, passing through tissue and muscle towards the great tubes filled with blood that ran up to and away from his enormous pulsing heart. The point stopped just before it pierced the wall of this organ.

Cuchulainn plucked out the spear and looked at the blade smeared with his blood and the fat and brain and all the other substances it had touched that day.

'Now I wish I'd gone back, Laeg,' he said.

He remembered eating the dog meat and the pain he felt afterwards on his left side. He realised that from that moment on this wound in his left side was inevitable.

To stop the blood flow Cuchulainn put his hand over the hole. The blood that came out went through his fingers and dripped on to the chariot's floor. His blood could no more be stopped, he realised, then the sea-tide as it ran in or out.

Cuchulainn took the reins and shook them. But instead of going forward the Black twisted and turned, pulling the chariot this way and that as he tried to break from his harness. It was hopeless to try to go on. Cuchulainn cut him loose. The horse galloped off, leaving the chariot beached on the grass.

He looked around. He saw where he had come to a halt was near a standing stone. It immediately reminded him of a sword: the handle was buried in the earth, leaving the blade sticking up above the ground. This was the place. Of course it was. From the moment of his birth this was the spot towards which he had been headed and now, at last, he had arrived.

He unfixed the ties and found, under the driver's seat, a piece of rope. He clambered down from the chariot and went slowly over to the standing stone. He walked one end of the rope around the standing stone, returned to the point where he had started and made a cunning slip knot. He worked the rope up to the level of his chest, then he got in behind it so his back was to the rock and he pulled the knot tight. The rope went under his arms and around the rock. As the rope took his weight he felt his hero-light was flickering above his head. He swallowed: his mouth was dry. He stared at the men of the new army in the distance and they, in turn, stared back at him.

'Come on,' he said, 'why don't you come and get me?'

The men of the new army remained motionless.

'Frightened, are you . . .? Isn't that it?'

The new army moved forward and formed a circle around the standing stone. The light over Cuchulainn's head waned further.

'He took your father's head off,' Erc said to Lugaid. 'Now here's your chance to return the favour.'

'He took your father's head off too,' said Lugaid to Erc. 'Why don't you?'

'Not until his hero-light goes out,' said Erc to Lugaid, 'but you can try now if you want.'

'I'll wait,' said Lugaid.

The new army waited and watched. At the end of the afternoon the light finally went out.

Lugaid walked forward with his broadsword, Erc following.

'I'll pull his hair to stretch his neck out,' said Erc, 'and you can have the honour of making the blow.'

'Good enough.'

The standing stone was about as broad as Cuchulainn was. The body was supported by the rope and the head lolled forward. Erc grasped Cuchulainn's hair at the crown and yanked forwards so the neck was extended and exposed.

'Don't disappoint me now,' Erc said to Lugaid.

'This is a hard blow to make,' said Lugaid. 'I mustn't catch the rock with my blade and I mustn't catch you.'

'You won't disappoint me,' Erc said to Lugaid.

'You know that, do you?'

'I do. You'll finish him with one cut.'

Lugaid raised his sword right above his head. He let it hang there for an instant and then he brought it down. The blade went in just above the point where Cuchulainn's back shaded into his neck. The edge sliced through the tendons and the muscles, then the windpipe, then came out the far side, a little shower of blood droplets following behind.

Now the head was away from the body Erc took the weight. He was anticipating the weight so he did not drop the head though it was surprisingly heavy. He lifted the head high so the whole of the new army would see it was separated from the body. Then Lugaid raised his sword and Erc put the pulpy neck over the end and then jammed the head down until the point of Lugaid's sword banged against the inside of the skull.

Then, with his sword held high so that all could see the head on the end, Lugaid strode towards the new army. Erc followed.

As Lugaid and Erc got closer, the massed ranks of the new army parted to reveal Maeve standing up in the back of her chariot. Lugaid walked up to her and proffered the sword with the head on the end. Maeve stared at the face.

The eyes were open and the mouth was turned up at the sides. It was a smile, a little smile that was playing on the face of the severed head and the smile, she thought, was for her.

Maeve reached forward and slapped first the right and then the left cheek. The mouth closed and the eyelids dropped.

'Your smiling days are done,' she said. 'You'll never smile again . . .'

After plundering Ulster, the new army returned to Rathcroghan. The druid who kept Maeve's heads now did the work necessary to preserve Cuchulainn's.

He cut the skin carefully away from the crown and sawed through the bone. He took out the grey brain and rolled it in white burning lime. He put the skull back and sewed up the skin so the head looked almost as good as new. Then he hung it up in a chimney. After a year, the head was wrinkled and brown, the eyes were gone and the tongue was shrivelled. Meanwhile, the brain, which was still in lime, had become a grey and black ball and hard like stone.

As she grew older Maeve would often have the head and the brain brought to her. She would look at the head and hold the brain in her cupped hands and think, I have your soul, Cuchulainn, and I hold it in my hands.

After Aillil died and Maeve was left alone at Rathcroghan, she would take her trophies to bed each night. And while she slept, they would lie beside her. And while she slept, though she was unaware of this, Cuchulainn's dead eyelids would tremble and his mouth would move, making a small smile, while the brain on the bolster nearby would pulse gently.

Maeve died and Fergus, who had asked to be told as soon as this happened, came straight away. In the royal bedroom he found the queen in her bed, she had died in her sleep, with Cuchulainn's head and brain beside her. He put these in a basket lined with linen and hid them. In the atmosphere of grief that followed Maeve's death no one noticed the trophies were gone.

Once Maeve's body was buried, Fergus retrieved his basket and slipped across the border. He went to Emer's grave, which was near to where Cuchulainn's compound had been, and buried Cuchulainn's head and brain beside his wife.

Fergus died not long after this.

Epilogue

The Tale's end and new beginning

Muirgen, his eyes firmly closed, declaimed what he had heard in the mist to his father, Senchán, and everyone else in the hall. He began with the story of Crunnchu and he ended with Maeve, alone in her bed in Rathcroghan with Cuchulainn's head and his brain. And as he spoke he became the people in the story.

Everyone present, including Bresal, listened very carefully. The scribes wrote it all down on large portions of thin vellum stretched over writing boards.

Then the day ended. Bresal in his place at the side was filled with that full feeling of pure pleasure that only a story brings. He heard people standing and the room emptying but he did not move. This pleasurable feeling was so powerful that he wanted to hold on to it for as long as possible. He sat on the bench with images springing up, one after the other, before his inner eye. Then he heard footsteps and looked up. Senchán was standing in front of him. Everyone else, he realised, had gone.

'You listened?' said Senchán.

'I listened.'

'And what did you think?'

'That's a story to keep men quiet for twenty nights in a row,' said the apprentice enthusiastically

'And could you tell this tale, do you think, for twenty nights in a row and keep your listeners happy?'

Bresal thought about this for a moment.

'Oh absolutely,' he said, 'and I can hardly wait.'

A note on the Irish chariot

The typical Irish fighting chariot was made of wood. Each wheel was a single continuous piece of wood with spokes and shrunken-on iron rims. Iron linchpins with decorated brass heads were pushed through the axle ends to hold the wheels in place.

The square wooden base frame was covered in at the sides and front with wickerwork attached to upright poles. A range of mounts was attached to different parts of the inside of the chariot to hold different weapons.

A long pole, to which a pair of horses was yoked, was fixed to the front. There were loops or terrets attached to the yoke through which the reins passed as they fed back.

There were two seats running across the chariot. Both seats lifted away and in spaces below clothes, food and extra arms would normally be stored.

Two shafts projected from the chariot's rear. These balanced the yoke at the front and helped to ensure that if the wheels hit a hole or a stone the whole chariot didn't flip over. In addition, in battle, scythes and blades might be attached to these: animals could also be fixed to them.

Bibliography

Cross, Tom Peete and Slover, Clark H., *Ancient Irish Tales*, London, 1937

Dunn, Joseph, *The Ancient Irish Epic – Táin Bó Cuailnge*, London, 1914

Flanagan, Laurence, *Ancient Ireland, Life Before the Celts*, Dublin, 1998

Ganz, Jeffrey, *Early Irish Myths and Sagas*, London, 1981

Gregory, Augusta, *Cuchulain of Muirthemne*, London, 1902

Hyde, Douglas, *A Literary History of Ireland*, London, 1901

Hull, Eleanor (ed), *The Cuchullin Saga in Irish Literature*, London, 1898

Hull, Eleanor, *Cuchulain – the Hound of Ulster*, London, 1909

Joyce, P.W., *A Social History of Ancient Ireland*, Dublin, 1913

Kinsella, Thomas, *The Tain*, London, 1969

Raftery, Barry, *Pagan Celtic Ireland, The Enigma of the Irish Iron Age*, London, 1997

O'Rahilly, Cecile, *Táin Bó Cuailnge* (from the Book of Leinster), Dublin, 1967

O'Rahilly, Cecile, *Táin Bó Cuailnge* (from the Book of the Dun Cow), Dublin, 1978

Pronunciation of Irish names and words

Irish word	Pronunciation
Aidan	a-den (hard 'a')
Aillil	all-ill
Airmed	arm-id
Almu	alm-oo
Amergin	am-er-gin ('g' as in 'gun')
Aoife	ee-fa
Art	art
Badh	bow
Blai	bly
Bodb	bub
Borrach	borrack
Bresal	bresle
Bricriu	bree-crew
Calitin	cal-i-teen
Cathbad	cah-bod
Ceithlinn	keth-lin
Condere	con-dirra
Connacht	con-act
Connla	cun-lah
Conor	conn-or
Cooley	coo-lee
Croach	croak
Crunnchu	crun-coo
Cuchulainn	coo-cull-en
Culann	coo-lunn

Cúr	coor
Daire	da-ra
Dechtire	deck-tear-a
Dun Breth	doon breh
Dundalk	done-dawk
Eithlinn	Ethlyn is the English version of the name
Emain Macha	ow-in mocha
Emer	ee-mir
Eogan	o-in
Erc	erc
Erigu	air-ig-oo
Etarcomol	etar-chom-al
Fannall	fonn-ull
Felimid	fell-ee-mead
Ferdia	fur-dee-a
Fergus Mac Roi	Fergus mock rec
Fernmag	fern-mag
Fiacha	fee-ack-a
Fial	fee-al
Fidchell	fid-kell
Findias	fin-dee-as
Finnabair	finn-bar
Finnchoem	finn-co-um
Finnian	finn-ee-un
Fionn	fee-un
Fionnuala	finn-oo-la
Foill	fwill

Folaman	ful-a-mun
Forgall	fur-gill
Fraech	frey-ock
Gae Bolga	gay bul-ga
Gamal	gom-all
Geis	gay-sh
Goibniu	gub-nu
Ibar	ee-bar
Laeg	lay-egg
Laoghaire	lear-a
Lerga	ler-ga
Levercham	lev-er-ham
Lir	lear
Lothar	low-har
Lough Echtra	lock ek-trah
Lugaid	lug-id
Lugh	lug
Mac Roth	mock wrath
Macha	mock-a
Maeve	may-vuh
Morann	more-an
Morrigu	morr-ig-oo
Muirgen	mweer-gin ('g' as in 'gun')
Nadcranntail	nad-crown-tall
Naoise	knee-sha
Nechtan	knock-ten
Niamh	knee-ave
Ochall	ock-al

Ogham	ohm
Orlam	oar-lum
Rathcroghan	wrath-crogan
Sainglain	sawn-glon
Sencha	sen-ka
Senchán	sen-kawn
Sétanta	set-an-ta
Sidhe	scythe
Slieve Mourne	sleeve mourne
Sualdam	soo-ul-dum
Táin Bó Cuailnge	tah-in bo cooling
Tuachell	too-ack-ill
Tuatha De Danaan (also Danu)	too-a day don-un (don-oo)
Usnach	ish-nack